Beyond
the
Storm

Beyond the Storm

A Novel of a Mother's Faith
and Her Son's Trials

Johnny Neil Smith
and
Susan Cruce Smith

SUNSTONE
PRESS

SANTA FE

Quotes from the Bible are from:
King James Version
New American Standard Bible
New International Version Bible
New King James Version

Sunstone books may be purchased for educational, business, or sales promotional use.
For information please write: Special Markets Department, Sunstone Press,
P.O. Box 2321, Santa Fe, New Mexico 87504-2321.
Cover art by Tamara Haase
Body typeface › Minion Pro
Printed on acid-free paper
∞
eBook 978-1-61139-560-0

Library of Congress Cataloging-in-Publication Data

Names: Smith, Johnny Neil, 1939- author. | Smith, Susan Cruce, author.
Title: Beyond the storm : a novel of a mother's faith and her son's trials /
   by Johnny Neil Smith and Susan Cruce Smith.
Description: Santa Fe : Sunstone Press, [2018]
Identifiers: LCCN 2018023938 (print) | LCCN 2018024459 (ebook) | ISBN
   9781611395600 | ISBN 9781632932334 (softcover : alk. paper)
Subjects: LCSH: United States--History--Civil War,
   1861-1865--Veterans--Fiction. | Families--Fiction. | GSAFD: Christian
   fiction. | Historical fiction.
Classification: LCC PS3569.M5375514 (ebook) | LCC PS3569.M5375514 B495 2018
   (print) | DDC 813/.54--dc23
LC record available at https://lccn.loc.gov/2018023938

WWW.SUNSTONEPRESS.COM
SUNSTONE PRESS / POST OFFICE BOX 2321 / SANTA FE, NM 87504-2321 /USA
(505) 988-4418 / ORDERS ONLY (800) 243-5644 / FAX (505) 988-1025

Dedicated to
Reverend Billy Graham
in appreciation for the words in his book *Angels*
which gave the vision for this story
and
Joseph Frederick Williams, my great grandfather,
who was a member of Company K, Fifth Regiment of CSA Mississippi
Infantryand who was wounded, captured, and spent the winter
of 1864 at Camp Douglas, Illinois.

Prologue

The drifts of smoke hovering above the earth shut out the light of a hot July afternoon. Down the line, regimental flags fluttered ever so slightly with the faint breeze. As the cannons ceased their firings, over the field came a hush like the stillness that follows a thunderstorm. Only an occasional faint musket shot broke the calm. Up the hill stars and stripes proclaimed that the Union line had finally held. The stench of burnt sulfur from black powder saturated the air as exhausted men, gasping for breath, laid down their muskets. In front of them and all about them lay the dead and dying. Moans, shrieks, screams, and pleas for help and for death, blended into a constant mournful din. In some places, bodies lay in piles. In other places, they lay in neat rows where they had been taken down by musket fire. Those fortunate, or perhaps unfortunate, enough to have breath reached out their arms, pleading for assistance, begging for water, and desperately trying to free themselves from the mass of carnage that held them captive. Defeated, the Southern troops, dragging their comrades with them, withdrew from the pit of hell. The hope of another Southern victory, one that might end the tiring and seemingly interminable war, had vanished on that hillside.

Gaining strength from the realization they were alive and had survived a massive, brutal frontal attack by Pickett's division of the Army of the Northern Virginia, the Union soldiers began to rise to their feet, shouting in unison, "Fredericksburg! Fredericksburg! Fredericksburg!"

Across the field, a southern soldier, bloodied and drenched with sweat, ran from one returning soldier to the next, searching for his brother. The struggle to survive and sheer exhaustion of the soldiers he questioned caused his search to fail.

"He's got to be out there somewhere," he thought to himself. "He's got to be alive!"

"I've got to find him!" he bellowed to a soldier who had reached to him for assistance.

The man who had been pushed aside cried out to him, "You're a fool to go to that slope again. It'll be sure death."

What the soldier had not told his comrade was the pledge that impelled him forward. He had given his word that he would look after his younger brother. His word now drove him more than the fear of imminent death.

The Union command knew this three-day battle was finally over. An officer ordered his men to separate the dead and care for the wounded the best they could. One of his soldiers asked about the Southern boys who were injured. The officer replied, "They're God's children just like us. Give them mercy. We hope to see the day when we will all be brothers again."

A private, looking at the mutilated mass, wondered aloud how a loving God could allow what he now surveyed. A comrade answered, "It isn't God's will. It's man's sinful nature."

Thus, what was to be the largest and bloodiest battle ever fought on American soil ended as July 4, 1863, drew to a close. Various hometowns and communities had now lost most of their young men. The sickle of war had swung viciously through the fathers, sons, and loved ones of this new nation whose country had declared its independence on July 4, 1776, a country now seemingly bent on self-destruction.

1

Unbearable Loss

Now faith is the assurance of things hoped for, the conviction of things not seen.
—Hebrews 11:1

Southern Mississippi

A steady rain had fallen for the past several days and, finally, became a drizzle as a brisk artic wind gushed in from the North quickly dropping temperatures below freezing point, sending animals scurrying for cover and people to the warmth of their fireplaces. An elderly couple cuddled in their bed under a heavy layer of quilts and watched a fire slowly turn to embers. At times, the gusts outside were so strong the loose windowpanes rattled and the wind whistled an eerie tune as it turned the corner of the old log house. It was December of 1864.

"Lott, you know it'll be Christmas before too long," said Sarah, nudging her husband.

"I know," replied Lott, not interested in making conversation.

Cuddling closer, she continued, "We didn't decorate last year."

"I didn't think it appropriate. Not under the circumstances," mumbled Lott.

"You remember two years ago, all the children were here. Thomas and James Earl got a furlough to come home from Virginia. Thomas was supposed to raise troops for Mr. Lee, and James Earl, sickly as he was, needed to come home to heal," stated Sarah.

"James Earl was always sickly. He had no business volunteering for no fighting. He didn't have a dog's chance for survival," murmured Lott. "He should have never left home."

"Well, like I was saying, Sister wanted to decorate the place for Christmas, so John invited Rebecca to help with the trimmings. I can see them dragging that little cedar tree into the house, and you were just fussing about bringing that bush into our bedroom. You said it might have bugs on it." Sarah chuckled. "John, Thomas, and James Earl strung popcorn and wrapped it around the little fellow while Sister and Rebecca took some of my sewing scraps and made white and red ribbons to place about the tree."

Lott pulled the covers closer about his shoulders and mumbled, "Do we have to talk about this?"

"I'm about through. Try to be a little patient for once. After we finished the tree, it was a sight to behold. Remember, it was John's idea to decorate the mantle above the fireplace with some of the short cedar branches that were cut from the tree, and it was your idea to place four large red candles among the branches on the mantel - one red candle for each of our children."

"I can remember," replied Lott. "That's part of the problem."

Taking a big breath, Sarah said, "I can see them all sitting, smiling, and happy, and you could tell they was proud of what they'd done. All my boys were there - Thomas, James Earl, and John while that sweet Rebecca nestled as close as possible to John. Sister, as usual, was trying to irritate John about his courtship with Rebecca, kinda teasing him." Then after pausing for a moment, she remarked, "You know John and Rebecca have known each other all their lives. No wonder they seem to have such love for each other. You remember that Christmas?"

Lott pursed his lips and twisted his neck to relieve some tension. "I told you, I remembered it. Woman, what are you getting at? This has been a long day. I'm tired."

Lott remembered too well and often kept his feelings to himself. He thought there was no sense upsetting others with problems he had no control over. To him, talking about the loss in the family only upset him more. The feelings stayed where he harbored them, locked deep inside his mind. His soul cried for a release, but no freedom would ever enter.

Sarah eased closer to her husband. "I think we ought to celebrate Christmas like we used to. You know, invite folks over. Read the story from Luke, and decorate like we did back then. Don't you think so?"

Lott slipped out of bed, wrapped a quilt around his shoulders as he walked to the low burning fire, and firmly stated, "Sarah, it ought to be a sin to love a woman like I love you, but there ain't gonna be no more decorations around this place."

Lott paused for a moment before speaking, "There's no reason to celebrate. Look over there at that sword. I still can't force myself to even touch it. Sometimes, I wish I had never come to this country. It would have been better for my parents to have stayed in Ireland than to come over here. Least, there ain't no war going on over there, taking their boys. Now let's quit talking about this nonsense. You know I don't like to talk about it."

Sarah eased out from under the covers and tipped to where Lott held the quilt open for her to join him.

"You got to let go and see how we are blessed," said Sarah. "When this here war is over, Thomas will likely come back home, and we got that darling daughter to raise. She needs us more than you know. God is going to bring our joy back to us one day, and we need to be expecting it."

Lott thought for a moment about their daughter Lucretia, known to the family as Sister, and realized that she needed him to be strong, but sometimes, the loss was just too great. Loss and bitterness fueled his anger about the deaths of his two sons and the other son who was as well as dead to him. It wasn't enough that his sons had gone to a war he wasn't sure he believed in, but Sherman's troops used his fence railings for firewood and took all his livestock for food, even the chickens and geese. They didn't stop there. No, they took everything in the house they wanted. Hadn't been for Toby hiding a couple of horses and cows in the swamp, there would be nothing left.

Lott pondered the time he and his younger brother Jake came to this land as young men. He remembered how hard they worked for the surveyor who was mapping out the Mississippi land after the Choctaw had ceded it to the United States government in the 1830's and the thrill he felt when he found some excellent farmland, then decided to stay. Jake and he built one of the finest log homes in the area complete with three large rooms down the left side of the house, and across an open hall called a dogtrot, they added two additional rooms. It was indeed an exceptional home for the time.

Two years earlier, John, with Lott's assistance, had bought Toby, a local slave, off the blocks in Meridian only to issue him his freedom. Even though Toby had his papers, he chose to stay with the Wilson family. His friendship led him to take the Wilson name for his own.

Interrupting Lott's memories, Sarah whispered, "You got to have faith, Lott. The Lord will provide. He always has."

Lott shook his head and silently pondered his feelings about faith. Maybe the Lord would provide, but he just didn't believe it. All he could feel was that his life was like Job's, the one who the Lord let the devil take everything he had except his life. What good was his life compared to those he loved.

Sarah, the daughter of a Methodist minister, began and ended each day in prayer and meditation. She got up early in the mornings and, in the quiet, found special time with her Bible and her Lord. Recently, during this time of deep meditation, she could feel God speaking to her.

Taking Lott by the hand, she led him back to their bed. Settling in for the night, Sarah kissed him and whispered, "You need stronger faith, Lott. Things will get better. Ever since I heard about John, the Spirit has been visiting me, and when I think of him, I have an unusual warm, joyous feeling."

"Hush it right now," said Lott. "That's crazy talk. I don't want to hear no more about it, and I don't need no Christmas this year."

All was silent for a while except for the whimper of the wind grasping at the house and the rhythmic repeated beats of the clock on the mantel.

"What about James Earl? I guess you got a cold feeling about him?" Lott asked.

"My heart aches for him, but it was time for him to go. He is at peace with the Lord. He's doing just fine."

Camp Douglas, Illinois
December 1863

John felt like his home and loved ones were an eternity away. After the battle, John was placed with other prisoners in confinements and then spent weeks on a train. After reaching their destination, they had been herded off the boxcars by bayonet and paraded through town like cattle going to a slaughter. People stared and hurled insults and objects as they had trudged their way to the prison camp. Many were barefoot and coatless. True, they had survived the bloody battle, but now they would be faced with a different type of survival, an even more difficult one.

"Line up and make it fast!" yelled the prison guards.

The snow blanketed the ground, and temperatures were below freezing.

"Listen up," the lead guard spoke. "Strip down. We gotta check for concealed weapons. And don't try anything."

Slowly, the prisoners removed their clothes, and the guards searched each article of clothing as the cold intensified within each prisoner. Even though the search made sense, the time without clothes stretched into more than two hours. The guards were ordered to confiscate any valuables found. Valuables could be used as a means of bribery, which was strictly forbidden. Their bodies began to shake and shiver, reaching a light blue as several prisoners collapsed, never to take another breath. The wind stirred the smell of human waste and filth into the air. John noticed long rows of buildings built perhaps three feet off the ground about one hundred feet long and twenty-five feet wide. Some had a chimney located at the end of the building while others had stovepipes protruding from the center. No smoke drifting from the chimneys indicated that heat would be a luxury unattainable by the prisoners.

John could feel fear and despair creeping into his soul as he entered the building and saw over one hundred thin and hollow-eyed men huddled near the back wall. The overpowering smell of unwashed men filled his nostrils. John saw no fire and felt only a piercing cold. Men huddled together for warmth as the beds on each side were left empty. In this gloom, John knew his chance of surviving to see those he loved was bleak.

"Welcome to eighty acres of hell. Some call this here place Camp Douglas, but we call it Camp Extermination. Welcome home, boys," whispered one prisoner.

"I can't afford to die. I will not die in this place," John mumbled.

"What'd you say?"

"I said, I ain't gonna die here."

"Well. Good luck to you. They's killing us here as fast as they do on the firing line. Some of us made it through one winter. God's willing, we'll make it another'n."

Suddenly, a crack of a musket from a guard outside sent slithers of wood sailing across the room as the ball hissed overhead.

"You know the rules," shouted a guard outside. "No talking after dark. I shot high this time. Next time, I'll aim lower."

The prisoner who had first spoken explained, "We are killed when they shoot into the barracks, and we are killed if we cross the dead line, which is a low-lying fence built to keep us away from the main security walls. Some hopeless prisoners wander into the area on purpose to end their misery. What's worse, the Federal guards are rewarded for killing us, so you better be careful."

The cold wind pushed against the building and gushed through the cracks in the walls and floor as prisoners huddled even closer to conserve body heat. When the cold was unbearable, the men would huddle together on the floor and share blankets instead of sleeping on the flea and louse-infested beds. Early each morning, the bodies of those who did not survive were removed and carried for burial. Before the dead were carried out, inmates took their blankets, coats, underwear, and especially shoes.

"'Bout morning, boys," a man called out. "Ole Santa'll be here soon. Better make your list."

The men didn't respond but got to their feet and wrapped themselves in their blankets as gale force winds off Lake Michigan howled across the open grounds. In a few moments, a bugle sounded, and the men rushed around, preparing for the morning formation. Sergeant Roper, in charge of the barrack, closely scanned the room for any who had died during the night or were too sick to stand formation. After close inspection, he found that four had died and eight were too sick to venture outside. Smallpox, cholera, dysentery, mumps, and pneumonia were taking their toll. Medicine had been sent from the Confederate government but had been seized and sent instead to the federal troops in the field.

As the sun tipped the horizon, sending slashes of light glistening across the snow and light puffy clouds skirting above, John looked down the long line of the once grand army of the Northern Virginia. They were not the invincible force he once knew but, instead, a pitiful group of barefoot soldiers in rags - no weapons, no caps, no pride, no hope, and only considered traitors, vagrants, and worthless men by their foes.

Sergeant Roper looked down the line of men. "Stand tall. Show some pride," he called out. "They're bringing up a new commander this morning."

"New commander," whispered a man in the line near John. "That makes three since I've been here."

"They say too many have escaped from this compound," whispered another prisoner.

"I heard the words out about too many of us dying," echoed another.

"Do you really think folks up here care if we die?" the banter continued.

Sergeant Roper turned to his men who were far from the Federal soldiers and said, "Truth is, any decent Union officer is needed at the front. What they send up here are those who ain't fit. They can't command men in the field, they don't want the job here, and they don't care whether we live or die. In fact, the fewer of us here, the easier it is for them."

Sergeant Roper snapped to attention and called his men to order as the Union officers arrived.

All was quiet except for the wind whistling across the snow, dusting the men in rank and the prisoners' blankets frequently flapping with each gust. The group of Union officers headed to the center of the parade ground and upon reaching the flagpole, stopped, pivoted, and faced the prisoners.

An introduction was made, but due to a strong gust of wind, John missed the name of the new commander. The wind grew calmer, and John heard the name Colonel Benjamin Sweet.

"Men, this is going to be short. Up to this point, it's been too easy for you. Expect the worse from now on. No prisoners will walk away from my compound and head home or return to their fighting units or socialize in the city. No one will leave, and no one will break you out. This will never happen under my supervision. Those who escape will be hunted down and executed, and those knowing about an escape and keeping quiet will face severe consequences. And if, and I say if, an escape is made, there will be no food or fuel for your barracks for five days," stated the colonel. "In fact, we've been feeding you too good. From here out, expect no vegetables or fruit and very little meat."

The colonel spotted some local citizens who had paid to watch from a high platform. He turned and, in a loud voice, said, "For the dear citizens of Chicago who might feel some sympathy for you, I'll deal with them too. Now, get the wagons out, and organize the burial detail," he said, turning toward one of his officers. "By the way, Merry Christmas, but forget about Santa this year, prisoners."

As the prisoners heard about the cut in rations, a murmur, like a wind, covered the grounds."Why don't you just line us up, and get it over with," a voice called out.

Colonel Sweet turned sharply to the prisoners and, dismissing them, shouted, "There won't be any meals today nor tomorrow. Maybe that will correct your attitude. Now we have details to perform." The prisoners slowly began to shuffle silently toward their barracks.

"Sam, I ain't served on one of them details yet, and I shore hope today ain't a start," commented John.

John had met Sam Harris, a fellow Mississippian, while being loaded on the train outside of Memphis, and with time, a strong bond had developed.

"John, you still got a limp. Now how did you say you got it?" asked Sam, walking along behind John.

"Don't rightly know. We were advancing on the Yankee line, and all I remember is a flash of light and a sharp pain," explained John. "When I woke up, I was in a Union field hospital. They told me I was a lucky devil. A piece of spent shell hit me on the head, and a ball went through my leg between the two bones and out the other side. If the ball had shattered the bones, they would have taken my leg, and if the piece of iron had hit me full force, it would have taken my head off. Yeah, I was some lucky."

"Show me the place on your leg," stated Sam.

John pushed up his britches leg and pointed to a round scar on each side of his calf.

"Hey, you. Private Lewis!" came a shout. "You're loading 'em up."

Sam shook his head. "Least you ain't gonna have to dig no graves. That ground is frozen solid."

After stripping the dead of their blankets and belongings, the prisoners carried them to wagon beds. Sadness filled John's heart as he realized the soldiers were being discarded with no loved ones to mourn and no prayer to send these precious souls on their way. John quickly said a few words to the Lord for each one he lifted to the wagon.

Later that day as John and Sam shared a piece of stale bread Sam had confiscated, he asked John, "Why do they call you Private Lewis? Don't they know yore name?"

"Well, when I was captured, I didn't care much what them devils called me. I just signed on as John Lewis. I didn't say nothing about me being John Lewis Wilson. It don't really make no difference what they call me, does it?"

"Well, tell me this? You got any other kin in this here fight?"

"I got two older brothers in it, Thomas and James Earl. When the war started, I was too young to enlist, but when I turned seventeen, I joined up with them."

"They know you up here?"

John shook his head. "Naw, I don't see how they could."

Later that night, John could not sleep, so he shook Sam and whispered, "You think we'll ever make it home?"

"Best not to think about it. Just take one day at a time," Sam replied, realizing that if the war continued, odds were that none of these prisoners would be alive.

"I got to get home," John said."My family needs me, and I got the prettiest girl you've ever seen waiting on me. Her name is Rebecca, but we call her Becca. She's got light red hair, emerald green eyes, and the Lord has blessed her in every way, if you know what I mean."

"Well, if she's that pretty, some other fellow may find her fancy." Sam laughed, pulling his blanket over his ears. "How about her? She know what happened to you?"

"I don't see how she could," answered John. "You know, I think we've loved each other as long as I can remember. Actually, I think I loved her before I even knew what love was."

A few days later, Sam was called for the burial detail and returned unusually quiet. John figured he was just tired or getting sick. The following morning, Sam was stirring about as usual but still un-talkative. John decided it was time to find out his friend's trouble and eased over to Sam and sat down beside him. "You got a problem, Sam?"

Sam waited, then shook his head and replied, "Yesterday, when we got them bodies loaded in the wagons, I noticed there weren't no shovels. We carried them pore souls down past the graveyard and kept on going. When we reached the lake, they had us unload 'em on a big boat, and once out in the water, they had us dump 'em in. They laughed and called 'em fish bait. They said that the ground was too hard for digging."

"Surely that can't be," muttered John.

"As the Lord is my witness, that's the truth," Sam said despondently. "Who we been kidding. It's gonna take a miracle for any of us to get out of here. Most likely you won't be seeing that green- eyed girl you been talking about."

"Ain't so. You gotta have faith, Sam," said John, placing his arm around his friend's shoulder. "We just got to do some praying."

"Praying," answered Sam shaking his head. "I'm not sure about that. I think the Lord's done turned His back on us. You've seen what I have. Men killed by the thousands, and those that ain't is crippled for life. Look what's happening here. They treating us worse than animals. No sir, I'm not sure about the Lord. If He loved us, wouldn't things be different? It'll take a miracle for me to believe."

John shook his head. "Can't think like that, Sam. Times are hard. The Lord might be testing us."

"You could be right. You look at yoreself lately? I bet you've lost thirty pounds since we got in here. You're might near skin and bones. You most near died last winter from that smallpox. You think you gonna make this winter? Your good Lord better give you more food."

When John joined the army at seventeen, he stood six feet tall, weighed about one hundred and eighty pounds, and was in perfect health, but now he was a mere shadow of that body.

Later that night as they huddled together, a prisoner whispered, "You boys see them sawhorses they built out front. They kinda tall for saw work. What you think they gonna use them for?"

"I think our Colonel Sweet is a little on the crazy side. Who knows," remarked one of the men.

"Shhh, we best quiet down. Don't want them fool guards shooting us."

Shivering in the cold, John began to shudder at the thought of survival. He knew the Lord was in control and that miracles did happen, but he felt no one could survive Camp Douglas if the war continued. There would be no return home, and John realized his last days might be spent at this forsaken place. For tonight, his hope was gone.

2

Prayers and the Pit

You are my hiding place; you will protect me
from trouble and surround me with songs of deliverance.
—Psalm 32:7

Little Rock, Mississippi:

Several days after Christmas, Sarah threw a shawl around her shoulders, gathered her bonnet, and walked out on the porch where she found Lott near the barn throwing hay to their lone cow. "Going to town. Would you please harness the rig for me," Sarah called out.

"What you going for," replied Lott, "we ain't got money to spend."

"I'm gonna make Sister a new dress. I got some things to barter," she explained. "I might do a little socializing too."

Lott went inside the barn and soon came out leading a dark brown gelding harnessed to a buggy. As he helped his wife into the buggy, he figured there was more to this trip than Sarah was telling.

Handing her a blanket, he remarked, "It's cold out here. You better cover up."

The village of Little Rock was only a half a mile from their home, and even though the road, once a Choctaw Indian trail, could be difficult during the winter season, it was passable. Little Rock contained a gristmill, livery stable, blacksmith shop, a church used also as the local school, and most importantly, a general store that served as post office and stage stop. It was here at Walker's Store that people met to purchase goods and socialize.

Pushing the horse through several large washouts, Sarah soon reached Little Rock. She secured the horse and made her way up the steps and onto the porch of Walker's store.

"I guess I'm the only one foolish enough to be out on such a cold day." She laughed to herself as a flock of crows soared high and found shelter in a barren oak tree down by the creek. Sarah walked across the rough-cut boards and lifted the latch to enter. The general store supplied everything the local farmers needed - plowshares, harnesses, saddles, cloth, seasoning, canned food, shotguns, powder and shot. The smell of hickory smoke, leather and salted hams hanging on large beams gave her a warm welcome as she strolled inside. Supplies were depleted because of the war that continued to rage.

"Anybody here," Sarah called making her way down the aisle to a large woodstove.

"Be out in a minute," replied a voice from the back room post office.

In a moment, Thomas Walker, the owner of the store, strolled through the back door. He straightened his coat and pushed what little hair he had in place. His face beamed a smile that emanated energy even though his thin, stooped body showed signs of poor health for a man in his late forties.

"Good gracious, Mrs. Wilson, what in the world are you doing out on a day as this!" Mr. Walker exclaimed, extending his hand. "Can I help you?"

Sarah shook her head and glanced around the store. "I'm just going to look around." For the next few moments, she walked about the place examining the goods.

Mr. Walker followed her and finally asked, "Is there something you want?"

"Oh yes," Sarah replied. "I need several yards of material, and if Becca is about, I would like to visit with her."

"Well, the material is over there, and Becca should be out as soon as she's sorted the mail. Just take your time, and I'm going to unload some items that got here on the stage."

"Don't bother about me," Sarah smiled.

"By the way, what are we trading today?" questioned Mr. Walker.

"We had a hog killing a couple of weeks ago. I've got you two fine hams in the buggy."

"There's nothing like ham and eggs. Yes ma'am, that's what we'll have come supper time." Mr. Walker laughed as he left. "Becca will settle with you."

Times were hard, and cash was short, and Mr. Walker allowed his customers to barter even though he often didn't need what they had. With prayers and hard work, he felt things would get better.

Soon, Rebecca walked from the back mailroom, "I knew it was you, Mrs. Wilson. I could recognize your voice anywhere. Sorry it took me so long."

Holding out her arms for a hug, Sarah embraced Rebecca and motioned her to sit in the chairs at the woodstove. For a moment, Sarah enjoyed looking into the face of this young woman who seemed like a daughter. Her curly auburn hair was pinned back behind her ears, and a few unruly strands fell across her cheeks. A glint of sunlight streaked across her face, showing the sparkle in her eyes. "*She is so beautiful,*" thought Sarah. "*I wish John could see her.*"

"Tell me, dear, what have you been doing with yourself. I've missed your visits."

When John was reported missing and presumed killed, Rebecca was devastated. She remained in her bedroom for weeks until her parents feared they would loose her forever. Then one morning, Sarah came to see Rebecca and stayed for most of the day. When she left, Rebecca slowly returned to normal and began making morning visits to see Mrs. Wilson but, lately, the visits had stopped.

"It's hard times, Mrs. Wilson. I stay pretty busy helping father here at the store, and you know my mother hasn't been well lately."

Sarah smiled at Rebecca. "You can't give up on John, child. I have a warm feeling about him. I don't think the Lord has called him yet. You need to keep the faith."

Rebecca looked doubtful and remembered how she had hoped John was alive and that the report of his death was a mistake. She had hoped she would hear that he had joined another unit, or was captured and in a federal prison, but after a year with no word, she had lost hope and faced the reality that the love of her life wasn't coming home.

Rebecca cleared her throat and, clasping Sarah's hands, said, "You know I've always been honest with you and it isn't easy to say this, but I just don't believe John is alive. There's been no word, and when I visit with you, it's harder for me. I've got to accept what has happened and try to go on with my life." Tears began forming in her eyes and slowly trickled down her cheeks. Rubbing them from her face, she murmured, "I just can't come anymore."

Clasping her hand, Sarah said, "It's alright, child. I understand. I'll just have to have enough faith for the both of us. There's things I could tell you, but I probably shouldn't."

"What do you mean, Mrs. Wilson?"

"Do you believe in the Word?"

"Yes, ma'am, you know I do."

"If you do, then you know there are angels about - both good and bad ones, and they minister to folks in strange ways."

"What are you saying, Mrs. Wilson? Have you seen an angel?"

Sarah smiled and nodded her head. "The Lord works in strange and wondrous ways. Don't you give up hope, child. Not yet. They talk with me sometimes."

Rebecca gave Sarah a hug and led her to the cloth section. Holding up a roll of light blue material, she said, "I think this would be perfect for Sister. What do you think?"

"I think it will do just fine."

"Mrs. Wilson, "I hope y'all had a good Christmas."

"Child, we struggled with it. Maybe next year."

"Tell Sister I asked about her."

"I'll do just that."

After Sarah left, Mr. Walker returned and, pausing for a moment, replied, "You know, I worry about Mrs. Wilson. She's been through so much, and I couldn't help but catch part of your conversation. Did she say she's been visited by angels?"

"Father, you know what a strong faith she has. She thinks she hears voices. Maybe there are angels," replied Rebecca as she straightened the cloth. "I think she really believes that John is alive."

Mr. Walker shook his head. "There is a point when the pain of losing loved ones is so great that the mind can't handle it."

"Are you saying she is losing her mind?"

"I'm saying something just ain't right with her. By the way, Frankie came by earlier and said he'd stop for a visit as soon as he took care of business."

Getting no reply, Mr. Walker peered around the counter to see if Rebecca was still in the storefront. "Did you hear me, daughter?"

"I heard you, Papa."

"Well, say something."

"What do you expect me to say?"

"Rebecca, Frankie is a man of means, and some say his family is one of the richest in the state of Mississippi. I'd say you'd be wise to give him a little of your time. Who knows what could happen," replied Mr. Walker. "You've got to start thinking of your future."

"Future. I don't want to think about that." Rebecca frowned.

Rebecca had known Frankie Oliver all her life. True, his family was wealthy, but she had heard that Frankie's father had exploited many to gain his wealth. Although Rebecca knew a son shouldn't be held responsible for a parent's actions and Frankie did bring fun back to her life, she still had reservations.

Frankie had been John's best friend, and when Frankie enlisted in the army, John had been quick to sign up too. As a boy, Frankie would start fights that he could not win, and John would step in to help. Rebecca knew John was worried about Frankie because his recklessness in a war could mean death. She also knew John had to feel betrayed when Frankie never showed up at the Newton Station. Rebecca had heard that Frankie's father paid a four – hundred - dollar fee so the State of Mississippi would release Frankie from service.

"Father, if Frankie comes by, I will probably see him. He has always been a friend," replied Rebecca, knowing this would please her father.

All was quiet except for the crackling of the hickory, burning softly in the stove and the wind howling around the corner of the old frame building. "Papa, you know you're right. I do need to look to my future. No matter what I think right now, it's coming."

Later that afternoon, Mr. Walker heard a horse whinny outside. A tall young man entered the door and quickly shut it behind him. "Gracious, it's cold outside. That wind will cut you in half," he muttered, removing his hat and overcoat.

Mr. Walker hurried to meet the young man and grabbed his hand. "Let me take your duds, Frankie, and you best get to the stove and thaw yourself up." He quickly called out to his daughter, "Becca, we got company."

Rebecca straightened the supply room and quickly smoothed her skirt, removed her apron, and pushed her hair from her face. "Frankie, you ought to have more sense than to be out on a day like this." She smiled. "What's so important that took you out today?"

Frankie, a tall, lanky but handsome young man of eighteen pushed his long straight blond hair back and smiled at her. "I had to run an errand for Papa this morning and thought it proper to come see how you all are getting along," he explained. He could hardly contain his emotions as he looked into Rebecca's eyes. She seemed more beautiful every time he saw her. Maturity was surely blessing her in every way. As cold as he was, he flushed as he gazed at her.

Embarrassed at the intent in his eyes, Rebecca quickly stepped away and reached for a broom leaning against a support timber and began sweeping up ashes around the stove. "So how are your folks doing?"

Frankie regained his composure and eased down on a chair next to the stove to watch Rebecca for a moment. "They're all fine. Papa is somewhat upset. When that Yankee group came through here a while back - "

"You mean Grierson," Rebecca interrupted.

"Yeah, that's the devil. Well some of our slaves tried to run off with him. That didn't work too good 'cause Grierson was on the move and didn't want them slowing him down."

"What happened to the slaves? You get them back?"

Frankie smiled. "We got 'em back, and I promise you they won't think about leaving no more."

Rebecca shuddered to think about the treatment that the slaves probably received. Even though she understood that slaves were needed on large plantations, she still saw the cruelty and lack of fairness. She was glad that her father did not own slaves.

The two talked for a while as Rebecca helped her father prepare to close the store. Frankie took Rebecca by the hand and walked her to the door. "Mama is planning a social for some of the young folks Saturday night, and I wondered if you would like to come? We'll have some music, a little dancing, and some mighty tasty treats."

Rebecca shook her head. "I don't think I can do that," she murmured. "I've got things to do. You know Mama's sick, and it's a pretty good piece to your place. I'd be late coming in."

"Rebecca, you need to get out and socialize some," Frankie whispered. "I could send one of our drivers to get you, and you could spend the night at our place. I think you would have fun. Suzanne would love to see you."

Suzanne was Frankie's younger sister and about the same age as Rebecca, but like Rebecca, she also had feelings for John. Suzanne's desire for a relationship with John had quietly kept them from friendship.

Rebecca glanced at her father who was watching the two and knew he wanted her to go. *Going to the party doesn't necessarily mean I will be with Frankie*, she thought, *and it will give me a chance to get out.*

"I should be ready by six," Rebecca said.

A big smile crossed Frankie's face. "I look forward to it."

As the door shut behind him, Rebecca peered back at her father. "Yes!" he exclaimed slapping his hand briskly on the counter top.

With the wind on her face, Sarah pushed the horse over washouts that had grown larger. Pulling the quilt snuggly around her shoulders, she slowly made her way home. A smile crossed her face as she saw the bundle of cloth beside her. There had been no presents for Christmas, but Sister was going to get a new dress, and Sarah began singing and praising the Lord. As she remembered her talk with Rebecca, she realized how ridiculous it must have sounded. Folks read about angels all the time in the Bible, but somehow, they seem to dismiss their existence. *I might be an old fool but I know what I feel, and I know the Lord is trying to tell me something. I just don't know exactly what,* she thought. As she topped the hill overlooking Little Rock, something compelled her to stop. Reining the horse in, she sat, looking at the bleak woodlands. The wind quit blowing, and all became quiet. She shut her eyes, and in the rustle of leaves, Sarah heard a voice whispering, "Your faith will make you whole."

The horse snorted suddenly and nervously shook his harness as the wind pushed the barren limbs of the old oak trees.

Sarah opened her eyes and looked to heaven and whispered, "Thank you, Lord. I understand."

Lot left the warmth of his fire when he heard Sarah's voice.

"I could hear you coming a mile off, woman. Sounds like an old time revival," teased Lott. "Here, let me take the rig, and you get on in the house where it's warm." Lott noticed the bundle under Sarah's arm and smiled. "Sisters back there making supper."

Sister left the kitchen to greet her mother. At fifteen, Sister was already as tall as her mother and had blond hair, blue eyes and a petite figure. She was a striking young woman who, many said, resembled her mother when she was younger.

Sarah hid the bundle behind her back but could not hide the joy she felt. "Here, Sister, it's a little late but Merry Christmas.

Unwrapping the bundle, Sister exclaimed with joy at the sacrifice her mother had made and at the beauty of the material.

***

Rebecca did attend the social at the Ollivers', and to her surprise, she enjoyed herself. Since the war had taken most of the young men from the community, the girls had to dance with boys not only shorter but also younger. The boys enjoyed their newfound status, but the war would soon call them away too.

Frankie thoroughly enjoyed the evening and danced every chance he could with Rebecca. At first, she seemed distant and totally disinterested in the social, but soon, a smile emerged and finally a laugh. Frankie planned to gain her acceptance and favor but knew he must go slowly. Frankie began stopping by briefly to see Rebecca and often brought Suzanne with him. Soon, the three were spending more time together, and Frankie felt Rebecca was beginning to consider him more than a friend.

Camp Douglas
February 1864

As promised by the new commander, life for the prisoners became more difficult. A cut in rations meant the starving men must find food elsewhere. The infestations of rats, once a hindrance, now became the men's primary source of protein. The Southerners jokingly made a meal they called squirrel stew. The few vegetables they were issued mixed with water, salt and pepper made a tasty stew. Once a young man from Alabama trapped a ground hog above the latrine, and it became a legend of luxury for the prisoners. The soldiers tried to keep their spirits high and hoped for better days.

A knock on the door caused Colonel Sweet to adjust his glasses, lay down his pen and straighten himself. "You may enter," the colonel stated harshly.

The door eased open, and an officer dusting the snow from his cape and hat entered. "You send for me, sir?"

"Captain Moore, I sent for you two hours ago. Is something wrong with our line of communication, or is this the normal procedure for Camp Douglas?"

The captain hesitated then came to attention. "Sir, I was in town talking to some leading citizens about our past problems. I got the message twenty minutes ago and hurried as quickly as possible."

"Hang your overcoat on that peg by the door and have a seat," directed Sweet. For a moment, the colonel sat, staring at the captain and finally spoke, "Captain, how long have you been at Camp Douglas?"

"Over two years, sir."

"Two years. Well, you should know a lot about past operations of this camp."

"Yes sir, I suppose I should," the captain replied, not certain of the colonel's intent.

The colonel smiled and stroked his beard. "I've been here a little over a month and have done a lot of investigation about this camp and have discovered that this is an ill-run prison camp where prisoners have literally walked out and headed home or rejoined their old units fighting us all over again. Maybe we should change the name from Camp Douglas Prison to Camp Douglas Social Club. The last report was of prisoners sneaking out and going into Chicago partying with young women. After getting arrested for drunkenness and spending a night in jail, they were released and never came back here. What do you think about that?"

"I've heard those stories, sir," replied the captain, squirming uncomfortably in his seat.

"I'm sure you have since you've been here for over two years and spend a lot of time in town," stated Sweet stroking his long mustache.

Sir, I know the condition here, but I'm not the commander. I just take orders from officers who outrank me. It's the military way, and I do my duty," answered the captain, trying to defend himself.

"Well said," replied Sweet. "You will take orders. First, double the guards around the compound where leaving will be all but impossible. Next, place informers among the prisoners to gain information about plans of escape. Third, make sure escapes are stopped before they occur."

"Yes sir, Colonel."

"That's not all, Captain. You continue spending time in the city talking to civilians, but this time, get the names of Southern sympathizers who have assisted in prison escape. Round them up, and bring them to Camp Douglas immediately. Now about the major breakout being planned at this very moment, what do you know about it?"

The captain pursed his lips in frustration. "Sir, may I speak openly?"

"You may."

"Sir, there are some Southern sympathizers in nearly every town, and I know this camp has not been run well, but I've heard nothing from the camp or from the citizens of Chicago indicating a breakout. Nothing. It's the dead of winter. If any of those fools broke out, they would either freeze or starve to death."

"Captain, that's exactly why you are captain, and I am colonel. It is coming, and we will put a stop to it. Double the guard, place informants in the barracks and spend time in the city. I want a report from you soon. Do you understand?"

"Yes sir, I'll do my best, Colonel."

After Captain Moore left, Colonel Sweet leaned back, lit a cigar and thought about how he would tighten control of Camp Douglas. He knew the history of the camp and even though he had heard of no escape plans, he was determined to put pressure on the prisoners and the citizens of Chicago to gain information. Next, he planned to reduce the number of prisoners with the new program where Southern prisoners signed an oath of allegiance to the Union and were sent to the western frontier to join Calvary units dealing with Indian uprisings. He rose from his chair, made his way to a large window and glanced about the compound and murmured quietly to himself, "If they didn't keep sending captured Rebs to the camp, with time and the number dying, my job would be less complicated. But for now, let's see who wants to go west."

The bugle sounded as the prisoners made their way from the barracks and fell into formation. The sun tipped the horizon, and a soft wind from the south brought a touch of warmer air that melted patches of snow under the feet of the prisoners. As water seeped into their shoes and surrounded the feet of those barefooted, the roll call was made and the burial details were assigned. This time before being dismissed, a captain came to the platform, unrolled a document, and asked, "Men, who would like to leave this place?"

The prisoners stirred and murmured among themselves.

"I'm serious," the captain stated. "There is a new program that allows you to leave. All you must do is sign an oath of allegiance to the United States of America, and you will be transferred out west to a Calvary unit. You probably are aware of the problems we are having with the Indians out there."

The prisoners began, once again, to talk among themselves.

"Go ahead and talk," said the captain. "When you finish, let your unit commander speak for you."

After a few moments, a Southern officer down the line raised his arm.

"You may speak," ordered the captain.

A tall lanky officer stepped forward. "Sir, does this mean we would be part of the Union Calvary?"

"You would," the captain stated.

"Would we have to wear the union blue?" the Southern officer asked.

"What else would you wear?"

"We wouldn't have to ever confront one of our own Confederate units, would we?"

"Since you would be operating out west, how could you?" assured the captain.

The Southerners were allowed to talk more among themselves. They knew if the war continued, chances were that many of them would never make it home to see family. Even though they may never look into the eyes of girlfriends, wives, or children, could they explain giving up the cause.

Finally, the captain raised his hand clasping a pen. "Step forward and you will be free. Inside the supply house to our rear is a hot bath, new clothing and delicious meal being prepared as we speak. You'll be on your way to Kansas by daybreak tomorrow. What do you say?"

Inside the commandant's office, Colonel Sweet stood rigid, arms folded behind his back, glaring out the window as no one accepted the offer.

The Southerners wondered if anyone would step out. They knew in their hearts they were Confederate soldiers who represented the South, their states and communities. They had fought to protect their country and their way of life and had shared hardships. They were bonded. They were one. All remained in line.

Colonel Sweet slapped his gloves against his leg in anguish and stormed out of his office. He proceeded to the parade ground where the line of men stood. Nudging the captain aside, he glared out at the prisoners and exclaimed, "You see the bodies brought out each morning? Those folks won't be going home, and if you will think about that for a moment, you probably won't either. This is a chance for some of you to survive. You want to live?"

A hush came over the grounds. A prisoner slowly stepped out, looking neither left nor right afraid to see the eyes of his comrades. One by one, others stepped forward and were immediately ushered away from the ranks. In all, thirty-seven Southerners left for service in the West.

That afternoon, as John and the other prisoners huddled around the fireplace in the rear of the barracks, the talk centered on those who had left to serve the Union. One prisoner, lighting his pipe with contraband tobacco, quickly inhaled and blew a large circle of smoke as he drawled out, "That there was an Indian smoke signal. They has spotted the Calvary, and they is fixin' to kill every one of them boys, especially them Southern fools."

The men laughed and nodded their approval and began breaking up into groups for the usual afternoon of playing cards and telling stories. John, who had obtained a Bible from a dying prisoner, settled on his bunk and read. Sam, tired of cards, came to John and eased next to him. "You believe in that book, don't you?" Sam asked.

John thought for a moment and nodded his head to Sam. "You know, it's the only thing that seems to make sense."

"Make sense," Sam answered. "John, you've seen what we did on the battlefield. You see how we're treated in this pit on earth. The way I see it is that mankind is the most evil and destructive animal yore Lord has created. Give us enough time, and we will destroy not only all mankind but everything else as well. To me, it's all senseless."

John placed his arm on Sam's shoulder and spoke, "Sam, the Lord works in strange and wondrous ways. You know, the Word tells us there's gonna be wars and rumors of war. You just got to have faith to know that God is going to bring good from all this, and at least in the Word, we do have hope."

Sam shook his head. "I do hope you're right, and if'n we ever get out of this place, you might want to become one of them preacher men. In fact, you might want to work on me first." He laughed.

***

Later that afternoon, Colonel Sweet looked over the list of newly recruited men and glanced at the captain sitting patiently and waiting for a comment. "Well, Captain, I wanted more, but these will have to do. They'll be out of here tomorrow."

At that moment, there was a knock at the door, and a soldier with a telegram came in.

"A telegram for you, Colonel," the soldier stated.

Sweet quickly studied the telegram and slammed his fist upon the table. "I can't believe this! I get rid of some of these devils, and they're sending me more."

Captain Moore, regaining his composure, said, "Sir, they always send us more."

"You don't know what's coming in here tomorrow, Captain."

"And who would that be?"

"You ever hear of Morgan's Raiders?" stated the colonel.

"Yes sir, I have," replied the captain.

"About fifty-six of them will arrive tomorrow, and our hands will be full," informed the colonel. "With their reputation and attitude, there's going to be trouble. They are not regular soldiers; they are murderers. They know no discipline."

***

Awakened by the smell of smoke and fatback frying, John sat up, rubbed his eyes and pushed unruly hair from his face. A few men with blankets wrapped around their shoulders were standing near the fire, rubbing their hands together for warmth while the barrack cook prepared breakfast. Fatback, fried corn patty, cooked in the grease from the pork, plus a cup of watered-down coffee made from crushed peanuts was all the prisoners knew.

Men were accounted for at the morning formation, burial details were assigned, and today, orders for a wood detail were requested. To warm the barracks and have cooking fuel, the prisoners were required to cut, split and distribute wood to the compound barracks. If the weather was too bad for details to go out, there would be no heat for preparing the meals. All would suffer. The best part of the wood detail is that prisoners enjoyed the freedom of the countryside.

As luck would have it, John and Sam were selected, and they began the long march of three miles. As the high walls of the prison faded from sight, they rejoiced. Here in the fresh open air, the smell of oak trees and damp leaves unearthed beneath the snow met their noses. The occasional flash of a deer bounding away or the scamper of a squirrel darting from limb to limb would remind the men of home. Here on the road, war seemed a bad dream. Freedom seemed so close John could reach out and touch it.

Since dry wood was needed, trees had been felled several weeks earlier, and the men cut them up and split the pieces into two-feet lengths. About mid-afternoon when the wagons were sufficiently loaded, the men headed to the barracks. As they approached the camp, they heard a loud commotion.

Sam pointed toward the prison. "What do you think's going on in there? Sounds like a riot. Reckon some men have done tried to break out?"

John, watching an eagle soaring overhead, was preoccupied and mumbled, "Could be anything."

The guards nervously hurried the wood detail back to the barracks. As they approached the camp, they saw a large detachment of Union troops escorting a mass of men into the gateway. Unlike the other Southern soldiers, these were not dressed in the normal gray and butternut colors. They had various colored coats, and their pants were tucked neatly into knee-length leather boots. Most wore wide brim hats with bright-colored peacock feathers at the hatband.

The sergeant in charge halted the wood detail because entering was impossible. Sam and John observed the new arrivals as they walked past. These prisoners kicked, cursed and spat at the soldiers who were prodding them along with fixed bayonets. One was able to break free from his bonds of cord, and instead of trying to escape, he grabbed a rifle from a guard, threw it down, plunged the guard to the ground and began beating him with his fist. The brunt end of a rifle butt quickly ended the fisticuffs.

Suddenly, a murmur came over the group.

"What's going on, Sam?" John asked.

Since Sam was taller than John, he stretched up on his toes and said, "You ain't gonna believe this!"

"What?" John exclaimed.

"There's a Negro in there with them dressed like one of our soldiers."

"Can't be," replied John.

Then John saw the man. He was indeed dressed like them. He was dark, and his wiry black hair protruded from all sides of his hat. He wore a bright-red wrap around his neck, and as he passed, his dark brown eyes met John's. A smile crossed his face, and he gave John a nod, then walked on toward the entrance. Suddenly, an explosion erupted from the gate and smoke filled the air. The Negro flew backwards, flinched a few times and lay still in the snow. He tried to raise his hands, but they only quivered. The white of the snow faded into red where the Negro lay.

At first, all was quiet; then one prisoner after another began to shout in confusion. Remembering the look and smile on the man's face, John pushed through the guards, knelt by the Negro and placed his arm under the neck of the soldier. The Negro looked up at John and tried to speak, but nothing came. His eyes glazed over, and he became still.

Outraged, John rose and lunged for the guard who had fired the shot. "You had no right to murder that man!" he shouted as he flung himself at the surprised man. "You just can't kill unarmed men like this!"

A hard blow to John's back sent him reeling to the ground, knocking him unconscious. As he was being dragged off, he heard a loud voice that seemed to echo in his mind.

"We're fighting this war to free the slaves, and it's costing us thousands of lives. Any Negro caught in a Confederate uniform or with a fighting Rebel unit will be shot. Those are the orders."

***

January finally faded into February, and the fresh spring breeze pushed from the Gulf, giving a taste of the quickly approaching weather. Spring planting would be in a few weeks, so Lott and Toby worked constantly, sharpening plow shares, inspecting and repairing harnesses, and hoping their lone mule, Ole Dusty, would be as steady as last year. Toby sat on a stool made from hickory and cranked the handle turning the sharpening stone. Sparks flew as the share head gained a point. "Time to work, time to play, time to push dat sun away," he sang.

Lott leaned over a fence rail bordering the farmyard, studied the field soon to be cultivated, and after listening to the tune, asked, "Where'd you learn that song?"

Toby laughed. "I don't just know, Mr. Wilson. It just come to me, I reckon. You like it?"

For the first time in months, Lot was talkative and laughing. He even spoke of going to church but still refused to speak of the boys. "I like it. It's got a catchy tune," he smiled and began to hum along.

Lott headed to the barn and lay down on a pile of straw not far from where Toby was grinding and watched as the strong arms carefully worked. Toby's right hand was turning while the other led the blade across the whirling stone. Checking the sharpness, Toby gently brushed his thumb across the blade. "This should do." He nodded. "You think the war is over?" Toby asked. "Ain't heard much about it, and ain't seen no Yankees about."

Lott shook his head. "Ain't much happening around here, but it's still simmering up yonder."

In South Mississippi during the winter of 1864, it appeared that the struggle was nearing its end. The Union armies with their large numbers and endless supplies were squeezing the life out of the Confederacy. The mighty army of Tennessee under the command of General John Bell Hood was all but destroyed at the Battle of Franklin and Nashville, Tennessee. The Southern men had mostly given up hope of a victory and didn't fight with the confidence they once had.

Lee, in Virginia, was also facing problems. In trying to protect Richmond, Lee had his army stretched all the way from Richmond to Petersburg. With the numbers dwindling from casualties, illness, and most of all, desertions, his line was thin. He knew, if something didn't happen soon, the line could not hold and the sun was setting on the Southern Confederacy.

Finished for the day, Lot and Toby straightened up the barn and put their tools away.

As Toby shut the door of the barn, he spoke in a worried tone, "Mr. Lott, is Miss Wilson ailing? She walks 'bout, talking to herself, and don't look jest right. I'se worried 'bout her."

Lott stopped and shook his head. "Too much has happened to her. I think she's just putting up a front. Being Godly as she is, she says things is gonna be fine, but I'm pretty concerned about her. It's like she's in another world, one where she hears voices, maybe angels talking with her. Folks are beginning to notice."

"What d'ya mean 'bout angels, Mr. Lott?"

"She's told others about angels speaking to her. Folks is making more out of it than they should."

"Is an angel kinda like a hant?" questioned Toby.

"Toby, I don't believe hants exist, but if they do, I guess they would be like an evil angel. You know, one of Satan's devils."

Parting ways, Toby headed down the trail to the small building where cottonseed was once kept. He had added a fireplace, new oak siding, and some furniture, and it had become his home. It was much better than the room in the barn where he had been staying. Even though it was just a little better than slave quarters, he was free and content.

"Don't like that talk about hants, and them devil angels," exclaimed Toby walking away. "That's why I'se got that old horse shoe over my door."

It was near dusk, and Lot saw no sign of Sarah as he approached the house.

Usually at this time of day, a light from a lamp flickered through the windowpanes of the bedroom, and a curl of smoke rose from the opening of the chimney, swirling and disappearing in the wind. He trudged up the steps into the open hallway, but the house seemed vacant, and a feeling of unease crept over him.

***

The sound is deafening. A constant roar is causing my ears to ring, and blood flows freely from my nose and mouth. My brain will soon explode. I won't exist much longer. The boom of cannons, the crackle of muskets, and the shouts of men destroying each other is overwhelming the very life from me. I try to stand, but my legs will not support me. We are ordered to attack. "Aim for the cluster of trees beyond the stone wall," I am told. "We will prevail. This will be the last battle." The roar stops, and I am left in absolute silence. Sound does not exist. I sit up and see vast human destruction. The hillside is covered with the dead. Even though no wind is present, a flag flutters here and there, but all else is deafening still. We've destroyed each other. Suddenly I hear thunder in the distance, a dark cloud forms, a slight streak of lightning, and a gentle breeze turns into a violent gush of wind spinning as it approaches me, spinning as it gains force. It becomes even more powerful as it reaches the edge of the battlefield. Sweeping forward, it lifts the bodies into the heavens, leaving the ground as fresh as spring. The grass is now glistening, and the flowers dotting the fields reach their heads upward. God has come to collect the fallen and has carried them home. What a harvest has been made today. I hear a voice calling me. There's someone beckoning to me. With all my strength, I raise myself up. Now on my feet, I look to the storm, and it is reaching to me and pulling me in. Immediately I am amazed at the change - no more clouds, thunder, or lightening. Voices are calmly calling my name. Snow is warmly falling, and peace has settled on the land like a curtain of light.

"You need to come with us, John. It's time to go," came a voice.

"Where are you taking me?" I ask.

"Where's your faith? Here, take my hand."

Slowly I reach out, but I know I can't go. It's not yet time. I began to run as best I can. The farther I run, the closer I feel the presence. I finally drop with exhaustion to my knees and scream, "Who are you?" The sun sparkles through silky hair and skin that is bright without blemish. "It's time for you to go home," the voice reaches out to me. I try to clasp her hand, but it is out of reach. Suddenly, I'm cold and my body begins shivering, and I feel the darkness.

John woke but his mind stayed on the dream. Was it a dream or a vision? He coughed and shook his head. Is this what death is like? What beautiful peace. But now it is so dark and so cold. Where am I?

Moments passed and John began to sense feeling in his body and was aware of a warm breath crossing his face. Reaching to rub his nose, he realized he had to be alive but why the darkness? Where am I? He felt a cold wall, and slowly, he crawled following the wall until he found a corner and another. He realized he was in a room that was perhaps three by six foot. He reached upward about two feet above his head and found a ceiling of wood. His body shook with the vast dampness and severe cold. His body ached with pain, and he was unable to move his arms and fingers. He screamed loudly.

Moments later, a stream of light flickered from above, and a screeching sound was heard as snow fell upon him. The ceiling opened into a large door of light so bright John had to shield his eyes.

"Well, sir," a voice called out. "This is one bet I seem to have lost."

John tried to speak but couldn't.

"I guess you are alive," the soldier said. "I best go get the lieutenant."

"Where am I? How long have I been down here?"

The soldier laughed. "About four days. Most of the time ranting and raving like a crazy man. You two shouldn't be alive. You're mighty lucky souls. Few people survive the Pit."

John now remembers hearing about the White Oak Dungeon or the Pit, a hole three feet by six and boarded on all sides capped by a heavy wooden door for the ceiling, and well-guarded. The pit contains a small bench, one blanket, and a hole at one end that serves as a privy. The floor is mud but frozen solid. He knows the pit is a form of execution with intense heat in the summer and deadly cold in the winter. Few have survived.

While one guard lifted the heavy door, the other who was on his hands and knees looked into the pit and asked, "Where's your buddy?"

"It's just me," John whispered, unable to say more.

"Ain't so, soldier, I heard another voice down there with you.

"Come on, it's cold out here. Let's get the man out and take him to the colonel. You probably just heard the wind blowing. Look down there. Ain't nobody else," said the guard, holding the door back.

John tried to walk, but after a few steps, he sank to his knees. The guard beckoned several prisoners nearby to carry John to the colonel.

"Get him a chair," ordered Colonel Sweet. "Keep him back there. He smells terrible."

"Yes sir. He's been in the hole for quite a while."

The colonel noted that John's eyes would not focus, his skin was a light blue and his toes were black and swollen.

"Am I free to go home?" John breathed the words.

Sweet pursed his lips and frowned, "Where'd you get a notion like that? You are lucky to be alive." Studying John closer, he shook his head. "You best pray that you'll be around tomorrow."

"Why was I put in there?" muttered John.

"Soldier, you jumped a guard and almost beat him unconscious. You remember that?"

"No sir, I don't," mumbled John as he began to drift off again.

"I should have had you shot," Sweet added. "I had so much on my mind with that Morgan group arriving I guess I didn't use good judgment."

Rousing, John remembered. "Why'd … you shoot … the Negro?"

Sweet smiled. "We got orders. Southern Negro soldiers are to be executed when captured."

"That's murder," said John, drifting off again.

"Private, take him on back to his outfit, and keep an eye on him. He seems to be a trouble maker to me," ordered Sweet. "I won't forget this one. No sir and I probably won't have to worry about him much longer."

After John had been carried away, Sweet looked over to Captain Moore writing the account of the day's activities. "What do you make of that boy?"

The captain carefully laid his spectacles and pen down, rubbed his nose in thought. "Sir, a few have made it during the summer, but none have survived the pit in the winter. He probably took no food or water, and the temperature had to be in the single digits. He shouldn't be alive, and all of this for a Negro. Who would have thought Johnny Reb would care?"

3

Faith and Fear

For you have been my refuge, a strong tower against the foe. I long to dwell
in your tent forever and take refuge in the shelter of your wings.
—Psalm 61:3-4

As the sun slipped away and darkness approached, Lott usually felt a sense of peace. The daily tasks were performed, the horses and mules were stabled, the chickens had gone to roost, and he looked forward to settling in for the night. During the summer after supper, they would retire to the porch to reflect on the day's activities as the fireflies flickered in the darkness and locusts sang their screeching melodies. Off in the distance, a hound pushed some critter across the swamp while an owl hooted its presence in a soft rhythm. During the cold winter evenings, the warmth of an open fire lured them to the hearth.

As Lott walked down the open hallway, he remembered that Sister had spent the night with a friend, Susan Crawford, who was teaching her to cross-stitch. Increasingly aware of the missing sights and sounds, Lott called out, "Sarah." The darkened room gave evidence to a problem, and Lott headed to the kitchen.

"Sarah, where are you!" he muttered. He headed back to the open hallway and shouted, "Sarah, for God's sake, answer me!"

His mind began to systematically think of the places she could be. He calmed as he thought about how Sarah worried that a hawk might get the baby chicks and headed to the chicken coop. Still not locating her, he headed to the creek to see if Sara had taken a walk and maybe got hurt.

As he returned to the house, he heard a low moaning from within the house. The sound was coming from the bedroom, and he realized Sara must be sick.

"Sarah, what is it?" he asked, pulling the covers from her face.

"It's so cold out there," she murmured as she pulled the cover back over her head.

Lott was wearing a shirt because the day had been comfortably warm. Once again, he tried to remove some of the cover, but Sarah jerked it back. Lott knew that Sarah must be sick and running a fever.

"Let me feel you," Lott said. To his surprise, she felt normal but was now shaking more than ever. "Do you hurt anywhere?"

"Lott, I don't hurt," Sarah whispered. "Would you please make a fire? It's terrible cold."

Lott was perspiring, but he built a fire and pulled his chair to the bed as close as he could get. If Sister were here, he could get Doc McMahan. Pacing the floor, checking her body temperature, and keeping the fire alive, Lot fought the long hours of night.

As dawn broke, Lot, exhausted and afraid he could loose Sarah, settled himself on a chair near the fire and bowed his head in prayer, "Lord, I know you and me ain't been on too good of terms lately, but I just can't understand why a loving God like you would take a man's sons from him. Anyway, I just ask that Sarah stay here with me." As tears filled Lot's eyes, he held them back and thought he had not darkened the church doors in over a year. Why would the Lord listen to him now?

At one time, Lott was a faithful member of the Little Rock Baptist Church and was even an elected deacon and Christian servant to the community, but the sadness of war shook his beliefs, and he no longer entered the church doors. With his spirit broken and his fear of losing Sarah, Lott cried, "Lord, forgive me, a sinner as I am, and don't place the burdens of my sins on her. Please place your healing hand upon her. She deserves your mercy. Amen."

The sun tipped the horizon, sending slashes of orange and pink clouds across the sky, and Lott remembered that Toby would not be coming to the house. He was to go to Union, a small town to the west, to check on the price and condition of a mule that he had heard was for sale. *He was probably already half way there by now*, Lott reasoned.

He found Sarah fast asleep, but she still clung to the covers and was mumbling.

"You feel better, Sarah?"

"Leave me be. You are interrupting us," Sarah answered softly.

Sister, proudly wearing her new dress, returned early from Susan's home. Lott beckoned her into the bedroom to explain about Sarah.

The weather had turned colder, so Lott put on his woolen overcoat, placed a wrap around his neck, and pulled his hat tightly down over his stubborn bushy hair. "Sister, stay with her, and make sure she's comfortable. I'm going to find Doc McMahan.

Doctor McMahan, a highly skilled and experienced doctor, was the pride of the community. After graduating from college, he chose to practice in his home community, giving up the fortune that could be made in a larger city.

It took Lott only minutes to reach Doc McMahan's place. Remaining in the saddle, Lott wasted no time, "Doc, there's a problem with Sarah. I'll tell you about it on the way, but let's hurry."

Removing the saddlebag of drugs and medical equipment, the two hurried into the house. Doc McMahan was a tall thin man in his early forties with long, brown well-oiled hair parted in the middle and clean-shaven except for a fashionable mustache. Doc quickly raised Sarah on the pillows and checked her temperature for fever, her throat for signs of irritation, her pulse and breathing.

"Sarah, can you tell me what's ailing you?" he asked.

Sarah gave a hint of a smile and shook her head. "I'm just so cold," she replied. "I'll be fine. They say all is well."

"Who are they, Sarah?" Doc McMahan inquired with a frown.

Sarah eased down and settled back into her bed. "It really don't make any difference. The Lord is in control. All is well with him now."

Doc McMahan stepped to the fireplace and warmed his hands behind him. Minutes passed as he stood and thought. Lott and Sister settled in chairs nearby.

Sister finally asked, "Doc McMahan, Papa, could y'all use some hot coffee?"

Both men nodded. The rich aroma of coffee filled the room, and finally, Doc McMahan spoke, "You know, Lott, I've been doing this for a long time, and to tell you the truth, I can't find anything wrong with Sarah, physically that is."

"Well, what do we do, Doc?" stuttered Sister, taking their empty cups.

Doc shifted in his seat. "Just get liquids down her and maybe make some chicken broth. She's got to have nourishment. Try to get her up, if possible. I'll come by each morning, and if things change for better or worse, come get me."

After Doc McMahan left, Lott and Sister sat silently, pondering the diagnosis. Although they were comforted that nothing was physically wrong, they were concerned about her mental state, especially since Doc McMahan didn't seem to know either. Lott now knew that loosing the boys could actually cause him to lose Sarah.

For the next two days, Doc McMahan came and was pleased with the way Lott and Sister had ministered to Sarah. They had been able to give her nourishment, and she was talking to some extent but still did not want to leave her bed.

On the night following the fourth day of her illness, Lott crawled into bed, exhausted, and slept soundly for the first time.

With the sound of a rooster crowing outside and a hound at hard chase in the woods below, Lott awakened suddenly. Drowsy from the long sleep, he was startled by the sounds coming from the kitchen. The smell of freshly brewed coffee and fried bacon filled the house, and a familiar melodious voice singing Rock of Ages was heard. He instantly reached to feel for Sarah, but she was not beside him. Throwing the cover back, he jerked on his housecoat and ran to the kitchen, barefooted. He found Sarah rolling dough for the morning biscuits and frying eggs crisply in the pan.

Sarah, without stopping, turned slightly and smiled. "Morning, love. I thought you were going to spend the day in there. Coffee's ready."

Lott placed his arms around her. Feeling the warmth of his caress, she turned and gave him a quick kiss. "Don't let me burn the eggs, dear," she said.

"Sarah, are you alright? How do you feel?"

"Well, I feel just fine. Why shouldn't I?" Sarah replied, wiping the flour from her hands, and turning to Lott. "But I am concerned about you keeping this house so hot. You must be getting old. You know what they say about old folks? Their blood gets kinda thin." She laughed.

Lott and Sister were amazed at the change in Sarah, but her lack of memory over the past days troubled them.

The prisoners carried John from outside of Sweet's office where he had collapsed, across the frozen grounds. One of the prisoners slipping on a sheet of ice sent the men tumbling. John lay motionless. To the men, he appeared as one ready to be placed with his maker, but a slight movement of his head indicated life, so they carried him into the barracks. Once inside, the men crowded around him as he was carried to his bed. John's hair was matted with ice, his face was a pale white, and his body seemed frozen. Whispering to each other, his comrades were sure he was dead. They knew that no prisoner had ever survived the pit in the winter.

Sergeant Roper slammed the door and shook the snow from the blanket wrapped about his shoulders. He noticed the huddle of men and wondered what had their attention.

"Is that Lewis?" he said, leaning down for a better look.

"Yes sir, what's left of him."

The sergeant pushed John's hair back and placed his hand on his cheek. He shook his head and pulled the blanket back that covered his feet. Concerned, he flinched, stood up, took a deep breath, and thought for a moment.

"Alright, move away and give us some room," he ordered. "This man is alive. That is for the meantime, and if we're lucky, we might just keep him that way."

He had two men move John to a pallet on the floor next to the cook stove and cover him with as many blankets as they could spare. Four men had died the night before, and their covers were a blessing. The sergeant sent a detail to the other barracks, asking for any extra wood that could be spared. He instructed another soldier to bring in a bucket of snow and told him to rub some on John's feet. Along with the rubbing, the feet were to be massaged to improve circulation. Hours later near the toasty heat, John, who was wrapped under a mountain of blankets, began to moan. At first, only a faint sound was heard, but soon, John began to scream out in pain.

"Cover him up, and hold him down," ordered the sergeant. "How's his feet coming?"

"They ain't as cold as they was, but they shore don't look healthy," the soldier replied. "You think he'll keep 'em, Sarg?"

The sergeant walked to the stove and thought that John probably wouldn't see daylight. Sergeant Roper realized he was tired of trying to survive. "Here I am, trying to lead these men, comfort, and keep them alive, but maybe we'd all be better dead and at peace," he muttered to himself.

"What'd you say, sir?" a soldier asked.

"Nothing important. Time to hit the bunks, boys. Tomorrow's another day."

As the days passed, John improved. His color returned, and to the amazement of the camp doctor, his feet were a more natural pink. The doctor now knew John would not face amputation.

John's fellow soldiers carried him wherever he needed to go, which was basically to the latrine out beyond the barracks. He took his meals in the barracks and was not expected to stand formation. His day consisted of sitting on a blanket-padded chair next to the stove and talking with fellow prisoners who still marveled at how he survived the pit. One afternoon, as the men were settling in for the night, a group of prisoners from North Carolina accumulated for the preparation of supper.

"Lewis, tell us about that hole you spent time in?" asked a tall, lanky prisoner.

"I really don't know what to tell you," John answered. "As strange as it seems, I can't recollect much that went on down there."

"John, you must've remembered something. Were you afraid?" Sam asked.

John thought for a long while but finally answered, "They tell me I was knocked unconscious and thrown in the pit. All I know is when I came to, there was no light to be seen, it was extremely cold, and I didn't know where I was or if I was even alive."

"That seems strange," one of the soldiers remarked.

"It was strange. As cold as it was, I felt warmth, and voices were speaking continuously to me," John continued.

"Voices? You was probably out of your head. That Yankee guard hit you pretty hard. You were just hallucinating," suggested Sam.

John shook his head. "I really can't explain it. When I came to, I was bundled up next to this here stove just like I am now."

***

In poor weather, Sweet seldom ventured outside. Since his office was located on the second floor of the main building overlooking the camp, he could view the entire prison. While his officers conducted formations, supervised the order of the guards, and held inspections, he could comfortably stand at his large window and enjoy a good smoke of tobacco. As days slipped into months, Sweet became more pessimistic about his position. Other generals like Grant, Sherman, Sheridan, and Thomas were making a name for themselves in the field and were constantly mentioned in the press for their gallant efforts that were shutting down the South. These names haunted him more and more each day. Sweet knew his chance of recognition was nonexistent. When this war ended, there would be no position for him unless he made a name for himself. If there were a prison outbreak and he could stop it, then maybe they would let him return to the field. Because there were Southern sympathizers in the city and spring was on the way, he began to plan a way to get noticed. I think it's past time for a report from Captain Moore.

Sweet beckoned to a guard who was posted at the door of his headquarters. "Private, go get Captain Moore for me, and tell him I wish to see him immediately."

Within fifteen minutes, the captain gasping for breath knocked on the Sweet's door and was ushered in by the guard. Once in, Sweet ordered the guard on duty to leave them alone.

"Take a seat, Captain," Sweet ordered. "You might as well get comfortable. We're going to be here a spell."

Captain Moore removed his overcoat and nervously arranged himself on the chair in front of the colonel. Moore knew Sweet could command, but at times, he seemed downright irrational. *Often, war can do strange things to people,* he reasoned. *Maybe that's why he's not on the front in Virginia.*

"Care for a smoke? I've got some fine cigars," offered the colonel.

"No, thank you, Colonel."

Sweet took a long draw from his smoke and blew a floating circle through the air until it eventually disappeared over the captain's head. "You remember the conversation we had a while back about getting information from the prisoners and perhaps some of our locals in the city?" Sweet queried.

The captain took a deep breath and moved his head to relieve some muscle strain in his neck. After a moment, he replied, "I didn't know how seriously you were taking the matter."

"Captain, did you not understand the order? Are you telling me you have done nothing?"

Glancing down, he shook his head. "I've not really done much about it except that day you brought it to my attention. But I have thought about it."

Sweet got up, wandered to his window, and looked out on the compound below in silence, then asked, "What has your mind accomplished, Captain?"

"Sir, there are citizens in the city who do sympathize with the South and have criticized what is happening here at the camp. I have witnessed this, but it is pretty much impossible to place informants in the barracks."

Sweet returned to his desk and began tapping his pen. "Captain, I want the names of those citizens, and I want informants placed among the prisoners. You find someone that can be bought, and we'll bring him in with the next group of prisoners who are sent to us. Remember, money is not an issue here. You understand?"

"Colonel, like I said earlier, I've heard nothing about any breakout."

Sweet clinched his teeth in anger and glared at the captain.

"Yes sir, I understand," replied the captain.

With the news of a possible break in the Southern line in Petersburg, Sweet realized that time was vanishing, and if he didn't move soon, it might be too late. "Captain, I want those citizens' names tomorrow, and for informants, I want one in the barracks by the week's end."

***

March in the South could see snowfalls and frigid temperature, but usually, the tender touch of spring would fill the air and days became warmer. Rebecca stayed busy to keep her thoughts from John, but she also felt the spring and a new beginning in the few socials she had allowed herself to enjoy. As the morning sun filtered into her bedroom, she pulled the comb through her tangled hair and stared at herself in the mirror. Deep in thought, she worked with her hair until each hair was laid perfectly. Perfection did not stop her comb, and time elapsed as her thoughts raced back to childhood days and John. Memories of riding horseback through the big woods, having picnics on the creek banks, holding hands secretly during the church service, stealing kisses when no one was looking, trading notes in school, and holding lengthy conversations about their future cluttered her mind. Rebecca could not remember a time when she was not in love with John. The reality of death was an enormous black wall of separation. As a Christian, she knew that John was waiting for her to come home to heaven where her Lord and Savior would be, but today, she longed to hold John and see his smile.

As the sun rose higher, Rebecca turned her thoughts to the words of Mrs. Wilson. Her only hope that John had survived came from Mrs. Wilson, but even that hope was replaced with the knowledge that Mrs. Wilson was overwrought with worry for her sons. Rebecca had heard of soldiers in the confusion of battle joining other units, but she also knew that once the conflict had ended they would return. There was a young soldier from over near Meridian who had received a severe head injury and lost all his senses and wandered into a federal encampment thinking it was his own. She also knew that thousands of soldiers were captured and sent to prison camps, and maybe, just maybe, John was among them. When this war ends, those prison gates would be opened, and she would know the truth. But for now, she had to trust Mrs. Wilson's feelings and keep hope alive in her heart but also continue with her life and be ready for what would come.

Mrs. Walker, concerned that Rebecca had not yet left for the store, called out to her daughter and went upstairs and knocked on Rebecca's door. She eased the door open and saw Rebecca combing her hair deep in thought.

"Darling, are you all right?" she said, walking over to her and tenderly taking the comb from her hands. "You've been up here a long time. Is something wrong?"

Rebecca continued to look into the mirror for a moment, then a slight smile crossed her face. "Mother, I'm fine. I was just thinking," she replied.

Mrs. Walker sat down on the padded bench beside her daughter and placed her arm around Rebecca's waist and asked, "Did you enjoy the party at the Ollivers the other night? I heard you all even tried some Scottish gigs. I bet it was a lot of fun. You know, Frankie would not be a bad catch. He seems to be a fine young man."

Without replying, Rebecca got up, tied a ribbon around the back of her hair to keep it out of her face, and began pulling on her sweater.

"Rebecca, did you hear a word I said?" questioned Mrs. Walker, following her out of the bedroom.

Rebecca nodded her head and murmured, "I guess you could say we had fun. But I'm not sure fun is what I need right now."

Walking to the front porch, she turned and asked, "Mother, do you think the Federal army keeps records and names of our soldiers who are captured?"

"I guess they should. Why?"

"Oh, I was just thinking. You want me to tell Papa anything?" asked Rebecca, making her way down the path that led to the road. Since the store was only a couple of hundred yards down the way, she knew she wouldn't be very late.

"I'll have lunch ready about noon," Mrs. Walker called back, concerned over Rebecca's mood. As much as Mrs. Walker liked Sarah, she wished that Sarah would quit putting those ridiculous ideas in Rebecca's head. From what she was hearing around Little Rock, Sarah was experiencing some emotional problems, and Rebecca surely didn't need to get involved with her apparitions. She had heard that even Doctor McMahan was confused over Sarah's mental state.

***

Even though John had miraculously survived the pit, regaining his strength was slow. When John was finally on the mend, all the soldiers in the barracks were stricken with dysentery, including John. With little medical aid, the death wagon stopped each morning for those bound for the lake. In a week's time, over a third of the prisoners were gone. Along with those who remained, John struggled with bouts of fever and nausea. What the pit had not done, dysentery was trying to do. Hours of lifelessness with sudden ravings and screaming could be heard throughout the barracks.

Sam was one of the few prisoners who escaped the disease and kept a constant watch over John, and when John's temperature rose, a cold damp cloth was applied to his head. Sam wasn't sure about all the Bible talk John gave and wondered if John's God would rescue him from this fever. Sam looked around to see if anyone was looking, and when all seemed clear, he eased down on the bunk where John was lying and closed his eyes and whispered, "Lord, I don't know much about you, but if'n you are around, John sure needs some help. As for me, I'm kinda ignorant about your ways, but Lord, if you can, please don't take him right now. Let him go home. Well, that's about it, Lord."

Following the meeting with Captain Moore, the city of Chicago was in a state of pandemonium. Fearing the wrath of the colonel, Moore did his duty. By day's end, the captain presented Sweet with a list of eighteen citizens who were known to have either aided or collaborated with the Southerners in some form or fashion. To the colonel's surprise, there were three women's names included on the list. The facts behind the accusations of some were scanty, but Moore had performed his duty. Among the list were some of the more prominent people of the city. In fact, one gentleman, Horace Gainey, had served as mayor of the city at one time. Most of the town felt such an arrest was unfounded, and the city folks were in an uproar. Without meeting with the group, Sweet had the men assigned to the barracks with the Southern prisoners, and the women were housed in a room adjoining the medical clinic.

Early the next morning, the serving mayor, James Stevenson, requested a meeting with the colonel but was denied. A quick telegram to Senator Douglas in Washington, who donated the land for the prison, opened the colonel's ears. Douglas, who had battled

Lincoln in the political arena and was stalwart in the United States Senate, was not happy about the arrest made in his home city. Sweet was at first enraged that Senator Douglas had been contacted but later felt that this might fit into his plan perfectly. With this in mind, he cordially invited Stevenson to his quarters. In fact, he sent his own buggy to bring Mayor Stevenson to the camp.

To the mayor's surprise, the colonel warmly welcomed him to the camp and offered him a choice of coffee or tea complimented with slices of hot, fresh baked apple pie. Expecting animosity, Stevenson was taken by surprise. Seated, the two talked vaguely about the war and the problems with running the prison, but with time, the mayor pressed his point. Sweet, elated over his exposure to Washington, sat comfortably, caring little at what was to come.

"Colonel, I thank you for seeing me, but I think you know why I'm here," stated Stevenson finally getting to the reason for the meeting.

Sweet sat nonchalantly while lighting a cigar and peered out at the mayor. "Tell me about it, Mayor. Perhaps I've missed something."

"It's about the citizens you had arrested. We feel there was no cause for that," replied Stevenson, knowing well that the colonel was aware of his mission. "I think there must be some mistake."

The colonel's tone changed. "Mistake! There's no mistake, sir. There's a war going on. I have prisoners here, and there are those who are working against the cause. I don't see a mistake at all. Mayor Stevenson, you should be congratulating me."

Knowing from the colonel's tone that nothing he said would be heeded, Stevenson rose, gathered his wrap, and looked directly at Sweet. "Colonel, some of our citizens are from the South or have relatives in the South, and others are very concerned about the conditions in this prison. You know, as citizens of the United States, people do have the protection of free speech granted by our constitution, and I am not aware of any threatening actions taken by the citizens you have arrested. Colonel, I don't know what you're trying to prove ,but Senator Douglas wants me to keep him updated on this situation. He will get a report."

"I think that would be wise, sir," replied Sweet, smiling. "In due time, I will sort out this lot of Rebel lovers, and I promise you if they are innocent, they will be released. You can tell Mr. Douglas that. I'll have your ride brought up."

***

As the citizens were brought to the prison and assigned to quarters in the barracks, the Southerners were confused about why Northerners were being placed among the solders. When the door of the barracks opened, two Federal guards led a short, fat, and well-dressed man who appeared to be in his forties inside. "I'd like to see your acting sergeant," ordered one of the guards, pushing the gentleman inside.

"Hey, Sergeant, we got company!" called out a prisoner.

Sergeant Roper, playing a hand of poker, laid his cards down and pushed his way through to where the guards were waiting. For a moment, he stood there gazing at the little man in front of him who appeared to be overly nervous and became hopeful that these citizens would see the deplorable condition of the quarters and effect some changes. "I'm in charge. What can I do for you?" answered Sergeant Roper.

"You got you a new one to keep up with. Give him a bunk, and treat him like one of your own. He'll have mess with you as well, and he might even loose some weight before he gets out of here." One of the guards laughed, pushing the man into the sergeant as they proceeded to leave.

Once inside, the sergeant took the man with him to the warmth of the stove and introduced to the other soldiers their new mate, Barrett Tucker, a teller of one of the local banks. Mr. Tucker informed the men that he had no idea why he was arrested or how long he would be detained.

John wrapped a blanket around his body and shuffled to the men who stood talking. A lot of questions were asked, but the man could not answer them. Edging near, John reached out and extended his hand. "Sir, you can call me John." One of the soldiers quickly offered John a chair, and John eased down, keeping his cover cloaked tightly around his body.

"Mr. Tucker, this here is a Federal prison camp. The folks you see around here all fought against the Union," John stated, feeling weaker with each breath. "It appears to me that if you're here, then you also are a problem to the United States or to the war effort in some way," suggested John in staggered breaths.

The prisoner shook his head and said that as far as he knew, he had done nothing to warrant his arrest. Finally, Roper showed him to a vacant bunk and told him if he got too cold, he could bring his cover to the stove area, if there was any room. The space around the stove was always first come, first serve. In the days that followed, Mr. Tucker was treated just like all the prisoners. He stood formation with the men, worked details, and ate the same food as the others.

To keep the prisoners occupied, they were allowed to march for two hours a day. Sweet kept stating that an idle man or body is the devil's workshop. One morning while the prisoners were outside practicing their maneuvers, Sam was ordered to clean the barracks. He stood leaning against his broom, watching the men outside when Tucker, who knew nothing about drilling and was not allowed to participate, walked up to Sam.

"Sam, I really don't know your last name, but I've been doing a lot of thinking about what that man said the first night I was here. I think his name was John. Well, one day after hours, a group of my friends got together for a drink or two, and we got into a heated conversation. Some of them said they were tired of this war and felt we should let the South go its way. With the massive casualties, they just didn't think it was worth the cost," Tucker explained. "We even criticized the way this camp was being run. You know, the only thing I can recall ever saying is I wish all you men would sneak out of here and go your way and leave us be."

"Well, Mr. Tucker, that just seems like idle talk to me. Nothing to get you placed in here. When men get to drinking, their mouths run loose and full of nonsense. Sometimes, we even get to bad-talking our own government. You know they say President Davis was some kind of a war hero down in Mexico, but he shore don't know how to control his generals and run a war. It's gotta be something else they got against you. You don't seem a bad sort."

"How long have you been in here?" Tucker asked.

"About a year and a half." Sam frowned. "Why?"

Tucker looked about the barracks, taking notice of the poor conditions. "I don't see how you've made it. You ever consider taking off?"

Sam thought a moment. "I guess you could say I've thought about it. Heck, we've all thought about it at one time or the other. Who wouldn't?"

Tucker laughed. "Why don't you try it? If you stay here, you'll either starve to death or die of some disease."

"If I knew I had a chance of making it, I'd sure enough do it. Yes sir, I'd take off in a minute. You want to go with me?"

Tucker laughed again. "I hope it doesn't take that drastic of a move to get out of here."

With time, family members were allowed to visit, but yet no hearing was scheduled for the citizens. When questioned about due process, Sweet just laughed and informed the people that this is a time of war and that the military handles such cases differently. In time, all would be resolved.

Late one Sunday afternoon, Sweet called Captain Moore to his office to ask him about the progress he had made placing informants in the barracks. Moore informed the colonel that he had secretly talked with several of the prisoners and that he only found three who he somewhat trusted to agree to listen and report. If the informants should get the word out about what was transpiring, then all would be in vain.

"How many days ago was that, Captain?"

"Three days, sir."

"And what have you heard?"

"Nothing, sir. The men said there has been no talk of escape," informed Moore. "They're just trying to survive the winter."

Sweet shook his head. "That's what I thought you would say, Captain. Nothing is going on in there. Well, I figured as well, so I took matters into my own hands. You know a while back when we brought our illustrious citizens in? One of those is a well-paid informant who will be reporting to me in the morning. It should be interesting."

4

Informant

And let all the angels of God worship Him. Are they not all ministering spirits, sent out to render service for the sake of those who will inherit salvation?
—Hebrews 1:6b & 14

A sharp wind whipped the curtains as a slight hint of dawn crept inside the bedroom where Sister slept. A rooster crowed outside, and the sound of fluttering wings filled the air as the chickens flew from the chinaberry tree beyond the outhouse where they roosted. A horse whinnied from the barnyard, and the distant sound of a hound giving chase in the swampland issued in the Sunday morning. With nature's call and the kitchen sounds of dishes clattering blended with soft voices, Sister awakened. Rubbing her eyes and pushing some strands of silky unruly hair from her face, she snuggled deeper within the warmth of her feather bed, laden with blankets.

March is an unpredictable month in Mississippi, she thought. Some days are so warm that winter is forgotten, yet nights are a reminder that old man winter is still holding on. It was rare, but she had heard that there had even been snowfalls during this transitional time. Shutting her eyes and trying to return to her dreams, she realized how quiet their house had become. *I know the difference*, she thought. *The boys ain't here. They say girls are loud and unruly, but the truth is not in it. Those brothers of mine could be the noisiest. Expected to be up, fed, and ready to work by sunup, they were in no mood to be mannerly.* She still remembered how they taunted and teased each other to the point that Papa would have to threaten to bring out his belt that hung from a nail on the kitchen wall in order to restore peace. They were constantly bickering in the field, afraid that the other was not carrying his fair load. More than once, the boys had come home from the field with bumps and bruises where disputes had been settled with fist-a-cuffs. Even though John was the youngest and smallest, his quickness made up for his lack of size and strength. To his brothers' frustrations, John could throw a punch and then outrun them racing about the field. Papa, always quiet and reserved, would let the boys settle their affairs if no major injury threatened, but at a point he deemed necessary, would intervene, and the plow lines would settle the issue. Sister laughed out loud as she remembered how tough Papa could be as he swung those long leather plow lines while the boys promised to never act up again. Pulling the covers around her neck, she yearned for those lost days and the irritating brothers who loved her beyond question.

Suddenly, a wide smile crossed Sister's face as she remembered. "It's Sunday," she called out. "It's church Sunday." Sister threw the covers back and pulled on her night robe to dash across the open hallway to the kitchen. She found her father sitting close to the stove drinking his first cup of morning coffee while her mother stirred the grits and watched the ham sizzling in the pan.

"My, you're happy this morning, child," said Papa reaching for his good morning hug. "What's happening in your world today?"

Giving him a hug and a light kiss on the cheek, she smiled. "Today's church day. Do you think we will have dinner on the grounds?"

In the rural areas of Mississippi where pastors were hard to come by, church services were a rarity. Services were usually held once a month and, in the Little Rock community, the Baptist and Methodist shared the same building but worshiped on different Sundays. When church services were possible, all effort was made to make the most of the day. The singing would begin at ten in the morning and by eleven the pastor was ready to present his sermon that continued as long as the Spirit moved, which was sometimes into the afternoon. If the weather permitted, families would bring covered dishes to spread on long wooden tables under the shade of aging oak trees. Although these Sundays were a special time of worship and fellowship, often a courtship was begun with many a young man and woman giving their hearts to each other. As hard as people had to work to eke out a living on these small farms, Sundays brought an opportunity to visit, share thoughts, voice opinions, and reveal emotions.

"Too cold today, Sister. Maybe next month when it's warmer," said Sarah, taking the ham from the pan.

"We are attending church today, aren't we, Mama?" asked Sister, helping her mother with cutting the biscuits and placing slices of ham inside.

Sarah gave Sister a frown. "Child, that must be the devil twisting that tongue of mine. It's Sunday meeting day. When the Lord's house is open, it's time to give him praise. You know we're going."

Lott shuffled out of his chair and wandered to the window sipping his coffee but making no comment. He had given his heart to the Lord years ago, but it seemed the Lord had turned his back on him. Over and over he wondered how a loving God could take his boys and all but destroy the farm he had struggled so hard to build. *What sin have I committed to deserve this*, he thought.

Noticing the effect the mention of church had on her father, Sister moved closer and reached up for a hug. "Papa, it's going to be alright. You've got mother and me who love you so much, and Thomas will come home someday."

Unable to respond, Lott sighed and hugged his daughter tightly.

"Papa, I sure wish you would go with us today," said Sister, taking a seat at the table.

Sarah returned thanks and began passing the plates of ham biscuits and steaming grits. "Times are hard, but we are still a family, and as the Word says, "The Lord gives and the Lord takes away. Praise be the name of the Lord," Sarah stated, looking to her husband. "You've got me and Sister, and you are the head of this household, and with that comes the responsibility of leading this family spiritually. Times like this, we've got to hold together and be strong."

Lott said nothing but got out of his chair, walked over to grab his coat and hat, then headed to the door. "I'm going for a walk in the woods. I'll be back after a while," he said, shutting the door quietly behind him.

Lott hoped a walk in the forest would give him time to think and find the peace that he needed. The upper woods had never been cut and the virgin timber, huge and majestic, stood as it had for hundreds of years. Nothing had changed since the Choctaw left for the territory, and except for the sound of birds and other wildlife, all was tranquil. This was his sanctuary. It was here that he talked to his Maker, made his complaints, and battled with his own spirit.

Sarah and Sister quickly cleaned the kitchen and went to Sister's room to prepare and dress for church. "Mother, do you think Papa will go today?"

"I don't know, child," answered Sarah, combing the tangles from Sister's hair. "He's a troubled man."

"I wish he was like before. He's changed."

Sarah laid the comb down in thought. "Sister, we've all changed. This war, the loss of our children, and an uncertain future is a lot to handle."

The news coming from Richmond and the riot of the Army of the Tennessee was evidence that the South was barely hanging on. Many felt the end was near and, with fear, anticipated the impact on the South.

As it neared nine thirty, Sarah and Sister put on their wraps and headed out the hallway, expecting a brisk walk to church. To their surprise, the sound of a horse met them, and Lott was bringing the buggy from the barn. As he approached them, he extended his hand to Sarah. In a full smile, she stepped up and settled herself next to her husband. Lott then stepped down to scoop Sister up into the back of the buggy.

"You give up on me?" he said, cracking the whip.

Sarah placed her arm around his waist as she turned and winked back at Sister. "Why would I give up on you? You've always been a godly man, and I never doubted it for once."

Lott shook his head. "Not so, Sarah. The Lord and me have still got a lot of unsolved business."

Sarah quietly reminded him so softly that Sister could not hear. "Mr. Wilson, the problem is not with the Lord."

The sun peeked through a cluster of puffy clouds being pushed by a blustering March wind as the family arrived at the churchyard. The grounds were covered with buggies, wagons, and horses and scores of children chasing each other in gleeful play. Men and women were in clusters, chatting and making their way up the steps to the church. The sound of singing beckoned the children from play. By the time Lott secured the rig and assisted Sarah and Sister from the buggy, several congregational hymns had already been sung. The building with its crisp white washed boarded wall and towering steeple caused Lott to swell with pride. The church was once a log cabin with dirt floor and large fireplace at one end, but the coming of a sawmill brought progress.

Rows of benches down each side separated by a wide aisle held families, and as creatures of habit, each family claimed its spot. Neighbors nodded and smiled while singing, and the Wilsons moved to the third bench from the front. Sister saw Rebecca, Suzanne, Frankie, and several other people her age across the aisle and, after getting her mother's approval, joined them.

As Rebecca glanced at the Wilsons, her heart drifted to thoughts of John and how she would wait at the top steps for him. When the buggy was in sight, she would wave her handkerchief to get his attention and then run to greet him. She sighed as she viewed his vacant seat.

The organist bellowed out hymn after hymn on the old foot-operated pump organ. "Rock of Ages" and "Amazing Grace" stirred the people and issued in the Spirit. At eleven o'clock, the singing ceased, and Brother Butler, the traveling preacher, rose from his prayer bench and stepped to the pulpit. He was an awkward man of six foot four and thin body but was dressed well-enough in black with a crumpled white shirt and matching black bow tie. With protruding Adams apple that jumped as he spoke and short trousers that revealed red socks with each step he took, he embraced the pulpit. Sister struggled to contain her laughter each time he got excited and his red socks danced in and out the legs of his pants. Her mother's raised eyebrows quickly settled her down, and she returned to God's message.

The preacher stood erect and clasped the corner of the pulpit as he looked across the congregation. With a deep, base voice, he called his people in, "Ladies, gentlemen, young folks, and children, the Lord has been talking with me, and what I have to say today is not from me but from above."

"Amen," chanted several men. "Tell us more."

Men often made supportive remarks and words of encouragement during the sermon, but women usually were expected to be silent. If a member wanted clarification on a point, a question could be asked, and even if there were a disagreeing opinion, the member could reverently voice that opinion.

"When you read the Book, they talk about them all the time, but yet, most feel they are a thing of the past, and they do not exist in our time. Some feel that with the coming of our Christ, there was no further need for them," Butler stated.

"Tell us about it, preacher!"

Sarah sat contently with a glance every now and then to make sure the young people were behaving. She felt a swell of pride in having her husband by her side and barely caught the nature of the sermon.

"I'm talking about angels! God's angels! God's messengers!" he shouted. "Folks now-a-days don't think they exist anymore. But if'n you believe the Word, it talks about them over and over. They ministered to Christ when he was in the desert. They shook the jail cell and led Peter out to safety. They talked with Paul when they were about to shipwreck. They spoke with John on the Isle of Patmos, and he gave us Revelation. You say angels ended with the coming of Christ. Well, I'll tell you folks, all that I just told you happened while Christ was here on earth and after our Lord was crucified. You hear me! It happened after the Lord's death. Angels are here with us, and they are at work this very moment!"

"Tell us more, brother!" shouted a man in the back.

"You got to make me a believer, preacher. I've got my doubts," stated another.

Lot shook his head in disbelief at the nature of the sermon. With the problems Sarah had been experiencing, this was the last thing he wanted her to hear. Dropping his head, he dreaded what would come next. Sarah immediately sat upright on the edge of the bench, tilted her good ear to the pulpit, and eagerly listened.

"Brothers, sisters, I know you are wondering why talk about angels," continued the pastor. "Times are hard here in the South. Loved ones are away fighting for our cause, and loved ones have been taken from us. I see vacant seats and pain on your faces, and no one knows what the immediate future holds. That's exactly why I choose to talk about angels. The Bible tells us they are God's helpers. They have been sent to warn us of danger, to comfort us in grief, to deliver messages to God's children, and to be our guardians. Angels can reach us in many different ways. Some come only as voices that we hear within our hearts while others talk to us in our dreams, and yes, angels do come in humanly form. Do we worship angels? No, we only worship our Lord and Savior, but God's angels are here among us, ministering to us. "

For the next forty minutes, numerous examples were taken from the Old and New Testament, showing how angels have intervened in peoples' lives under the direction of the Heavenly Father.

"Now in closing, we are in perilous times, and we need comforting support. Yes, we have the Father and the Son and the Holy Ghost, but we also have a host of heavenly angels to care for us and give us protection. We are not a forsaken people," he concluded.

All was quiet for a moment then Josh Adkins, the village blacksmith, raised his hand. "Preacher, I had two boys that went off to fight. They is both buried in Virginia soil. I don't see where no angels guarded them. I guess I'm one of them who thinks angels is for long ago."

"Amen," stated several others.

What began as a murmur developed into open conversations as members began to express their feelings. With each remark, the pastor tried to give an example to clarify his position, but to his dismay, the service was quickly getting out of hand.

Noticing the way the sun's rays were creeping across the wall of the room, Sarah followed their path until it rested on the delicately carved cedar cross that was stationed behind the pulpit. Rising, she pointed to the cross and reverently spoke, "There are angels as sure as I'm breathing. You spoke of loosing loved ones," she said faintly. "The Bible tells us there will be wars and rumors of wars, and if you read the Word, you'll find out that Satan also has his angels or demons doing their devilment. I guess what you got to remember is that the Lord's ways are not our ways. We aren't capable of understanding His ways. That's why faith is so important."

Embarrassed, Lot tugged on her skirt to sit.

Never taking her eyes from the cross, she seemed to be talking as if she were the only one in the room.

"So you see, our problem is our faith - that is, our lack of faith. You say you believe in the Father, Son, and Holy Ghost. Well, if you do believe, then you must also believe in angels because they are a part of his magnificent glory. They're here, all about us. It has been said that we have entertained angels unknowingly. I don't know why I deserve it, but they have been visiting with me for a spell, and I know my James Earl is with the Lord, but I do believe my John is not."

Not a sound could be heard as the congregation sat amazed and confused by the words Sarah spoke and at the sincerity and authority in her voice.

"Thank you, Lord. I hear you and praise your holy name. You are my shepherd, and I shall not want," she stated, closing her eyes while lifting both hands toward God. She then slowly eased back down to the bench, exhausted.

As Sarah sat, the minister spoke, "After those heartfelt words, let us close with prayer."

After the closing prayer, the people left the church troubled. Many would not look at Sarah at all while others had disbelief written on their faces, and still, others compassionately saw a mother in grief. Lott gently took Sarah's hand and assisted her out. Before they left, Sarah turned and looked directly at Rebecca. Their eyes met for a moment, and Rebecca turned away, wishing she had never attended the service.

Seeing the distress on Rebecca's face, Frankie extended his arm and, as soon as the Wilsons left, escorted Rebecca to the side door. "You alright?" he asked, but Rebecca didn't answer. "I've heard the talk about Mrs. Wilson, but I didn't know how serious it was. It's a sad thing," Frankie continued as he helped Rebecca down the steps.

"Frankie, I just don't know," Rebecca finally spoke. "I'd really rather not talk about it."

Suzanne who was already at the buggy called out, "You two need to hurry up. Mother's gonna have dinner waiting."

Frankie could barely take his eyes off Rebecca on the ride home. She was the woman he desired, but he knew her heart was sealed. The faint thought of John returning kept Rebecca from sharing her love with him, but with time, Frankie hoped he could gain her trust and affection. Young men were scarce during these times, and his family had the attractive means to impress any young lady, and Frankie, with all his heart, wanted Rebecca to be the one.

Lott and Sister were quiet on the way home and concerned over the church service, but to their surprise, Sarah was talkative. "Lott, I hate to tell you this, but I think I either daydreamed or napped during the service today. What did the parson talk about this morning?" she said, laughing.

Lott glanced back at Sister and shook his head, not knowing how to respond. Surely, she remembered, but as seriously as Sarah took her faith, he knew she wouldn't joke about a church service.

When they reached home, Sarah hurried into the house to prepare lunch while Lott put away the buggy. Sister led the horse to its stable, coaxed him inside, and closed the gate. Returning to her father, she said, "Papa, I don't think mother knows what happened today, and now she seems completely normal. I just don't understand."

Lott scratched his head in thought. "Darling, I'm at my wit's end. I don't have any answers, but at least, she seems to be herself most of the time."

Neighbors were already aware of Sarah's spells and had decided that her display at church was either an act of God or a touch of insanity due to her great loss and inability to face reality.

Lott was afraid he would lose Sara like he'd lost the boys, so he decided to pay Doctor McMahan another visit. The doctor reminded Lott that the mind was delicate, and in his medical study, not much research had been done on the mind and emotions. He advised Lott to care for his wife and enjoy each day and trust God for the rest. Lott tarried on the way home, deep in thought. He realized that maybe Sarah would get better, but if the worst happened, he would never admit her to an asylum. He shuddered at what he had heard about the asylum in Jackson. "No sir," he said to himself. "She'll be with me as long as she lives."

***

As Colonel Sweet had feared, the arrival of Hunt's Raiders had an instant effect on the camp. With the punishing cold weather and poor food and housing, tempers flared and violence occurred. Fights between individuals and groups within the barracks were constant. As long as the fights did not escalate, the guards ignored them, but when order was needed, rifles cracked, and men were shot. Use to freedom and lack of discipline, Hunt's men often intimidated the other prisoners and even taunted the guards. They had no respect for order and showed little fear. On several occasions, a raider would leap over the dead line that bordered the walls, knowing he could be shot but would quickly dart about dodging the line of fire, then race into the bystanders, blending with the masses. As more prisoners arrived, chaos prevailed.

Sweet knew he had to make a move to quickly restore order and discourage any possible escape. Calling for Captain Moore, he informed him to have all the prisoners, including civilians, standing in formation by seven o'clock the next morning and to have the mule in the front. The mule was a large wooden saw horse standing five feet tall. Captain Moore reminded him of the severe weather moving in, but the Colonel was unconcerned.

As darkness spread over the camp, a heavy snow swept in from the northwest, covering the grounds and banking up against the barracks. John and his comrades sat quietly around the stove wrapped in blankets, and talking softly. At the sound of voices, the men turned to the door and saw four guards entering. One of the guards called out, "Tucker, you in here?"

"I'm here," Tucker answered, rising.

"Get your belongings. You're being released," stated a guard.

The men were silent and surprised, but quickly, they began to congratulate Tucker. John clasped his hand and said, "It's about time you got out of here."

The wind howled, and snow fell into the night, but as morning neared, the storm cleared, and the stars twinkled brightly. All was quiet and peaceful at Camp Douglas. In the distance, only the lonely howl of a dog was heard amidst the soft snoring of the soldiers.

With the sun tipping the horizon, a bugle blew and the sound of guards scrambling about outside roused the prisoners. The doors of the barracks were unbolted, and guards rushed in. The prisoners were informed that there was to be a general assembly outside. Hurrying out, John observed men falling into formation across the parade grounds. Union officers were heading to the platform where addresses were made, and the prisoners were positioned so they could easily see and hear. There was a heavy posting of armed guards with bayonets placed around the prisoners. The sunrays sparkled on the snow, and a stiff wind sent chills through the shabbily dressed prisoners. Time passed as the Union officers milled around on the platform, and finally Colonel Sweet arrived.

"Men," he called. "I have treated you better than our soldiers in your Andersonville prison down in Georgia. Before I got here, you did might near what you pleased even going into the city for some fun. There were escapes. Yes sir, in coming here, my goal was to stop visits to Chicago and stop escape,s but I recently got word about a breakout."

A murmur rippled through the Southern ranks as they questioned his statement. A shot was fired to regain order.

"I have my means, and I will bring the instigator forward," shouted Sweet.

A detail of ten guards quickly marched across the grounds toward John's group. The guard in charge came to a halt in front of Sergeant Roper.

"You got a man named Samuel Harris in your ranks?"

"Yes sir, I do."

"Point him out," ordered the guard.

Sam stood motionless and dumbfounded. "You want me?" he asked nervously.

Two of the guards pushed through the men, seized him, and dragged him from the ranks.

"What do you want me for?" called out Sam as he struggled to free himself. "I ain't done nothing."

Prisoners began to break rank in protest but were instantly pushed back by bayonet.

Sam, unable to free himself, felt it was a mistake and walked freely with the guards who led him to the sawhorse positioned in front of the prisoners. Sam was ordered to climb upon the horse and straddle the main beam with his legs dangling down on each side. He was stripped of his upper clothing, and he sat uncomfortably, waiting for an explanation. Moments turned into an hour as Sam struggled to find a better position, but soon, pain shot down his legs and sweat ran down his face. Angered by Sam's misery, fellow prisoners shouted remarks to the guards, and more federal soldiers were brought into the compound.

Finally, Sweet held up his hand. "This is what happens to anyone who plans to escape," he stated. "He'll stay up here until he gives us the names of those involved, and when he does, he'll come down. Until then, he'll have a nice ride."

Wincing in pain, Sam called out, "I don't know what you're talking about. I ain't got no plan to escape."

"Bring up the buckets men," Sweet ordered.

Guards brought up two large buckets filled with snow and tied one bucket to each of Sam's ankles adding more weight and pain. An uproar covered the grounds as the Southerners hissed their discontent.

"This ain't right," John murmured. "I'm around him all day long and ain't ever heard of any plan."

The mule had been used in other camps to gain information, and its effects were deplorable. Men usually remained on the horse until they became unconscious or died, and those who survived were hurt so badly it was difficult for them to recover. Hours crept by as all stood witnessing the cruel ordeal of Sam fighting against the unending pain. Finally, exhausted, Sam collapsed and slumped down on the beam, and his comrades, unable to help, dropped their heads in shame.

"Cut him down," ordered Sweet. "He's not going to talk."

The guards got him down and, finding him alive, carried him back to the barracks, and prisoners were dismissed.

Sweet returned to his office in a cheerful mood and called to the guard posted at his door. "You can bring him in now, private."

In a moment, the private returned. "Any thing else, sir," the guard asked.

"That will be all."

"Have a seat, sir," Sweet said. "Care for a smoke?"

"No, thank you."

"Well, you did what I asked, and I hope the conditions weren't too uncomfortable for you considering the pay. I believe we agreed on one hundred dollars, Mr. Tucker," the colonel explained.

Tucker nodded in agreement and reached for the envelope. "Sir, the condition was every bit as bad as one could expect in a prison, but the truth is, I really don't think Harris intended to escape. It was just idle talk," Tucker said. "The prisoners talk about getting out and going home all the time."

The colonel bent down to light his pipe, and looked directly at Tucker, and said, "I paid you well, and that includes you keeping your mouth shut. I hope you understand."

As Tucker left, Sweet moved to the window, knowing he had made his point to the prisoners, and as for Harris, who was he to be concerned? He was just a prisoner that should have been killed a long time ago.

***

In the barracks, the men clustered around Harris, not knowing what to do. John hurried for a cup of water and knelt beside Sam to help him drink.

"I don't understand why they did that to me," he murmured. He looked down to his legs. "I don't think I can move them," he said in anguish. "It hurt worse than anything I've ever felt."

Exhausted, he listened as his friends talked about the punishment. One of the prisoners remembered hearing a similar case at another prison. Pushing through the men, he reached down to Sam. "We got to get you up and get your blood circulating. If we don't, you might never be able to walk again."

Catching him under his arms, the men dragged him around the barracks while encouraging him to take a step. With sweat rolling down his face, Sam finally managed two awkward steps.

Later that night, John lay on his bunk, and for the first time in a while, he began to think of home and his family. He knew he would probably never see Mississippi again, and hope only made living harder. He had always lived a peaceful life with a loving mother and father. In his home and community, he felt the presence of a loving and protecting God, and all was well, but when war broke out, the door of hell had been opened. He had seen men kill one another by the thousands, and some even seemed to enjoy the taking of another's life. The hardships of living in the open, marching endless miles, cold and wet, and never having enough food were difficult, but the cruelty he had experience and seen at Camp Douglas was worse. *If one believes in angels, Satan's angels, then they are here,* John thought, *and Colonel Sweet certainly must be possessed.*

John thought, *The politicians who were unable to compromise led this nation into a blood bath. Where were they now? They weren't here at Camp Douglas or on any of the battlefields I've been on, but probably curled up warm and snug in their beds, living for tomorrow and not for the moment.* Just the thought angered him. Finally, he thought about Rebecca. His breath shortened, and his heart pounded with excitement. Her smile, the sparkle of her emerald green eyes, her teasing to get his attention, the touch of her lips against his, and her goodbye wave at the station tore at his heart as he watched a full moon ease across the bright evening sky. Maybe, just maybe, she might be looking out at the same beautiful display of God's handiwork, and maybe, she still holds hope that we can have a life together.

***

An early spring whippoorwill sounded from down by the little rock creek, and an owl answered as the moon crept across its path overhead illuminating the room where Rebecca slept. A warm breeze fluttered the curtains nearby, brushing her cheek gently bringing her sleep to an end. Rebecca glanced around the room and saw that all was in order. Her clothes were neatly draped across the chair ready for the day's wear, and down the hall, she heard her father snoring. Then all was silent again. The birds had finished their song, and the wind had stopped its mischief. The mesmeric beauty of a full moon shone on her as she knelt upon the floor by her window looking into the heavens. She remembered the church service, the look on Sarah's face, and the words she shared with the congregation. Perhaps Sarah was hearing words from God or an angel. Maybe, just maybe, John was still alive. The thought warmed her heart, and she returned to her bed, snuggled under the covers, and slept soundly.

The next morning, Rebecca dressed, quickly finished her breakfast, and, throwing a shawl around her shoulders, told her mother about her plan to visit the Wilsons. She stopped to tell her father she would return to her store duties by mid-morning. Reluctantly, her father consented.

As soon as Mrs. Walker finished clearing the table and washing the dishes, she took off her apron, freshened her hair, and hurried to the store. The mid-morning stage from Meridian would bring goods to be checked and the mail to be sorted. Her hope was that Rebecca would be there by the time the run was made. As she entered the side door, she found her husband preparing the cash register for the day.

"Betty, Rebecca's not back yet," he said, closing the box. "I wish she would get the Wilsons out of her mind."

"They're good people," replied Mrs. Walker, heading to the store front to catch a glimpse of the stage. "I can't see no harm in it."

"I'll tell you this, woman. As long as Becca listens to Sarah's nonsense, the longer she'll hold on to her hope of John returning. The boy ain't coming back, and that's a fact."

"Then what do you propose? Deny her seeing them? Becca and Sister are friends you know," answered Mrs. Walker.

"As long as I can remember, that Olliver boy has cared for Becca, and with a little encouragement, it could lead to something more. I don't have to tell you about their assets. They could buy and sell this entire county," answered Thomas.

In a few minutes, Rebecca hurried into the store ready to help her mother with the mail. The stage usually arrived by ten o'clock, and the locals were already in the store. Mr. Walker waited anxiously for the customers to leave that day, so he could persuade Rebecca to think about a future with Frankie.

"How are the Wilsons?" asked Mr. Walker.

"They're just fine, father. I had a good visit," replied Rebecca continuing her work.

"What'd y'all talk about?"

"I don't know exactly. Just things."

"What about her visitors?" probed Mr. Walker.

"They didn't mention anybody coming by, father. Mr. Lott and Toby have been in the field plowing, and Sister and Miss Sarah are just doing women's stuff. Mrs. Wilson is teaching Sister how to sew, and Sister kept sticking her finger and calling out a few exclamations that had her mother scolding her. We all had a good laugh about it," answered Becca.

"What about the angels? She say anything about them?"

"Oh father, Miss Sarah didn't mention that." Rebecca smiled. "You know, folks think Miss Sarah is touched, but I don't see it that way. For the most part, she's as normal as you and mother."

"Humph," grunted Mr. Walker. "I still think something ain't right with her."

"That's enough, you two," interrupted Mrs. Walker. "I don't want to hear any more of this. Rebecca, I prepared dinner before I left. Go on up to the house, and set the table. We'll be along."

After Rebecca left, Mrs. Walker headed to Mr. Walker and stated, "Dear, this has got to stop. Rebecca is doing well and seems to be getting over her loss, and we need to leave her alone."

Mr. Walker shook his head angrily. "You don't see it, woman. She's not over John, and as long as Mrs. Wilson puts those ridiculous ideas in her head, she's gonna hang on for a lifetime of senseless waiting."

"So what do you recommend, husband?"

"Give her the facts," replied Mr. Walker. "John did not return to his unit after the battle. Next, his close friend, Tim, saw him blown into the air. And as for him being a prisoner, I plan to contact a friend in Jackson who can gain information from Richmond. If there is no John Lewis Wilson on their list, then that means he will not be coming home, and Rebecca can have a future."

***

As days passed, Sam regained the feeling in his lower body and was able to walk. Colonel Sweet, confident that his prisoners would never attempt an escape, sent letters to Washington about his progress at Camp Douglas and how he had stabilized an ill-run and chaotic prison. He failed to report the high death rate among prisoners or the poor sanitation and cruel and inhumane treatment.

When the prisoners thought they had seen the worst, an epidemic of smallpox swept the camp. The death rate soared as the disease took its toll. The prison was quarantined, and special precaution was taken. Each morning, the dead were removed, and their belongings were burned. Now that the ground was thawing, the bodies of the dead were buried in long trenches instead of thrown into the lake. Sweet worried about the death totals reported to Washington, but not much could be done about it.

For a while, it seemed that John's barrack might be spared, but a soldier from North Carolina became ill, and the disease had settled in. Sam was fortunate not to contract the illness, but John was not as lucky. There was no rhyme or reason as to why some died quickly while others recovered, evading death. While John lay there semiconscious and burning with fever, Sam never left his side. He tried to get as much water down John as possible and made sure John took the medication given him. Sam continually encouraged John.

5

Stranger at the Door

Be not forgetful to entertain strangers: for thereby some have
entertained angels unawares.
—Hebrews 13:2

On April 13, 1865, the sound of cannon fire shook the ground around Camp Douglas, and prisoners hurried from their shelters. For months, the war had not been going well for the South, and surrender was inevitable.

Suddenly, a cheer was heard from the guards posted around the perimeter. Next, each fieldpiece was discharged. Sam raced down the path toward his barrack.

"Get up! You won't believe what's happened! Lee surrendered two days ago, and they expect all the other generals to call it quits too."

John tried to get up, but was so weak he let Sam help him to a sitting position.

"'Lee's just in command of one army. How about the army of the Tennessee?"

"John, the army of the Tennessee took some kind of beating at Franklin and Nashville. I hear there ain't much fight left in them, and what's left of 'em was sent to the Carolinas under the command of Johnston. Since Lee has give up the fight that means General Johnston will have Grant and Meade to his north and Mr. Sherman to the south. He ain't got a dog's chance. This here party's come to an end."

" 'Bout time, Sam. I'm ready to go home, and as soon as we get there, I want you to stay long enough to be my best man," replied John.

John had been at Camp Douglas for almost two years and had barely escaped death three times. When he had entered the camp, he had been in excellent health, but now he was thin, his cheeks were sunken, and his face was covered with a dark beard. John had survived the largest military engagement ever fought on American soil and battled disease and the extreme elements of Camp Douglas, and now he would taste freedom.

On May 14, 1865, the prisoners were called into formation. Once assembled, Major Ben Anderson addressed the group, "Men, as you have heard, General Lee surrendered along with the rest of the Confederate Army. This war is over. You are no longer prisoners of the United States. In the morning at eight o'clock, you will be officially paroled. You will have three choices. You can sign a statement pledging your allegiance to the Union and enlist in the United States Calvary where you will be sent out west to deal with the Indians. Second, you can sign a statement pledging allegiance to the Union and with your parole papers receive a free train ticket home. Third, you can choose not to sign the statement of allegiance and find your own way home."

The next morning, John stood in line as each prisoner made his choice. Some chose to go west, others signed a pledge of allegiance to the Union and were moved near the railway, and others defiantly refused to sign the paper and were directed to the prison gates.

While in line, Sam nudged John. "I ain't signing. What about you? I fought this outfit for four years. I ain't about to join 'em now, especially after the treatment we got here."

The idea of having a free ride home sounded good to John, but like Sam, he would feel like a traitor if he signed. "I ain't too fit, but if you'll help me, we'll get home."

"Next," called the Union officer at the table.

"Ain't signing." Sam nodded.

"Me neither," added John.

"Get them out of here Sergeant," ordered the officer. "The gate's over there boys. I hope you like to walk. Next!"

John and Sam walked out the opened gates together as free men. As they approached the guard at the gate, Sam asked, "Yank, now that we's free, which way's home?"

"This Reb wonders which way's home. He could've had a train ticket. I don't think General Lee sent no extra tickets." The officer laughed. "Just use those legs, and keep the sun over your left shoulder in the morning and over your right shoulder in the afternoon. Sooner or later, you'll get home or run right into the Gulf of Mexico."

Sam looked at the ground for a few seconds and then back into the soldier's face.

"You know what's wrong with you? You weren't fit to fight us in the field. That's why they stuck you up here at this prison. At least, I'm loyal to our cause."

Several Union soldiers hurried over, expecting a scuffle.

"Hold back, men. This Southern trash doesn't bother me none. I doubt they'll even make it home. Let it be," stated the soldier coldly.

The bright morning sun shone on hundreds of ragged and mostly barefooted men as they emptied out of the compound rejoicing. As John looked toward the northern end of the camp, he could see the long burrowed areas that marked those who had died in this camp, and then he looked to the lake where thousands would remain never to see their loved ones again. John recounted that four years ago, they had been the grand army of the Northern Virginia, invincible and in decent uniforms with rifles, swords, bayonets, and flags flying high - the pride of the South. *But now*, he thought, *we look like tramps and vagrants, just like the Yankee said.* But rags and all, John couldn't remember ever being so happy. Raising his hands upward, John exclaimed, "I can't believe it. I'm finally going home. Thank you, dear Father."

John almost laughed out loud as he looked at his friend. Sam, with his unruly, wind-tossed hair, shaggy beard, clothes with holes and patches, and barefoot as the day he was born, gave way to a gigantic grin. John realized that even though Sam had tasted cruelty on the mule, he had never lost his spirit. John looked at his feet and laughed, "At least, I got some shoes even though I had to bind the soles to the upper leather with cord. Yes sir, I got shoes."

"I could have gotten me a pair, but I don't like the thought of wearing dead man's stuff," Sam replied. "Well, John, the sun's over our left shoulder. We must be headed south."

"Right, but I'm not sure I'll be able to make it home. It took us more than two weeks to get here by train." John said, realizing his weakness from smallpox.

Sam chuckled. "John, I ain't planning to do a heap of walking. We don't have no ticket, but I do know how to jump trains, and if need be, I can steal a horse or two. We going to get you home to that good-looking gal of yore's. We'll stay to ourselves so we can find food and not get caught."

They took the longer back roads, which were safer. They could forage and beg for food with no other prisoners to make people fearful. With the help of a walking stick, John trudged along, and when he tired, they would stop and rest. It took five days to work through Illinois, and after hiding on a barge crossing the Ohio River, the boys finally reached Kentucky soil. They skillfully sneaked off the barge and sprinted into thick woods near the riverbank.

Huddled in the cover of the bushes, John whispered, "Sam, we ain't eaten in three days. I can't go much farther like this."

They had covered thirty miles of desolate sparsely-settled countryside where land was covered with dense forest and farms were ill-kempt and unproductive. At each farm, they were told that there was not enough food for family much less strangers.

Stopping at a stream to water and wash, Sam sat with his back to an elm tree, deep in thought. "John, we got to change our plan. We got to head to the southeast and find some civilization and somethin' to eat. This has got to be the poorest country I've ever seen, but with farms about, there's got to be a town nearby."

After resting a while, they began their journey once more. Several miles down the road, they met a rider. He slowed his mount and approached cautiously, leading his horse away from the men. John called to assure him they intended no harm and just needed to find the nearest town. The rider was reluctant to reply, but resting his hand on his holstered pistol, he stopped and said at the next fork to take a left, and they would reach the town in a day. John and Sam, exhausted and footsore, hurried along with excitement about the possibility of food. With darkness approaching, they stopped for the night to rest.

At the town, they planned seek temporary employment, rest, buy decent clothing, and earn a little extra money to carry them on their way.

The men rested on a grassy slope covered in newly-leafed oak trees overlooking a small stream and gazed at the stars above as they listened to a chorus of tree frogs, and their thoughts wandered to home. "Sam, you say you're from Magnolia, Mississippi.

What's it like down there?" asked John, rolling out his blanket for the night.

"Well, it ain't much to tell, John. We got an eighty acre spread about six miles from town where we raise a little corn for the livestock, and Mama has a big garden to help feed the family, and we hunt for extra meat. As for Paw, he does a lot of odd jobs. Sometimes, he hires out when folks want to build a house, works in the local sawmill, and sometimes, hits the Mississippi River and works the barges."

"Sounds like y'all don't need slaves to work the place." John laughed.

"Slaves! You is looking at one right now," joked Sam. "You folks have any on yore place?"

"Naw, we don't believe in holding them. Papa says it's ungodly."

"Then why'd we go off fighting this war, John?"

"Cause we ain't got no better sense, I guess. You didn't tell me nothing about Magnolia?"

Sam laughed again. "Ain't much to tell. We got a general store, livery stable, blacksmith shop, carpenter's shop that makes furniture and a bank. We don't go to town much because it takes money to shop, and we don't have much of that. What about your place?"

"Well, it's a lot like Magnolia, but there's one difference. The gentleman who runs our general store has the sweetest and prettiest daughter you have ever seen."

"That's got to be Rebecca." Sam laughed.

"You got that right, and we live about a half mile up the road from Little Rock, and Sam, I don't want to brag, but Papa has got a pretty big place."

"How big?"

"Well, when Papa and my Uncle Jake came into Mississippi as young men working with some surveyors, they loved the country so well that they took all their earnings and bought about nineteen hundred acres," replied John.

"Nineteen hundred! That's a plantation," exclaimed Sam, rising up on his elbow.

"Not so," replied John. "Most of it is in woods, and some of it is Homer's, my uncle's only child. When Uncle Jake was murdered, my aunt who is part-Choctaw, gathered their belongings and left for the Oklahoma territory. One thing Papa and Uncle Jake did was built the largest and finest log house you'll ever see. They picked a location off an old Indian trail where they figured a road would eventually be."

"Did that happen?"

John yawned. "No, the road came one half mile south of our place. That's where Little Rock sprung up. Sam, I want you to come home with me and meet my family."

"I'll come if'n you'll have something good to eat," Sam laughed. "What happened to your Uncle Jake?"

"We never found out for sure, but we think that Uncle Jake was murdered because he helped a Choctaw friend keep his land - land that Mr. Frank Olliver wanted," replied John. "I guess we'll never know for sure if Mr. Olliver had him killed, but on the way home one day, Uncle Jake was shot. It was a difficult time for my father because he was real close to his brother."

The next morning John was wakened by splashing sounds at the creek. Since the hill where they slept sloped off sharply to the creek bottom, John couldn't see the stream but knew Sam was up to something. John walked to the crest and peered down and saw Sam by the waters edge with a long willow pole in his hand. Occasionally, he would slowly lift the pole and then thrust it into the water. "Sam, what in tarnations are you up to?" asked John, making his way down the steep bank.

"Trying to get us some breakfast," he said, making another thrust into the water. "Look over there," Sam continued, pointing to the grass where three brim lay. One was still flipping about. "How do you like this spear I made? I guess you can say I'm doing this Choctaw style," he exclaimed, holding up his willow pole with sharpened end.

"Sam, that's all and good, but we don't have any way to cook them."

Sam twisted himself around and, with a big smile, shook his head. "Who needs a fire? From what my Papa said, folks overseas eat 'em raw. He heard that from a China man working on the barge with him. We are gonna become Chinese today." He laughed. "If it was later in the year, I'd get us a mess of tadpoles."

With a piece of a knife that Sam had carefully confiscated at the prison, the fish were cleaned, and the two sat on the creek bank eating away, surprised at their tasty meal.

It didn't take the two long to finish the fish, and rolling and securing their blankets, they were soon on the road again. The farms became more numerous, and fields of young corn tipping the soil were seen. John and Sam sat down with their backs to a split rail fence face to the sun and admired the fine herd of cattle and horses that grazed in the field across the way. As they glanced down the road, they saw a group of Southern soldiers approaching.

Sam called out to them, "You Dixie boys?"

One of the men raised his hand. "Is there any other kind?"

John and Sam laughed.

"Come over and take a load off your feet," John shouted to them.

The group settled themselves about John and Sam and began to converse. They had all been soldiers and were on their way home to Arkansas. They had enlisted early in the war before the river was closed off and had fought with the Army of the Tennessee. When the regiment was formed, there were about nine hundred and thirty men. When they surrendered with Johnston in North Carolina, there were only eighteen of the original men present. They hadn't seen their families in over four years. When asked about sharing their food, they replied that they had walked from Carolina and had nothing to give, but hearing of John and Sam's breakfast, the sound of raw fish sounded good to them. They all shook hands and wished each other well. As the men walked away, one of them called back, "There is a town back yonder, but you need to watch them folks. They ain't very friendly."

John and Sam had only walked a few miles when they saw a boarded sign nailed to the side of a tree with the word Wickliffe printed across its front.

"Well, John, I guess we have found Wickliffe, Kentucky. Let's go see what this place holds for us country boys."

John and Sam walked into town cautiously, watching the people as they stirred about their morning business. Numbers of wagons and buggies proved it was a busy morning in Wickliffe.

"The place seems alive with people!" exclaimed Sam.

"Don't you know what day it is?" John replied.

"Naw, I don't reckon I do, John."

"It's Saturday. Folks are coming in to do their shopping," explained John. "Better get on down there, and see what we can do."

The villagers stared at John and Sam and would quickly look away. John realized that finding a job dressed in rags would be difficult, but it was necessary in order to reach home. Down one side of the street were a livery stable, granary, clothing store and bank, and across the street a large general store, land office and church. Boarded sidewalks lined the streets, and most stores had porches over the walkway. One building that caught their attention had a bold hand-painted sign reading, Happy Harry's. Curious, they pushed the door open, and in the dim light, they could make out two pool tables, several tables with chairs, a piano pushed up against the wall and a long bar with a massive mirror secured to the wall behind the bar.

"You know what this is?" Sam laughed.

"No. I have no idea," replied John, puzzled.

"I don't know where you've been, but this place is what you can call a saloon."

"What's a saloon?"

Sam laughed again. "A house of sin. Men come here to play pool, gamble at cards, drink liquor and most likely, get in trouble."

"How do you know about this?" John asked.

"I went with my father one time down to the Mississippi Landing at Natchez. If'n there was one of 'em, there had to be twenty of them saloons."

"Sam, we need to get our minds off Happy Harry's and start looking for work. It might be wise to split up. You take one side and I'll take the other," said John.

John inquired about doing chores to earn food with everyone who would speak to him, but no one seemed interested in helping. Finally, at the end of the street, John tried the general merchandizing store and introduced himself to the merchant in charge.

"Sir, I'm John Wilson from Miss'sippi, and I'm tryin' to make my way home. If you got any chores I can do to earn some food, I would certainly be thankful," said John, extending his hand.

The elderly man raised his head and adjusted his glasses to examine the young man standing in front of him.

"You one of them Rebs, ain't ya? One of them prisoners from up near the lakes. Look at yoreself, boy. I don't want the likes of you in my place. You'd run folks off, and that would be bad for business. Now get on out of here 'fore I call the law."

John still held his hand in greeting. "Mister, I'm just hungry. I need to eat."

"I said git. You ain't the first to come through here. You boys is about to steal us all blind. Now git out of my place," ordered the merchant.

"I ain't no thief, sir. I'm just trying to get home," John explained.

John quietly left the store and met Sam coming down the street.

"You have any luck finding chores? They all but kicked me out of that store." John sighed. "It appears some of our soldiers have been through here and caused trouble."

"Seems so, John. I ain't done much better, but go down near the end of the street, and wait for me. I got a plan."

A half hour passed, and Sam had not come yet when John heard a loud commotion and saw Sam thundering down the street astride a large gray horse with a loaf of bread under his arm and a ham strung across his saddle horn.

"Get ready, John! We got to get, fast!" screamed Sam.

As the horse approached, John could see a group of men in pursuit. Two were armed.

"Catch my hand, John, and swing up," shouted Sam, reaching to John.

As John reached to grab Sam's outstretched hand, he heard a thundering sound. Instantly, Sam toppled from the saddle and tumbled to the ground. The horse, startled by the loud gunshots, galloped out of sight.

Sam lay motionless on the dusty street. John rolled Sam over and knelt down by his side. Blood gushed from his chest. The bullet had gone completely through him.

"Sam, why'd you do a fool thing like that? You done gone and got yoreself shot," muttered John.

Gasping for breath, Sam whispered, "You 'member when I was hungry and you stole them crackers for me? You know, on that train carrying us to the prison? Well, I owed ya."

He tried to speak once more and then eased his head on John's lap.

"I weren't so hungry that yore life was worth this."

The men now encircled John with pistols drawn and motioned for him to stand.

"Boy, you has stole yore last horse in Kentuck'. We're tired of you thieving Southern boys taking what you want. You going to be jailed, and you is going to see the judge," growled a man with a marshal's badge pinned to his shirt.

"You didn't have to kill him. All we needed was something to eat."

"You can save it for the judge, boy. I don't care to hear your story," said the marshal, grabbing John by the arm and pulling him up.

"What's the charge, marshal?" replied John trying to pull away.

The marshal tightened his grip. "Horse thieving and stealing ought to do the job."

"I wasn't on that horse, and I didn't have possession of anything stolen," replied John defiantly, pulling away from the marshal. A blinding light and sharp pain sent John tumbling to the ground.

***

The smell of freshly brewed coffee and the sound of men talking awakened John. Trying to sit up, he immediately slumped down in intense pain. Later, he regained consciousness and opened his eyes to a fat little man with horn - rimmed glasses and chubby red cheeks wiping his face with a damp cloth.

"Well, Mr. Prisoner, I see you are back with us."

"What happened? What day is it?" muttered John.

"You best stay down, boy. You got a pretty hard lick to the head, and for the day, it's Tuesday."

"Tuesday? Who are you?" questioned John.

"I'm Doctor Jackson, local physician," replied the man, taking off his glasses and wiping them against his shirtsleeve.

John eased up on an elbow and looked about. "What am I doing here?"

"They got you for horse thieving and stealing. That's what they say," answered the doctor, tucking his instruments neatly into his medical bag. "You best get used to this place. You'll probably be here a spell."

John stayed in the county jail for three weeks until his case came in review to Judge Clarence Henry. After listening to witnesses and to John, the judge ruled that John had not actually stolen the horse or food, but because of his action to mount the horse, was clearly in on the theft. He was sentenced to one year in the county jail, providing he behaved himself.

As the heavy iron door slammed shut, John shouted, "I'm innocent! I had nothing to do with it! I never stole anything. I've been taught better than that."

He slumped down on the hard cot next to the wall and mumbled to himself. "The only thing I ever took in my life was a few stale crackers, just crackers. My friend is dead and now a year in jail. God, where are you? Don't you care about me? Don't you know I need to get home?"

***

Meanwhile, the South anxiously awaited the return of its heralded heroes. In a few cases, entire companies marched in formation over hundreds of miles of rough roads to be officially dismissed when they reached their home county, but for the most part, the men just trickled back into their homeland any way possible. Most walked but many jumped trains as the Southern conductors were instructed to look the other way in an effort to aid the men heading home.

During May and July of 1865, thousands of soldiers returned to the outstretched arms of their wives and parents. Many who returned had been listed as either dead or missing in action, and their arrival home startled friends and loved ones, bringing unexpected joy.

A May summer wind, both hot and early, swept across the porch of the Wilson home, but as usual, Sarah was out at dusk. With the last rays of light, an owl screeched in the distance, and the night came alive with buzzing sounds of singing locusts.

Lott, headed to the house after a hard day in the field, spotted his wife out front rocking and singing. "Sarah, when are you going to finish yore foolishness? All you do is sit and sing. You don't even keep the house any more. If'n it wasn't for Sister, this place would be in cobwebs. He ain't ever coming home. You got to face what's happened," Lott continued, removing his shoes. "All the boys is home now. That is, all that's coming back."

Sarah continued rocking. "You think what you might, husband, but he's a-coming. You'll see."

Lott slung his shoes to the floor. "Dadburn it, woman! I'll swear you are becoming as crazy as a fritter. Folks 'round here are beginning to talk. That boy's dead, and you best accept it."

Sister headed out to the porch worried. "Mama, Papa, is something wrong?"

"Wrong! I'd say something is wrong," muttered Lott.

"You best go on to bed, darling. Your father and I are just having a talk. You go on now," said Sarah, motioning her back to her room.

Sarah calmly continued her rocking and ignored her husband's outburst.

"Faith, husband. Just a little faith."

Finally, Sarah rose to wash up and retire for the night, but Lot remained alone realizing that he and his wife had lost their special evening time together because of his words.

As long as Lott could remember, he had never seen a May this hot. The livestock was taking shelter in the woods down by the creek, and the young corn barely peeking through the ground was parched. Lott found comfort from the heat in the shade of his front porch. As the evening waned, clouds gathered in the west, and a slight timbre of thunder rumbled. A brisk wind swept across the front yard, sending dust swirling upward like tiny snakes circling toward the sky. The tree limbs began to sway, and torrents of rain plummeted to the ground. Lott moved to the other side of the porch away from the path of the rain and enjoyed the gift for which he had prayed. As the storm passed, the warm ground was engulfed in a mist. The coolness of the air and the gentle drips of water off the house gave Lott a sense of peace.

"What in the world is someone doing out in weather like this," Lott mumbled to himself as he glanced down the road.

As the man cleared the mist, he waved.

Lott walked to the steps and waved back. "It's a bad day to be out. Where you headed?"

"Going home, that's where I'm headed," he answered.

The young man was barefooted and in the rags of a Southern uniform. His hair was light blond, straight and hung to his shoulders, and his face was beardless. His dark blue eyes sparkled. He stood about five foot four and was very thin. *He is almost too pretty for a boy*, thought Lott.

"Come on up, and rest a spell," said Lott, reaching to shake his hand.

"Thank you, sir," said the boy, settling himself on the floor of the porch.

"How old are you, son?" questioned Lot.

The boy pushed his wet hair from his face. "I'm fourteen."

"That's kinda young for a soldier, ain't it?" said Lott. "What's your name, and where you from?"

The boy looked up as the clouds were breaking sending slivers of light lacing across the fields. "The South needed us. General Lee needed us. My name is Gabe Jacobs, and I'm headed west."

"You hungry? When you had your last meal?" said Lott.

He smiled up at Lott. "I ain't hungry."

They talked awhile, and soon, Lott found himself sharing his troubles and time quickly slipped away. Lott told about losing two of his sons to war and how he was afraid he was losing his wife as well.

Gabe listened as Lott opened his heart.

As the sun was setting, Gabe smiled at Lott and spoke, "You say your wife thinks she is being visited by angels? Do you think that's possible?"

"That's Old Testament happenings," Lott replied. "Not today."

"Mr. Wilson, I don't mean to be disrespectful, but you need to search your Bible. The Lord still reigns, and His angels are all about." Rising to his feet, he extended his hand. "I've got a piece to go. I do want to thank you for inviting me over."

"Wait a minute, son. I've got an old hat that will keep the rain and sun off your head, and I think James Earl's shoes might just fit you. You wait here, and I'll be right back."

Finding his old hat and collecting the shoes, Lott hurried back to the porch, but the boy was not there. Thinking he might have followed him into the house, Lott went from room to room looking for him. Opening his bedroom door, Lott found Sarah and Sister sitting in the light of a lamp, sewing. "Has anybody come in here?" asked Lott.

"What do you mean?" replied Sister, laying her needlework aside.

"Have you seen anyone?"

"No, dear, have we had company?" Sarah said.

"Haven't you heard us talking out front?"

Sister giggled. "We heard you talking. We figured you were just talking to yourself. You know, an old age thing."

"You all right, dear," said Sarah.

Lott returned to the porch and found no evidence the boy had been there. The earth had been refreshed, a cool breeze bathed his face, and a warm feeling came over him, and his burdens seemed lighter. He chuckled to himself, maybe he and his wife were beginning to lose their minds together and were seeing angels. Maybe angels were here among them. How else could he explain the disappearance of the young man and the comfort of his heart? Maybe God had not forgotten him and his family. Maybe God loved him and would see him through the deaths of his sons. Lott whispered a prayer of thanks.

6

Detained

God is our refuge and strength, an ever present help in trouble. Therefore we will not fear.
—Psalm 46:1-2a

John could not believe the verdict. He didn't steal the horse or food, but running to meet Sam and extending his hand made him a partner in the crime. *How foolish it all seems now,* he thought. *Here he came galloping down the street, and all I thought was this will make our journey easier.* "I deserve what I got," mumbled John as the marshal led him out of the church where the hearing and sentencing took place.

"What'd you say, boy?" asked the marshal who was handcuffed to John and was leading him toward the jail.

"Nothing important," replied John.

"We're going to spend a lot of time together. You can make it easy, or you can make it difficult."

The marshal, Hank Goss, was a man in his mid-fifties, short, stocky and almost bald. What little hair he had was cleanly shaven, and his long white mustache was waxed and curled. He was all business and tolerated no foolishness. The town could not afford a full-time marshal, so Hank made his primary living on a small farm on the outskirts of town.

John, sound asleep at the break of dawn, was awakened by a rooster crowing and the screech of a door. The jail was a small stone structure ten by twenty feet with only two rooms, the marshal's office and the adjoining cell. Since there was little crime, the accommodation was sufficient.

"Time to rise, Johnny Reb. Times a-wasting," called out Hank. "You got to eat and go."

John sat up and rubbed his eyes. "What are you talking about?"

"How about two biscuits with ham, a fried egg and some coffee," Hank said, unlocking the cell door. "You'll get supper too."

John walked to a small table next to Hank and sat down on a wooden box. "This is a lot better than at Camp Douglas. All we got was rice, beans and sometimes, a little pork, and there were days we got nothing."

Hank had the coffee brewed, and after John enjoyed his meal, Hank took out a set of handcuffs connected by three feet of chain and placed them on John's wrist. He then directed him to the door.

"Where are we going?" asked John.

"You going to work, boy," answered Hank, pointing to a wagon harnessed and waiting.

"What do you mean work? I thought I was to be jailed."

"We do things a little different around here," explained Hank. "Town has got to pay my salary, and the food we bring you costs us money. That's where you come in. When we got a prisoner, we put him up for hire to anyone who's got the money. That takes care of my salary, yore food, and if there is any left, it goes into our school fund. We're fortunate to have a fine institution of learning here in this little town. This whole program seems to work extremely well."

"What do you have me doing today?" asked John, climbing up on the wagon seat. "You going to take these chains off me? I can't do much with 'em on."

Hank laughed. "You know how to plow a mule, don't you?"

"Seems like I was born plowing."

"Well, you can still keep your hands on the plow handles, your feet will be free, and if you decide to run, you won't get far," Hank explained as he pushed a wad of chewing tobacco into his mouth.

The morning was cool and fresh, and John enjoyed the ride into the country. The winding road led through dense forest and scattered farmland, and after several miles, Hank made a turn up a small path. Soon John could see split rail fences and a house that centered the road.

"This here is Mr. Daniel Taylor's place. He's been a little under the weather lately, and since him and his ole lady don't have no children, that's where you come in," said Hank, spitting out a stream of tobacco juice.

As they pulled in, a couple of hounds burst out to meet them, barking raucously alerting the Taylors that visitors were here. In seconds, the door swung open as a small, thin man limped onto the porch.

"Brought your boy," said Hank. "You got him till sundown."

Mr. Taylor carefully made his way down the steps and came over to John. "He don't look like much," he said, eyeing John. "How do you know he can or will work?"

"Get on down, boy," said Hank, motioning to John. "He'll work or he won't eat, and like I said, I'll come get 'em at sundown."

John placed his foot against a spoke on the wagon wheel and jumped to the ground. Straightening himself, he looked at Hank. "You not gonna stay with me?"

"Stay with you?" laughed Hank. "I got a farm of my own to work. I ain't no full time marshal."

John watched Hank for a moment as he left in the wagon and then turned to Taylor. "I'd appreciate it if you'll show me where the mule and plow is."

"Not so fast," answered Daniel. "I ain't ever worked no jailbirds. How do I know you won't run off the first time I take my eyes off you? And don't you have some decent clothes? You look like a pauper."

"Sir, I don't plan to run off, and I do plan to give you a good day's work. I expect these chains would be a problem if I did decide to run," said John, holding up his arms.

"Come on then," Mr. Taylor answered as he walked to his barn. He sat on an old empty barrel and carefully watched John catch and harness a mule to the plow. Then he pointed to a field beyond the barn and said, "Boy, there's forty acres to be broken, and since it is already past the time it should have been done, you need to get on it. How long do you think it'll take you to do the job?" Taylor asked.

John paused as he looked over the field. "You've had a dry spring, and the grass hasn't taken over. I'd say, it'll take two days to break it up for planting and one more to get the seed out. I can do it in three days."

"Three days!" exclaimed Taylor. "More like six I'd say."

"Trust me. Three days and you'll have seed in the ground, and if you will, please leave me some drinking water by that old oak over there. I'd appreciate it."

John slapped the lines across the mule's flanks and headed to the fields. The plow burrowed into the soft soil as the grass was turned under displaying the earth beneath. Hour after hour, John pushed the mule and plow across the meadow laying out neat, straight rows. Occasionally, John would stop and rest a few moments, then the work went on. As thin and weak as John was, he was surprised and relieved that he had the stamina to do hard work. As midday approached, Mr. Taylor walked out to see what John had accomplished and was surprised at the acres that had been turned.

"Hey," he called out. "Want to see you."

When John reached the end of the row, he pulled the mule in and walked to Taylor. "Sir, is something wrong?" asked John, wiping sweat from his brow.

"Don't you think you're pushing it a little too hard out in this heat? You've made a big dent in the field," commented Taylor elated over the amount of field that had been plowed. "Is your leg giving you trouble?"

John shook his head. "No sir, it's a lot hotter down in Mississippi. I'll be fine, and for my leg, it'll be fine. A minie ball went slap through it."

"My wife has cooked up some chicken and dumplings, if you care for some. You've put in some hard work this morning."

John took a large swallow of water and wiped his brow again. "Thank you, sir, but I plan to put seed in the ground the day after tomorrow, but maybe, she could fix a plate for me to take when I leave today."

John kept a steady pace for the remainder of the day, and as the sun was setting, he saw the marshal returning. As John was putting the mule into the stable to be fed and watered, he saw the marshal and Taylor talking. He took care of the mule and headed to the wagon that would take him back to jail.

The next two days went by quickly, and as the sun set, John left the field. As John was getting in the wagon with the marshal, Taylor hollered out for them to wait a minute. He went into the house and came back with a bundle and handed it to John. John looked at it and was surprised to see a newly-made shirt. "Thank you, sir, and tell your wife the shirt is greatly appreciated," John replied.

"Couldn't stand those rags you're wearing. The misses thought this might do you better. You did me a fine job, young man. I appreciate it," Taylor said, extending his hand to John.

"You gonna make this little town some money, boy, when word gets out. Yes sir, maybe the judge will extend your stay," Hank said, hurrying the rig along. "That job should have taken you about six days. Why the hurry up with no lunch?"

"The man said he was behind on his planting schedule. I just wanted to get him caught up."

Hank pulled the wagon to a stop. "You don't get it, do you, boy!" he scowled. "You're suppose to make us some money. This ain't no party. You understand?"

John looked away in disgust. "I guess I don't understand. I just did my best, but it certainly isn't a party, and I do realize I got to make you money," he stated sharply.

"Boy, you trying to get smart with me!" Hank said, grabbing John's arm.

John jerked loose. "Didn't intend no disrespect. I was just trying to help the man."

The cell door slammed shut, and John began unbinding the cloth that held the upper part of his shoes to the soles. No sooner had he loosened the knots, they fell into pieces. *There would be no fixing up these*, he laughed to himself.

"Hey Marshal, that field ate my shoes."

"What do you mean ate your shoes?"

John held the pieces for Hank to see. "Nothing left to 'em. If you expect me to work on my feet, especially on rough ground, you'll need to get me some, or this ole boy ain't gonna make you much money."

Hank remained silent, ignoring the remarks.

"Hank, I need to send a telegram to my folks, so they'll know where I am and that I'm alright," said John, lying on his bunk and pulling his pillow under his neck.

"You got money for that?" stammered Hank.

"Nope, you know I don't."

"What kind of a place you think I run here, boy? You think we got room service," answered Hank, shutting his desk drawer and preparing to leave for the night.

"How about a letter? That don't cost much," probed John.

"Same old song, boy. You got to realize your station in life and face reality. You know what reality is, don't you? See you about dawn."

"If you'll take these here chains off me, I could work even better," John called out.

"Dream on, boy," shouted Hank, stepping up to his wagon seat.

John listened to the frogs croaking down by the town's millpond and locust singing their sharp evening songs. For those moments, he was at home. Mother and Father were next door, Sister was trying to master the mandolin, and a half-mile down the road, Rebecca was waiting for him. He tried to hold on to those thoughts, but the reality of one year in jail destroyed his dream. His mind could hear his father tell him that no matter what circumstance you find yourself in, make the best of it, and learn from it. John shuddered. He had survived battles. He had endured Camp Douglas, and now he was serving a one-year jail sentence. He knew this would be difficult if he remained behind bars in a cramped cell. Working outside, no matter what the task, was much better than the isolation of a cell.

When word got out about John's hard work, barely a day would go by without his employment. Many of the local farmers were behind with their spring plowing, so John was kept busy for most of late May and early June. In addition, he mended fences, hoed weeds, repaired houses and buildings and once it was known he was good with horses, he was called to break and train them. Hank was pleased with the money John was bringing the community, and John did receive some shoes.

Outside, a brisk wind whipped the trees about and a hard rain beat upon the roof of the jail. There would be no work today, thought John as he got up to stretch and headed to the window to see the rain.

Hank settled in his desk seat with his feet stretched up upon the edge and studied John. Most prisoners had tried to get out of working, but this one thrived on it. He knew this young man was not a criminal, but the town was benefiting from his mishap with the law. *I just hope he slips up, just one time*, thought Hank, *then we could easily extend his stay*. When John was first arrested, Hank saw an arrogant and too-educated Rebel. Kentucky was a border state where men fought on both sides, but Hank was a Union man. Despite this, his affection for John was growing.

Hank pulled out a checker table and checkers. "I've got a job for you, boy," said Hank walking over to the cell and pulling a small table over next to the bars. "I want to see you try to beat me in checkers."

John laughed. "I don't want to play you," and sat back down on his bunk.

"Why's that? You afraid I'll embarrass you?"

John laughed again as he got up and pulled his stool up next to the bars. "Cause I've seen you play before. You do alright at first, but then when your opponent jumps you or you loose, your temper gets the best of you. You only beat the ones that don't know much about the game."

"You know that's a lie, boy! I'm better than that! You're just trying to cut me down so I might loose. Now stick those arms through the bars, and line your checkers up. I'll show you how we play in Kentuck."

"Hank, we play the same game in Mississippi."

Hank played well at first, but with one jump after another, John ruled the board. On his last move, John claimed three at one time, and Hank fumed. He threw the table aside sending checkers rolling in all directions, sailed the checkerboard across the room, and stormed out of the jail.

***

About mid-day, a rider with dust floating down the street behind him headed to Walker's store. Stopping at the entrance, he dusted himself off and walked down the open aisle to Thomas who was reading the paper that had just arrived on the Meridian stage.

"You Thomas Walker?" the rider asked.

Thomas adjusted his glasses, studying the man carefully. "I'm Thomas Walker. How can I help you?"

The rider reached inside his coat pocket and retrieved an open envelope containing a letter. "You need to sign this telegram from Washington D.C.," stated the man.

Thomas took the letter, and after signing for it, thanked the man and hurriedly sat down. He could hear his heart beating as he began to go into its contents, and a smile of satisfaction formed on his face as he read.

"Hallelujah!" he shouted, jumping up and waving the paper above his head. "It's about time I got word. Thank you, Lord, thank you."

Mrs. Walker rushed in to check on her husband. With the widest smile she had ever seen, Thomas still waving the letter skipped down to meet her. Elated, he pulled her to him, swung her around, and gave her big hug.

"Darling, you won't believe this! Come on over here, and sit with me," he said, leading her to several chairs placed where men could sit and talk while their wives shopped.

"You know a while back when I told you I was going to do some checking up to find out from the government who was being held in them northern prison camps?" Walker spoke waving the letter in his hand.

"I vaguely remember it," answered Mrs. Walker.

With the confidence of a lawyer closing a strong case, he continued. "First, I sent a telegram to Richmond, hoping to get the information I needed, but about that time, the Union Army had broken our lines and taken the city. Our soldiers and politicians fled and Grant torched much of the city. That put a damper on things, so I thought to myself, why not go straight to Washington. It was indeed their prisons holding our soldiers. They surely had to keep records."

"Thomas, don't be foolish. Those men don't care about problems we have. To them, we are nobodies," said Mrs. Walker.

"You're right, Bet. We are nobodies, but Mr. Frank Olliver Sr. is a man of means. When he wrote them that he did not support the secessionist movement and his son was not allowed to join the army, things began to happen, especially with one senator."

"What happened next?' stammered Mrs. Walker, becoming more interested.

"Well, let's just say a large amount of money switched hands."

"Thomas, you know what they say about Olliver money," stated Mrs. Walker.

When this country was opened for settlement, Frank Olliver had come in with Lott and Jake working with a surveyor's crew and, like the Wilsons, decided to stay.

But unlike them, he had brought in a lot of slaves from Louisiana and made money on cotton, which he used to buy more land and more slaves.

"Talk is he cheated both whites and Choctaws along the way to get the land and money he has accumulated," interrupted Mrs. Walker.

"I don't know about that, but I do know that few Choctaws decided to stay, and those that did stay didn't know how to work the land and just abandoned it," explained Thomas, not interested in the specifics.

Mrs. Walker shook her head. "What's in that letter, Thomas?"

He smiled. "This report came straight from the war department. There were quite a few John Wilsons held in the camps, but when it came to John Lewis Wilson, there were only two. One died before John even joined up, and the other man was from Texas. They did cross a man named John Lewis up at Camp Douglas, but he weren't no John Lewis Wilson."

"Now that you've got the information, what do you intend to do?"

Thomas folded the telegram neatly and placed it in his pocket. "Stop all this foolishness, that's what I'm gonna do. I'm going up to see Lott and Sarah now, and when I get back we'll sit down with Rebecca. Have you noticed every time any of our soldier boys come through here heading home, Rebecca rushes out to meet them?"

"I think we all want to go talk with them and thank them for their effort."

"Not Rebecca. she's always asking them if they know anything about John. I've heard her myself," stammered Thomas.

"Maybe, but Thomas, you don't need to bother the Wilsons. They've been through enough. No sir, you need to leave them be, and for Rebecca, this ain't gonna sit well with her. Her hopes will be dashed just like before."

"There's a thing called reality, and it's time she faced it," answered Thomas. "I always liked the Wilson boy, but it's time Rebecca realizes that life ain't always fair and you have to take what comes and move on."

"By the way, what's in this for Mr. Olliver? Why would he be willing to pay such a sum?" frowned Mrs. Walker.

Thomas tipped his hat, gave a slight bow and smiled. "A few thousand dollars don't bother Frank much, and I can definitely say he is very much interested in our family, if you know what I mean."

"Where's Rebecca now?" asked Thomas.

"She's walked down the way to visit her friend, Betsy. They had a new colt born last night, and Betsy wanted her to see it. She should be back in a while."

Thomas took a deep breath. "I started all this business, and tonight when we all get home, I'll talk to her. I just pray I'll say the right words. The last thing I want to do is cause her more heartache, but she needs to get on with her life."

***

Rebecca reached home about dusk and hung her bonnet on a peg in the hallway, and eager to share her visit with Betsy and the beautiful colt, she went to find her mother.

"Mother, you should see her!" she exclaimed. "She's light brown with a touch of white right between her eyes and another patch running down the lower part of her back. She is simply beautiful!" exclaimed Rebecca, rushing into the parlor.

As Rebecca shared every detail of her visit with Betsy, her father came from the back porch after enjoying a late afternoon smoke. He took the telegram from his pocket and began reading the note. When tears accumulating in Rebecca's eyes, Mrs. Walker eased closer and placed her hand on her daughter's. After Thomas finished, all was quite.

Rebecca wiped her tears away and stated, "Why did you do that, Father?"

All was quite for a moment while Thomas collected his thoughts. "For your own good."

"Did you ever think how painful this would be for me?" murmured Rebecca.

Thomas cleared his throat. "I know you've struggled with the loss of John, and all that nonsense from Mrs. Wilson only made it worse. I had to do something."

"Darling, we're only trying to help, and God knows we have tried everything," added her mother.

Rebecca took a long breath. "I know you love me, and I know you've tried to console me, but I don't think you understand me. I need someone to talk to, but you wouldn't allow it. When I went to Mrs. Wilson, we talked, cried, prayed and sang."

Tears trickled down Rebecca's cheeks. "It was at their home I found peace, and I felt comfort."

"What about all this angel talk, Rebecca?" interrupted Mr. Walker.

Rebecca shook her head and wiped away the tears. "I don't really know, but I do know I felt hope and healing."

Thomas rubbed his nose in thought, knowing he needed to be tactful. "Then, do you believe that John is gone?"

A smile formed on Rebecca's face. "He'll never be gone, not for me. I've loved John all my life. No, I've adored him. He was always kind, thoughtful, humorous and exciting. Even as a child, after a visit, I could hardly wait until I could see him again. I remember when the older boys would tease Frankie or Tim. It was John who stood up for them. That's the way he was. I loved him for it. I love him now, and I'll love him forever, but I do think the Lord has taken him from me. If for some strange reason that should not be the case, then I, along with Sarah and her angels, will rejoice."

All was silent as the three sat together. Rebecca broke the silence with the words her father had been longing to hear. "Father, I had already made up my mind to go on with my life. I think that's what John would want me to do."

***

Frankie dipped his comb into the basin of water and slowly brought it through his long blond hair as he studied every feature of his maturing face. As a youth, he had always been thin and lanky and not very coordinated, but with years, he had grown to be over six feet tall and had filled out quite nicely. Still, to his disgust, his facial hair was behind schedule with only a trace of sideburns sprouting. He straightened his shoulders, stuck out his chest, and smiled. Not bad, he thought. As he was pulling on his boots, he heard a horseman approach and voices downstairs.

"Frankie, your father just got in and wants to talk with you," his mother, Judith, called out.

Bounding down the stairs, Frankie found his father sitting in the parlor talking with his mother, and from his expression, there was trouble.

"'Bout time you got up, son. It's might near ten o'clock. I've been up since daybreak and have covered the whole place," said Frank Sr. as he pointed to a vacant chair across the room.

Frank Sr. was indeed a workingman. He came into the county as a young man with nothing and now farmed over three thousand acres of land, owned over sixty slaves before the emancipation, and had numerous business enterprises. To accumulate such wealth, he made his own rules, was not afraid to gamble, and was ruthless with anyone who opposed him. In general, he got what he wanted. One thing he didn't do was give his son sound direction or spend quality time with him. Suzanne, his older daughter, saw her father for what he was and relied on her mother for direction, but as a young boy, Frankie longed for his father's attention and approval. Reaching manhood, things changed, and a breach had developed.

"What did I do now, Frank?" said Frankie, expecting a reprimand.

"You think you did something wrong?"

"It's always the same old story. Frankie, do this. Frankie, do that. When are you going to take some responsibility? You ain't worth the food I give you. So, Frank, what have I done wrong now?" replied Frankie, eyeing his father.

Judith went to sit next to her son. "Don't be so hasty. Give your father a chance."

Frank Sr. regained his composure and took a deep breath. "How are you and the Walker girl doing? You still seeing her, I hope."

"That's entirely my business. I don't ask about your love life," muttered Frankie, knowing that there were other women in his father's life but ashamed he had spoken this in front of his mother who never believed the accusations and dismissed them as worthless gossip.

In anger, Frank brought his fist down hard against the coffee table, shattering an empty cup to the floor. "Listen to me, boy. I just spent a large sum of money to get some information from Washington about the Wilson boy stating he was not a Union prisoner, which means for once and for all, the boy is dead."

"So what!" exclaimed Frankie.

"So what!" shouted Frank, looking toward his wife. "What have we raised here, an idiot?"

Returning his stare on Frankie, he replied, "That means Wilson is out of your way, son."

Frankie's face turned red in anger, and he began to grit his teeth as he chose his words. "Some folks say I'm a chip off the old block, so if I'm an idiot, what does that make you? As for responsibility, you talk a big show, but you have never let me stand on my own two feet and take on responsibility. You never have given me a chance to learn and grow. You thought you were saving me when you bought my way out of the army, but you made me the laughing stock of the community. And now, you are doing the same thing again. I don't need your help when it comes to Rebecca. So don't do me any favors. Don't expect me to be thankful for your interference."

Frank got up, walked to the window, and remained silent for a moment. "You had five close friends who joined up. How many of the Clearman boys came home? All three are buried in Virginia. Your best friend John is dead. Tim Johnson is missing his leg. How do you like those statistics?"

Frankie smiled. "I wish I'd been with 'em. Dead and in hell would be better than trying to satisfy you."

"Both of you need to settle down," interrupted Judith, trying to soothe the family feud. "Rebecca is a fine, beautiful young woman, and we just want what's best for you."

Frankie spoke only to his mother. "I've been on buggy rides with Rebecca and have visited her at the Walkers, but Suzanne always initiated the visit and was with us. Rebecca does seem to enjoy our company, and we are growing closer."

Frank made his way back to the sofa and, for a moment, sat there eyeing his son. "Frankie, there ain't many young men around here for Rebecca to court. You are a handsome young man with a pleasing personality, and someday, could be the richest man in Mississippi. I don't see how in the world that girl wouldn't want you."

Judith nodded her head in agreement. "What your father said is true. You've got to keep letting her know you are interested, and in time, she'll come around."

Frank got up and extended his hand to Frankie. "You'll have to excuse my outburst, but I do wish to have Rebecca as my daughter-in-law, and I don't like you to call me Frank. There ain't but two people in the world can call me father, and that's you and Suzanne."

Frankie scowled and murmured under his breath, "I'm sure there's more."

7

A Young Heart

And there is a time for every event under heaven – a time to plant and a time to uproot what is planted; a time to kill and a time to heal; a time to weep and a time to laugh; a time to mourn and a time to dance; a time to search and a time to give up as lost; a time to be silent and a time to speak; a time for war and a time for peace.
—Ecclesiastes 3:1b, 2b, 3a, 4, 6a, 7b, 8b

The spring rain had cleared and a dense fog covered the ground, making the dark night darker. No one stirred outside John's cell window. He had said his evening prayers and settled into a sound sleep. Late into the night, the screeching of a rocking chair woke him. Sensing a presence, John threw off his cover, leaned up, and looked toward the sound. He could see nothing and felt blinded by the dark. All was quite, and John thought he must have been dreaming. Just as he laid his head on the pillow, the sound started again. John sprang to his feet, clasped the bars, and peered into the night.

"Who's there?" John whispered.

The rocking ceased. "I'm sorry I woke you."

"Who are you?" asked John.

"I'm on my way home, and the weather like it is, I decided to take cover until it clears. I'll be moving on soon."

"Why the jailhouse?" questioned John.

The stranger chuckled to himself. "It was the only place open. What are you doing in here?"

John began to share his story and opened his heart to the stranger. He told him in detail about his war experiences, Camp Douglas, and the reason he was in jail. He talked about his family in Mississippi and how his heart yearned for them and for Rebecca. The hours passed, and when he had finished, he realized that all the talk had centered on him and how rude he had been. He quickly apologized and thanked the man for listening.

The rocking stopped, and he heard the man get up. "Well, John, it's time for me go. I enjoyed listening. I know things seem helpless right now, but I feel you'll be home by Christmas, and you will see Rebecca again."

"You never told me who you are," John spoke.

"Oh, I'm really no one of importance. Just remember, take care and keep your faith."

The door eased shut, and all was quite again.

What an unusual visitor, John thought. With a start, he realized that the man had called his name. In all his talking, he did not remember mentioning it.

The clouds broke, and a full moon illuminated the cell as John drifted off to sleep.

John woke as the door squeaked open, and Hank cleared his throat as he entered, bringing in the morning sunlight. John sat up, rubbed his eyes and looked about. "Hank, you always lock me in at night, don't you?"

"Shore do. I'm afraid you'll find a way out of the cell and make a run," answered Hank, walking over to his desk and slinging his keys down. "Why'd you ask?"

"Did you forget to lock the door last night?"

"Boy, do you listen to me? I take my work seriously, and yes, I locked the door last night. Why?"

John sat down on his bunk and ran his fingers through his hair in thought. I did sleep pretty soundly last night. Sometimes, dreams can be so real that it is hard to separate them from reality. It's when you wake up, you realize it's all in your mind.

"Nothing, Hank. I just had a dream, that's all."

"What about? Trying to escape to your dreamland in Mississippi?" joked Hank.

"Well, in my dream I was told I'd be home by Christmas."

"Christmas! That's a good one. You might be home for Christmas come 1870," Hank laughed.

John had been in jail for more than six weeks, and the time had rushed by. His work was hard and tiring, and when he lay down at night, it seemed only seconds when he would be up and going again.

When John joined the army, by the cotton scales in Hickory he weighed about one hundred and eighty pounds, but at the time he was jailed, he was frail, weak and down to one hundred and fifteen pounds. Due to his illness, he had lost some of his hair and was pretty unsightly. No wonder people shied away from him when he entered town. But with time and some good home-cooking, John had recovered. His hair was growing back, and he was gaining weight with his handsome features returning. It seemed like no job was too hard for him and there wasn't much he couldn't do. Not only had he been employed every day except Sundays, but with his reputation, he was now booked many days in advance. On some days, when more than one person wanted his service, Hank would actually auction him off to the highest bidder.

John finished some fence work for the day, and since it was Saturday, he was unshackled and looking forward to some rest. As the cell door slammed shut, the jail door opened, and a tall, thin man dressed neatly in black entered.

He walked to Hank and took a chair across from him.

"How you doing, Parson?" Hank said, straightening himself as he slid a half empty whiskey bottle down into the lower drawer of his desk. "Good to see you."

The parson smiled. "I'm doing fine, and no need to hide the bottle. If I didn't see it, the Lord did."

"Yes sir, can't hide from you or the Lord." Hank laughed. "What do you want?"

Hank answered his own question. "I know what you want. I ain't been to services lately. That's it, isn't it?"

The parson shuffled about. "That ain't it, and it ain't about your lack of tithing. That's between you and the Lord, but I do feel you're on a slide."

"Slide! What do you mean by that?" exclaimed Hank, somewhat apprehensive.

"I've known you for more than twenty years, and if you don't change, you're on a slide away from the Lord and straight to the devil."

Slightly angered but knowing the parson was probably right, Hank slowly shook his head in agreement and laughed. "Now, Parson, tell me what you really want."

The parson went to the cell where John was sitting. He stood a moment peering intently at John. "Hank, I've got a way for you to redeem yourself and perhaps save your soul."

"Pray tell, preacher. I sure need to get off that slide," he said, taking the parson more seriously.

"Well, our church needs painting."

"You want to employ the boy. That's it, ain't it, Parson?"

The parson walked back to Hank. "You got it, Hank. The church wants to employ the boy, but we don't have the money."

"No money! That don't sound like employment."

The parson chuckled. "Let's look at it like this. We work the boy, and you kinda don't charge us. You could say that this is a sort of tithe for you. How do you like that?"

Hank mumbled to himself and pursed his lips in thought. "How many days would it take?"

"I figure about a week."

"A week!" muttered Hank. "I'll loose a lot of money on that."

"Hank, it might stop that slide you're on, and the folks would truly be beholding to you. You might even become the town hero."

"Town hero." Hank chuckled. "Well, I don't see how I've got a choice then."

"Your church's got a steeple, don't it?" interrupted John.

"That's right young man. Why?"

"No disrespect. I'll paint your church, but I don't paint steeples."

"What do you mean you don't paint steeples? You will do what I tell you to do," said Hank, becoming angry again.

The parson studied John for a moment. "What's the problem with steeples?"

"I've faced a lot of frightful and agonizing things in my life, but I do have one fear that I've never overcome, and that's the fear of heights. You get me up more than ten or twelve feet, and I'll probably fall."

The parson walked to the cell and extended his hand. "Thank you for your honesty, and we'll just let the Lord work out that problem for us. Are you a believer?"

"Yes sir, I am. I accepted the Lord when I was eleven. I guess you can say I'm a baptized Baptist," John said, taking his hand.

The parson turned to Hank. "This boy has been in your jail for over a month. Why hasn't he been to church?"

"Church!" laughed Hank. "He's a criminal. Criminals don't go to church."

"He's also a Christian. Come Sunday, he belongs in church," replied the parson.

"You want me to bring him there shackled and all. That'd be a heck of a scene."

"Hank, we're all sinners, and I'm not sure this boy deserves what we've given him. You bringing him to church would be good for him and just think what the congregation would think of you. I can just hear Miss Lucy say, our marshal has done some backsliding, but he still loves the Lord so much that not only does he come to church but brings his prisoner as well. Well, you might even get elected deacon before you know it."

"Preacher, you are one convincing soul. I'll tell you what. The boy ain't got no decent clothes. You get him something decent, and I'll get him to church."

"What about the shackles in the Lord's house?"

Hank took a deep breath in disgust. "There won't be no shackles, but I will have my pistol in my coat pocket. Anything else, Parson?"

"That's about it, Hank. I think we can say we've got you off that slide."

As the preacher was leaving, Hank laughed to himself. I wonder if deacons are allowed to drink whiskey? Probably not. No sir, no deacon for Mr. Hank.

On Sunday, John was ready for church with his new clothes, recent haircut and shave. At ten thirty, Hank arrived stuffed into his clothing with bulges popping at the seams, white shirt crinkled and a mismatched tie. John couldn't help but chuckle.

"What are you laughing about? You think I'm overdressed?"

John tried to restrain himself. "Hank, you look just fine. I'm just not used to seeing you dressed up. That's all."

At the church, John noticed the outside walls and understood why the parson wanted them painted. He took a glimpse of the tall steeple, then quickly looked away. John felt at home in the sanctuary. The clapboard walls of white, the clear glass windows, and the line of benches in front of an elevated podium brought back memories of his Mississippi church. John and Hank walked down the aisle to a vacant bench as the congregation turned and was impressed with the handsome man in gray homespun trousers, a dark blue cotton shirt, black leather suspenders and clean-shaven with neatly trimmed curly black hair. The women couldn't help but give him a nod and slight smile.

After Hank and John settled on the bench, the preacher nodded a welcome and began the service. The preacher had purposely chosen the topic of the spirits, that is the love of whiskey. As the service ended, the preacher asked if anyone had anything to share. Several had prayer request for ailing friends and neighbors and when it appeared that all request had been made, John raised his hand.

"Mr. Wilson, what is your request?"

John stood and spoke clearly. "First, I want to thank the marshal for allowing me to attend service, and I want you to know I'm sorry. After three years of war and surviving Camp Douglas, I guess I was still suffering from the effects of smallpox and starving and just wasn't thinking. I just wanted to get home to my family. I know the Lord has forgiven me and hope you will too."

All was quiet as John took his seat then a clap was heard in the back of the room and others joined in.

On the way back to jail, Hank seemed troubled.

"What's going on, Hank? You didn't like church, did you?"

Hank slapped the reigns down hard against the flank of his horse. "Wasn't that. I didn't care for the sermon."

"You mean about drinking?"

"You got it. You may think I'm hell-bound but I do read my Bible, and it don't say you shouldn't drink. What it says is you drink in moderation. I do drink, but you'll never see me drunk. The preacher was wrong."

"Are you planning on going back?" probed John.

Hank snickered. "Sure, I'm going back. How can I become a deacon man and not go back? By the way, I appreciate what you said about me bringing you to church."

John looked at Hank and said, "You know your problem. Underneath all your talk and threats, hides a decent man. You just don't let him out much."

"You say I'm getting soft! Boy, I know how to deal with lawbreakers, and you can't be easy on them. If they think you're soft, they take advantage."

"Then this is a game you're playing. Is that it?"

"Game! No sir, this ain't no game. I keep peace, and I run a good jail and being tough is smart."

"Hank, I've been in jail for almost two months, there ain't been any other arrests made. Seems like this is a pretty peaceful town."

"Well, that's because I do my job well."

"I just mean, you don't have to be so gruff all the time."

On Saturday, John relaxed and reflected on all that had happened. Making bad situation tolerable seemed to be succeeding. He was developing positive relationships with the people of the community and had earned the marshal's respect. No longer was he shackled while working, and people were bringing to the jail treats such as cakes, pies, home-cooked bread, as well as meals. At first Hank resented this but quickly changed his mind after John began to share the bounty.

While John dozed, his nose began to twitch with a musty, sweaty smell. Next, he heard hard breathing and opened his eyes to a man's face pressed against the bars inches from where he lay.

"You a soldier boy?" the stranger asked in a hissing voice.

Startled, John sat up. "Who are you?"

"They say you are. I bet you won you a medal," the man replied, stomping his feet and laughing.

The man's shabby clothes, shaggy beard, ill-kept hair, and the way he spoke and acted convinced John that the man had some mental problems.

John extended his hand and smiled. "I'm John Wilson, and who might you be?"

The man had been squatting on the floor but eased back for a moment, then leaned forward and cautiously took John's hand. "I'm Wally."

"Wally who?"

The man released John's hand and began scratching his head as if some insect had found a home among the tangles. "I don't know. Just Wally. You a soldier?"

John sat up. "Not any more. I'm just a prisoner."

John pointed to a chair. "Take a seat, Mr. Wally. Why'd you come in here to see me?" John asked.

Wally took his chair and began to clap his hands and shake with laughter. "I want to make money, and they say you are a good worker. I want to work for you."

John felt sorry for the man and knew there was no way to make him understand that he couldn't help him.

"Wally, I'll talk to the marshal, and if he needs some more help, I'll tell him you are available."

Elated, Wally jumped up and laughed and chattered to himself. "I'se gonna be rich, Mr. Soldier Boy."

John reached over to a sack and retrieved a large red apple and crunched into it. The pulp filled his mouth, and the sweet juice ran down his chin. Wally instantly stopped his outburst, took his seat and watched John intensely. With each bite that John took, Wally would take a deep breath and swallow.

John laid the half eaten apple down, reached to the bag and handed Wally an apple. A large smile crept across his face as he took the apple and immediately bit into it. "You my friend, Mr. Soldier Boy?"

"Wally, I think we are the best of friends. Why don't you call me John?"

Wally heard the door open as the marshal entered. He threw what was left of the apple and quickly ran for the rear entrance.

"What's that moron doing in here? Git out of here, boy!" Hank yelled after the man. "How long has he been in here?"

John shook his head. "I don't know. Perhaps an hour. Maybe less."

Hank closed the door, mumbling as he worked his way back to his desk.

"Who is the man?" asked John.

Hank fumbled through some papers on his desk. "His name is Wallace Jeffcoats. We call him Wally. He was born that way. Dumb as a bat. His paw left when he was a baby, and his poor mother is pretty near destitute."

"Can he work?" asked John.

"Not much. He mops and sweeps floors and does odd jobs. That's about it. If it weren't for the church folks, they'd both starve to death. Did he bother you?"

John shook his head. "I didn't know how to take him at first, but he was fine."

Hank placed the papers he had been studying in one of his drawers, collected his keys and walked toward the door. "He won't bother you no more. I put the scare on 'em."

***

The morning sun tipped the horizon, speckling its way through the heavily leafed trees that bordered the garden. Long rows of corn swayed as a light breeze rustled their young leaves. Straight rows of butterbeans and peas grew strong as well as potatoes, carrots, lettuce, beets and tomatoes. On the far end of the garden, the land sloped into a damp bottom where sweet potatoes and watermelons were spreading their vines in an unruly fashion. Only a short distance away near the creek bottom, sugar cane had been laid out and was already knee high.

Come fall, the cane would be cut, crushed by a grinder pulled by mules, and the juice would be processed into molasses syrup. With the vegetables the Wilsons grew and the meat from their own hogs and beef cattle, they were practically self-sufficient except for purchases of flour, sugar, salt and simple necessities.

The women pulled up and bound their skirts below the knees, showing their bare feet. Using hoes, they carefully loosened the earth around the plants, taking the unwanted weeds and briars away. Even though it took a lot of time, harvest time would be even more time consuming. To process and preserve the vegetables would take from morning until dark for several weeks.

Sister stopped her work and used the sleeve of her blouse to wipe the perspiration from her brow. She leaned against her hoe and blew gnats from her face, then said, "Mama, do you think I'm pretty?"

Sarah stopped, looked at Sister and laughed. "Well, Sweetie, you have looked better than you do now. Why do you ask?"

Sister retied a cloth binding that kept her long hair off her shoulders. "I turned sixteen a few months back, and I wonder if it's time for me to start courting. The boys do seem to take note of me. They like to tease me and enjoy talking to me. What if one of them wants to call on me?"

Sarah resumed her work. "First thing, you are a very pretty girl, you're smart, and you have a good heart," she answered as they toiled along together. "Are you trying to tell me a young man has caught your fancy?"

Sister stopped again. "You know Johnny Jenkins, don't you? He's regular at our church services."

"Known him all my life, darling."

"Well, last Sunday after the service, Mrs. Olliver invited a group of us to their home for a social next Saturday. She told us that Suzanne would be returning from a visit at her grandfather's plantation in Louisiana, and they wanted to surprise her."

"What are you trying to say, Sister?"

"Well, Johnny asked me to go with him. He said his father would accompany us in their buggy. You think I can go?"

Sarah smiled. "Sister, I think you are old enough to start courting, but you know your father, he's very protective of you."

"Then Mama, you are saying I have your approval?"

Sarah laid down her hoe and wrapped her arms around her daughter. "You have my approval, but you still have to talk with your father," she said. "He'll be tired when he and Toby leave the fields this afternoon. Wait until he has rested, had his supper and is relaxed, then talk to him about your courting Johnny."

"I'm afraid to do that, Mama."

"I'll be there with you. You'll do fine. It's getting kind of warm. I think it's time to go to the house."

As the sun faded in the west, Lott and Toby unharnessed the mules they had been plowing behind since morning, gave them water and hay, and turned them out into the barnyard for a much-earned rest. Lott climbed the porch steps, took off his shoes and stretched out on the boarded porch exhausted. When Sarah heard him approach, she left the kitchen where she had prepared supper, collected a cup of water and ventured out to him.

"Here, darling, this should help," she said, handing him the cup.

"Thank you," he grunted.

"You going to be alright?"

In a matter of swallows, the water was gone. "Just let me rest a spell, and I'll be fine."

Finally, Lot mustered his strength and went to the well beyond the kitchen, washed himself and changed clothes. During supper, Sarah and Sister tried to involve him in conversation but to no avail. His energy was spent. Thanking Sarah and Sister for the meal, Lott wandered back to his front porch rocker. A cool, gentle breeze brushed by as the locust and tree frogs sang. Off in the woods, a whippoorwill filled the air with its lonely tune.

Even though Lott loved his wife and daughter, he missed the boys. It was almost as if he could hear them joking and arguing with each other. He could see the plow lines around their necks as they called to the mules and did a man's work. His heart ached as he imagined them married with children and always in his life, making old age easier. It would be only a matter of time before he wouldn't be able to work as he did today, even with Toby helping. How would he provide for his family then?

The screeching of the door interrupted his thoughts as his wife and daughter joined him. They talked for a while with Sister less talkative than usual. Nervously, she would get up out her chair, wander around on the porch and in a few minutes, take her seat again.

Lot first thought it was just teenager peculiarities, but because he was tired, her restless activity was becoming irritating. "Sister, what's going on with you tonight? You're about to get on my last nerve," he muttered.

Sister had been talking to her father in her mind since she had gotten her mother's approval, but now she could not find the courage to begin the plea.

"Sister," Sarah said, nodding to her.

Sister cleared her throat and took a deep breath. "Papa, I want to talk to you about courtship."

"Courtship! What about it?" Lot replied, looking directly at her.

Sarah nodded for her to continue, and Sister began to become more confident.

"Papa, I turned sixteen three months ago, and I think it's time to consider courtship," she nervously stated. "What do you think?"

Lott took a deep draw from his pipe and blew out a circle of smoke. "You're too young to be thinking about that. Your time will come."

All was quiet for a few moments. "Papa, can I ask you something?"

"I've said all I care to, but speak on."

"Papa, how old was Mama when you two met and married?"

Lott took a deep breath and cleared his throat.

"Answer her, husband," said Sarah quietly.

"I don't rightly recall, dear."

"I was two months older than Sister when we met, and you married me one month before I turned seventeen. I think you need to listen to your daughter."

Lot went to the edge of the porch and tapped his pipe against a porch beam, spilling the burnt tobacco to the ground. "I guess I've been hoodwinked by you two, haven't I? Some young man has caught your fancy. Is that right?"

"Johnny Jenkins wants me to go to a party this Saturday night at the Olliver's," Sister blurted out. "His father will ride with us, and there will be adults there to supervise us. What do you think, Papa?"

"I think I haven't noticed that you are about grown, and you should have brought that to my attention, Sarah," he said turning to his wife. "Sometimes, I think I'm becoming a senile old man." He chuckled. "You can go to the party, but when Johnny and Mr. Jenkins come, you bring them into the house so I can set some ground rules. You understand what I'm saying?"

"Oh Father," Sister exclaimed, reaching to embrace him. "Thank you."

After Sister had retired for the night, Lott and Sarah sat rocking, talking and enjoying the comfort of the cool evening. As they were ready to retire, Lott placed his hand on Sarah's arm. "Were you really sixteen when we married?"

Sarah laughed. "I hope the Lord will forgive me, but I was almost eighteen."

"I knew it! You two ganged up on me, and I received a good hoodwinking," laughed Lott, picking up Sarah and carrying her down the hallway to their bedroom.

***

John stood looking at the church as Hank unshackled his leg irons. The building was larger than he remembered and the steeple higher. *There is no way I would go up there*, he thought.

"What are you looking at so hard?" questioned Hank, throwing the chains into the bed of his wagon.

"I can't do it, Hank. I can't paint that steeple."

Hank covered his eyes from the morning sun and looked up. "I don't care how you do it, but when this job is over, that steeple better be as white as the rest of the building."

Parson Wilcox came from his study located in the rear of the sanctuary and headed to the men. After a few minutes of talk, Hank climbed into his wagon and left.

"Mr. Wilson, I do believe we have a job in front of us. Are you ready to get started?"

"I'm at your service, sir and you can call me John."

"John you'll be and you can call me Parson. If you'll look in the shed behind the church you'll find a ladder, brushes and plenty of paint."

The old paint that covered the building had not chipped but was just faded so no scraping would be necessary. By mid-morning he had covered the lower side of the western wall and began to work upward toward the roofline. He heard a noise and turned to see a young woman approaching with a pitcher and cup in her hands. She had long brown hair flowing down her back, deep brown eyes and a figure that caught his eye. John found her face to be flawless. *She was indeed a beautiful woman*, John thought.

"Papa thought you might need some water. The morning has become warm," she said.

John wiped the perspiration from his face with a cloth from his pocket and took the cup. Welcoming a rest, he wandered over to the shade of an oak tree and sat with his back to the trunk. The girl followed him with the pitcher.

"What's your name?" asked John.

The girl blushed. "My name's Angie, Angie Wilcox."

"I'm John Wilson."

"I know. I've seen you in church," said the girl, pouring him another cup of water and stepping away cautiously.

"You don't need to be afraid of me. I won't hurt you," said John. "Thank you for the water."

John soon returned to work and completed the western wall in one day. Each day at mid-morning and around four in the afternoon, Angie would bring him water. At noon, the parson would bring John his dinner, and they would talk about everything from religion to politics to farming techniques. As usual, on the fourth day at mid-morning Angie promptly brought his water but continued to keep her distance.

"Why are you afraid of me? Do you think I'm a hardened criminal?" John asked.

"That's not it. You shouldn't be in jail."

"Then what's wrong?"

Angie glanced at him. "You are a Rebel soldier. You probably killed people, didn't you?"

John shook his head. "I was a soldier, a member of the Army of the Northern Virginia. When the war started, I was too young to enlist. I joined later. As for killing, I don't know if I ever shot anyone. We stood in the firing line and exchanged fire, but all I could see was smoke and a mass of blue across the way. I don't know if I ever killed any of them."

"But you tried to."

"Yes, I guess I did. That's what war is. I don't think anybody likes the idea of taking another man's life. I know I don't. The Bible says, 'Thou shalt not kill,' then it turns right around and talks of Joshua and the Battle of Jericho. Men have been killing one another since Cain slew Abel. I know the Lord can't be happy with the way we keep killing each other."

For the first time, a smile crossed Angie's face.

"Why did you ask me such a question?"

Angie dropped her head. "My brother was killed at Fredericksburg. He was in the Union army. Folks here fought both ways. Some were Unionist and others Secessionists."

A lump formed in John's throat. "I'm sorry. I didn't know."

"Were you there? I mean at Fredericksburg."

"No, that was before I joined," John explained.

"Mother died two months later. The doctor said it was from a heart attack, but I think it was from a broken heart."

A horse galloped up, and a well-dressed young man dismounted and led his horse to John and Angie. Slightly stockier than John and with a box shaped face, neatly groomed, light red hair and an air of arrogance, he walked up and embraced Angie.

"You must be the jailbird I keep hearing about," he said, looking condescendingly toward John.

"I'm John Wilson, and I do dwell in the town's jail," he replied, extending his hand.

With a smirk on his face, he looked down at John's extended hand. "I don't shake with thieves."

John flushed with anger but knowing he didn't need trouble, excused himself and went back to his painting. In a while, the young man left, and Angie walked over to John. "You'll have to excuse his behavior. He's really not that bad. I just think he didn't like seeing me with you," Angie explained.

"What's his name?"

"His name is Amos Henderson. His father owns the bank," she replied.

"Angie, if you don't mind me asking, are you two courting?"

Angie nodded yes.

"You deserve better," murmured John under his breath.

When John finished painting the lower section of the church, the parson came out to inspect and then pointed to the steeple. "What about that?" he said.

John looked up at the steeple. "I can't do that."

"That's right. You're afraid of heights."

"Yes sir, I am."

The parson thought for a moment. "Then we'll work together. We can climb a staircase inside the steeple tower, and if you'll man the ropes. I'll get out there and do the painting," suggested the parson.

"What do you mean by man the ropes?"

The parson laughed. "That means you can stay inside the tower, and your job is to be sure the ropes supporting me are secured. How does that sound?"

A sense of relief swept over John.

After a week of painting, John sat on the front steps, accompanied by the parson, and waited for Hank.

"You did a fine job, son," the parson said. "Angie has enjoyed talking with you. She said you weren't like the other young men around here, not as self-centered. I guess you have a young lady waiting for you back home?"

"I hope I do. It's been a long time."

***

Mrs. Olliver worked diligently decorating her home, preparing plenty of food, games and music.

Since it was late July, there would be sliced watermelon fresh from the field, several specially-prepared Creole treats from her South Louisiana homeland, and most important, a string band for dancing. Some of the parents frowned on the idea of dancing, but the young people justified it by mentioning folk dancing, and parents relented.

"Son, I'm in the kitchen with Zelda. I need to see you," Judith called to Frankie above Zelda's clatter. In the culinary arts, Zelda had even surpassed her mother who had also served as the Olliver's cook.

"Yes ma'am," Frankie said, walking up and embracing his mother. "You need me?"

"Zelda, we'll be in the parlor. I know you've got things under control in here. If you need me, just call."

Frankie and his mother headed to the parlor, and Judith walked to the front windows and pulled them closed to keep out the afternoon sun. "Did you get the band scheduled for the party?"

"I did," he replied.

All was silent for a moment as Judith sat there thinking.

"Is that it, mother?"

"No. No, wait a minute. I think we need to talk."

"Well, I'm here," said Frankie, puzzled by her behavior.

"Son, I'm a woman ,and I certainly know about women's feelings and emotions, and I believe we need to talk about you and Rebecca."

Frankie shook his head. "Mama, there ain't much to talk about. I've tried to make her interested in me, and Suzanne and I have had outings with her, but it was always the three of us. I don't think she's ready for a relationship. It's like she's in a locked chest and won't let herself out."

Judith sat next to Frankie. "Son, the girl's experienced a great loss. You have to expect such a reaction, but with time, she will be fine. In the meantime, I think you should show her attention, be kind to her and do not press her as to a relationship with you. Just be there for her. As your father said, you are a handsome man and a man of means. There's nothing you can't give her. It may take a while, but this young woman is certainly worth the wait, if you think you might fall in love with her."

Frankie leaned over and embraced his mother. "I've always loved her, but there's always been John. Now that he's gone, I'll do my best, but you know patience is not my virtue. If things should work out for us and if she should become my wife, I want to make sure that it is me she loves and that she's able to let John go. I couldn't live with her wishing I was John every time she was in my arms."

***

After her talk with her father, Sister was happy. With the devastation of war, Sherman's raid through the community, and the loss of two brothers, life had been more than difficult. Nothing seemed normal, but for the first time, she felt life was getting easier. Her mother kept encouraging her to trust in her faith in God, but even her faith had given her little reassurance that life would ever be the same. Now she knew it would never be the same, but that God would bless their lives again. It seemed a storm had passed, and a beautiful rainbow graced the heavens. For the first time in years, she actually looked forward to the future.

Lott and Sarah couldn't believe the transformation as they watched Sister sing and laugh when she worked, and she even offered to help her father and Toby with the fieldwork. Sarah remembered how it felt to receive callers and decided to make this evening special. With the extra money she had saved, Sarah went to Walker's store and purchased material to make Sister a new dress. Sarah had made her a nice winter dress, but with this stifling July heat, that dress would not do. She selected refined white cotton and white imported lace border to compliment the dress. She wanted the dress to have a high collar, to be form-fitting at the top and waist and then fall freely to her ankles. Sister could pull her hair back and tie it with the same border material that graced her dress. For the first time in years, there was an air of happiness at the Wilson's.

***

Late July in South Mississippi is usually hot, dry and humid with an occasional late afternoon thunderstorm. This year was no different. Rebecca made her way home after work, took off her shoes and ventured to the shade of the front porch to relax and read. She selected a book of poems by Emerson and got into her favorite rocker. She had only covered a couple of poems when movement caught her eye. She closed the book as the man carefully dismounted and reached for something. To her surprise, it was a crutch. He placed it under his armpit and hobbled up the walk.

"Tim. Tim Johnson. Where in the world did you come from?" she exclaimed, wrapping her arms around the young man and squeezing him as hard as she could.

"Well, woman." He laughed. "Do I get a kiss?"

Rebecca gave him a kiss on the cheek and hugged him again. "Come on up to the porch. We've got so much to talk about. I just can't believe it's you."

Tim was John's best friend, and even though they came from different backgrounds, they had always been close.

Tim had lost the lower part of his right leg in the war and carefully grasped the step railing with one hand as he cautiously made his way up the steps. Rebecca reached out to him to help, but Tim waved her away. "I'm fine. I've got to learn to cope with it." Rebecca still followed him closely up the steps. Rebecca told Tim to have a seat and went inside to quickly make lemonade.

For a whil,e they reminisced about old times and talked about how the families were faring. Both seemed to evade the topic that burned inside of them, but finally, Rebecca collected enough courage to ask the question. "Tim, you don't have to, but would you tell me about John?"

Tim got up from his seat, hobbled to the porch railing, and with his back to Rebecca, stared out across the way. For a long time, he stood motionless, and Rebecca was sorry she had asked.

Turning, with tears watering his eyes, he returned to his seat and looked at Rebecca. "I'm not sure I know how to answer that, but I'll tell you what I know, and I want you to listen --- because I won't ever tell it again."

Rebecca placed her hand on Tim's.

"When we formed up at Gettysburg, we were a sight to behold. There were twelve thousand of us standing shoulder to shoulder. Flags flowed in the breeze, bayonets glistened in the sun, officers shouted orders and music could be heard. John was four men down the line from me. It was glorious. Even though our spirits were high, we knew what was ahead. We had to cover a mile of open ground to reach the Yankee line where they were crouched behind a long stone wall waiting for us. It was like Fredericksburg where the South slaughtered them Yanks, except this time, the Yanks were behind the wall. When we stepped out, the Yankee cannons hurled solid balls at us. It didn't do much damage, but when they hit someone, there wasn't much left to 'em. About halfway down the slope, they changed to exploding balls that sent iron pieces in all directions. We walked as fast as we could, pulling our hats down over our faces trying to ignore them devils. Large gaps were ripped in our lines. As I marched, even though I was with thousands, it was like I was alone. I thought of home and my family, and I prayed as hard as I ever prayed, but in my heart, I knew I would soon be dead. I looked down the line at John, and he shook his head and pointed upward. I think that's the last time I saw him."

All was quiet for a moment.

"Tim, you don't have to tell me anything else."

Tim took a deep breath, then another. "When we reached the bottom of the slope down by a road picketed with fences, all order ceased as we struggled to climb over the timbers. The smoke from the guns was covering the field, and the roar of cannons and musketry was deafening. We just wanted to kill them before they killed us. I was so afraid I could barely walk, and I prayed for the Lord to take me. We were only two hundred yards from the stoned wall when the cannons threw canister shot at us like a giant shotgun, and the Yanks rose up from behind their cover with rifles, and the slaughter began. Men were dropping like flies, and others were literally blown to bits. Balls were whistling by and nipping at my clothing. As I tried to load my rifle, an explosion to my front blew my hat off and what was left of an arm hit me in the chest knocking me down. At first, I thought I was blinded, but it was dirt and someone's blood that caked my eyes."

At this point, Tim closed his eyes and began to mumble to himself.

"Tim, are you alright?" asked Rebecca, placing an arm around his shoulder.

"I wiped it away and being able to see, I turned and ran toward the road. Men reached up for help, but I just ran faster."

"Tim, did you actually see John fall?"

"Those of us who made it back, tried to re-form at the wood's edge where the attack began, but most just collapsed, completely exhausted. I sat down with my back to the trunk of a tree and cried as hard as I have ever cried. I don't know when, but eventually I fell asleep. To this day, I don't know why I was spared. About dark, I felt someone tugging at me, and I saw Thomas, John's older brother. He asked me if I had seen John. I told him not since the first of the battle. We headed back to the field to look for him, but didn't get a quarter of a mile out when an officer stopped us and ordered us back to the ridge. Thomas objected but the officer pulled his pistol on him.

The next morning, rain was pouring down, and Lee ordered us to withdraw. My heart was broken thinking about John, and I felt guilty for not trying harder to go and look for him. Rebecca, I did search to see if by mistake, he had fallen in with another regiment, but I couldn't find him."

The two sat quietly for a moment. "I know this was hard but, with all my heart, I thank you," Rebecca whispered. "When did you get hurt, Tim?"

"It was later near the end of the war at a place called Cold Harbor. Rebecca, thank you for asking. I needed to share this burden. Thanks for listening."

The sun began to set, and Tim placed the crutch under his arm and started slowly down the steps. Rebecca, remembering the coming event, grabbed his arm. "Tim, the Ollivers are going to have a surprise party for Suzanne next Saturday. Are you going?"

"Naw, they didn't invite me."

"They probably don't know you're home," reasoned Rebecca.

"They know."

"What do you mean? You and John and Frankie were friends."

"Rebecca, I want you to listen to me. If you go to the party, look around. You won't see a single soldier there. You know Ted Harrison and Buddy Adkins. They were in the same regiment as I was, and we all grew up together, and they live close to the Ollivers. Rest assured, they won't be there."

"Why not?"

"Cause like me, they won't be invited."

"Tim, what do you mean?" asked Rebecca, puzzled.

"You can call it a guilty conscious, but I don't think Frankie would feel comfortable with us around."

"Tim, I don't understand what you are saying."

"Do you remember back in sixty-two when that recruiter set up shop in your father's store? He said it had been a hard year and that General Lee needed more men. Well, me, John, the Clearman boys and Frankie had been out hunting that morning and had killed us some squirrels. We decided to stop by the store and get some cheese and crackers. While we were sitting on the porch of the store, the sergeant came out to see our kill. Well, he started talking to us about how good the war was going and how he thought we would be some fine soldiers, and we got excited about the prospect. To tell the truth, it really got Frankie stirred up, and he walked right in and signed his name. Well, John turned to me and said, as reckless as Frankie is, he wouldn't last six months in the army much less a battle. After walking the porch for a while, he turned and told me he was joining up. He said he had to look after Frankie. So the whole lot of us signed up. When we got down to Newton Station to catch the train to Jackson, our friend Frankie didn't show."

"I understand that he was sick with an illness," interrupted Rebecca.

"Illness." Tim laughed. "That was in 1862. The war lasted until April of 1865. You telling me he never got well. I'll tell you what happened. A man down at Hickory owed Mr. Olliver a large sum of money and had a son at war age. He told the man that the debt would be excused if his boy would take Frankie's place. Well, he joined our unit and told us the truth."

Rebecca was speechless. "I can't believe that, Tim."

"Believe what you will, but just see if those boys show up at the party."

"By the way, of the five of us that joined up that day, not counting Frankie, you want to know how many came home? You are looking at him."

As Tim was mounting, Rebecca followed him across the yard. "Tim, I'm sorry about your leg."

"Ain't so bad. I never did like farming like my Pa does. Being pretty good with the numbers, I could probably be a clerk of some kind." Then reaching into his pocket, he pulled out a large roll of bank notes and waved it to Rebecca. "Fact is, I'm pretty good with the cards, and if that don't work out, I'll just marry me a rich woman, if I can find one."

Rebecca couldn't help but laugh. "Tim, I can see one thing. That war hasn't changed you a bit. You're just as crazy as you always were."

Tim started to leave but reined his horse in. "Rebecca, I think I know how you feel about John, and if I know John at all, he would want you to get on with your life. In a way, you and me have to keep on living. We have to move on, but at the same time, he'll always be here in our hearts."

As Rebecca watched Tim ride off, she was confused about Frankie and the war and all Tim had shared with her. She knew Tim was truthful, but surely Frankie would not have been a coward. Since she had decided to attend the party, she guessed she would see for herself who showed up.

8

Defending the Defenseless

For the love of money is the root of all kinds of evil.
1st Timothy 6:10

Time stopped for Sister the week before the party. She paced about more than normal and had become excessively talkative. Sarah had even assigned Sister more household responsibilities, but she finished them so quickly Sarah had to create new jobs. Sarah finally sent her to the field with a hoe, but as soon as Lott saw his daughter dusty and sweaty, he sent her back to the house.

Saturday seemed to never come, and Sister worried that something might happen to keep her from attending. What if she or Johnny became ill? What if Johnny couldn't come get her? What if Suzanne were detained in Louisiana and the party was canceled? What if Johnny didn't show up at all?

Saturday dawned bright and clear, and Sister got up earlier than usual to prepare for the social. She hurried to her brother's vacant room where her dress had been neatly ironed and laid out on the bed, and she stood for a moment to admire the work of her mother and to daydream about the party.

Lott had a few chores to do that morning but decided to finish early so he could clean and get his best clothes on for Sister.

"What time did the young man say he would be here?" Sarah asked as she stood behind Sister, carefully combing the tangles from her long straight hair.

"Mother, there's some sticking out from behind my right ear," Sister remarked pointing to several stray hairs. "Four o'clock. I think that's what he said. What time is it now?"

Sarah looked to the mantle. "A little after two."

"I'll never make it in time. What am I going to do?"

Sarah laughed. "Well, the way I figure it is that we need twenty minutes to finish combing your hair and tie the ribbon around it and five minutes for you to slip the dress on. Now, that's not very long."

"What about my dress? What if I pop a button?" muttered Sister.

"I sewed it well, and that won't happen. Now when Johnny arrives, you will wait in here until I come get you. Your father will want to speak with him and Mr. Jenkins, and we want Johnny to get a little anxious in the mean time.

"Mama, I'm nervous. No, I'm really scared."

Sarah embraced her daughter and whispered, "You'll be fine. You are a beautiful, charming young woman. You have nothing to fear."

The clock on the mantle struck four, and Sister sat impatiently on the edge of her bed, waiting. To her joy, she heard a horse and buggy approach and pull to a stop. Her heart pounded as she recognized the voice of her father welcoming the Jenkins to their home.

Johnny who was dressed in a dark gray suit, white shirt, black tie, and clasping a bouquet of flowers, stepped down from the buggy. His hair was parted down the middle and with a nick on his jaw, he had evidently attempted to shave. Having grown a lot since the last time he wore his best outfit, the pants legs were a little short, but overall, he was quite handsome.

"Hope we're on time," said Mr. Jenkins, extending his hand.

"You're fine. You two come on in the house. Care for something to drink?" Lott asked politely.

"No thank you," answered Johnny, looking about nervously.

"Have a seat, gentlemen," Lott said, pointing to chairs near the fireplace. "I think we need to have a talk." All family gatherings occurred in Lott and Sarah's bedroom because it was the largest room, and during the winter, it was the only one heated. Even though the windows were open, a hint of oak smoke from the winter fires lingered.

Lott sat down and looked at Johnny. "I'm kind of new at this, so if I blunder, please excuse me. I understand that you and your father will escort my daughter to and from the party, and at no time will you and Sister be unattended. Is that correct?"

"Yes sir," Johnny blurted out in a shaky voice.

"That's good. And at no time will you take advantage of her in any way. You will treat her like a lady and always show respect."

Johnny was speechless, so Mr. Jenkins nudged him.

"Yes sir, like a lady."

"And what time will you bring my daughter home?"

"We'll have her home by ten," Johnny answered politely.

"What time?"

Johnny looked over to his father and then back to Lott. "Nine o'clock?"

"That's better. Sarah, you can bring sister in now."

Johnny instantly stood holding his bouquet of flowers and shuffled his feet uneasily.

The door eased open, and Sister entered followed by her mother. Nervous, Johnny dropped his bouquet and quickly tried to retrieve the flowers. Embarrassed, he stood up and handed the tangled bouquet to Sister. "Sorry," he said. "You are so beautiful," he added without thinking.

Sister smiled and handed the flowers to her mother. "I've never seen you better dressed, Johnny. I'm looking forward to the evening. I know it's going to be fun."

The parents smiled at one another as they watched the two, realizing that their little girl was maturing and things would now be different. Mr. Jenkins gave Lott an approving smile, and asked to be on their way. Lott and Sarah followed them to the porch and watched them as they climbed into the buggy. Sister leaned out, waved to them and was soon lost in the dust of the road.

Lott and Sarah stood watching as long as possible, then Sarah headed to her favorite rocker while Lott eased down on the top step of the porch with his back resting against a beam. A sense of loneliness filled him as he realized that though Sister would be back in a few hours, this was just the beginning. It wouldn't be long until some young man would steal her heart, and she would be gone. All of his children would be gone.

"Sarah, I've done a terrible thing, and I hope the Lord will forgive me," Lott said solemnly.

"What have you done now, dear?"

"I don't know why I couldn't see it happening, but I gave the boys far too much attention and Sister too little. And then when I lost them, I didn't give her any attention at all and just wallowed in self pity. I guess she must have thought she wasn't important to me.

"They worked with you everyday. You depended on them to help us keep the place going. Lott, all farmers do the same around here."

"May be, but that don't make it right. She's always been special to me and always will be, and I need to let her know, especially now since the Lord has taken all my sons."

"Lott, I don't believe the Lord has taken all of your sons away. You know Thomas is probably still alive, and John -"

"Stop right there. I don't want to hear this," interrupted Lott.

For the past several months, Sarah had not mentioned John nor angels. She had seemed normal, and Lott didn't want anything to cause a reoccurrence of strange behavior.

A tint of dust rose in the air as the buggy made its way out of sight, and Lott's mind went back to another day when steam was rising from the dampened ground following the thunderstorm. No matter how hard he tried, he could not forget that afternoon or the stranger. He could not understand what had happened nor why no one had heard the voice but him.

"Are you alright, Lott?" asked Sarah.

"I'm fine. Just a little lonely tonight."

"I feel the same."

All was silent as the sun slid behind the hills, and its rays slowly faded in the dense canopy of the leafy forest, losing their glow to the evening. A dove cooed in the distance, and peace overcame sadness.

"Sarah, do you believe there is such a thing as a ghost?"

"Ghost! Are you serious?" replied Sarah. "I don't believe in any ghost, but the

Holy Ghost. The Bible don't say anything about ghostly apparitions, but it says a lot about angels. Why'd you say that?"

Lott pursed his lips. "Well, the other day Toby and I were taking a mid-morning rest, and he brought up the subject of hants. You know, a hant is kinda like our ghost except they are more into devilment. Toby said the other day that if someone dies and has been mistreated, then his spirit comes back looking for revenge and puts the scare on those who did the mistreating."

"Lott, that's all nonsense. You know better."

"Now listen to me. It's not just Toby's hants, even the Choctaws have their spirit. They call him shilup. If one of them dies and has not prepared himself for the hereafter, then their spirit lingers a spell until he has done what was necessary to go on to the other world. They believe that this spirit, shilup, even hangs around a while."

"So what do you think, Lott? Do you believe in all that nonsense?"

"If all these folks believe in spirits, then there must be something to it."

Irritated, Sarah got up to leave. "Lott, I have never seen a ghost, a hant or a Choctaw spirit, and there is no mention in the Bible about such. I don't know what's wrong with you tonight. First, you are sorry about the way you have treated Sister, then you start talking about spirits. I'm not listening to any more of this."

"Well, I think there is just as much a chance of having ghost around as there are angels," Lott blurted without thinking.

Sarah went into the house and soon returned and dropped a Bible in his lap. "You say you're a Christian. You need to spend some time reading the Book. It's all here. All your answers are in here."

***

The buggy soon rounded a bend in the road and ascended the long drive that led to the Olliver house. Both sides of the drive was lined with rows of massive oak trees and bordered by split rail fences that opened into plush grass fields. Horses grazed lazily and briefly lifted their heads as buggies approached. The Olliver house was built on a rolling hill overlooking at least one thousand acres of rich river bottomland. Endless rows of cotton displayed their purple blossoms, announcing another good year for the Ollivers.

The Olliver mansion had massive columns supporting the roof and circling the house. The lower floor contained a study, parlor, dining room, library, master bedroom and large social room. Winding stairs led to the upper floor where four bedrooms were located. Each bedroom had doors and windows that led to the porch that circled the house. The kitchen was located a short distance from the house and had a covered walkway leading to the dining room.

The sound of laughter and music filled the air. A dozen saddled horses were tied to hitching posts out front, and at the edge of the pecan orchard nearby, buggies were securely posted.

As they pulled to a stop, a Negro dressed in a black suit walked out to meet them.

"Sir, may I secure your ride?" he asked politely.

Mr. Jenkins shook his head. "No, thank you. Ill be going on home and will be back to pick them up later."

"Yes sir, I understand."

Even though the war was over and slavery had ended, most Negroes enslaved by Mr. Olliver remained on the farm performing their same duties. They could still stay in their homes and would receive wages to purchase food and clothing, but it was required that they make any purchases at Walker's store on credit with debts to be settled monthly. Olliver's workers quickly purchased more than their salary could support and became indebted to the establishment. With the support of the local sheriff, Mr. Oliver made sure his workers could not leave the area until their bill was cleared. In turn, Walker gave Frank a cut from the profit and Olliver had his laborers. Mr. Oliver had found a way to thwart the Emancipation Proclamation and was pretty proud about it. He didn't really care about politics but was just greedy for the wealth slavery brought him.

Johnny leapt from his seat and politely helped Sister as she stepped down from the buggy. As he held out his hand to assist her, the afternoon sun sent rays of light across her face, and he embraced her beauty.

They climbed the stoned steps to the entrance where Mrs. Olliver, Frankie and Suzanne were welcoming the guests. Mrs. Olliver's father was French, and her mother was Creole which is a blend of Caucasian, Negro and Indian. Sister quickly compared the mother and daughter and noticed both were tall, olive skinned, with dark black hair and high cheekbones. Even at her age, Mrs. Olliver was still beautiful, but most impressive was her air of dignity, poise and manners. Most people could not understand why she had ever been attracted to Frank Sr. who was common in appearance, rude even to his friends, untrustworthy, and would let nothing interfere with his drive for power and fortune. Worst of all, he treated his children with little respect. Frankie did not look like his mother or sister except for his height. He was light skinned, thin faced and had long blond hair that fell to his shoulders. Tonight, he was wearing a white silk shirt with full puffed sleeves and dark blue pants neatly tucked into knee-length polished riding boots. Sister couldn't help but blush as she took his hand when he welcomed them to their home.

"Sister, you surely have grown up and are looking lovely tonight," Judith said, smiling at her. "And, Mr. Jenkins, you are a most fortunate young man to be escorting her."

"Yes ma'am, I surely am that," replied Johnny, proudly taking Sister's arm under his.

"You two, go on in. We'll be cutting melons in a moment. I think most of the young people are already here. We're waiting for one more to arrive," stated Mrs. Olliver.

As Sister and Johnny walked away, Frankie could not take his eyes off Sister. He hadn't seen her so well-dressed, and the change was unbelievable.

"Suzanne, later on tonight, when we have our dancing, your brother here has got to hold that young lady," he whispered, still watching Sister as she gracefully walked away.

Mrs. Olliver cleared her throat. "Frankie, you and I had a talk the other day about a woman of interest, and it didn't include that one. You do have a priority, don't you?"

"Mama, I'm nineteen, and it's hard for me to ignore such beauty."

"Son, she's a Wilson. Don't forget that."

In a matter of minutes, another buggy arrived and Frankie and Suzanne walked out to greet them. Mr. Walker pulled the horse in and handed the reins over to the Negro awaiting them.

"Will you be staying, sir?" asked the Negro.

Mr. Walker walked around to the other side of the buggy and held his hand out to assist Rebecca. "I'll be staying. I have business with Mr. Olliver tonight."

Rebecca stepped down and took her father's arm as they walked over to Suzanne and Frankie. She wore a light green satin dress and her auburn hair was pulled into a fashionable bow. She glowed as she smiled at them.

"Sorry, I'm late," she said, giving Suzanne a light hug. "You look nice tonight," she said, reaching up and pushing some unruly hair from Frankie's face, a habit she had begun when they were childhood friends.

After they had talked briefly, they climbed the steps to reach Mrs. Olliver's embrace and welcome.

It had been a long time since Sister had visited the Olliver home, and she had forgotten how beautifully and elaborately it was furnished. The deep red imported mahogany flooring ran throughout the home, and in every room, large hand-woven rugs from India added more beauty. The ceilings were over fourteen feet high, and the walls, board and batter, were smoothly plastered and painted beige. The house sparkled with the most exquisite furniture money could buy.

Mrs. Olliver stepped on a platform that had been erected for the band and spoke, "Guests, we welcome you to our home as we celebrate the return of our daughter, Suzanne, who has been visiting her grandfather in Louisiana for the past two months. I hope you all have a wonderful time."

The group of twenty-five clapped and cheered as Mrs. Olliver thanked them several times for gracing their home. It was obvious to Rebecca that she, Suzanne and Frankie were the oldest ones here. She knew few of the young people and saw no one who had fought in the war. *There was no question about it*, reasoned Rebecca, *the war had taken its toll, and few men her age were left.*

Mrs. Olliver invited the guest to the patio for watermelon and games. One of the most popular events was a scavenger hunt where clues carried them throughout the house, barn and gardens and offered the boys the best chance to steal a kiss. At six o'clock, Mrs. Olliver rang a bell, and the group assembled to eat plates of barbecue, slaw, baked beans and freshly baked rolls. Strawberry cake would be brought out later.

Throughout the games, Rebecca had been paired with younger boys since the only boy her age was Frankie, and he didn't seem interested in spending time with her. She was feeling out of place and wished she hadn't accepted the invitation when a voice interrupted her thoughts. "Well, who have we here? May I join you?" Frankie asked, smiling as he took a seat across from her. "You are having a good time, aren't you?"

Rebecca returned his smile. "I am having a good time, but ---."

"But what?"

Rebecca paused. "I feel a little out of place. Except for you and Suzanne, I really don't know anyone here. Are we what's left of a lost generation? I used to go to parties, and all our friends would be there. Where are they now?"

Frankie took a swallow of tea. "Lot of the girls are married, and most of the boys were either killed in battle or have moved on looking for work." Frankie hesitated, noticing the expression on Rebecca's face when he mentioned battle. "I'm sorry. I should have been more thoughtful."

Rebecca placed her hand on his. "I took no offense. You told the truth."

Hearing the band warming up, Frankie took Rebecca's hand and walked her to the social room. "Maybe a little music will raise your spirits."

As they entered, they found Frank Sr. on the stand in front of the musicians, and by his looks, he had been partaking of the spirits.

"Oh no," muttered Frankie. "I don't know how this will work out."

"What do you mean, Frankie?"

"Nothing, I hope."

"Boys and girls, I know you've been having fun. I want you to know that Miss Judith and I am more than glad to have you in our home. By the way, my office window lies right next to the rose garden, and I have witnessed some fine display of emotion from that position." He laughed.

Several girls blushed, and an undercurrent of laughter was heard as the boys tried to see which ones had been lucky.

Weaving slightly, he continued, "This party is to honor my beautiful daughter, Suzanne, and we're glad she's home. Now for the rest of the evening, you will have a foot-stomping good time, but for me, it's just a little too loud. Farewell and good night."

"Whew," breathed Frankie, glancing over to Suzanne. "He made it."

Once again, Mrs. Olliver took the stage. "The band is tuned and ready, and since some of you don't know how to dance, we'll start with something easy. So boys, take a partner, and form a line facing your lady. Girls, on the next dance you may choose your partner."

A loud round of applause shook the room as the boys ran to select dancing partners. In the mean time, Frank Sr. retired to his office where he and Mr. Walker had been talking.

"Thomas, aren't you driving your daughter home tonight?"

"You know I am," slurred Thomas.

"Then no more drinking. Now tell me how we're doing?" inquired Frank.

"We're doing fine. I think all of your hands have overextended their credit, and when they get in that shape, they have to pay more for their goods, and thus, the profit becomes greater. The moneybag is bulging. You came up with a good idea, my friend." Thomas smiled, pushing his empty glass away. "You know, Frank, I've got even a better idea. Just think about this. What if you raised their salaries? Then they'd spend more money at my store, and you'd get a bigger cut when they get overextended."

Frank shook his head as he packed his pipe with some fresh tobacco that had just arrived from Cuba. "Thomas, sometimes I think you are fairly intelligent, and at times like this, I think you are as stupid as that brass doorknob over there. Don't you realize that if I paid them more in salary that they might just figure a way to pay off their debt, and I'd lose my slaves. Plus, I'd be paying more out to begin with. No, our deal is good the way it is."

Thomas laughed. "Well, at the moment, I thought it sounded reasonable, but, I'll tell you a little secret. I took the plan you introduced to me, and I've offered it to several other farmers who work the colored. Now I may be a stupid old man, but I'm becoming a rich old man too."

Frank thought for a moment as he took a long draw from his pipe and began to laugh. "Well, maybe you just gained some intellect with that. Is there any way I can get in on the action? I'd certainly like to invest in that program." Then Frank looked closely at Thomas and asked, "Thomas, does your wife know about your financial dealings?"

Thomas sobered at the thought. "No, all she and Rebecca do is stock the shelves and wait on the customers. I take care of the money matters myself."

"Do you think she'd approve?" probed Frank, taking another draw from his pipe.

"Approve. You know she wouldn't," he responded.

Frank pointed over to the Bible lying on the edge of his desk, seldom used. "How can you go to church on Sunday and explain to the Lord how you exploit folks?"

All was quiet for a moment. "Thomas, I'll tell you one more thing. Looking at you and me, I'm a lot better person than you."

"I sure can't see it," replied Thomas, angered.

"The way I see it, is you and I both take advantage of the colored, but the difference is that you get dressed up and do church where I seldom darken the doors. That makes you a hypocrite. Anyway, I figure you and I will be rooming together one of these days."

"You mean we might be jailed for what we've done?" frowned Thomas.

Frank laughed so loud and hard it almost took his breath. "Jail! Naw, it's not jail I'm thinking about."

Thomas frowned at that and began to wonder why he had become involved in this business of Frank's. He tried to rationalize it all, but when it came down to it, it was the money. Money was a powerful motive for going against what was right and good.

***

Since most of the young people didn't know how to square dance to the music of the fiddle, guitar, banjo, mandolin, string bass and accordion, and Mrs. Olliver had taught the steps to Suzanne and Frankie at an early age, they in turn served as tutors for the party guests. After a few mishaps, all the young people quickly caught on and in a matter of minutes felt like masters on the floor. Next, Mrs. Olliver introduced the three-step waltz using Suzanne and Frankie. The waltz was more difficult than square dancing, but because the boys could get closer to their partners in the waltz, there was no returning to the square dance.

At first, Johnny had trouble staying with the beat and stumbled over Sister's feet, but with time, he learned the steps and relaxed. As he swept Sister around the floor, Frankie came up and tapped Johnny on the shoulder.

"Mind if I cut in," Frankie said, taking Sister's hand from Johnny.

"What do you mean by cut in?" said Johnny, reaching to regain Sister's hand.

Frankie pushed him away. "That is an act of courtesy. You can do that at dances. You'll have her back soon enough." Placing his hand on Sister's waist, the two swirled around the floor, leaving Johnny angry.

"I hope Johnny was not upset," said Sister softly.

"Why didn't you turn me down, my dear?"

"I didn't know I had a choice."

"I'll take you back to him, if you choose."

"No, let's finish the dance," she answered. Because Frankie was such a smooth and experienced dancer, Sister wanted to continue, but she felt bad about leaving Johnny. Still after the dance had ended, Frankie asked for another, and she consented.

Mrs. Olliver finally introduced the two-step in which the boys could hold the girls even closer in their arms. The music slowed, and the lights were dimmed.

Time was quickly slipping away, and the party would soon end as Rebecca sat watching the couples on the floor. She had hoped Frankie would dance with her, but he had been dancing with all of the female guests. Several younger boys had asked her to dance, but she declined. Finally, she saw Frankie heading her way.

"Rebecca, would you care to dance?"

She smiled. "It would be a pleasure."

He took her into his arms and pulled her to him, and the two danced smoothly. Not used to being held so close and in this fashion, she blushed. Her breath was short and her heart pounded as the two embraced and flowed with the music.

As the party ended and the guests were leaving, Rebecca thanked the Ollivers for having her. Frankie politely offered to escort her to her father's wagon.

As they approached the steps, Rebecca asked, "Frankie, why have you ignored me for most of the night? You are the only one here that is my age."

"I didn't mean to ignore you," he said. "I just felt like as a host it was my responsibility to move around the group to be sure all were enjoying themselves."

How foolish I must have sounded, she thought.

"Please forgive me. I should have known better," she said.

Frankie took her hand and gave it a soft kiss. "It's alright. I would love to call on you, if you will permit."

"I would like that," she replied.

After all had left, Frankie and his mother wandered to the swing in the flower garden to relax and enjoy the peace of night. Suzanne, tired from the night's activities, retired to her room.

"Mother, I'll give you credit. You certainly know women."

"What do you mean by that, son?"

"I did everything you said. I was polite to Rebecca, but I kept my distance for most of the night."

"So what are you trying to tell me?"

"As the evening wore on, I occasionally would go over to talk with her or ask for a dance, then I would leave to socialize with the other guest. You know what happened? She actually said she wanted to be with me more, and when I walked her to her father's wagon, I asked her if I could call on her."

"And she said yes," interrupted his mother.

"How did you know that?"

"Son, as you said, I know women."

As Rebecca lay in bed that night, she examined all that had happened and thought about the words Tim had spoken. She saw clearly that everything Tim had stated was true. Frankie had made excuses why the older boys were not in attendance, but in Tim's account, those boys were at home, uninvited.

***

As the days shortened and the leaves showed traces of gold and brown, a touch of fall was in the air. John had been hired out for cutting and splitting firewood for one of the locals and was now enjoying the comfort of his cell bunk. Usually, he didn't like being isolated within the cell, but today it was different. His back was stiff, and his muscles ached from the long hours of using an ax. The thought of Saturday and a day off was invigorating. His mind wandered back to the night he had the unusual dream. The man's voice was clear, and it was as if he could hear him take a breath before he spoke. John remembered telling the stranger all that had happened to him and his hope to return home, and the stranger had assured him he would be home for Christmas. Next, John's thoughts changed to the incident in the Bible when Peter was in jail in Jerusalem and an angel came to him. The angel unlocked his chains, opened the door and led him out to safety. Before he could pursue that thought, the door swung open, and Hank strolled in.

"John, I'll be leaving soon, and there will be food brought over later. Tomorrow morning, be ready about half past ten for church. You'll be having dinner with the parson, and his daughter will bring you back to jail."

"She's gonna lock me up?"

"Yeah, I trust her."

"Hank, you're telling me that I'm having dinner with the parson and then his daughter will lock me up. I don't want her to do that."

"Well, you got a better idea?"

John thought for a moment. "How about this? I walk in here by myself, take the key off the peg, lock myself up and throw the keys over under your desk."

"What if you decide to run?" muttered Hank.

"You've always said you had some of the best blood hounds in the county. I don't think I'd get very far."

Before he could answer, the door swung wide open, and Harry Stamper, the owner of Happy Harry's saloon rushed in. Harry's nickname was Happy due to his pleasant disposition, and with that came his establishment's name, Happy Harry's.

"Hank, I need some help! Now!" Harry gasped.

"Now take it easy, Happy. What's got you upset?" Hank asked.

"The place is suppose to open at seven, and I just got word that my mother-in-law has come down ill," explained Happy, gasping a breath.

"Well, Happy, I ain't no doctor. How can I help you?"

"My wife wants me to take her to the doctor. I got a man to run the place for me, but I still got glasses to wash, dry and shelf before he gets there. This is Saturday night, and you know the crowd that'll be showing up later. I need some help. I got someone for the mopping."

Hank pushed his chair back and propped his feet up on the corner of his desk studying the situation. "Happy, I know about your Saturday nights, and it has been a problem for me at times. Folks gonna close you down one of these days. But what I think you are asking is that I hire out my boy to you. Right?"

"Won't take long. Maybe an hour. Not much more."

"Whoa right there!" exclaimed John who had been listening to their conversation. "I've had my full day."

"Hey boy, you ain't running this show," stormed Hank, giving John a hard look.

"Tell you what, Happy, I'd normally charge you about two dollars, but since your place has been a sore in my side so to speak, you can have him for four."

"Four! That's nothing but stealing."

"Take it or leave it. You got him for one hour, and no more."

Happy walked John down to his place, and when he entered, John was surprised to find Wally diligently mopping the floors. A big smile formed on Wally's face as he recognized John, and he dropped his mop and extended his hand.

"Wally's got a job like the soldier boy," he said, grasping John's hand. "I bet you is proud of me, ain't you?"

John shook his hand. "I see the job you're doing, and yes, I'm proud of you."

"I thought so, Mr. Hero, Mr. Medal Man." Wally laughed, dropping John's hand and skipping around the floor.

"Wally, stop that foolishness, and get back to work!" Happy sternly exclaimed. "Times a-wasting."

Wally picked up his mop and watched John as he headed to the bucket and clutter of dirty glasses waiting to be cleaned.

"Soldier Boy, we friends, ain't we?" Wally whispered.

John smiled back. "Yes, Wally, we're friends."

Happy quickly left, trusting John to get the job done right, and John, after finding soapy water in the bucket and a cloth, began to wash and dry the glasses. With the massive amount of dishes, John figured that he would certainly not be finished in an hour.

Around seven o'clock, the door bolted open. Two men entered, placed their hats on pegs on the outer wall, rolled up their sleeves and walked over to one of the pool tables. With the floor still wet in spots, one of the men almost slipped. Catching himself on the edge of the table, he regained his balance and then saw Wally near the piano holding his wet mop and smiling.

"You think that's funny?" he said, glaring at the unusual-looking man.

Wally ceased to smile and edged behind the piano.

"You ain't talking? What's wrong with you?"

The man picked up a pool stick and in a threatening way walked toward Wally. John quickly laid his cloth on the bar and edged closer.

"Wally didn't mean nothing by that. He's just a little unusual," John explained.

"Ain't you that jailbird? You know, Hank's slave," the man said, turning his attention from Wally to John.

"You can call me what you like, but Wally didn't mean nothing, and we don't need any trouble."

"Yeah, you're the marshal's boy. We rough you up, and then we might be in there with you. We'll let it slide this time."

The men racked the balls and began playing and laughing, and John was relieved that nothing had happened. Later, another man entered.

"Sorry, I'm late," he said, rolling up his sleeves and taking a stick from the rack. Turning, he saw Wally staring at him.

"What are you doing in here, dummy? Happy must be in bad shape to hire the likes of you." He laughed.

John cleared his throat. "He's doing alright."

"Well, look who else is in here, boys. You remember me?"

"You're Amos Henderson," John answered as he continued to dry a set of glasses.

Amos walked close to John so that their faces were inches apart. "And I know you, John Wilson. You're the one that's trying to spark my girl."

John continued drying a glass. "I have no intentions toward the young lady. Her father has befriended me. That's all."

Satisfied, Amos walked away, laughing. "You hear 'em boys, no intentions. Let's forget these two nothings and how about some cards. If you two can beat me, you can have what I've got in my pocket over there. Let me give you a hint. It's liquid, and it'll make you frisky."

Dropping their sticks on the table, the other two men walked to the table, laughing. "Deal 'em, big boy, deal 'em."

It had now been over an hour, and John expected Hank to walk in any moment to escort him back to his cell, but no one came. John cautiously watched the men. Wally hastily pushed his mop across the floor.

Another fifteen minutes passed, and John ventured to the doorway. There was no marshal to be seen among the shoppers, completing their Saturday business. *If the crowd would hurry and show up, some of the attention would be diverted away from Wally and me*, John thought. The clock above the bar showed twenty minutes after seven. John remembered that Happy had a man coming, and John was sure hoping it would be soon. The men continued to laugh, looking frequently toward Wally.

One of the men called out loudly, "Hey Wally, come over here a minute."

Dragging his mop, Wally waddled to the men. "Wally is a good worker," he mumbled over and over.

The men laughed. "We know you are an excellent worker, Wally," Amos stated. "That's why we asked you over." He then spat a big glob of tobacco juice on the floor near his seat. "See that? You need to get that up." He laughed, pointing to the floor.

Wally looked at John, and John shook his head no. Not understanding what John meant, Wally got his bucket and began to clean up the juice. Once it was clean, another one of the men spat across the floor. "You can get that up too" he said sarcastically. John stopped his cleaning as he realized that trouble had just come.

Before Wally could clean up the last spit, one of the men looked at John, smiled, and taking a deep breath, spat a wad across the floor. Frustrated and confused, Wally rushed to clean it up and, in the process, knocked the glass Amos was using, and it crashed to the floor. All was silent for a moment. Then Amos looked at John and then Wally and said, "Wally, you've gone too far. That mop just ain't gittin the job done. I think it best if you clean up the glass and then try licking it up with your tongue. You might even learn to like chewing."

Wally looked again at John. The desperate look in his eyes was more than John could stand. He untied the apron he was wearing and walked over to the table. Before John could turn the corner of the bar, he saw Amos kick Wally as he bent over to begin cleaning. The kick sent Wally sliding across the floor.

John was furious. Even in combat, he had never seen such cruel treatment. "Men, this show is over," he said helping Wally up. "This ain't about him. It's me you want."

"You got that right, thief," said Amos who had now risen from his seat. Before John could react, Amos kicked him in the back, sending John sprawling to the floor and onto pieces of the broken glass. Stunned, John lay for a moment. Then placing his hands under his body, he struggled up, pulling Wally with him.

Wally looked strangely at him. "Soldier Boy, I think you got shot," he said, pointing to John's hand. Blood was seeping from between John's fingers and dripping to the floor. John turned his hand over and noticed his palm had been sliced open by a piece of the broken glass. Turning, he found Amos standing next to the table with a smirk on his face.

"Amos, this card game is over," John said and with a hard swing, struck Amos on the jaw, sending him flying over the table and to the floor where he lay motionless. Before John could regain his balance, one of the other men grabbed him from behind and began choking him. The two wrestled about, knocking over several chairs until John could get a hold on him and, with a twist and swing, threw the man off of him and through the front window of the establishment sending glass and framing sailing across the sidewalk outside.

Women in the street began to scream, and people began to quickly gather.

As John was turning, he felt a sharp pain in his back and head, and he drifted into darkness, losing all consciousness.

***

The rain had ceased falling, creating a cool, comforting breeze flowing into the bedroom where Thomas and Betty, his wife, slept. The constant drip of raindrops falling from the roof overhead and softly falling to puddles below and the faint roll of thunder off to the east were barely audible. Outside, a quietness covered the land like a new blanket of snow.

Betty began to rouse at the sound of moaning, but sleep called her back as she dismissed the sound. Only when it became louder did she awaken, and lying still, tried to collect her thoughts. Realizing the sound was coming from Rebecca's room, she quickly got up, lit the wick on her lamp and walked down the hall. As she entered, she found Rebecca curled up on her side clasping her hands to her head and making a constant murmuring noise. Betty tried to pull Rebecca's hands away but was unable.

"Darling, are you ill?"

Rebecca's eyes immediately flashed open, surprised and horrified. Then she looked about the room wildly and took her hands away from her head. Even in the cool night, her bed clothes were soaking wet with perspiration. "Mother," she whispered, curling back up.

"Yes, dear, it's me," said Betty, leaning over and smoothing the hair from her face. "I think you just had a bad dream."

Rebecca relaxed and reached for her mother's hand. "Mama, I have the worst headache I've ever had and the strangest dream."

"You don't have to tell me about it, dear. Maybe in the morning, if you can still remember it."

Rebecca leaned up and placed the pillow behind her back. "I want to tell you about it now. As I was sleeping, smoke began to filter through the window into this room, and no matter how hard I tried to get up and close the window, my legs would not move. It kept streaming in until the ceiling halfway down to my bed was a solid cloud. Then, it began to swirl about until there was a circular space formed above me."

"You sure you want to tell me more, darling?"

"Mama, an image of a man lying face down in the cloud appeared. His legs were spread and his arms were in the same position but reaching out for help. One hand was bloodied, and a puddle of blood formed around his head. He had dark curly hair, and his head was lying to the side. I tried to see who he was, but his hair covered his face. Mother, I think it was John."

Betty pulled her daughter to her and held her close and began a rocking movement like she had done when Rebecca was a child. "Darling, you need to forget that dream. It was probably caused by the sound of thunder we had earlier tonight."

All was silent as the two huddled together. "Mother, the other day when Tim came by to see me, he actually made sense. He told me that he would love John like a brother as long as he lived, but believed John would want us to go on with our lives. Mama, I believe that, but why this dream?"

"Darling, maybe if it was John in your dream, he was telling you that he was gone, and you should move on."

"Mama, I'm so confused. I gave my heart to him years ago, and as hard as I try, I can't forget him. I do want to go on living, and I do want a life that includes marriage and children."

A rooster crowed outside, and a hint of dawn filled the room. Birds began singing, and the smell of moistened soil was invigorating. Rebecca hugged her mother. "Mama, I will always love John even though he's gone. It's like my love for our risen Savior who died and was resurrected bringing us new life. Even though Jesus is no longer with us, His Spirit is always close to us. Mother, I think I'll always feel John close to my heart no matter what tomorrow brings. I do hope God will bring me a man who will love me as John did, and I know I've got to be willing to open my heart, especially if it's God's will. I just hope God will give me the strength to face the future without John."

9

Struggle with Death

For I know the plans that I have for you; declares the Lord, plans for welfare
and not for calamity to give you a future and a hope. Then you will call
upon Me and come and pray to Me, and I will listen to you. And you will
seek Me and find Me when you search for Me with all your heart.
—Jeremiah 29:11-13

A lamp's flickering light danced images against the shadow of the cell walls as the doctor labored over his patient. Slowly, he made the stitch and carefully pulled the thread through. Finished, he rolled down his sleeves and sat on a chair next to the bed exhausted.

"Will he live doctor?"

"I put ten stitches to the back of his head and another twelve to close the cut across the palm of his hand. It appears the bluntness of the force from the chair struck him across the back. If it had been to the lower head, you wouldn't have needed me. Come here, I want to show you something."

The doctor pushed the tangled hair from John's face exposing a jagged scar at the hairline. "What you see is an old head wound. I suspect this was caused by the blunt end of a musket or a piece of iron from a percussion shell. He probably had a concussion with the old wound, and now has a concussion with this new one."

"Will he live?" asked Hank.

"I'd say no, and if he does live, his mind may not come back. Only God knows because I've done all I can do."

"Ain't there something I can do, doctor?"

The doctor wiped the sweat from his brow. "Well, get some rags, roll them in rolls, soak them in cold water, and place them on his forehead. That will keep the swelling down in the brain. Do this every fifteen minutes. Remove as much clothing as possible to allow for circulation. Keep him completely cool."

As Hank cut off John's pant legs, the doctor leaned down to study a scar on John's leg about the size of a ten-dollar gold piece.

"Hank, look here. What do you think caused that?" the doctor asked.

Hank brought the lantern closer to get a better look."Looks like someone held a lit cigar to the boy."

The doctor shook his head. "May look like it, but it ain't."

He then turned John's leg to the backside of the calf revealing a larger scar. "This was done by one of Mr. Lincoln's minié balls. The ball entered where I first showed you, and it exited out the backside. It went right between the fibula and the tibia, the two long bones in the lower leg. This is one lucky boy. If that ball had gone one-sixteenth inch to either side, the bone would have shattered, and the leg would have been amputated. It does seem by the calcium build up that some damage was done. Either it chipped or broke the bone. Does the boy limp when he walks?"

"He did when we first locked him up, but it seems to be better now," said Hank.

"Doc, how you know about those minié balls?"

The doctor scratched his head. "About two years ago, General Hood sent out riders looking for doctors, and I got conscripted into the Army of the Tennessee. I went along with him through the Franklin and Nashville campaigns. I've seen a lot more than a man should see."

The doctor collected his hat and medical bag.

"Doc, you've had a rough night, ain't you?"

"I've got to go back to my office to finish work on the other two. As for Amos, he's got a fractured jaw, so I'll bind his jaw with a strap, and he'll live on liquids for a spell, and for the other, he just needs some stitches. From what I've heard, that was one fierce brawl, and I imagine Amos started it," the doctor replied as he headed out.

Hank prepared the cloths and gently placed one on John's forehead. *Oh Lord*, he thought, *I should have picked him up when I was supposed to. Time got away from me. If this boy dies, it's all going to fall on me.*

At nine o'clock, the sound of church bells echoed across the valley, calling everyone to church. Hank had slumped down on a chair near John's bunk and was sleeping soundly. The door of the jail squeaked open, and Parson Wilcox strolled in.

"Hank!" he called out.

Startled, Hank blurted, "Where? What's going on?"

"It's me, Parson Wilcox."

Hank blinked and rubbed his eyes several times, and said, "Morning, Preacher. What's up?" Then remembering the doctor's advice, quickly took the cloth wrap from John's head and soaked it in cold water, squeezed it out and placed it back on John's forehead. "Preacher, what time is it?"

"Little past nine. Why?"

"Oh no!" he exclaimed. "Doctor Jackson told me to change this here cloth every fifteen minutes. It is supposed to keep his brain cool."

"'When was the last time you changed it?" asked the preacher.

Hank shook his head. "I don't know, maybe three or four o'clock this morning. This has been one long nightmare of a night."

The preacher leaned down to get a better look at John. "He's still breathing. Does the doctor think he's gonna live?"

Hank got up and stretched. "He don't think so. Said it was in the Lord's hands."

"Do you know what happened down there last night?"

Tired and frustrated, Hank shook his head. "I don't have a clue. When I got down to Happy's place, John and Amos were laid out cold, Randy was running around, bleeding and screaming he was dying and the other boy had run off."

"Who was the one that ran?" asked the preacher.

"Ed Johnson from the county over, and they tell me he's wanted for attempted murder. We won't see that boy again. He's probably crossed the river and is in Missouri by now."

"How long do you have to keep changing those cloths?"

"Doc told me every fifteen minutes, and he'd check on him sometime Monday."

"Hank, you're gonna need help. I'll send Angie down for the afternoon, and I'll find someone to relieve Angie for the night. I would come myself, but I've got some sick members to visit this afternoon."

Angie arrived after lunch, and Hank showed her what to do.

"You're going to be just fine, John Wilson," she whispered, as she carefully bathed his face. "John, you've got to try hard to get better."

She knelt down by the bed where John lay and prayed, "Lord, place you healing power upon this man. Lord, give him strength, and heal his broken body. If possible, return him to his family."

Soon, a church member came to relieve Angie. She quickly explained what needed to be done and whispered another prayer for John's healing before heading home.

After a good night's sleep, Hank saddled his horse and headed for town. He found Tad Miller, a church member reading an old Paducah newspaper.

"How's the boy?" asked Hank.

"He ain't moved an inch. I just changed his cloth."

Hank thanked him for helping, pulled a chair to the bed and watched for any positive sign of recovery.

"Boy, can you hear me? It's time you woke up. You hear me?"

"Hey, Marshal!" a man called out.

Hank recognized Mr. Andrew Henderson, Amos's father and owner of the local bank. This is just what I don't need right now, he thought. "What can I do for you, Mr. Henderson?"

Henderson pointed down to John. "I want that man arrested."

Hank took a deep breath and pursed his lips. "Can't do that, sir."

"And why not?"

"He is already arrested. If you'll look around, I think you will see that this is a jail, and the room we're in is a cell," muttered Hank.

"You trying to get smart with me, Marshal?"

"No sir. Just giving you the facts, Mr. Henderson."

Henderson paused. "Well, Marshal, I'm drawing up charges against Wilson for assault with the intent to kill, and I'm expecting a conviction."

Hank squeezed out the cloth once more and placed it on John's forehead. "May not do any good. The doctor don't believe Wilson's gonna live. Now yore boy just has a broken jaw, and he's gonna live," Hank said sarcastically. "Intent to kill. You're right. One of 'em 'bout killed Wilson."

"I don't care. If that boy lives, I'm taking him to court, and when I get through with him, he'll be sitting in the Kentucky State Penitentiary in Louisville. Nobody's gonna break my boy up and get away with it."

Hank got up and walked to where Henderson stood. "First thing, your boy has been looking for trouble the past two years. Now, Ed Johnson was with him, and he's wanted for attempted murder, and Randy was in jail a year ago for breaking in Billy Baker's house. Now, I plan to find out what happened last night. If John's guilty, then he will be punished, but if I find out your boy is guilty, then he will be here in jail with Wilson."

"Humph," grunted Henderson. "My boy won't spend a minute in your jail, and as for you, come next election, you'll be a full time farmer."

Hank gritted his teeth as he restrained himself. "Mr. Henderson, I love farming, but I don't particularly care for being threatened, so I think maybe it's time for you to leave."

Henderson fumed out and slammed the door behind him.

Later that morning, Doctor Jackson stopped to check on John, and was pleased to see there was no swelling, and his pulse was strong even though he was not consciousness. He advised Hank to continue the cold cloths and to get liquids down John as soon as possible.

Hank could find no one who witnessed the brawl even though he talked to almost everyone in the town. Hank knew it would be Amos and Randy's testimony against John's, which meant that justice would not be served.

Tuesday dawned bright as the sun eased over the horizon. The leaves were beginning to show their fall colors, and a cool breeze out of the north hinted a taste of what was to come. Angie brushed into the jail, hung her cloak and bonnet on a peg on the inside wall and wandered over to Hank.

"How's he doing, Marshal Goss?"

"Not much change. Really ain't much we can do until he wakes. Then Doc said we have to get fluids down him or he will die."

Angie watched John intensely for a few moments and noticed John's eyelids quivering, and ever so often, she detected a jerk in his lower arms. A hint of a smile formed. Then a frown pushed it away.

"Marshal, come here a minute," she called.

"What the matter?" answered Hank, pulling his hat on.

"Looks like he may be waking up."

Angie wiped John's face with the damp cloth while Hank poured a cup of water.

"Angie, turn his head a little towards me, and I'm gonna try to give him some water. If he chokes, we'll turn him on his side and try to get it out. Hank brought the cup to John's lips and began to trickle water into his mouth. At first, it simply ran out from the corners of his mouth, but finally John swallowed, got strangled and started to coughed.

Hank and Angie feared that he might choke to death.

John could hear soft voices that seemed to echo as if inside an empty barrel. Eking his eyes open, slivers of light blinded him, and he reached to cover his eyes. Then he opened them and tried to focus on the images about him, but he could only see shadows.

"John, can you hear me?" said Hank.

John turned his head toward Hank but said nothing.

"What happened to my horse?" he whispered. "The clouds were beautiful and so refreshing. I guess I lost my horse. Father is gonna be disappointed with me. I almost choked on that water when we ran through the creek."

"What's he talking about?" muttered Hank. "Angie, you best go fetch the doctor."

"I'm talking about how I lost my horse! Can't you understand that?" John shouted out.

Hank then turned John to face him. "Do you know me, John?"

John raised his head and studied the figure in front of him. "You're the marshal." He then raised himself up again and looked around the room."

Hank reached for the cup. "You need to drink some water."

John slowly began to swallow the cold water and, lying back down, slipped off to sleep.

Hank pulled the cover over John's body and tucked it neatly about his shoulders. He then kneeled by the bedside and prayed. "Lord, thank you for your mercy, and place your healing hand on this child of yours. Please make his mind right, dear Lord. Please forgive me for how I've wronged him. And, Lord, please listen to this prayer even though I don't deserve to be heard by you. But this boy, he does."

***

Fall was in the air, and Lott picked up his crosscut saw and got Toby. The two ventured into the forest beyond the fields where barren cotton stalks stood in long rows. It had not been a good season, but several bales of cotton had been carried to the gin, and Lott felt assured he could now pay his bills with a little left.

Toby had taken care of Frankie and John when they were boys, and when the Ollivers decided to auction him off, John bought Toby and granted him his freedom. Toby asked to work for the Wilsons, and Lott helped him fashion the crib in the barn into a comfortable room with an added fireplace. During the spring, they had cut six large oak and hickory trees and left them lying to dry. Today, with the use of the crosscut saw, the two men would cut the limbs and trunks into firewood and accumulate enough wood for both households.

Lott loved walking through the woods during this time of year. The trees had taken their full, fall colors, and with the slightest breeze, some would flutter to the ground like a gentle rain shower releasing its drops. Easing through the underbrush, Lott and Toby observed squirrels scurrying seeking fallen acorns, and occasionally, a turkey would stroll in front of them. It was a beautiful morning, Lott thought.

When the men reached the trees, they removed their coats, rolled up their sleeves and began to saw. By midday, they had completely cut one of the trees into desirable lengths and decided to take a break. They strolled to the nearby creek, and drinking their fill, walked back to the work area and sat down to rest.

"Toby, you know the other day when we had that conversation about spirits," said Lott.

"I remember. We talked about hants, ghosts and the spirit world," answered Toby, unconcerned.

"Well, when I got home and told my misses about it, she thought I was being ridiculous. Do you really think your hants exist?"

Toby thought for a moment. "Mr. Lott, the way I sees it, is hants is them bad angels the Bible talks about. You know, when Satan was kicked out of heaven, he took some angels with him. They scare folks and cause trouble. Them hants ain't nothing but the devil's angels. That's the way I sees it."

"That's why y'all put them horseshoes over your door?" questioned Lott.

"That's right. It's kinda like them children of Israel when they was about to leave Egypt, and they placed the blood of sheep around their doorway. The death angel passed them over."

"How do you know so much about the Bible?" asked Lott surprised. "Can you read?"

Toby laughed. "Ain't suppose to. Slaves ain't suppose to do no reading."

"Well, can you read or not?"

"Mr. Lott, my mama was brought over here across the waters when she was just a girl, and being smart and good natured, she was bought by a plantation man near Savannah. Instead of going into the fields, they let her take care of the master's chillun. She dressed 'em, played with 'em and took care of 'em all day long, and when they had their schooling, my Mama would quietly listen in. Well, with time, she picked it up. When I was growing up, she secretly taught me the words. So, yes sir, I knows how to read."

"Sounds like you've read the Bible?" Lott probed.

"Mr. Lott, when I got to be about fourteen, times got hard, and the master sold me off. I was sent down to Louisiana, and that's where Master Bourdeau, Mrs. Olliver's pappy, bought me. When Master Olliver bought all this land up here in Missi'sip, he talked Master Bourdeau into letting me go with him. Then one day, Master Olliver told me to clean out an old closet and throw away everything in it. Well sir, as I was cleaning it out, I came across an old dusty Bible, and I guess I kinda sinned a little. I hid it in my coat pocket and took it home. At night, I'd take it out and read. I shore had to be careful though."

"How many times you read it?"

Toby scratched his head. "Not sure, maybe ten or fifteen times. Some of it don't make sense, especially that last book. You know about the revealing."

Impressed, Lott smiled and patted his friend on the back. "Times been hard on you, hasn't it? I'll tell you what, if you will stay with me until I get back on my feet, I'll deed you forty acres down on the south side of our section. There you'll have some good bottomland for corn and sugarcane and enough hill country to plant cotton. How's that sound to you?"

Toby realized Lott meant it and asked, "Why would you do such a thing?"

"First, because it's the right thing to do, and second, I can't work this place without you."

"Mr. Lott, you know I got a woman over at the Ollivers. I'd like to bring her to my place. She won't be no trouble."

"Slavery days are over. Why haven't you already sent for her?" replied Lott.

"Master Olliver won't let her go. He says she's carrying a debt."

"Carrying a debt! What kind of nonsense is that?" said Lott. "I'll tell you right now as soon as we get through with this cutting, I'm paying Frank a visit. Who does she owe?"

I think she owes for food and such, maybe at Walker's store," Toby explained.

For the first time in years, Lott felt the family was finally healing from its terrible losses. Sister was happier than he could ever remember, and not only was Johnny calling on her frequently, but other young men were dropping by as well. Sarah couldn't be more loving and content, and no longer did she talk of spirits or angels, nor did she ever mention John in their conversations. As for the strange boy, Lott decided that he probably was just a soldier passing through.

Weeks went by, and the first taste of winter swept across the South. A hard rain out of the west preceded a strong north wind, temperatures dropped and frost settled on the land. Lott pulled on the sweater Sarah had knitted him the previous winter and, with a hot cup of morning coffee, ventured to the porch for a cool breath of air. He sat in his rocker and listened to the sound of chickens feeding and the bellow of livestock across the fields. The sounds of the farm were interrupted as Lott watched a horseman approach. As the rider reined his mount, he took off his hat and spoke, "Sir, are you Mr. Lott Wilson?"

"I am," answered Lott, getting up to greet the man. "Why don't you get down and join me here on the porch?"

"No, thank you. I haven't seen my family in over three years. I live down below Newton," said the man, shaking Lott's hand.

"What can I do for you, young man?" asked Lott.

"I'm Jack Yates, and I served with your boys in the army. We were all in the same company. I got shot up, and your boy, James Earl got sick, and we ended up in the hospital together."

Lott's heart began to tremble as he listened to the man.

Jack reached in his pocket, retrieved a pocket watch and handed it to Lott. "James told me if anything happened to him that this watch should go back to you. He said it was your father's watch," he explained as he handed the watch to Lott.

Lott held it for a moment as he remembered the Christmas he gave James Earl the watch. Times were hard, and that's all he had for the boy. Lott returned his mind to the young man.

"Now you boys were in the infantry. How'd you get that horse?"

Jack laughed. "It was a long way from where we were paroled to home, so I took any available job in the towns I entered. Over time, I saved me about thirty dollars. Then one night, I got into this card game, and I got lucky. One of the men ran out of money, and all he had was this here horse. So now it's mine."

Lott paused, choosing his next words carefully. "Before you leave, may I ask you one more thing? Did my boy suffer?"

The young man shook his head. "He just went to sleep. In fact, he had a smile on his face. Yes sir, the Lord took him gently."

The words comforted Lott's heart and brought him peace.

Jack reached down once more and shook Lott's hand and turned in the saddle to leave. "You know, I lost two good friends in one day. There was a boy in there that couldn't have been more than fourteen years old, too young to even have a trace of beard. He had long blond hair and had fair skin. I lost both of them."

Lott recognized the description he had given and at once asked, "What was the boy's name?"

Jack smiled and replied, "His name was Gabe Jacobs."

"Are you sure about that name?" he questioned.

"Yes sir, I'm positive. His name was Gabe Jacobs."

"And you know he died?"

"Why, yes sir. In fact, I was holding his hand when he passed. Are you alright?"

Lott nodded and then watched as the man rode off. Over and over, he rethought each word spoken, thinking perhaps he had misunderstood what the man had said. Minutes turned to hours as he tried to put the conversation into perspective. As hard as he tried, the comments were direct and simple.

***

Since it was almost bedtime, Sarah glanced over at Sister who was reading. "You might want to check on your father. He doesn't usually stay out this late, and it's cold outside."

Sister laid her book down, threw a shawl around her shoulders and walked to the open hall. There was no sound of rocking nor the dim light of her father's pipe. "Papa," she called out. All was silent. "Papa, are you out here?"

"Right here, darling," came a voice from the dark, so soft that Sister could hardly hear it.

"Are you alright? It's getting late. Mama wants you to come on to bed."

"I'm fine. Just tell your mother I've got to do some thinking. She'll understand."

Sister returned inside and walked to the fireplace to warm herself. "Mama, Papa's acting mighty strange. He said he had a lot of thinking to do and you'd understand."

"Darling, I don't know what's troubling him, but something has been on his mind for a spell. You know men are different from us. They hold their feelings in and won't talk about their problems. Us women, we have to share it. Your father lost all of his boys, and with old age slipping up on him, I'm sure he's worried about running this farm and providing for us."

"Are we to leave him out there? He's only wearing a sweater," Sister answered.

"Sister, get his heavy coat and take it to him. Kiss him good night, and tell him you love him. He'll come in when he's ready."

Lott suddenly remembered the watch that his father had brought with him from Ireland. Lott pulled his coat collar up around his neck and thought about the man and the watch. He wished he had never heard about Gabe Jacobs. Angered, he reached back and threw the watch as far as he could toward the woods. The words were haunting him because maybe Toby was right, and Gabe was one of the devil's angels intent on tormenting him. Lott continued to think about the strange occurrence and the watch, but eventually, his thoughts turned to the time when all his children were home. It was such a happy time, before the despair of loss filled his heart.

On the eastern horizon, dawn approached, and Lott's thoughts wandered to the time he had spent with Gabe. He remembered opening his heart to him and sharing his personal grief and troubled heart. The boy had sat patiently and listened while he had talked about losing his boys and how he was afraid he was also losing Sarah. He clearly recalled how the boy had questioned his belief in ministering angels and that if he would only read the Word, he would understand.

It was there all the time, and I was too blind to see the truth, he thought. There was no way an angel of the devil could say such a thing. The warm feeling I had while we talked could not be anything but a gift from God. Lott now knew that he had kept company with an angel of the Lord. Lott had his answer. He walked slowly in the yard until he found the precious watch and knew James Earl was with the Lord as was John. Lott was at peace. Never again would he question his wife over her religious feelings nor would he discourage her from talking about angels. Without question, she was walking in the light while he traveled in darkness, blaming God for what had happened to his family. Suddenly, he remembered a verse Sarah often said about how the Lord giveth and the Lord taketh away, but blessed be the name of the Lord.

"It's time for me to get back to the Word," Lott said, walking down the hall to their kitchen. "I've been away too long."

***

The doctor followed closely as Angie hurried to the jail. He adjusted his glasses and lifted John's arm to feel for a pulse while watching the second hand on his pocket watch. "You say you got some water down him?"

"Yes sir, we did, and it almost strangled him. I did see him swallow though."

"And Angie said he spoke to you."

"He did but it didn't make much sense. He talked about losing a horse and that he was riding in the clouds. Said his father was gonna be upset with him for losing the animal."

"He did seem to recognize you," Angie relayed.

"But he seemed blind and had an unusual look in his eyes," explained Hank.

The doctor rubbed his chin and thought for a moment. "Hank, if you got the lick on your head like that boy did, you would have a problem focusing too. He did regain consciousness, and you did get fluids down him. That's a good sign. Now the boy's unusual statements about horses and clouds are probably just a dream or hallucination which is completely normal."

"You want me to wake 'em up where you can see for yourself?" asked Hank.

"Heavens no. Let him sleep. When he does wake up, get as much fluid down him as possible and give him something like chicken broth. It's natural the way he's sleeping. You'll probably find each time he awakens, he will stay awake longer, and when he does rouse up, talk to him and keep him up as long as possible. Write down what he says. You got all that?"

Hank nodded, and the doctor left for his office. Angie offered to make some chicken soup for John and have it ready before nightfall. She also let Hank know that she would get some church members to help with taking care of John.

Several times during the night, John woke up and talked about his dreams, then would drink the water offered and doze back to sleep. Those who attended him tried to keep him awake as long as possible and jotted down notes about his words.

When John awoke at two o'clock in the morning, he was given some warm chicken soup. As dawn neared even though he was sleeping soundly, he began talking incessantly. His talk ranged from family to boyhood experiences, but primarily his mind dwelled on the war. He continued to describe events in vivid detail. Unable to take such extensive notes, his keeper, Patrick Cooper, finally laid his pen down and just listened.

Early that morning, Doc Jackson returned.

"Wake up, son. It's morning," Doc said, gently shaking his arm. John didn't move but kept mumbling.

Doc brought his hands up near John's face and clapped them as loud as he could.

John's eyes shot open, and for the first time, he sat directly up in his bed and pointed to one of the inner walls of the jail. "We got to get out of here!" he shouted. "Those shells will tear this place apart. You hear them muskets. This place ain't safe."

"Where are you, John?" asked the doctor.

"I'm not sure I know you."

"I'm Doctor Jackson."

John grabbed the doctor by his arm. "I don't care if I die, but you're not taking my leg." John then held his right leg up. "You've got to promise you won't cut it off. You can hear me, can't you?"

The doctor patted John on the arm. "You'll keep your leg soldier."

John smiled. "Thank you, sir. I'm obliged. Could I have some water, please?"

To the doctor's surprise, John sat up and drank the entire cup and then asked for more. The doctor looked at his watch and was pleased that the boy had now been awake for more than eighteen minutes.

"Son, do you know what your name is?"

John looked about for a moment. "I'm not rightly sure."

At ten minutes after seven, Hank strolled in, surprised to see Doc out so early.

"Morning, Doc. Morning, Patrick. Mighty early, ain't it?"

Doc Jackson collected his bag and spoke to Hank who was going through his mail. "Now listen to me. The boy's started talking, and I want to know every word he says. It's important. You understand?"

A puzzled frown came over Hank's face. "What's so important about that? If he's talking so much like you say, how do you expect someone to write it down?"

"Listen to me, Hank. You won't be able to write everything down, but tell those that stay with John to listen and write the general idea of what's being said, and you can stop the cold compresses. The swelling is gone."

"That's a lot of trouble, Doc. What's so important about all of this?"

"I'm in a hurry. I'm already late. Just do what I ask."

"Before long, I'm gonna have to start hiring people to sit with him. That would be asking a lot of folks to spend their nights down here, especially just to listen to him talk," Hank yelled out as the doctor was leaving. "Did you hear me?"

"I heard you. I'll cover the cost if need be," the doctor called as he waved goodbye and walked across the street.

Later that morning, Angie stopped by the jail to pick up her empty bowl, and she gave Hank a list of volunteers. Angie then checked on John.

"I heard he's been talking a lot," she said.

"He talks a lot, and then he might not say a word for an hour. I'm supposed to listen to everything he says and keep note of it. That's what Doc Jackson ordered. Sounds crazy to me."

Angie eased down in a chair next to the bed. "I don't know. Doc Jackson is a pretty smart man. He must have a good reason. By the way, I heard Amos's father might press charges against John. Is there anything truth to it?"

Hank suddenly struck his fist against his open hand. "Dadgummit! I've forgot all about that. Here it is Thursday, and I ain't got the first statement. I've got to go see those boys and right now. Angie, do you think you could stay a spell until I can get back? It might take several hours."

"If you'll go by the church and tell my father where I am."

"I'll go right now, and remember, if he starts talking, listen to him," exclaimed Hank, leaving.

John slept peacefully and sometimes would mumble to himself but not loud enough for Angie to understand what was being said. Outside, a dog barked loudly as it chased a wagon down the street. John immediately awoke. He saw Angie, and reaching out, he clasped her hair and pulled her closer to him. For a long time, he looked directly into her eyes then releasing her hair, he gently tried to smooth out the tangles he had made.

"You've been here a long time. I've seen you giving me water, and you spooned me some soup. Are you my wife?"

Angie chuckled to herself and thought how lucky she would be if that were true.

"I volunteered to sit with you, but we are not married. Why did you think so?"

John removed his hand from hers. "I don't rightly know. I guess it was the way you looked at me and have taken care of me. You are a pretty thing, you know. I would be a lucky man to have you for a wife."

Angie blushed and gave him a quick smile, but she hoped he had not noticed the growing feelings she had for him.

Before noon, Hank stormed back into the jail, frustrated and angered over the morning's investigation. "Hogwash!" he exclaimed. "All lies!"

He quickly apologized to Angie and asked her how John was doing. After Angie left, Hank hoped he would have no more interruptions so just maybe he could get his thoughts together about John's problem. Taking out his pad, he was about to review the statements when the door squeezed open, and a shaggy head peeked in.

"I come to see the General," Wally whispered. "You know we's friends."

Hank dropped his pen in disbelief. "You want what?"

Wally eased the door open a little further. "The soldier boy. Is he gonna live?"

Hank got up and spoke in frustration, "Wally, I don't need this right now. You best go on your way. I've got work to do."

"The General and Wally was in that war together. He needs to see me."

"That's it! Now you get out of here right this minute. Now get!" shouted Hank, running toward him hoping to scare him away.

Wally ducked out and ran as fast as his short legs would carry him. He stopped and saw that Hank was not in pursuit, then called out, "Tell the General that Private Wally can save his life. You get 'em that word. You hear?"

Private Wally can save General Wilson's life? Now I've heard it all. I've a good mind to just go back inside, lay my badge on the desk and call it quits, thought Hank.

Hank soon cooled off, and the afternoon passed quickly as Hank studied his findings on the brawl. He now realized he should have interrogated Amos and Randy immediately after the fight before the two could get together and adjust their stories. Their tale just didn't make sense.

"Hogwash and double hogwash," muttered Hank to himself. "It's all lies. They're telling me John went over to the three of them to start a fight. Nothing they've said sounds like John. They almost killed the boy, and in court, it will be two men's word against John's, and he won't have a chance."

Late in the afternoon, Doc Jackson came by to get his daily report and noticed that Hank was pretty unhappy. Hank told him about the statements and his belief that John had no chance of defending himself. Doctor Jackson reminded Hank that the truth would win out, but Hank still felt that the future was pretty grim for John even if he did fully recover.

As the days passed, John continued to improve and was now only taking short naps during the day and sleeping soundly at night with the revelations continuing.
By Saturday, John was awake and up as if nothing had happen, except that John had no remembrance of his earlier life. He knew his name was John because that was what people were calling him. He had no knowledge of the war or what had happened to him. To the doctor's surprise, John still maintained his math abilities and enjoyed reading. After finishing a book, he could sit down and recall every detail of the story.

On Monday morning, one week and one day following the fight, Doctor Jackson walked into the jail about the same time Hank arrived, and the two sat calmly having a cup of morning coffee.

"Been a wild ride hasn't it, Hank?" the doctor said, blowing across the hot coffee to cool it.

Hank shook his head. "Normally, there ain't a touch of trouble in this little town, but since I shot that boy off that stolen horse and put this boy in jail, my life's been pretty mixed up. And it ain't over yet."

"What do you think is going to be the outcome?" asked Doc.

Hank took a swallow of coffee. "I don't rightly know. If Henderson decides to press charges against John, it don't look good for the boy. I wish the judge would just say the boy has made his restitution and let him go on home."

"Through John's stories, I've gotten to know him quiet well. He seems to be a fine lad and well read. From all accounts he was raised a Christian. Physically, he's well and strong, but mentally he doesn't know who he is or what happened that night. Does he go to court and get punished for something that he can't recollect? Doesn't seem fair to me."

Hank sat quietly thinking. "Doc, the whole thing is crazy, and talking about crazy, you know who's about to drive me wild?"

"Probably Mr. Henderson," answered Doc.

"No, it's that crazy Wally. He keeps poking his head in the jail, wanting to see John and he keeps saying that Private Wally can save General Wilson's life and that there's a big battle coming. He then covers his ears and tells me that he can even hear musket fire. Heck, I've even started playing his game. I run him out and tell him to go see General Lee or Grant. He then comes to attention and gives me a salute and runs off down the street calling for the general. You ever heard of such?" laughed Hank.

"I don't reckon he's took to the bottle," laughed Doc.

"Bottle! The boy don't have sense enough to know what that is." Hank laughed, spilling his coffee in the process.

Two days later, a cold rain was falling, and soon, winter snow would be covering the ground. Hank put on his heavy woolen coat, wrapped a scarf around his neck and pulled his hat tightly down to cover his ears as he began his daily walk around the town. Hank enjoyed this time with the storekeepers. It was a relief from the boredom of the office and a chance to catch up on the local gossip.

A light drizzle forced him to stay under the porches of the establishments as he made his way down the sidewalk. He methodically stopped at each store, chatted a spell and moved on to the next one. As he approached the bank, he pulled his collar up and hat down close above his eyes and hurried past. Henderson got a glimpse of Hank and excused himself from a customer seeking a loan and rushed outside.

"Hey Marshal!" He shouted. "Hold up a moment."

"Yes sir," he replied turning slowly to face Henderson.

Henderson extended his hand, but Hank rejected it. "Got my paper ready. Do I give it to you or the judge?' he replied, dropping his hand.

"I suppose you mean a charge against Wilson."

"What else? I told you I was going to press charges, and since the boy has come around, it's time to get on with business," Henderson explained with a grin.

Hank dropped his head and pursed his lips. "Henderson, all yore boy got was a broken jaw and a little embarrassment about getting whipped. He's gonna be fine, but they almost killed Wilson. He still ain't right in the head. Why don't you just drop the whole thing?"

"Drop it! You must be out of your mind. My boy has already lost over ten pounds because he can't eat solid food, and how'd you like to be thrown through a window? No telling how many stitches it took to sew the boy up, and you want me to drop it?"

Hank rubbed his hand across his face, trying to control himself. "Henderson, you know what your problem is? You don't give a hoot about that boy that got cut up. All you care about is that your boy got whipped, and that hurt your pride."

A smirk crossed Henderson's face. "You don't like justice, do you? Should I give the charge to you or the judge? Either way, Wilson will be spending Christmas in the Louisville Penitentiary."

Hank gritted his teeth in anger. "Mr. Henderson, you best deliver this to the judge. If you hand it to me, I'll tear it up right before your eyes."

Henderson laughed. "Come on, Marshal, do your duty," as he handed the summons to Hank.

Hank took the paper, ripped it to pieces and let it flutter to the ground.

Henderson laughed as the bits of paper covered the walkway and, reaching inside his coat pocket, pulled out an envelope. "I thought that would be the way you would react. This one is addressed to Judge Henry. How does that sound to you?"

Hank thought for a second. "Henderson, maybe your money and power can buy you anything, but you ain't God Almighty. You ain't above Him, Mr. Henderson."

Life was pretty boring for both John and Hank, but at least, John enjoyed reading and it seemed that someone was always dropping off books for him. Hank finally remembered how the two used to play checkers before the accident. Bringing out the board, Hank patiently taught John the rules of the game, and to his delight, he finally was able to claim victory. It was such an afternoon while the two were playing that there was a tap on the door, and Judge Henry walked in.

"It's cold out there!" he exclaimed, removing his hat and coat.

"Afternoon, Judge. What brings you out on a day like this?" said Hank, getting up to shake the judge's hand. "Have a seat here near the woodstove."

The judge adjusted his glasses and peered at Hank. "What in tarnations is going on down here? Sounds like you had some kind of rout."

"You must have heard from Henderson."

The judge pulled a letter from his shirt pocket and handed it to Hank. Hank looked it over and then handed it back.

"Assault with intent to kill? Battery? Destruction of property? Sounds like some serious accusations, Judge."

"That him back there?" asked the judge, walking to where John sat.

"You looking at him."

Getting up, John extended his hand. "Afternoon, sir. I'm John."

The judge shook his hand and looked him over for a minute then walked back to where Hank waited. "Is this the same boy I sentenced a while back?" he asked.

"That's him, Judge."

"He sure don't look the same. That boy was skin and bones and in rags. You must feed 'em good down here."

"We been hiring him out, and to tell you the truth, he's earned his keep and more. You're right. He's gained more than forty pounds, and folks have been giving him clothes."

"Marshal, all I got is what I showed you on that document and what Mr. Henderson told me, now I want what information you've collected, and I want the truth."

For the next few minutes, Hank disclosed all he knew about the incident, and when finishing, the judge sat quietly for a spell.

"You think the boy's innocent, don't you, Marshal?"

"Yes sir, I do believe that," answered Hank.

A frown crossed the judge's face. "You got a problem. He's got no recollection of what went on, and as you well know, it will be two statements against one. No, with Wilson's amnesia, it'll be two against zero."

Hank took a deep breath and shook his head. "What can I do, Judge? How can I make sure justice is upheld?"

"I don't rightly know, Marshal. You might try praying."

"When will the hearing be, Judge?"

"Weather permitting, I'll be making my way back here in about four days."

"Four days! That soon!" exclaimed Hank.

Hank knew why Henderson wanted the case to move forward so soon. He'd have his boy in court all bound up and looking pitiful, and the other boy would still have his bandages, and John would be sitting there looking healthy and spry. *Goodbye Mr. Wilson, you'll be in Louisville, Kentuck when that day is over*, Hank thought.

The weather was clearing on the following Sunday morning, and Hank surprised John by taking him to church. John washed his face, combed his hair and put on his best clothes. Members welcomed him as they made their way down the aisle because John had gained the respect of most of the people in the community. Angie smiled at John and motioned for them to share her family's pew. After a special song, Angie's father preached a sermon on the Good Samaritan, and even though John had heard it many times before, this day, he heard it for the first time. As the pastor concluded his sermon, John looked at Angie and formed the words thank you and covered her hand with his. Angie blushed, then smiled and whispered, "You're welcome."

The preacher closed by asking for prayer requests, and after a few had been acknowledged, he then asked for any unspoken ones. All was quiet as the members looked about, then Hank slowly raised his hand.

"Yes," said Angie's father, looking to Hank. "If the Lord wills, may it be."

10

Court of Justice

Now to Him who is able to do immeasurable more than all we ask or imagine according to His power that is at work within us. To Him be the glory in the church and in Christ Jesus throughout all generations, forever and ever, Amen.
—Ephesians 3:20-21

After harvesting time, the whole family would venture into Little Rock to pick up mail, buy necessities and visit with friends. Since the weather was beautiful, the Walker's store was quite busy. Mr. Walker had been sick with influenza for several days and was home resting while Mrs. Walker and Rebecca were exhausted from waiting on customers, restocking shelves, checking and handling mail. About a quarter of six, the crowd dwindled, and a colored man and his wife walked into the store.

Mrs. Walker looked to Rebecca. "Darling, I'm worn out. Tell them we're closing."

"I'll help them, Mama. You need to get off your feet." Rebecca walked quickly over and asked, "Can I help you?"

"Yes ma'am," the man turned to his wife and asked, "Lucy, you remember what all we gots to have?"

"We needs about a pound of sugar, pound of coffee beans, a side of pork, bag of flour and some salt. That ought to get us by fer now."

Rebecca smiled at the neatly dressed woman. "I'll get those things for you. Won't take but a minute."

Rebecca soon had the items collected and on the counter for payment.

"That will be seven dollars and twenty-two cents," Rebecca said.

The man took his items and mumbled, "Put it on the paper."

"Excuse me. What did you say?" asked Rebecca.

"Mr. Walker writes them down, and we pays when we can," explained the man.

Rebecca's mother said, "That means they're charging it, dear. Write it down, and your father will post it in his ledger later. A lot of our customers charge. Some pay once a month or when their crops come in. Others just pay along as they can."

When the store was closed for the day, Rebecca decided to help her father by catching up his ledger.

"Mother, where does father keep his book of charges?" she asked.

Mrs. Walker, weary and ready to leave, answered absentmindedly, "In the drawer under the counter by the cash register. When you come, bring the moneybox with you. Just leave the charge notes in the drawer on top of the ledgers."

Rebecca opened the drawer and found a black notebook and looked for the place to write the charges. She found all the accounts neatly arranged in alphabetical order by the customer's last name. Listed were dates of purchase, items bought, prices and a running tab. Over on the opposite column were dates and sums of payments. It looked simple.

She then looked at the receipt for the charged items and saw the man's name was listed as Theodas O.

"Mama, who is Theodas O? You know the colored man that came in here."

"Oh, that's probably Theodas Olliver. He works for Mr. Frank. When the Negroes were freed, a lot of them took their owner's name."

As Rebecca turned the pages, she could not find Theodas Olliver. Frustrated, she decided to look for a second ledger. She found a slightly smaller one and noticed it was organized the same, but most of the names were O's. She found the name Theodas O and wrote the items purchased, then sat back and relaxed as she perused the man's past accounts. The more she studied them, the more she saw discrepancies. For instance, a pound of sugar in July cost ten cents, the same as it was that morning, but in August, it was listed as costing fifteen cents, and in September, eighteen cents. Each month the price had increased.

"Mother, could you come here a minute?"

"Yes, dear."

Rebecca showed her mother the ledgers and the increase of charges, and they began going through the books. Finally, Mrs. Olliver took the books from Rebecca and placed them back into the drawer.

"Rebecca, all I do is take inventory, stock shelves and wait on customers. Your father handles the finances. I'd say he was charging them interest on carrying their debt. I wouldn't worry about it."

"But mother, the cost on some of those items have doubled in three months."

"Like I said, your father will handle this part of the business," Mrs. Walker explained.

"Okay, Mother. I'll stay and close up," Rebecca said. Mrs. Walker, eager to check on her husband's condition, thanked her daughter and headed home.

As soon as her mother left, Rebecca went directly to the ledgers. She carefully scanned Theodas O's account and took note of the increases. Next, she studied the paid column and added the amount charged for the purchased items at their normal base price and was shocked by the difference. Next, she studied other customers in the smaller ledger and found that all had been overcharged in the same manner. She then picked up the larger ledger and reviewed each account and saw that no one had been overcharged. Her heart sank as she realized that her father had been unfair to those in the smaller ledger. She replaced the ledgers, tried to scratch out her markings and with a heavy heart, headed toward home.

The inviting aromas of ham frying and coffee brewing brought Lott to the kitchen. With a blanket around his shoulders and the cold against his bare feet, Lott headed to his favorite chair near the woodstove and window.

"Good morning, Sarah. Looks like a young snow covering our yard," he said, viewing the heavy frost.

Sarah laughed. "And you look like a Choctaw chief with that old blanket wrapped around you and your hair all mussed up."

"A chief sounds good to me. I know breakfast ain't ready yet, but do you think you could fetch this old chief a cup of coffee?"

Sarah opened the oven door and slipped a tray of rolled biscuits inside and, pouring a cup of coffee, walked over to Lott. To her surprise, he asked her to set the cup on the table, and before she knew it, he pulled her into his lap and wrapped his blanket around her. "Time for some good morning loving, dear," he said, cuddling her close.

Sister tipped in, pulling her night coat tight as she edged across the floor in her thick woolen socks. "Gracious, is that necessary?" she exclaimed.

Sarah quickly got up and headed back to the biscuits. "Well, you know we are married."

"I know, but children don't like to see their parents, you know." She frowned and gave her mother a hug. "I'm about to starve. How long 'til we eat?"

"Let me tell you ladies something," interrupted Lott. "The other day I was talking with Toby, and you know what he asked?"

"Probably how your hants are doing," answered Sarah with a smile.

"Well, it wasn't about hants. Toby said he wanted to bring his wife home."

"I didn't know he was married, Papa. I thought the slaves kinda just lived together," Sister said.

"Heavens no, child, they get married in their own way. They have a big party, and after a while, one person holds one end of a broom while another grabs the other. Then they just jump over the broom together. It's quick and easy. I'll tell you girls something. A man sure better know what's he doing because one second, he's single and the next, he's married."

Sarah and Sister were amused at the unusual ritual.

"Just think, Sister, how easy that would be when you decide to get married."

"Papa, you're so funny. Without a preacher, it wouldn't be right."

"Well, I guess you could invite the preacher, and when you got ready to jump, he could say 'Dearly beloved,' and when your feet hit the ground, he could say, 'Amen.' It sure makes sense to me."

Sister just shook her head and replied, "Papa, you can forget that idea, because I plan to have a beautiful church wedding."

As they enjoyed breakfast, Lott continued his line of thought. "Toby does have a wife and I know of two grown sons."

"Why isn't she here with him?"

"Toby said something about a debt that keeps her from leaving," Lott explained.

"Slavery days are over. A person can go where they want," said Sister, clearing the table.

"You're right, daughter. I told Toby I'd check on it, and I guess it starts with Frank since she works for him."

After breakfast Sister tidied her room while Sarah and Lott enjoyed another cup of coffee. Sarah clasped Lott's hand and gave him a loving smile. "It's good to hear you laugh. It seems like old times."

"The other day, I ran into Jim Clearman. You know he had three boys that went off to fight, and none came home. His wife died of the fever several weeks back. I felt for him and realized that even though we've had losses, the Lord has truly blessed us. We've got a roof over our heads and food on the table, and I'm living with two of the finest women the Lord has ever made. And I do believe Thomas is still alive, and he'll come home one of these days."

The next morning, Lott saddled his horse and headed for the Ollivers. The idea of stepping into Frank's home brought bad memories. The two had come from Savannah as young surveyors of the Choctaw lands and fell in love with the country, but after acquiring land, their lives took separate paths. He and his brother Jake struggled to create a productive farm while Frank, with slave labor and unethical methods, carved out an empire and became one of the richest men in Mississippi. As much as Lott detested talking with Frank, he knew his intervention was necessary.

Despite the beauty of Frank's land, Lott could only think of how it had been obtained. The head of a Choctaw family could file an application, and if the Choctaw agreed to give up his tribal alliance and follow the laws of the state, he could be granted a section of land. One fortunate Choctaw had been granted such a section, but a little alcohol and a card game took it from him. The six hundred and forty acres that Lott was admiring had belonged to his brother's Choctaw friend. Frank's desire for this land had cost his brother, Jake, his life.

"Well, what a surprise." Judith Olliver smiled. "I'm so glad to see you. Won't you come in?"

"Thank you, Judith. I can't stay long. I need to speak with Frank, please," he said, dreading the coming moments.

"Frank has just returned from Jackson on business and got a late start this morning. He should be dressed by now. Just take a seat in the library," Judith said, pointing to the room to his left. "I'll have some refreshment brought in."

Instead of the expected maid, Suzanne whirled through the doorway, bringing him a steaming cup of tea and a cupcake. The two talked for a few minutes, and Lott enjoyed the pleasant person Suzanne had become. When Suzanne saw her father in the hallway, she politely asked to be excused.

"Well, I thought I'd never see you darken my doors." Frank laughed, extending his hand and taking a seat across from Lott.

"Strange things do happen," Lott answered, shaking his hand.

Even though their hands met just as their lives had been intertwined, there was no friendship found in either of their eyes. For a while, the men talked of old times and the trials and hardships of starting new lives out in the Mississippi wilderness while Frank anxiously awaited the real reason for Lott's visit.

Frank lit his pipe and blew a circle toward the ceiling. "Lott, what do you need from me?"

Lott smiled. "Well, I guess you know this is not a friendly visit?"

"What can I do for you?"

"The other day, Toby, the colored man on my place told me his wife, Sadie, was still working for you. He wants her to come live with him but said she owed some kind of debt and couldn't leave your place. Can you shed some light on this?"

Frank blew another circle of smoke and thought for a moment. "The old winch is still trying to work for me, but at her age, she ain't worth much. She don't owe me anything." Frank thought to himself, *The woman well up in age had seen her better days and was of little help in the fields. It would be better for him if she were off the place.*

"Then what's holding her, Frank?" Lott asked, confused.

Frank thought about his options. He knew he could tell Lott about the debt she owed Walker's store, but that could cause some repercussions. Since Frank didn't care about the new deals Walker was working out with other farmers, he decided to be as truthful as possible and let the cards lie where they would.

"The problem ain't with me. You might want to go talk with Walker. As far as I'm concerned, the old gal can leave anytime she wants."

Lott and Frank shook hands, and after thanking Mrs. Olliver and Suzanne for their hospitality, Lott bade them goodbye. Lott couldn't understand why the debt would keep her at the Olliver's.

Since it was only four miles from the Ollivers to Little Rock, Lott soon arrived at the Walker's store, secured his mount to the porch and entered. Only one man was shopping, but he had paid and was headed out the door. Lott walked to the counter where Thomas was placing money from his sale into his cash register. Before he could speak, Rebecca came in from the side door that led to their home.

"Morning, Mr. Wilson. How's the family?"

Lott embraced Rebecca and gave her a smile. "The family is all doing well. You sure are a lovely sight to behold. How have you been doing?"

"I'm fine, Mr. Wilson."

Lott smiled again at Rebecca, then turned his attention to Mr. Walker. "Thomas,

I been over to Frank's place, and he sent me to talk with you," Lott said, leaning against the counter.

Thomas's eyebrows lifted, and he was filled with apprehension. Thomas quickly asked Rebecca to head to the front and meet the Meridian stage bringing the mail and goods he had ordered.

Rebecca could hear a little as she walked to the front of the store, and Lott asked, "Thomas, Frank told me that Toby's wife Sadie couldn't leave the Olliver's because of the money she owes you. Is that right?"

"Lott, a lot of folks owe me money these days. Lot of them buy on credit," Thomas explained, wondering just how much Frank had said. Thomas decided to get to the point and get Wilson out of the store.

"Lott, business men are trying to protect themselves during these hard times. If a man runs up a big bill and decides to take off, we'd loose money and have to close our doors. To protect us, the sheriff has agreed to help by stopping anyone who owes us before they can leave the county. It's a pretty good idea, I think."

Lott tapped on the counter as he considered what Thomas was saying. "There's one problem with that story, Thomas. Toby's wife ain't wanting to leave the county. She'd be only moving about four and one half miles to where we live. I think you need to see if she owes you anything."

Because of the ledgers, Rebecca had eased her way closer to her father and Mr. Wilson.

Frank took out his ledger and slowly turned the pages. He closed the book and stated, "Sadie's not listed here. She must be shopping elsewhere."

Walker reached out to shake Lott's hand, hoping he would leave, but Rebecca reached for the other ledger and said, "You might want to look in your other register under the name of Sadie O."

Thomas flushed with anger and embarrassment as he frowned at his daughter. "Oh, I forgot about that one. It holds our questionable accounts. Quickly turning through the pages, he stopped and studied the account. "Appears she owes me about eighteen dollars and five cents," he muttered as he closed the book.

Lott took a small pouch from his pocket and reaching inside pulled out two ten dollar gold coins and laid them on the counter. "If you will please write me a paid in full note on Sadie so that I can for some reason carry it to Frank, I'd appreciate it. And don't worry about the change. You can give that to the sheriff."

Folding the note for Frank, Lott was headed out when Frankie came through the front door. "Morning, Mr. Wilson," he said, tipping his hat. "Rebecca, are you ready to go for a ride? I've got my rig outside and plenty of blankets to keep us warm," he said, reaching for her hand.

Lott looked up and thought of John and Rebecca and could see that Rebecca was thinking of the past. As Lott left, he gave Rebecca a smile and nod, letting her know that even though it hurt, he understood.

That afternoon, when Rebecca returned from her outing with Frankie, her father was waiting for her.

"Why, daughter, did you interfere in my business today? How do you know about my ledgers?" Mr. Walker questioned.

"Father, I see those ledgers all the time, but the other day when you were sick, I tried to record the order that one of your customers charged," she replied, holding her judgment for another day.

Her reply set his worries at ease, and he hoped there would be no other ramifications. As Rebecca walked the path to home, she was pleased she could help Toby but was sadly disappointed in her father.

Lott reached home at midday and hurried to tell Toby the good news, "Toby, hitch up the wagon because we are headed to the Olliver's plantation to fetch her."

***

Doc Jackson laid his glasses down to rub his tired eyes, then folded his arms and rested his head on the desk. For the past two hours, he had reviewed the notes taken while John slept. At first, it was confusing to decipher, but Doc was slowly piecing together John's life. For the past several nights, he had talked about the walk from Camp Douglas and how he had lost his friend Sam. The doctor hoped John would soon reveal what had happened at Happy Harry's because the hearing would be in only two days, and the truth might not be revealed in time.

A light tap interrupted his thoughts, and he got up to find Angie at the door.

"Well, good afternoon, Angie. I pray no one's ill." Feeling the cold afternoon breeze, he motioned her in.

"No sir, we're all well. I just wanted to talk with you if you have time."

The doctor took her cloak and wrap, then pulled up a chair.

"Now, what can I do for you?"

"I'm worried about John and what might happen to him," said Angie anxiously.

"What about Amos? You've been kinda sweet on him, and for all we know, John is guilty of starting the fight. Amos got hurt too."

Angie dropped her head. "I think I know both of them. I can't see John starting trouble in there. He seems to want to do what is right and is very self-disciplined."

"What about Amos?" repeated the doctor.

"He's a Henderson. His father controls a lot of people and yes, I am fond of him, but sometimes his arrogance gets the best of him."

Pointing to the stack of papers, the doctor said, "You've listened to a lot of this, but if you like, I don't care if you browse through it."

Angie quickly began reading the accounts. Minutes passed into hours as she studied the writings.

Angie gathered her cloak as she looked at the clock. "I was supposed to be only going to the store to get father some writing paper for his Sunday sermon, so I better head home," she said, pausing. "What if you don't find out what happened? What's your next plan?"

"To tell you the truth, there is no other plan," he answered, opening the door for the young woman.

***

The morning of the hearing dawned bright and crisp. Not a sign of a breeze was felt as people made their way into the village. The normally quiet town was alive with movement. Wagon after wagon weaved down the muddied street heading for the Methodist church at the south end of town. The farmers in early November had finished the harvest and had free time for entertainment. The son of a prominent banker was accusing an incarcerated stranger of assault with the intent to kill. Many citizens' sympathies were with the young man who had worked so diligently for them. Others supported Amos who had grown up in Wickliffe.

Hank trudged down the sidewalk, dreading the outcome for John. The church bell rang nine o'clock, so he hurried his pace. The hearing would begin at ten, and the church would be packed. The church was the only building large enough to appropriately accommodate the crowd, and the local school, which also met there, had been cancelled today. Hank found the doctor in the jailhouse adding some extra oak to the stove. John was washing his face and had trimmed his beard.

"How long you been here, Doc?"

Doc straightened up and looked at Hank. By his mussed hair and tired look, Hank didn't need an explanation.

"You been here all night, ain't you? You get anywhere with the boy?" questioned Hank.

Doc poured himself a cup of coffee and sat next to the stove. "Yeah, I got something. I had him walking down the street to Happy's place early this morning in his dream world, but then a bunch of dogs started chasing a cat around the back of the jail, and he sat up wide-awake and has been up ever since."

"Has he had breakfast?" Hank asked, pouring himself a cup.

"They brought it about seven."

"How about you, Doc? Have you eaten?"

"Eaten. I haven't even thought about it. How can a man eat when an innocent person is going to be convicted of a crime?"

Hank shook his head. "I didn't have no appetite either."

"I'll tell you something unusual though. John started talking about how he had an uncle named Jake who had married a Choctaw woman. He talked about how much his uncle loved horse racing and that he and one of his Choctaw friends came all the way up here to Kentucky to buy a long-legged thoroughbred."

"That ain't unusual, Doc. He's just going back to his beginnings again."

"That ain't it, Hank. The boy was telling me this when he was awake, not while sleeping."

"So he may be remembering his past?" questioned Hank.

"Could be, and if what he told me is the truth, he may be getting his senses back. Time will tell," added Doc.

John, cleaned and dressed in his best clothes, asked as he smoothed the wrinkles from his pant legs, "How do I look?" John was dressed in a pair of gray homespun woolen trousers, a white cotton shirt, black leather suspenders and a pair of ankle high military shoes that had been dropped off by a veteran who had recently returned home.

"You'll do, boy," Hank said, looking him over.

Hank looked at his pocket watch. Twenty until ten. His heart fluttered, and his breath shortened. "Time to go, boy," he said, motioning to the door. "We'd better put these on," he added, taking a set of handcuffs from his pocket. "I got to make it look like I'm doing my job."

"Is that necessary?" questioned Doc Jackson.

"Well, he is my prisoner, and I don't know how the judge would like it if I bring him in without them. Don't want to upset him up front."

John held out his hands, and the cuffs clicked tight. Hank looked back to Doc. "You going with us, ain't you?"

Doc dropped his head and mumbled, "You two go on."

"Now Hank, what did you say I did?" questioned John as the two walked away from the jail.

In all of his years, Doc could not remember feeling so helpless. In the quietness, his mind drifted to when Jesus was arrested, beaten and crucified. He knew how the disciples must have felt seeing an innocent man put to death. Doc breathed a prayer, "Lord, justice is up to you today. We need a miracle, and I know your power can make this right. Lord, just turn it loose today in the courtroom."

As Hank approached the church, multitudes of wagons, buggies and horses caught his attention. Throngs of people milled about, and children chased each other in play. The loud murmuring of people socializing was like a whirlwind of unconnected words. He had seen crowds at church revivals, funerals and all-day service but nothing could match this gathering.

As Hank and John made their way through the crowds, they were greeted by both words of encouragement and whispers of accusation. Hank was not surprised that every pew was filled and people were standing along the outer aisle. A hush came over the mass as they watched Hank and John move to the front. In the place of the pulpit, a desk and chair had been stationed for the judge. Below the pulpit platform, a table and two chairs were placed for the plaintiffs and the accused. Only the aisle separated the parties.

Since the town marshal collected and presented information for both parties in a fair and unprejudiced fashion, no lawyer was needed. Each defendant would have the opportunity to disclose their account of the altercation. Finally, the judge would deliver his decision.

John took his seat and looked at the people nearby. He was comforted to see Angie and her father directly behind him, and with cuffed hands, John took the parson's hand and smiled to Angie. At his right, he found the seats for the plaintiffs vacant.

"Hank, you think they're gonna show?" John asked.

"They'll be here. They'll come at the last moment and walk down that aisle looking like they been attacked by a herd of buffalo." Hank glanced at his pocket watch. "In fact, it's about time now."

No sooner had he replaced his pocket watch, than the door opened, and a hush came over the church. Amos walked in first followed by his parents. Amos had a white towel folded and tied around his head. He looked thin with loosely hanging clothes. A slight limp was noticeable, and occasionally, he grasped the edges of the pews to steady himself. Behind him came Randy with his mother who held to him tightly. Never had Hank seen so many bandages on one person. *Certainly, he couldn't still have bandages this long after the fight*, John thought.

Hank nudged John. "Have you ever seen such a sideshow? I hope the judge sees through their play-acting."

At ten o'clock, the church bell rang, and the back door leading to the pastor's study opened and Judge Henry walked in. The people didn't notice the judge's entry at first, but stopped talking when Hank called for order.

"This hearing will come to order!" shouted Judge Henry. "Marshal, do you have a deputy present?"

"No, Your Honor, I don't"

"Then deputize two of these folks. Place them in the center of the aisle. If anyone gets disorderly, I want them removed at once. If they resist, take them to jail. Do you understand me?"

"Yes sir," replied Hank.

Hank chose his deputies, posted them where the judge had ordered and waited for the judge's instructions.

Raising Hank's report above his head, he looked to the men sitting before him. "I'd like to thank Marshal Goss for trying to get the truth about this altercation and the contents are disturbing. Assault? Battery? Intent to kill? The truth may be difficult to find, but I plan to do just that."

He looked at Amos and Randy and spoke, "Looks like you boys have had a round with a pack of wildcats and lost."

A slight laughter covered the room.

The judge slammed his gavel down against the table to silence the crowd.

Next, Judge Henry addressed John, "Wilson, I don't know what to make of you.

You're already in trouble, and here you are again. The two boys over there look like battered men, but you're as fit as can be. How is that?"

Hank raised his hand. "You Honor, Wilson was hit in his back and head with a chair, and it's a wonder he's still alive. He may look fit, but he still ain't got his right senses."

Judge Henry rubbed his face, then looked to the paper lying on his desk. "I've read the accusations, and Marshal, I want to hear from the plaintiffs first. Take this Bible, and swear them in, and because of their condition, they can give their accounts seated."

Hank swore Amos in first and took his seat next to John. Amos informed the judge of the difficulty to talk due to his broken jaw, but he would do his best.

"The other afternoon Ed, Randy Polk and me decided to meet up early at Happy Harry's to shoot pool and try our hands at cards," Amos mumbled through his teeth. "When we got there, Wilson was washing and shelving glasses. Well, while we were playing cards, Wilson started making remarks about Angie Wilcox, the preacher's daughter. He knew I was courting her, but I think he has a fancy for her. I told him she was a fine Christian girl and not to make such remarks. He said he kissed her when he was supposed to be painting the church."

"That's a lie, Amos Henderson," Angie called out.

"That's enough, young lady. Now, Mr. Henderson, continue."

"I told him I'd heard enough and for him to hush. He came over and pushed me out of my chair, so I got up and pushed him back. He then drew back and hit me. Last thing I remember was him saying he was gonna kill me. Then I was on the floor knocked cold as a flitter."

The judge sat quietly for a moment, rubbed his beard and looked to the other man. "Polk, are you able to talk?"

"Yes sir."

"Then proceed."

Polk recalled the same exact story and added, "Judge, when I saw Amos lying there, I didn't know if he was dead or alive. I know'd Wilson meant business. Wilson came around the table, picked up a pool stick and headed for Amos. I was scared, but I had to help my friend, so I jumped on his back and put a hold around his neck. He tried to get me off, but I hung on, until he swung me around so hard I sailed through the glass window. When I come to, I was cut to pieces and covered in blood. If it hadn't been for Ed Johnson, Wilson would have killed both of us."

A surprised murmur sifted over the crowd.

"Where is this Ed Johnson now, Marshal?" asked the judge.

"As far as I know, he's left the state. There's a warrant for his arrest in our neighboring county, so he took off."

"Wait a minute, Marshal. Are you trying to taint these boys' statements, insinuating they are associated with a wanted criminal," interrupted Mr. Henderson.

"Just giving the facts, sir. That's all," answered Hank.

Judge Henry brought his gavel down hard. "Sit down, Mr. Henderson. One more remark, and you'll be out of here."

The room grew silent.

"Boys, do you have anything else to add?" the judge asked.

Both said no, and the judge turned his attention to John. "Now, Mr. Wilson, I've heard some strong damaging statements, but this is America, and you are innocent until proven guilty. You've heard what they've said, so it's time to tell your story."

After John was sworn in, he stood and straightened himself to face the judge.

The judge lowered his glasses. "Tell me this, Mr. Wilson? How do you plead to these charges? Innocent or guilty?"

As John looked at the judge, he suddenly had a flashback to that afternoon.

"Judge, I drew back and hit him as hard as I could. He slid over that table and crashed to the floor. Did I intend to hit him? I certainly did, but I don't think I intended to kill him."

The crowd became livid with the emotion John displayed. Hank grabbed John's arm. "Judge! I need to talk to John. You know, he ain't just right in his thinking. We need a few minutes, sir."

"You got fifteen minutes, and I want this room cleared except for those involved with the case!"

Confident that John would be convicted, Mr. Henderson and his wife strolled out of the church.

Amos smiled at Randy. "This thing's over. Wilson just sentenced himself and made himself a fool."

Hank spent the next fifteen minutes preparing John for his plea. "Son, you need to plead innocent. If you say you are guilty, the judge will automatically sentence you. If you maintain your innocence, you can at least defend yourself," the marshal said.

The judge allowed the spectators to return and called the hearing to order. "Mr. Wilson, how do you plead?"

"Your Honor, I'm innocent of the charges," replied John.

"Then have your say, Mr. Wilson."

John stood thinking as hard as he could, but could not remember what happened. Minutes passed, and the judge became impatient.

"Mr. Wilson, did you hear me?"

John turned to the judge. "Your Honor, I don't know what happened. All I know is that I was angry, and I did hit Amos," he said. "Could I do those things they said? I really just don't know."

Hank shook his head, realizing that John was destroying any chance he had.

The judge paused. "Wilson, this is a serious problem. If found guilty, your sentence could be ten years in the state penitentiary. Choose your words carefully."

Hank got up and stated, "Judge, with his mental condition, he can't defend himself. There's got to be another way to conduct this hearing."

"Marshal, I've served this bench over twenty years. I go by the book and draw from my experiences. Now, there were three men in there and only three witnesses. You've heard them. Those two gave the same story, and the accused stated he intended to hit Mr. Henderson. I'm retiring to the study, and when I return, I will have a verdict."

The sanctuary was unusually quiet while the people waited. The stillness of the afternoon seemed to suck the air from the church like a vacuum. Even Pastor Wilcox was finding it hard to breath and noticed something unusual seemed to be happening.

***

Doc, crossing his arms on the desk to rest, reached down with one arm to pull out his pocket watch. "Twelve thirty," he mumbled, not hearing the door ease open. "It's about over by now."

Feeling a cold breeze cross his body, Doc looked up to see Wally standing just inside the door and at military attention. His first thought was to ignore him and hope he would leave, but the sense of helplessness and loneliness dictated differently.

"Come on in and shut the door," Doc said, motioning to the boy.

Not an eye blinked nor a muscle moved as Wally stood there.

"Wally, I said to come on in."

"General Wilson got hurt. It was a big battle! Three cannons was a-shooting at him," Wally exclaimed, getting more excited with each statement.

How does the boy ever come up with such nonsense? Doc shook his head and decided to play along. "You say Wilson is fighting the Yanks again?"

"Big fight! The general was fighting hard, and I was there to mop up. One of them cannons got 'em," added Wally.

"I guess you were shooting one of those muskets, weren't you, Wally?"

Wally frowned. "No sir, I was armed with a mop. The general is hurt. You need to go fix him up." With that Wally saluted, pushed the door open and ran away.

Doc shook his head and marveled at such a ridiculous story. *What in the world was he trying to tell me?* The words Wally had spoken began to play across his mind. Wilson was hurt in a big fight, and the three cannons could mean three men were involved. Wally was there but was armed with a mop. Doc jumped up, slammed his fist against the table and ran from the jail.

***

The judge would soon be returning with his verdict, so the spectators sat anxiously quiet. The judge walked in, headed to his desk and took a seat. "This has not been an easy decision for me," he said, adjusting his glasses. "Mr. Wilson, you may stand."

Hank gritted his teeth while Angie clasped her father's arm. The crowd held its breath.

"Sir, you are already serving a year's sentence for participating in a crime, and with no evidence in your defense, I have no other alternative but to sentence you -"

"Hold up!" shouted a voice from the back. "There was another witness to the fight," shouted Doc, hurrying down the aisle.

Surprised, Amos looked at Randy and then back to his father.

A rumble of talk filled the room, and once again the judge called for order.

"You may approach the bench, sir," ordered the judge, hoping the man could shed some light on this case.

"I'm Doctor Jackson, the local physician. I believe there is another witness, and if you'll give me a few minutes, I think I can get him here."

"You believe or do you know, doctor? There is a difference."

"Your Honor, I'll stake my reputation on it. There is a witness."

The judge looked at his watch. "You've got thirty minutes, and that's it."

Doc smiled at Hank. "Come on, we've got work to do."

Concerned, Amos turned to his father. "I thought Ed was gone."

"He is gone. He should be in New Orleans by now," explained his father. "I don't know what's going on here, but no need to worry. Nothing anyone can do at this point."

Doc hurried Hank out and headed to Wally's small two-roomed house located on the northern edge of Wickliffe. A swirl of smoke floated from the chimney, and clothes hung on a line beside the house. The rackety porch made both men step cautiously to avoid falling through. Hank tapped lightly on the door, and footsteps inside were heard. A frail woman cracked the door and peeked out.

"What you want, Marshal?" she asked through the small opening.

Hank took his hat off and placed it politely under his arm. "Ma'am, this is Doctor Jackson."

"I know who he is. What do you want?"

"Ma'am, we need to talk to Wally."

"Wally! What'd he do now?" she asked.

"Ma'am, there's a man named John Wilson who's in trouble, and we don't think he did what they say. We think Wally might have seen or heard something that could help clear him."

"You talking about General Wilson?"

"Yes ma'am, we are."

"Then you best come in," said Mrs. Jeffcoats, pulling the door open.

For the next few minutes, Doc told her all Wally had said and that Wally might be the only one who could help.

"Gentlemen, my boy lives in his own world. Some say he's touched, but he has more sense than most give credit. I'm not sure if he'll even speak at court because he don't like crowds, but if he does, you'll have to listen carefully and translate his thinking. Now, for Mr. Wilson, the boy talks about him all the time. He's like a hero to him and shows Wally respect and kindness. Wally ain't used to that."

Doc looked at his watch. "Where can we find him?"

"He's likely to be out back behind the chicken house in the big old chinaberry tree. Most likely, he'll be sitting up on a limb doing his bird-calling."

They found Wally exactly where his mother said with his hands cupped together blowing between his thumbs making the sound of a dove.

"Afternoon, Wally," the marshal called. "If you will, I'd like you to go downtown with me."

Wally climbed a little higher in the tree and kept on blowing his fist. "I ain't going nowhere," he mumbled.

Hank tried to coax him down, but Wally wouldn't budge.

"Wait a minute, Hank. You're going at it wrong."

Doc came to attention at the base of the tree and called, "Private Wally! I've got a mission for you, and if we don't get this message to General Judge soon, General Wilson might not make it. He may be imprisoned or could die. That's an order, Private."

Wally immediately jumped to the ground. He came to attention and saluted. "Reporting for duty, sir!" he exclaimed. "Where am I going?"

"Private, we got to hurry. The battle is raging over at the church. We got to get there fast," explained Doc.

Hank rolled his eyes in wonder. "Doc, how in tarnations did you think of that?"

Doc patted him on the back and smiled. "Didn't you listen to his mother? It's all in translation. Now come on, we got ten minutes."

As the group approached the church, Wally stopped and wouldn't budge. "Can't go in there. Too many Yanks."

Doc replied, "Private, battle is hard. Your general is in there wounded. You're the only one who can save him. Corporal Goss and I will be going with you, and both of our muskets are loaded. You got to be brave."

With that, Wally climbed the church steps.

The door squeaked open, and the people looked to see who had entered. Many of the women and men covered their mouths as they whispered to their neighbors while others just laughed openly.

Amos nudged Randy. "Is that their witness? This will be a circus before it's over."

Because of all the whispering, Wally once again balked. Doc could not get him to move. Finally, Doc said, "Wally, close your eyes. I'm going to lead you to your duty." Doc led Wally to the front. Terrified and shaking, Wally faced the judge.

John nudged Hank who was standing close by.

"What's he doing here?"

"Sh...," whispered Hank. "He's your witness."

John tugged on him again. "Can't you see how scared he is? He won't talk before this group."

"Is this your witness?" asked the judge.

"Yes sir, Your Honor. This is Wally Jeffcoats."

Laughter rippled across the room. Wally cringed at the sound.

Tired, the judge took a breath and said, "Well, swear him in, and let him tell his tale."

"He ain't got no tale to tell, Judge. The boy's touched. Can't you see he ain't got no sense." A man in the back laughed.

The judge adjusted his glasses and pointed to the man who had spoken. "Remove that man, and arrest him."

The judge stood up and stated, "In our Declaration of Independence, it states that all men are created equal, and that means this man standing before me has got the same rights as the rest of you. Now, Marshal, I want to hear what Mr. Jeffcoats has to say."

Wally hands began to tremble and he jerked his head in a rapid fashion then just closed his eyes.

"Mr. Jeffcoats, have you something to share with us?" questioned the judge.

Minutes passes with Wally saying nothing.

Amos whispered to his father, "How much better can it get?"

The judge motioned to Hank to approach the bench. "Are you trying to embarrass me?"

"No, Your Honor," answered Hank.

John motioned to Doc and after the two talked, Doc asked to approach the bench and asked if he could question Wally. The judge consented but informed him this was their last chance.

Doc took two chairs and placed them facing each other. He asked the judge to take a seat next to John. Reluctantly, the judge agreed. Doc then placed Wally in the seat with his back to the crowd, and he sat facing Wally and the people. Doc asked for complete silence. After a moment of silence, Doc leaned close to Wally.

"Private Wally, do you ever work to earn money?"

Wally twisted his head and thought. "Wally works. Wally can work hard."

"Have you ever worked at Happy Harry's?"

"Sometimes. Wally works there," he mumbled.

"What do you do there?"

"I mop the floor. Wally knows how to mop good."

"Were you there when the big fight broke out?"

Wally began to fling his hands and glanced back at Amos and Randy. His eyes widened and his breathing became rapid. "Don't like fights. Wally don't like fights."

"Did you see a fight at Happy's?" Doc probed.

"Wally was mopping fast, trying to get my job done, but them boys kept talking ugly to General Wilson and started spitting 'bacco juice all over the floor. They spit faster than Wally can mop."

"What happened next, Private?"

Tears began to roll down Wally's face. "Wally got in a hurry and knocked that man's glass to the floor. It broke all up."

"Whose cup was it?"

Wiping the tears from his face with the sleeve of his shirt, he turned and pointed to Amos.

"Judge, this has gone too far. They're baiting the boy," shouted Mr. Henderson.

The judge spoke to the deputy, "Take Mr. Henderson out. I've warned him."

The people were amazed that Mr. Henderson was being escorted from the hearing.

When Wally settled down after the outburst, Doc directed his attention back to the fight.

"What happened next, Private?"

"When Wally bent down to pick up the glass, he kicked me to the floor. They laughed and called me names."

"Who kicked you, Private?"

"The one with that tie around his head. He kicked Wally hard. That's when General Wilson saved me. He reached down to help me up, and he got kicked down like me. He cut his hand bad, and it was bleeding."

"What then, Private? Was that all?"

"The general said they ought to be ashamed and that the general had enough. He hit the man over there and knocked him over the table. That other man with them sheets all over his body jumped on the general's back and tried to hurt the general. It didn't work. The general chunked him through the window."

"Did the general get hurt?"

"I told you, he cut his hand. Didn't you listen?"

A muffled laughter was heard as people tried not to upset the judge.

"There was another man there. He hit the general with a chair and ran out the back. The general was dead. I mean, I thought the general was dead."

"What did Private Wally do then?" asked Doc.

"Everybody looked dead. Wally was scared. Wally was sad. My general was gone. I ran outside and hid."

"What about your pay? When did Harry pay you?"

"He paid me before I mopped. My dollar was in my pocket. They weren't gonna steal my dollar."

The courtroom was completely silent as Doc sat smiling at what Wally had revealed.

"Is the owner of the saloon present?" the judge asked.

"Yes sir," came a voice. "I'm here. Harry Stamper's my name."

"Marshal, swear him in," ordered the judge.

After swearing Harry in, the judge asked, "Does Mr. Jeffcoats work for you?"

"Yes sir, he does at times," answered Harry.

"Was he employed the afternoon of the fight, although you were not present?"

Harry hesitated.

"Mr. Stamper, you have a problem, sir?" asked the judge.

"I just don't remember, Your Honor. There was so much going on that day."

A man in the back raised his hand. "May I speak, Your Honor?"

"Granted. Speak."

"I'm Tim Russell. I own the general store here in town, and about an hour after the fight, Wally came in upset and laid a dollar on my counter. I asked him where he got it, and he told me he was doing some mopping at Happy's. He wanted it to go on his mother's account."

The judge adjusted his glasses and frowned down at Harry.

"I'm going to ask you one more time, and if you lie to me, not only will you face time in jail, but I'll do everything in my power to shut your place down. Did Mr. Jeffcoats work for you on the day of the fight?"

Harry dropped his head. "Yes sir, he worked for me, and I did pay him a dollar."

Knowing the hearing had turned against them, Amos raised his hand.

"Your Honor, what does all this really mean? What if Wally was working there that day? It's still two men's word against a boy we know ain't just right," stated Amos.

"I'm going to take a few minutes, and when I come back, I'll tell you what this means," stated the judge, leaving the courtroom.

The judge soon returned and motioned for Hank to approach the bench. "Marshal, I'm going to allow Mr. Henderson to return to the courtroom. I want him to hear what I've got to say."

When Mr. Henderson had taken a seat, the judge called the room to order.

"Ladies and Gentlemen, this has been an unusual and frustrating case. The charge was assault with intent to kill plus damages," stated the judge. "Most disturbing is the deception I've heard today. First, this charge should've never been brought before me. In all my years on the bench, I've never been so misled. I almost sentenced an innocent man to the penitentiary."

The judge turned to face the plaintiffs and spoke, "Mr. Henderson and Mr. Polk, you stated Mr. Wilson initiated the fight and intended to kill you."

The judge faced the people. "The only witness for the accused was a boy who has some mental difficulties. I know you may be thinking we can't take his word, but in my years on this earth, I've met a lot of Wallys. They may not know how to express themselves, and they are definitely different, but I'll tell you something, I've never heard one tell a lie."

Next, the judge looked at John. "So, Mr. Wilson, I'm dropping the charges against you."

A loud applause erupted as the spectators realized the truth and felt justice had been served.

The judge asked for order and continued, "Now, Mr. Henderson and Mr. Polk, you should be ashamed of how you treated Mr. Jeffcoats, and I admire Mr. Wilson for defending the boy's dignity. However, you two have also lied and misled me and the people of this community, and for this I am sentencing each of you to thirty days in jail and a one hundred dollar fine. Since Mr. Wilson is already occupying the jail, I'm dropping the jail time, but you will be fined and will do 30 days of community service."

"That's outrageous," shouted Mr. Henderson, rising from his seat.

"I think you're right, Mr. Henderson. The fine will be one hundred and fifty dollars each. Speak again, and I can continue the increase," stated the judge.

"Now, for you, Mr. Wilson, in reparation of the damage done, I'm fining you twenty dollars. Do you have that kind of money?"

"No, Your Honor. I don't have any money."

"Your Honor, I'd like to pay that twenty dollars for Mr. Wilson," spoke a thin elderly woman from the back of the room.

"You don't have that kind of money to spend, Mrs. Jeffcoats," Hank softly said as she walked past him.

Taking a small pouch from her pocket, she handed the judge two ten-dollar gold pieces.

"Sir, I appreciate how Mr. Wilson stood up for my boy. It's the first time anyone around here has shown Wally any respect. We need more like him on this earth."

The courtroom was silent, contemplating their own behavior toward Wally.

The judge stated, "This trial is now over. The verdict is complete, and the sentencing is just."

Doc and Hank shook John's hand, elated over the verdict and the relief it brought. John looked back to thank the pastor and Angie for their support and found Angie instead holding out her arms to him. John hugged her and put his arm around her shoulder.

Amos who had been talking to his parents, left and walked to Angie. He grabbed her arm and snarled, "Well, I see where your sentiment lies. If you want to socialize with trash, that's your right, but you won't see no more of me."

"I suggest you take your hand off my daughter, and I wouldn't allow you to see my daughter anyway. You need to take a good hard look at yourself and ask the Lord to forgive you," advised the pastor.

As the courtroom cleared, John found Wally. He was alone and in his own world not realizing his impact on justice. John placed his arms around him as he hugged and thanked him.

Wally smiled. "General, did we win the battle?"

"Private, you won this battle, not me."

Late that night, John lay on his bunk under the full November moon, knowing the Lord's hand had prevailed.

11

Letting Go of the Past

And this is my prayer that your love may abound more and more in knowledge and depth of insight, so that you may be able to discern what is best.
—Philippians 1:9-10a

Since the trial had been prolonged, Judge Henry decided to stay for the night and leave early the next morning. After a good night's rest at a local boarding house, he decided to talk with the marshal before leaving town. He quickly dressed and ate breakfast then walked down the street to the jail. He tapped on the door and listened for a response.

"It's open," came a voice from inside.

"Judge Henry, this is a surprise," Hank exclaimed as the judge walked in the door.

"Come on in," Hank said, pulling a chair out from behind his desk. "Thought you'd be long gone by now."

The judge removed his hat, sat down and placed his hat on his lap. "I thought I needed to talk with you before I left."

"What about?" asked Hank puzzled. "I thought all went quiet well."

"Quiet well you say? Marshal, you did a lot of things right, and you seem to have your heart in the right place, but you made a big mistake."

Hank edged to the front of his chair and dreaded what he knew was coming.

"Marshal, the Wilson boy was in your custody, wasn't he? That means he was your total responsibility at all times. What you did to him was like putting a fat worm on a hook and then dangling him over a pool of hungry fish. You left that boy totally unsupervised. If it hadn't been for Wally Jeffcoats, Wilson would be facing a lengthy prison term in Louisville, and you know what, it would have been your fault."

Hank dropped his head, knowing all along the mistake he had made. He sat for a moment, then reached over and started removing the marshal's badge pinned to his shirt pocket.

Before he had it completely detached, Judge Henry pushed Hank's hand away and pinned the badge on again. "That's not necessary," he said. "I think you are a good marshal, and a good marshal learns from his mistakes. I should know. I've made plenty."

When the judge left, Hank pondered the error that could have sent an innocent man to prison. Except for the grace of God and His miracles and the testimony of Wally, his mistake could have cost John his freedom. For the first time, Hank realized that God does take care of his children when his children pray. Hank bowed his head and whispered, "Thank you, Lord, for loving me and John enough to bring about the events of yesterday. Help me to always seek your will, dear Lord. Please forgive me for all the sins and wrongs I have done, and stay with me and in my heart each day. Thanks most of all for your precious Son who gave all for me."

For the next several days, Doctor Jackson continued to monitor John while he slept, but those who listened had little to report. His dreams were either no longer occurring or John was no longer talking as he dreamed. Doc decided that he would begin investigating the stories John had shared with him and Hank. This morning, he asked Hank to step outside so that they could talk without John hearing them.

"It's cold out here, Doc," Hank said, pulling the front on his coat closer to his body. "Can we make this fast?"

"John's been telling us all kinds of things that happened to him down in Mississippi and about his family, and I need to know if the stories are real," said Doc.

"Well, why don't you send a wire to his hometown and try to locate someone who knows the boy?" stated Hank, packing his pipe for a smoke.

"I would, but in all his tales, he doesn't tell me directly where he lives. All I know is he lives somewhere in South Mississippi."

"Doc, the other day, he got to talking about Camp Douglas and shared some rough tales about a Colonel Sweet who made life hard on them. Sweet cut their rations to almost nothing, and when they died, he had the bodies thrown in Lake Michigan. Yanks called their bodies, catfish bait. John talked about a tall sawhorse that Sweet made men straddle until they passed out. Sweet even had his soldiers tie buckets of sand to their legs to make it more painful. John said they called it riding the mule and that some of the prisoners were lame for life and others were crippled for quite some time. I can't believe that could happen."

"Hank, wasn't Camp Douglas somewhere near Chicago?"

"Yeah, from what I know, it was located southeast of Chicago, right in town. The property was owned by Senator Douglas and was given to the government. Why?"

Doc slapped his leg and jumped up. "Because one of my good friends in medical school has a practice up there, and they do have wire service. I may not be able to get anything out from Mississippi, but ole Doc here can tap into the Chicago line, and we will get some kind of answer."

Hank continued to hire John out, but after the talk with Judge Henry, he was careful. He made sure that John was supervised by reputable people at all times. With winter approaching, there were fewer requests for labor, and Hank thought about stopping the whole program, but the town needed the money. Hank's one delight was that he could easily beat John at checkers, although lately John's improvement was beginning to test his skill.

The cold weather brought winter rains that kept people confined to the warmth of their homes. Fewer visitors dropped by the jail to visit except for Doc who made time every day to converse with John. He found John to be educated and well-read. Their conversations would run from politics, Greek philosophy, and flaws in the American court system to training and racing horses. Another daily visitor was Wally, and since the trial, even Hank welcomed his visits.

With each passing day, John became more restless. As long as people brought books for him to read, he could tolerate the long days. The bright spot of his week was Sunday services with his newly acquired church family. Many of them were becoming close friends, but of them all, he enjoyed the time with Pastor Wilcox and Angie the most. Hank would drive him to church, sit with him during the service, but once it ended, he would turn John over to Parson Wilcox for the afternoon.

On such an afternoon, John was having dinner with Parson Wilcox and Angie. Following the meal, the three of them discussed the sermon delivered that day and how it should be applied to daily life. A light rain gradually turned to sleet, and the parson put several pieces of oak wood into the stove and returned to the table.

"It's gonna get nasty tonight. Old man winter is slipping up on us," said the pastor, retuning to his seat. He asked John and Angie, "What did you think of my sermon today?" His message that morning from the Old Testament was Hannah's dedication of her son Samuel to the Lord at an early age.

"Papa, I'm not sure I could give my son up at an early age and see him just every once in a while. That had to be a great sacrifice," Angie stated.

"What about you, John? What's your thinking about what Hannah did?"

"First, she prayed many years for a son, and she never gave up hope. That shows the power and faith in persistent prayer, and once she conceived, the glory of his birth was overwhelming. As much as she wanted to rear the child to manhood, she felt that God had finally listened to her yearnings, and the greatest thing she could give back to Him was Samuel. The boy Samuel grew into the prophet Samuel, truly a man of God, and until his death, he was the religious leader of Israel."

The parson nodded his head in approval. "I should have let you preach today. Tell me, John, what is your religious background, if you don't mind sharing it with me?"

Bits and pieces of John's prior life were returning to him, but names seem to evade him.

"Parson, I wish I could answer that. I think my grandfather on my mother's side was a minister of some kind. It seems like he traveled around preaching. Does that make sense?"

"Those preachers are called circuit riders or circuit preachers."

"I also envision a white clapboard church with a tall belled steeple resting on a crown of a hill. There's always someone waiting on its steps waving to me, and when I read the Word, a warm feeling comes over me, and I have a deep sense of hope in myself and in humanity and that God does reign on high."

"Amen, John Wilson, you answered my question after all."

A little later that afternoon, one of the parson's closest friends dropped by for a visit. Directing him to the parlor up front, the parson left the warmth of the kitchen to John and Angie. The two sat silently for a few moments, a little shy because of the time alone. The sleet was now turning to snow as it gently floated to the ground speckled with drops of sleet.

"We don't see much of this in South Mississippi," John said, walking over to the window. "I wonder if I still have a family down there?"

"I'm sure you do. At least, I hope so." Angie remembered John's hug and protective arm after the trial and asked, "John about the other day?"

"We were both excited over the outcome of the hearing, and I was just thanking you for standing by me during the trial," John said, returning to his chair.

Angie flushed. "John, I've only been that close to one other boy. In fact, I've never really been kissed before."

"You're only sixteen. I can understand that."

"You know I'm almost seventeen. Have you kissed many girls?"

John laughed. "I surely hope so if it is as pleasurable as the hug the other day." Angie was relieved that he had wanted to hug her and sat a little closer to him.

"John, you really have grown special to me," Angie said shyly.

"Angie, I sure would like to kiss you. Would it be all right?" John asked.

Angie leaned in closer, and John touched her lips tenderly.

When they parted, John spoke his heart, "I don't really know who I am, and I probably shouldn't have done that. For all I know, I could be engaged or have a wife. I promise I won't ask you again until I know the truth."

Angie appreciated his honesty, but she hoped to be in his future. The more time she spent with John, the more she wanted to be near him. Even though she wasn't sure, she felt she could be falling in love with him.

Later that afternoon, the conversation turned to the life John had experienced at Wickliffe and what the future held for him.

"John, when you're free to go, what will you do?" Angie asked. "You know you could stay here. Wickliffe is a nice place, and you seem to be good at a lot of different tasks. You could make a good life for yourself here."

John got up from where he was sitting and walked to the warmth of the stove.

"Angie, I can't make any decisions until the Lord gives me back my memory. If I've got family in Mississippi, I'll have to go to them. Sometimes, I see faces of people that I think I know, and it's not just in my dreams. I want to know what my life used to be like. I hope you can understand that."

"Do you think you know someone named Rebecca?" Angie cautiously asked, afraid of what the answer might be.

John shook his head. "I just see faces. Tthat's all."

The clock back in the parlor struck five, and a knock on the door was heard.

"Hank's here. Thank you for the afternoon," John said, getting up to retrieve his coat and hat. "I hope to see you next Sunday."

As John left, Angie's heart was heavy with so many emotions. She worried that her heart would be broken when John remembered his past. Angie struggled with these thoughts for a while, but eventually, she realized that God knew what was best for her and John and that she must trust only God with her heart.

***

One Sunday afternoon, when John was spending time at the Wilcox's, Hank decided to take a much needed nap, but just as he had dozed off to sleep, a loud rap on the door awakened him, "Hank, you home?"

Hank's hounds were alive with yips and yaps.

"Humph," he grunted. "What'd you say?"

"Hank, it's me Doc Jackson."

Hank threw the quilt off, pulled up his suspenders and ventured to the door in his sock feet.

He looked out at the snow that was whirling and faintly covering the ground and then recognized Doc amidst the gathering snow.

"Doc, you must be out of your mind to be out there roaming around," he muttered, rubbing his sleepy eyes. "Come on in. I'll make us some fresh coffee."

Hank pointed Doc to a comfortable chair and headed to the kitchen to brew some coffee.

After Hank had settled down again, but this time, with a fresh cup of coffee for them both, Doc began sharing the meaning of the Sunday visit.

"Didn't mean to interrupt your Sunday nap, but I just got something interesting in the mail. Thought I'd share it with you," Doc said, pulling a letter from his pocket. "You know I said I was going to wire Chicago about John and Camp Douglas. Well, we don't have wire service around here, so I wrote a letter." Hank's eyes were beginning to close as he sat comfortably still. "Hank! Wake up and listen."

Hank's eyes shot open. "I ain't sleeping. You got a telegram from Chicago."

"No, I got a letter. Now listen to me," barked Doc.

"You remember me talking about the stories John was telling us about Camp Douglas? Well, my friend Dr. Joseph Miller wrote me back. Now listen, Hank."

"I'm listening."

"I'm going to skip the introductions and get down to the specifics. Now here it is."

Everything you related to me concerning the camp was accurate but even worse. I've never seen men treated as the Union generals in command treated those prisoners, and Colonel Sweet was the cruelest. The stench from the compound was almost unbearable, and when the winds came off the lake and into the city, we knew the nickname Camp Extermination was accurate. You wouldn't believe the filth that existed inside that compound. As far as reporting deaths, we know that the officers sent in reports highly deflated. Those boys died by the thousands, and some were even shot for sport by the guards. If any Southern soldier of color approached, they were shot at the camp's gate; it was nothing short of murder. As for Sweet, if the South had won the war, he would have been executed just like I heard was done to the commander down at the Andersonville Prison in Georgia. If you need more information, there's plenty more to tell.

"What do you think about that, Hank?"

Hank, now wide-awake, rubbed his beard and nodded. "Looks like our boy is getting his senses back. We gonna have to start taking him more seriously."

"More than that, Hank, he mentioned the name Sweet. That's the first time he's clearly identified a person by name when he wasn't asleep. The others he's mentioned, he doesn't seem sure about when he's awake. Like you said, it appears the boy is coming back."

***

As the sun set, a cold chill filled the air. Frank Sr. rode up to the steps of his house, and Andrew, one of his stable men, walked out to welcome Frank home. He took his mount to the barn to be brushed down and stabled. Suzanne went to the window to see who had arrived and was surprised to see her father. He had been on a business trip up north to Philadelphia, Pennsylvania, and was not expected until the end of the week. Suzanne bounded down the steps when she heard him whistling a tune, which was even more surprising. Usually, Frank Sr. was quiet, moody and often obnoxious. As much as she hated to confess it, the bottle seemed to bring out the best in him. Rarely did he show such joy without it.

"How's my beautiful daughter?" Frank said, closing the door. "Come here, let me give you a hug."

After embracing, the two walked to the kitchen where supper was being prepared. Lula, one of their cooks, was in the process of placing a tasty breakfast of fried ham, scrambled eggs, grits, buttered browned biscuits, blackberry jelly and steaming hot coffee on the table. What normally was considered breakfast became, on a cold night in the South, a most welcome meal.

As Frank was pouring himself a cup of coffee, Judith entered.

"Well, look who's here. You got back early," she said, giving him a hug. "I heard some whistling outside. Could that have been you?"

"It was none other than me, my darling, and I couldn't wait to get home to you all," answered Frank, pulling the chair out for his wife and then assisting Suzanne.

"Where's Frankie?"

"He's gone to Meridian for the evening," Suzanne answered.

Frank shook his head. "The boy needs to be careful. It ain't the safest place to be at night."

After supper, the three retired to the parlor, and Frank relayed his good fortune in Philadelphia. He shared the development of the railways in the East and told how he met with a group of businessmen to discuss the new rail line that would run across the western plains and connect a line from the Pacific, joining East to West, and that enormous profits for him were inevitable.

"Judith, you will not believe what the government is offering folks investing in the new railroad. Not only will I earn stockholder money, but Washington is giving large areas of land on both sides of the tracks to investors. It's like striking pure gold."

Judith smiled to her husband. "How much did you put into it?"

"Not much. About twenty thousand for now. If things go like I think, I'll add more later."

Judith raised her eyebrows. "Twenty thousand. That's a nice sum. I'm glad we've got it."

"Father, I didn't know we had that much money," said Suzanne.

"Darling, you don't have any idea of my assets. Twenty thousand is just spending money for me."

Frank had become extremely wealthy by hiding his money during the war. Frank knew the war was approaching, so he cashed all his bank notes and currency and exchanged it for gold that he in turn hid on his premises. When the war ended and the South's economy was in shambles, those who had money other than confederate could purchase land and goods at a deflated price and rapidly increased their earnings. Not only had Frank accumulated an enormous amount of wealth, but Judith's father who ran a sugarcane plantation down in Louisiana had even more.

Lighting his pipe, Frank remembered the letter in his pocket and pulled it out to give to his wife. Judith recognized her father's handwriting and opened the letter.

"Papére Bourdeau wants us to come down for the sugar festival next week. He wants me to tell you, Suzanne, that some handsome Cajun boys are already asking to have dances with you at the low country boil. He is going to reserve a suite for us in New Orleans at his hotel, and he will leave some money for shopping."

"Well, Suzanne, you just got home. You probably won't want to go back this soon," joked Judith, winking at her husband.

"Don't want to go back! You've got to be kidding. I would love to go back, and you know how I love to shop. I wish I could live there. I love Papére's plantation, and I love New Orleans even more. I think I'll start packing right now!" exclaimed Suzanne.

"Frank, do you think you can go with us?" asked Judith.

"No, I'm tired of traveling. I'll be staying here. I do think it would be good for Frankie to go. He hasn't seen his grandfather in a spell. One of these days, he'll be running the place and needs to learn the business."

The two sat quietly for a few moments, and then a smile crossed Judith's face. "Frank, I do think Frankie should go with Suzanne and me, and I think I have a proposition for that young man that should prove most interesting."

As the sun was breaking the eastern horizon, Frankie rode up; and after releasing his horse, he tipped up the stairs to his bedroom, trying not to disturb anyone. Judith heard him and got out of bed. She saw Frankie's horse still saddled, lazily grazing on the front terrace.

"Will that boy ever become responsible?" she whispered to herself.

"What'd he do now?" muttered Frank.

"I don't know. His horse is out front, still saddled and roaming."

"Well, at least he's home."

"Home, is that all you have to say? What about responsibility?" Judith exclaimed.

"Judith, the boy just turned nineteen. What do you expect?"

"It's time he became a man. When my Papa was Frankie's age, he was married with a child on the way and farming his own five hundred acres," exclaimed Judith, walking out of the room. "I'm gonna have a talk with the boy."

"No you ain't! You let him get his sleep first," Frank sternly stated. "And for your Papére Bourdeau, I'm tired of hearing about his exploits because his life was pretty easy with his inheritance. I had to work for mine. I might not have had much to call my own when I was his age, but my darling, as of this day, I believe I can buy and sell your papa."

Judith waited until midmorning to talk with Frankie. She found him partially wrapped in quilts, fully dressed and sleeping soundly. She could smell alcohol and cheap perfume and shook her head in disappointment.

"Time to wake up, son."

Frankie cracked one eye open, then closed it. "What time is it, Mama?"

"Time for you and me to have a talk."

Frankie turned over on his back, stuffed a pillow behind him and then looked down at himself and laughed. "These ain't my normal bed clothes, but I guess I got in a little late."

"You didn't take care of your horse. Your father and I were upset about that," Judith said, pushing his hair from his face. "Son, I don't like the things I'm seeing. It's time you took on some responsibility. At least take care of your horse."

"Well, that's what our stable men are for, Mama."

"Frankie, I want to know something. Are you interested in Rebecca, or is it just talk?"

Frankie threw his legs to the floor and sat on the edge of the bed, facing his mother. "She's everything a man could want. I'd be a fool not to pursue her."

"Then why do you go out with those women in Meridian?"

Frank twisted his neck to loosen it up. "Look at it like this. I'm nineteen and like to socialize with pretty women, and I don't even know if Rebecca cares about me. You talk like I should marry the woman."

"Would you?" Judith asked.

"Sure I would, if I knew she cared for me and had John Wilson out of her mind. You better believe I would."

"Now, Frankie, think about what I've told you. Be a gentleman, polite and caring, and let her feel that you are sincerely interested in her welfare. Where has that gotten you?"

Frankie stretched and thought for a moment. "She's seeing me socially and appears to enjoy my company," he said, realizing his mother's advice had achieved what he'd failed to do on his own.

"Alright, now you are ready for the next step. Your Papére Bourdeau wants us to come down for his sugar festival."

"Mama, I ain't going down because I don't care for the low country," Frankie mumbled.

"Hear me out, son. I want you to go with Suzanne and me, and I want to invite Rebecca to go with us. I think the only place she has ever been outside of this county is Meridian, and I want her to see the mansions of Natchez, the splendor of New Orleans and your grandfather's empire in the low country. I want her to see there is another world outside of Little Rock. One day, that sugarcane plantation will be yours, so you need to take an interest in the place. This trip will give you two a chance to spend quality time together."

Frankie rubbed his chin and nodded his head. "Mama, it sounds like you want me to buy the girl's love. I don't want her like that."

"Son, Rebecca is a fine young woman. I don't want you to buy her love, but I do want you to share what her life could be, if she gave you a chance. Don't you think it's important that she see who you are and where your life is headed?"

"It's probably a good idea, but I'm not sure she would go with us." Frankie said, giving his mother a good morning hug.

"Suzanne and I are headed to Walker's store today for a visit to invite Rebecca."

"That still don't mean she'll go," Frankie said.

"Darling, I know women. Believe me, she'll go."

When Rebecca heard Mrs. Olliver's plans, she was excited about the opportunity to see Natchez, New Orleans and sugarcane plantations. They would leave in two days and arrive in the bayou country the following week. Suzanne told Rebecca to pack for warmer weather.

After the Ollivers left, Rebecca was fascinated with the idea of venturing outside her small world. For two years, her life had been only work at her father's store, church and home. She couldn't wait to leave. All she had known was here in Little Rock where people lived on small farms with rustic dwellings. Rebecca's head spun with the images of mansions and luxury.

As she packed her clothing for the trip, Rebecca thought pensively of how her life had changed. Before the war, her plan was to marry the man she had loved all her life and have a home filled with children. Neatly folding her dresses, she could still not imagine life without him. She understood that memories of John would remain, but her life's dreams would have to change. She could not even, with God's help, hold on to the hope that John was alive; no, she must face her future and grab hold of it, and this trip would be her first step.

On Monday, the seventh of November, a carriage pulled up to the Walker's home. Rebecca walked to the front porch to greet the Ollivers. The sun had barely tipped the horizon, and the leaves were showing their fall colors. A cool breeze brushed across her face, tossing her auburn hair.

Suzanne waved from the carriage. "Are you ready for adventure?"

"I think I'm ready," Rebecca replied a little apprehensively. *Yes, this is the first step to a new beginning*, Rebecca thought.

While Sammy, one of the Olliver's stable men, picked up Rebecca's baggage and placed it on top, Frankie welcomed Rebecca and assisted her into the carriage. Dressed in a dark green skirt with a white-laced blouse, Rebecca's beauty was radiant. Clasping her around the waist, Frankie lifted her up the step and into the carriage. Just the touch of her body took his breath. Frankie directed her to the seat next to him and softly stared at her, amazed she had said yes and he would have a chance to steal her heart.

Judith smiled at Rebecca. "Darling, it is our pleasure to have you with us, and we are going to show you a world that most people around here could never imagine."

With a crack of a whip, the horses bolted forward; and with a swirl of dust, the carriage raced away. Rebecca leaned out of the window and waved to her parents who stood hand in hand and waved back.

"What do you think, Thomas?" asked Mrs. Walker.

"She may be our daughter, but as attractive as she is, she can have any man she wants, and what more could she desire than what the Ollivers have to offer."

"What about her love for John?"

"Well, he just don't exist anymore, does he? And if he did, what could he offer her in return? She would always be the wife of a farmer and only a step from the poorhouse. Yes ma'am, I hope she gives herself to that young man. Nothing would make me happier than a wedding."

After a two-hour ride, the carriage pulled up to the Newton station; and while Sammy unloaded and checked the luggage, Rebecca and the Ollivers were directed to the coach that would carry them westward as far as Vicksburg. At that point, they would take a boat to Natchez where they would spend two nights and then travel to New Orleans. Frankie escorted Rebecca to her seat next to a window where she could enjoy seeing the countryside, and he settled next to her.

As the train pulled from the station, Rebecca glanced back to Sammy who gave her a smile and waved. Her first ride on a train was amazing because of the speed. In a couple of hours, they had passed the towns of Forrest, Morton, Brandon and were approaching Jackson, the capital of Mississippi.

Rebecca nudged Frankie and said, "What will Jackson be like? Are there stately buildings like I've heard about in New Orleans?"

Frankie laughed. "No indeed. New Orleans is much larger. When this state was formed, the officials selected a place that would be near the center of the state and would have a waterway, the Pearl River, for transportation. The only stately building is the capital building itself, but the rest of Jackson is pretty primitive. There are few houses of grandeur, but most of the homes and businesses are rough-cut frame buildings, and the streets are not paved."

"You're teasing, Frankie. Certainly, our capital would be nice." said Rebecca.

At ten minutes before eleven that morning, the train pulled into the station at Jackson. Rebecca soon realized that everything Frankie had said was true. With an early morning rain, the streets were muddied and impassable. She saw several wagons that had sunk to their axles in the mire, and with the rain, the buildings appeared damp and dreary. The only bright spot was far up the street located at the top of a sloped hill where the capital building stood like a giant overseer with all of its tiny poverty stricken subjects below.

"I see what you mean," said Rebecca. "I expected more from our capital. Will Vicksburg be the same?"

"I'd say it is more stately than Jackson. It's an old river town that handles a lot of commerce. They have some fine buildings and homes there, and the main street is paved with bricks. It was really something before the Yankees took it. It has a lot of battle scars, and many of the businesses and homes are still in disrepair. It's too important of a port, so one day, I do believe, it will be restored to its former glory."

Rebecca marveled at Frankie's knowledge.

"How long will it take us to reach Vicksburg?" Rebecca asked.

"Once we get moving, I'd say about two hours, and then we'll be boarding a paddle boat for Natchez. We should be in Natchez by late afternoon. This will be our hardest day of travel. That's why we are spending two days in Natchez to rest."

Rebecca could hardly wait for what the next few days would bring. In one short day, she had traveled from the eastern part of the state to the Mississippi River; and now boarding the first boat in her life, she would reach Natchez as the sun was slipping beyond the horizon. Rebecca was also enjoying Frankie's company and the sincere attention he had given her. Perhaps Tim had been wrong about him.

12

Christmas Plans

If we say we have no sin, we deceive ourselves, and the truth is not in us. If we confess our sins, he is faithful and just to forgive us our sins and to cleanse us from all unrighteousness.
—1st John 1:8-9

A brisk November band of showers swept through the hill country of Southern Mississippi followed by a rush of cold northern air. The hardwood trees decorated in autumn shades of gold and brown were rustled by the blustery wind, which sent their leaves swirling up and down then finally settled them on the ground below. Winter was only days away.

Sister, wrapped in a snug woolen sweater, pulled the tail of her apron up and held it tightly with one hand at her waist. She began to fill the pouch with shelled corn for the chickens, then walking out to the yard beyond the house she began to call out to them, "Chick! Chick! Chick!"

Chickens flew from all directions as she vigorously threw grain to them. With a constant cackle and cluck, the birds fed in a frenzy. As she threw the last bit out, Sister shook the husk and pieces of corn from her dress, brushed her hands and walked back to the house. In her parents' bedroom, she found her mother sitting near the warmth of a fire, churning butter. It would be only minutes until they would be pouring out what was left of the buttermilk and would be dipping and scraping the butter from the churn. That night, Sarah would have a platter of large browned biscuits sliced in half, coated with fresh butter and complimented with thick molasses. A side of fried ham would cover at least half of a plate. The smell of freshly brewed coffee would permeate the air.

"It's cold out there, darling," commented Sarah as she churned away.

Sister removed her sweater and settled herself near the fire. "It's not that bad," she answered, holding her hands near the blazing fire. "I just hate feeding those devils. They have no manners at all. In fact, they remind me of the men folk at dinner."

"Well, Sister, I think men are usually just as hungry as those chickens. When you work as long and as hard as they do, I'd say they're might near starving."

While the fire popped and sizzled, Sister's thoughts traveled to the time when all her brothers were at home. There was always a disagreement or a good teasing, and their home was active with pranks, brotherly fights and lots of laughter. She received most of the teasing and had to endure it to keep from looking weak. As much as she resented their teasing, she would give anything in the world to experience it again.

Sarah looked at Sister's sad face and stopped what she was doing. "Sister, what's bothering you? You care to share it with me?"

Sister shook her head and spoke, "I was just thinking about my brothers and how much I miss them."

"I know, darling, but the Lord gives, and he takes away, and He has a plan that most times we don't understand until many years later. You'll always have your memories, so keep them close in your heart. And one day we'll all be reunited up in heaven. That will be a glorious time."

Sarah returned to her churning, and Sister sat, quietly thinking. "Mama, I want to ask you something."

Sarah glanced over the top of her glasses.

"Mother, I know James Earl has gone to be with the Lord and maybe Thomas is alive out there somewhere, but what about John? What's happened lately that you don't talk of him anymore? You said that you had visits from a heavenly being telling you that he was alive, but you never speak of that anymore."

Sarah's eyes twinkled, and a smile crossed her face as she reached for Sister's hand. "Darling, as I have said many times, the Lord works in strange and mysterious ways. His ways are not our ways. As I sit here, I tell you the truth, there are things that have happened to me I can't explain. To talk about it seems to cause the family trouble with the way people think of us, but I still pray and talk with the Lord. But, Sister, nothing has changed. Somewhere on this earth, there is no question in my mind that your brother is alive and will come home to us in due time. The time schedule is not in our hands. Now, I guess it is best that we keep this between you and me since everyone else can't handle what I know, but I do know, just as sure as you are sitting here with me, John will be with us too.

Sister squeezed her mother's hand. "I know that we'll see John in heaven one day. Isn't that really what you mean when you say John's alive?"

Sarah shook her head. "No, that's not what I feel. That's not what I mean at all."

"Then what are you saying?" questioned Sister.

"Darling, just keep the faith, pray and watch what wondrous things our God will do."

Sister thought about all her mother had said, and as hard as she wanted to believe that her brother was alive, doubt clustered her mind.

"Mama, I want to ask you one more thing."

"Go ahead, dear."

"It won't be too many weeks before Christmas. I wish we could celebrate like we once did, even if it's just a little bit, maybe by just reading the Christmas story. Do you think we can have a real Christmas this year?"

"It's left up to your father. The loss of the boys has crushed his heart. His spirit and faith have taken a beating. Christmas was always a glorious happy time for our family, and just the thought of it brings your father the memory of what we once enjoyed and lost. His heart has hardened, and he has to make peace with the Lord before we can truly have Christmas."

"Can I ask him about Christmas?" Sister spoke quietly.

Sarah looked out the window to where Lott and Toby were splitting firewood and throwing it onto a large pile that would then be brought and stacked on the front porch.

"I've seen some changes in your father recently. I don't know what has come over him, but something is happening."

"What do you think has happened?"

"Sister, I'm not sure. I asked him if anything was bothering him a while back, and he just said it was something he had to work out by himself. I knew he wasn't ready to share it with me. But, yes, I do think it's time we talked to him about wanting Christmas back in our home."

"Should I approach him or should you, Mother?"

"Darling, let's pray about it, and we'll just see what happens."

***

Everything Frankie had told Rebecca about Natchez was true. The city was one of the older ones of Mississippi, and resting on the banks of the Mississippi river, it flourished with commerce. Even though the war had done its damage, it still was prosperous. Bailed cotton was being brought in from the plantations and some still dotted the countryside. The rest of the days in Natchez went by quickly as Rebecca and the Ollivers scurried about, visiting local shops and enjoying some of the best food the area had to offer, but the most astonishing part was the tour of some of the local mansions owned by friends of the Ollivers. In the Little Rock community, the elegance of the Olliver home set the standard for the area, but here in Natchez, it would be the norm. As they left the last mansion they would visit, Judith asked, "Rebecca, what do you think about Natchez?"

Rebecca smiled. "I've never seen anything like it. The grandeur of the homes is almost unbelievable, and there are so many of them. It looks like the war never touched this place, and I thought Meridian was a busy city, but it's nothing like this. Thank you for inviting me to come."

Suzanne laughed. "Just wait until we get to New Orleans and to grandfather's place. You've seen nothing yet."

"I can't imagine anything more impressive than what I've already seen," said Rebecca. "Is there anything about Natchez I don't know?"

Frankie laughed. "Oh yes. Young ladies like you and my sister would probably feel a little uncomfortable in Natchez below the hill or what is called Lower Natchez."

Suzanne raised her eyebrows then spoke to Rebecca, "He means that there are places in New Orleans that one has to be careful, but just being in Lower Natchez is dangerous."

"How is it dangerous, Suzanne?" questioned Rebecca.

Frankie cleared his throat. "There's a lot of gambling and drinking allowed which brings fights and killings. Even the law is hesitant to venture down after dark. One of the most renowned fights that ever took place in Lower Natchez was between the famous Jim Bowie and another man. Word is that Bowie killed the man with only his knife."

"I've heard tell of Bowie," Rebecca said.

"And then, of course, there are the ladies of the night," added Frankie.

"Frankie, that's enough about Lower Natchez," Judith said, trying to change the subject.

Frankie was well acquainted with these establishments and had spent numerous nights in them. When traveling with his father, he was often left on his own, and Lower Natchez was a temptation too enticing for a young man to ignore.

Judith encouraged all to retire early when they reached the hotel.

Suzanne, who was rooming with Rebecca, talked for a while and decided to take her mother's advice and get plenty of rest.

Frankie, tired of the day's visit to mansions, walked to the lobby of the Grand Hotel and struck up a conversation with a couple of men who had arrived that afternoon from Memphis.

"Sir, what do you know about these parts?" asked one of the men not much older than Frankie as he lit a smoke.

"I've been here quite a few times. What do you want to know?"

The man smiled to the other man next to Frankie. "Well, I do a little gaming sometimes, and I do enjoy the company of a fair maiden. They are a precious item you know."

Frankie rubbed his chin in thought. He should probably keep quiet about Lower Natchez because of Rebecca, but the temptation to return began to gnaw at him. "Lower Natchez has numerous gambling houses, and they do have some fine women that will keep you company, but let me warn you, it can be dangerous. A man can get beaten and robbed, and worst still, he could get himself killed. If you decide to go there, I'd advise you to stay together at all times."

The two men looked at each other for a moment, then one said, "Sounds like you know the place right well. Why don't you escort us? We'll make it well worth your time."

Frankie's conscience told him to end the conversation and go upstairs to his room, but another impulse told him that the night was young and it wouldn't hurt to make a little money while he protected the men. Besides, he had spent three days in the company of women and needed a little time with the men folk. A few hours couldn't matter that much. "I might go with you fellows for a short while, but once I get you settled in, I need to come back to the hotel."

Snuggling under the covers, Rebecca thought about the past three days. Never could she have envisioned all she had seen and experienced in such a short time. Exhausted, she closed her eyes in prayer. She whispered, "Lord, thank you for your love and mercy. Lord, you know my struggles with all that has happened and the loss that has destroyed my will to live. I don't know where you are carrying me, but direct my every step, and let it be in thy will. If my heart is to be opened to another, so be it. I want to thank you for the love that I once had and will always carry in my heart. But most of all, I want to thank you for your grace that gave me life through the perfect love of Jesus. Amen."

"Are you talking to me?" asked Suzanne.

"No, just to the Lord."

***

A whisper of a breeze from a drafty jail cell window brushed across John's face as he lay on his bunk reading from the Bible that Parson Wilcox had given him. All was peaceful both inside and outside the jail with the exception of an occasional bark of a lonely dog. John's glance swept the jail, noting its solid construction. In his estimate, the walls were one foot thick of stone and mortar, and behind the stove was a small rear door. Half of the floor space was Hank's office and contained a desk, chest of drawers for paper work and a padded chair. There was a large barred and glassed window located on the outer wall facing the street, and next to the rear wall adjacent to the desk was a large pot bellied stove. Three chairs leaned against the wall. The back part of the building contained a barred cell with two bunks and a table. The ceiling above the cell was covered by soundly nailed three by twelve inch oak boards. The window that allowed John the pleasure of the woodland scenes behind the cell and breaths of fresh air and sunlight was now boarded over until spring.

What a home, thought John, taking a break from his reading. The low crackling noise of the wood stove gave John a warm feeling that would leave when the chill of the night would filter into the jail. "At least I should be thankful that Hank trusts me enough to allow me the use of a lantern for reading," he murmured to himself. John laid his Bible down, pulled up the covers, fluffed his pillow and began comparing himself to the story of Joseph he had just read in Genesis.

Young Joseph was favored by his father and was sent to find his brothers in the field. The jealous brothers seized Joseph and placed him in a pit and contemplated killing him but decided to sell him into slavery to a caravan of men traveling to Egypt. In Egypt, Joseph was bought by Potiphar, an Egyptian officer, and was a leader of the servants until Potiphar's wife desired him. Because Joseph was loyal to his master and disciplined in the way of the Lord, he resisted the wife's advances. In her frustration, she accused Joseph of attacking her, and believing his wife, Potiphar had Joseph thrown into prison. Joseph remained there for two years until by his God-given ability to interpret dreams, he was set free.

"Lord," he prayed. "I feel a lot like Joseph except I don't know anything about interpreting dreams. Like him, I was thrown in jail for something I didn't plan. Right now, I'm not sure if I'll ever get out of here. If it hadn't been for Wally, I'd be in the

Louisville Penitentiary for a long stay. Lord, I don't know what you plan to do with my life, but I accept your will, and while I am here, I plan to follow you. I'll continue to praise you no matter what happens in my future. If it is in your will and your grace, I pray that someday I'll return to my family and home. Amen."

The flame from the lantern flickered, and peace came over John. He pulled the covers tightly around his neck, reached over and blew out the light. The cell was completely dark, and John's suddenly remembered a visitor who had come to bring him hope. *Maybe even today, God still answers prayers and sends messengers of comfort,* he thought.

The next morning dawned dark and dreary as sleet turned into a steady rain. Hank eased into the jail, trying not to wake John, rekindled the stove, and now stood at the window gazing down the street. No one was stirring. Except for the popping from the damp wood burning in the stove and the patter of rain on the roof, all was quiet. The silence gave him time to think. He was in his forties, working part time as a small town marshal with a small salary to match and operated a farm on the outskirts of town. There was little crime in Wickliffe, but now because of John, he barely had time for his farm work. At first, he resented John and treated him harshly, but now, he actually admired the young man.

John began rustling his covers, so Hank called out, "'Bout time you woke up. Day's a-wasting."

Still thinking about Joseph, John answered, "Don't you think my sentence was too harsh?"

Surprised at how John's words matched his previous thoughts, Hank rubbed his beard and replied, "Where did that come from?"

"Hank, you know I didn't plan to steal a horse. I just got caught up in the moment. I was half starved to death and would do might near anything to get home."

Hank unlocked John's cell door and sat down beside John's bed. "John, to tell you the truth, I believe you, but as marshal, I can't go against the judge's ruling. Nothing would make me happier than seeing you go free."

"Hank, I'm proud you feel that way. It makes staying here easier, but tell me this? Do you believe in justice or balancing the scales?"

A frown crossed Hank's face. "You know I believe in justice."

"Well, the way I see it, is the man who stole the horse was killed, and I'd say with the money I've made for the town I could have bought seven or eight horses for the one that was stolen plus Sam Jones got his stolen horse back. Don't you think justice has been served?"

Hank was silent for a moment. "John, I see your point, but all I do is what the judge directs, no more or no less. Now, how about a game of checkies?"

John smiled and got out of bed. "Hank, I've gotten better at the game these past few weeks, and you surely are a poor loser. When I start making my jumps, your face turns as red as fire, and when I take your last checkie, you throw a fit. I don't understand why you want to play with me. It can't be any fun for you."

Hank walked up to his desk, pulled out the checkerboard and checkers, placed them on the desktop then motioned to John. "Today may be my lucky day."

Before they could get started, the door swung open, and Doctor Jackson, holding a newspaper over his head to keep from getting wet, rushed in. "Top of the day to ye, laddies," he joked with an Irish accent, and laying his damp paper aside, said, "I see we're checkering again."

"What brings you out on a day like this?" grumbled Hank, knowing his game was going to be disturbed. "Pull up a chair, if you like."

Doc took a seat near the stove, smiled at John, winked and said, "It sounds like you've already beaten him. I've told him a million times he just doesn't have the talent for this game."

Angered, Hank placed the checkers back in the box, folded the checkerboard up and placed all in his upper drawer. "Doc, you and me are sure enough friends, but sometimes, you can get on a man's nerves. Why'd you come down here anyways - to tease me?"

Doc patted John on the back. "No, I just wanted to spend the morning with my two best friends and be available to treat you for a heart attack when you throw your checker fit."

John and Doc burst out in laughter while Hank stood, not knowing whether to be angry or to laugh. Slowly, a smile began to form on his face, and he began to laugh with them. "Well, like the old saying goes, with friends like you, who needs enemies?"

The three sat around the stove, drinking coffee and chatting while the rain pattered on the roof overhead. A little before ten o'clock, Hank excused himself to run an errand.

"John, how's your memory coming?" questioned Doc, filling his pipe for a smoke.

"Doc, I'm remembering a lot more about who I am and where I'm from, and I've come to remember my family and how they all look. The strange thing about it is that I first started seeing fuzzy, distorted figures who became the clear images of the ones I love."

"That's not unusual at all, John. From what I've read, there have been other cases such as yours, and it should make you feel better knowing that in those cases, the person's memory completely returned."

With a frustrated look, John shook his head. "But, Doc, there is one image of someone very special that just will not return to me. In fact, this woman's image seems to be fading more each day. I really feel like it is important that I remember her."

"John, I can't answer that question for you. How the brain works after an injury is new to me. In fact, I have learned more these past few weeks than I learned in medical training."

"Doc, I keep praying that the Lord will reveal that person to me."

John looked carefully at Doc and then spoke his mind. "Doc, I don't mean to pry into your personal life, but I haven't noticed you at any of our church services."

"Doc dropped his head, sat silently for a moment, then murmured, "My sins are too great, and for that, the Lord has dealt heavily with me."

John eased closer to Doc and spoke earnestly with him. "Doc, we're all sinners. There's not a one of us who is spotless. It's through the Lord's grace and our repentance that all of our sins can be forgiven. There's no sin too great."

Tears began to form in Doc's eyes. "John, let's say a man was happily married to a woman, and through an injury, she was crippled. Then one night, he went out with another woman, a married woman, and while he was gone, his house caught fire, and his wife was burned to death."

Doc took a deep breath in an effort to push the words out. "That man should have been at home, taking care of his wife, but instead, he allowed her to perish in a horrible manner. After that, the war broke out, and being called, he saw more pain and death than any mortal should. It was like he was sentenced to a hell on earth. Yes sir, the Lord took his vengeance on his sorry, sinful soul."

Doc wiped at his eyes and cleared his throat. "John, that man was me. I killed my wife." He wept.

John reached over to hold his friend. "We've all sinned," whispered John. "Do you remember what David in the Bible did? He took another man's wife as his own and arranged to have her husband killed in battle, yet this man is known as a man after God's own heart. Oh yes, David paid the consequences for his sin, but he was forgiven and stood as Israel's greatest king."

"How could David be forgiven for such an act?" whispered Doc.

"It's because God knows our weaknesses and flaws, and most important, He is a forgiving God. Do you want to be forgiven for all that happened?"

"You know I do," murmured Doc, trying to hold back his tears. "It haunts me every day."

Then let's get down on our knees and ask the Lord to forgive you. By His grace and love, your sin will be forgiven, and I promise you, your life will be changed."

After a long searching prayer, Doc felt the wonderful forgiving grace of God. After so many years of running from God's love and harboring guilt in his heart, Doc let go of that guilt and walked into the loving arms of his Heavenly Father. John gave Doc another hug and welcomed him back into the family of God.

Doc now knew how wonderful it felt to have God's forgiveness and to forgive himself, and he hugged John then called out as he left, "Thank you, John. Expect to see me this Sunday at church."

John smiled as Doc left the jail, and for the first time in a long while, John knew that his time here in the jail was not all lost. He felt at peace, knowing his friend had entered into the presence of his Lord.

A little before lunch, Hank returned to find John sweeping out the jail and singing happily. "What are you so happy about? I bet you and Doc are planning something to get my dander up."

John shook his head and kept on singing, knowing that it was not his place to share the special moments that had occurred.

After lunch, Hank heard a rider and looked to see who was approaching. Hank frowned and said, "Here comes trouble."

As Amos Henderson dismounted and strode up the steps, Hank met him and warned, "We want no trouble here Amos. You've done enough."

Amos removed his hat and politely said, "I intend no trouble, sir. I'm here to see Wilson."

Hank stepped in front of Amos barring his entrance. "What about?"

"I need to talk with him. It's personal."

John motioned to Hank. "Let him come on in. It'll be all right."

Hank pointed to his desk. "I'll be right here, and if there's any trouble, there'll be two inmates in the cell tonight."

Amos meekly entered the cell and settled himself in the chair Hank had provided. For a moment, Amos looked about the room contemplating how to begin. He slowly extended his hand and said, "I want you to forgive me for what I did to you. I was wrong about everything, especially about how I treated Wally."

John took his hand and smiled. "I accept your apology, and I guess I need your forgiveness too. I know fighting never solves a problem."

Amos rubbed his chin. "You did hit me quite hard. I sure got tired of eating soft food, and it was pretty embarrassing for me. You know, you knocked me out with one lick."

The two talked for a while, and to Hank's surprise, laughter was soon coming from the boys.

Amos got up to leave and shook John's hand again. "I want to thank you for bringing me to my senses. I was head strong, arrogant, foolish and most of all, jealous of your relationship with Angie. I hope we can be friends."

John clasped his hand. "I don't see why we can't. It's a dreadful day when a person can't forgive another."

Hank stood with his hands on his hips in wonder. *I thought I'd never see the day when those two would be shaking hands and talking about being friends. Strange things do happen. Maybe this is my day for checkers after all.* "Hey John, you and Amos want to play some checkies?"

Both boys smiled at each other. "Not today, Hank," John answered.

"Not on your life. Not unless the Doc is here to administer to you," laughed Amos.

Hank smiled at John. "I bet you told him about that, didn't you?"

That night as John once again lay warm in his bunk, he thought what an amazing day he had spent. One prodigal son, the Doc, had returned to his Father, and two men at odds had settled their differences. "Thank you, Lord, for allowing me to see your glory in action," John whispered as he drifted off to sleep.

***

With the winter weather slipping into the deep South, there was less to do on the farms and in the homes. Lott and Toby were working in the barn, repairing farm equipment and planning for the spring planting. Sarah and Sister decided to bring out the quilting frame and start work on a new quilt. During the year as Sarah patched and made clothes for the family, she would always save her scraps for quilting. In the warmth of Sarah and Lott's bedroom, the two sat busily stitching the pieces of cloth together. Keeping her eye on the needle, Sister said, "Mama, you're happier than I've seen you in a long time. What's come over you?"

Sarah smiled over to her daughter. "Christmas is coming soon."

"I know, Mama, but I haven't seen you this happy in quite a while."

Sarah kept stitching. "It's probably best to keep it all to myself. You just don't fret. Your Mama is doing fine, and we will have a splendid Christmas. Have you approached your father yet about us observing it?"

"No ma'am, I haven't. I guess I'm a little scared."

"No need for fear, darling. He's your father and he loves you deeply."

That evening, as the family settled in for the night, Lott sat quietly, resting his tired body and watching the flames of the fire perform a flittering dance. Gathering up her courage, Sister left her knitting and eased down in her father's lap as she had done as a child.

Lott straightened himself and looked at Sister. "Daughter, what in the world are you doing?"

Sister looked into his dark blue eyes. "Papa, I just miss being your little girl, and I was just remembering how you used to hold me and assure me that all was well when I faced problems. I just miss those days."

Lott's eyes swelled with tears, and he gently placed his arms around her and stroked her long blond hair. "I do remember those days too, sweet one, and I do love you more than you can know."

As he rocked Sister, the moments slipped by as they both thought back to her childhood days.

Clearing his voice, he said, "Darling, with the loss of the boys, I haven't made life very easy for you nor your mother. I promise you I'm going to do better, and I plan to start with Christmas. It's about time I let the Lord back in my life. We will celebrate Christmas in every way except I don't want no bush brought into this house for decorating."

Sister hugged her father with all her might. "Thank you, Papa. This is the best Christmas present you could ever give me."

As Sister headed to bed, Sarah walked over to Lott to give him a kiss. "It's about time you made your peace with the Lord," she whispered, wrapping her arms around his broad shoulders. *My dear husband, you would not believe all the Lord has in store for us this Christmas*, she thought.

***

Judith woke earlier than usual, got dressed and hurried to wake the children since they had to be at the dock early for their departure to New Orleans. She tapped lightly on Frankie's door. He made no response, so she knocked a little louder. Still, there was no sound coming from the room. She took the extra key that was given to her at check in and unlocked the door. She found the room vacant, and the bed covers were undisturbed. A sudden fear grew as Judith contemplated what could have happened to her son. Natchez was a bustling and beautiful town, but it could also be a very dangerous place. Judith hurried to the girl's room and tapped on the door. To Judith's relief, she heard footsteps, and the door swung open.

"Morning, Mother," Suzanne said, buttoning her blouse. "I know we have to get dressed, eat breakfast and be ready to board by nine o'clock. We're on schedule."

Back in the dressing room, Rebecca called out, "Morning, Mrs. Olliver."

"Good morning, Rebecca."

With a worried look on her face, Judith peered into the room and quietly said, "Do you know the whereabouts of your brother?"

"I guess he's in his room," Suzanne said.

"Come out here in the hallway. I don't want to concern Rebecca," Judith said, taking her daughter's arm and leading her out of the room.

"Frankie's not in his room, and it appears he did not spend the night there. I'm worried about what might have happened to him. Maybe I should contact a law officer," whispered Judith.

Taking her mother by the hand, Suzanne said, "Mother, he is a grown man, and you know how he likes to ramble. He's probably fine."

Just at that moment, Frankie walked down the hall, waved at them and said, "Good morning, my fair maidens. How about us going to the Queen City?"

Judith rushed to him and pulling him to her, whispered, "Where have you been, young man? I've been worried about you. You weren't in your room when I checked on you." As she held him close, she could smell cigar smoke and perfume. "Is that smoke I smell?"

Frankie straightened himself and smiled at his sister. "Mother, is it one of your rules that a grown man has to get his sleep each night? To tell you the truth, I wasn't sleepy, and a couple of gents wanted me to escort them down to Lower Natchez for their protection."

Reaching into his coat pocket, Frankie pulled out a one hundred dollar bank note. "They paid me to keep them out of trouble. Now dear, I was in a smoke-filled gambling hall, and there were certainly some women around, but I stayed with the men all night.

In fact, we just finished breakfast, and I am on my way now to wash up and make sure you ladies are on time. Note too, Mother, that there's no smell of liquor on me."

Judith breathed a sigh of relief and reached to hug her son again. After Judith had returned to her room, Frankie smiled at his sister, and Suzanne knew that he had stretched the truth.

By nine o'clock, the group had boarded, been directed to their rooms and had walked up to the bow to say goodbye to Natchez. This boat contained three decks with the lower section below water level used for storing goods, the second level contained a large dining hall, a gaming room, a dance floor and bedrooms reserved for the captain and special guests, and the top floor had only sleeping quarters.

With a loud whistle, the steam engines strained and sent large puffs of black smoke curling into the air, and the mighty wheels began churning up waves of muddy water as the boat eased away from the wharf. Suzanne placed her arm around Rebecca's waist and waved at the people below. Rebecca quickly followed suit. Frankie, who had been standing by his mother, was now slumped down on a large wooden barrel and almost asleep. Nudging Suzanne, Rebecca asked, "Is Frankie feeling well?"

Suzanne rolled her eyes at her mother while Rebecca was still looking at Frankie. "I think he had a rough night. I don't think he's feeling well."

Rebecca walked to Frankie and placed her hand on his. "You don't feel well, do you?"

Frankie mustered a smile. "I'll be alright. If y'all will excuse me, I think I'll go to my room and get a little rest. I should be fine."

Rebecca spent the morning near the bow, observing the beautiful shores. She then realized that on her left was her home state of Mississippi and across the way was Louisiana. Down the river, she saw miles of deep forest and occasionally an opening revealing farmland or a small town. During the early part of the morning, she observed deer watering in the river and birds perched in the branches of the trees, but most astonishing were the long tangles of Spanish moss hanging from the large cypress trees at the water's edge.

After a delicious noon meal, the women decided to rest and later meet in the dining hall at six. To Rebecca's pleasure, it was announced that after dinner, there would be a dance with a band performing.

When they reached the dining room that evening, they found Frankie dressed in his best and apparently fully recovered. In his light blue suit, white shirt and dark blue necktie, he looked very handsome with his clean-shaven face and long blond hair neatly combed.

"Well, I've never seen three more amazingly beautiful women in all my life. Men would kill just to be dining with any one of you," he said, politely bowing to them.

Rebecca smiled but Suzanne raised her head arrogantly and teased, "I bet you say that to all the girls."

Frankie offered his hand to Rebecca and escorted her, his mother and sister to their table, then politely seated each of them. After another fabulous meal, they wandered to the upper deck walkway to watch the sun sink below the horizon, and their conversation turned to dancing.

"You know, I've never danced at an adult dance. The only dance I have attended was the other day at your house," Rebecca informed Frankie.

"Don't worry, Rebecca. I'll be with you the whole time showing you exactly what to do. We are going to have a grand time," reassured Frankie.

"I just hope you won't be embarrassed by me."

"Rebecca, I could never be embarrassed by you. You don't realize how beautiful you are. I think every man here would trade places with me tonight," Frankie told her softly.

Judith excused herself from the group to visit an old friend from the low country that she had seen earlier at dinner.

The chug from the steam engines and the whishing of the giant paddle wheels filled the night air as the boat seemed to glide through the dark, murky waters. A full November moon settled low in the southeastern sky, and an unusually warm fall breeze fronted their faces.

Suzanne patted her brother on the shoulder and said, "I need to leave the moon to you two if I'm to have dances for the evening. I need to go now and make my presence known."

Frankie leaned back and kissed his sister on the cheek and replied, "Sis, you won't have to worry about that. It won't take but one look, and you'll have plenty of suitors."

"Well, thank you for the compliment. It is always good to hear them from you, brother."

"It's more than a compliment. It's a fact. Dear sister, you have grown into quite a beauty. Of course, getting there has been hard on me!"

"Leave it to you to follow a compliment with a complaint," Suzanne teased. Smiling, she waved goodbye and walked toward the stairway leading to the middle floor.

The moon continued to make its slow rise in the sky as Rebecca lingered in the happiness of the past two days. As the night grew colder, Frankie placed his arm around Rebecca and brought her closer to him. Rebecca looked up, thankful, and smiled.

The sound of vibrant music filled the night, and after listening for a moment, Rebecca asked, "What are all the instruments I hear? One sounds like a fiddle, and I'm not familiar with the rest. The music seems a lot slower than what I'm used to hearing."

Frankie turned his head slightly and listened for a moment. "From what I can tell the so-called fiddle you're talking about, when played in a refined fashion, is called a violin. In fact, there are two violins playing. One carries the melody while the other plays the harmony part."

Rebecca's eyes brightened. "You mean like when one woman sings soprano and another alto in our church choir? Is that it?"

"Exactly," answered Frankie, placing his hand over Rebecca's. "In addition, I hear a string bass, a trumpet, and not unusual for these parts, an accordion."

"Frankie, you amaze me with your knowledge, first of the city and now of music?"

"In my visits to Papére Bourdeau, there have been many dances. He has a beautiful ballroom, and because he loves to dance, he employs musicians who usually practice before the dance. I guess I've taken all these experiences for granted and don't realize how blessed I am."

Rebecca continued to marvel at the sounds floating across the way. "I know the instruments now, but what about this style of music?"

Frankie laughed. "Well, by using the accordion, I guess you could call what we're hearing classical, Cajun music, and the type of song is called a waltz."

Rebecca's eyes brightened even more with anticipation. Squeezing his hand, she murmured, "You can dance to that, can't you?"

"You certainly can," assured Frankie. "It's just a one, two, three step, and it's really very easy." Frankie took Rebecca's hand and led her away from the guardrail. "If you'll look around, you'll see no one is watching. I think this would be an excellent place for a dance lesson. What do you think?"

Rebecca smiled at Frankie and nodded her head in agreement. Frankie placed one hand around her waist and directed Rebecca to do the same, and then he showed her how to gracefully extend her other hand in front. He counted one, two, three, and they began the movement together as the band in the distance played. After a few awkward movements, the couple was soon gracefully waltzing the deck.

Frankie led Rebecca down the stairway and to the ballroom. Suzanne was already in the arms of a young man, and Judith was sitting with her friend enjoying the music. Frankie took Rebecca's hand and led her to the dance floor. With the floor full of dancers, the music began, and the two glided about with the elegance of well-schooled dancers. Elated, Rebecca wished the night would never end. She and Frankie danced practically every dance, and as the night wore on, other young men asked for her hand to the floor. Even though she was flattered, she declined feeling safe in the arms of Frankie.

As Rebecca and Frankie were dancing, a woman made her way through the crowd to the table where Suzanne was sitting and took the seat next to her. "Do you know that man dancing with the beautiful woman?" she said, nodding toward Suzanne's brother and Rebecca.

Surprised, Suzanne turned to the woman. The woman next to her was very attractive and appeared to be in her early twenties. She was tall, dark skinned with deep brown eyes and long, straight black hair that fell down her back and rested near her lower shoulders. "You're from the low country, aren't you?"

The woman smiled. "It's quite obvious, isn't it? Is the man out there married to the woman?"

"Why no, he isn't. Why do you ask?"

"He's very handsome," the woman answered.

"What's your name, if you don't mind me asking?"

"I'm called Angel," the woman said, not taking her eyes off Frankie.

"That's a very religious name," said Suzanne, wanting to know more about the strange woman who had shown an interest in her brother.

With a sly smile, the woman laughed. "Oh no, I guess you could say I'm not that kind of angel. I do enjoy the company of gentlemen. Would you mind telling me the name of the gentleman out there?"

Suzanne was reluctant to give her brother's name, but finally spoke, "His name is Frank, Frank Olliver."

"Oh," the woman exclaimed. "Last night, he told me his name was Allen."

Suzanne took a quick breath. "You must be mistaken. You probably have him confused with someone else."

As the woman rose to leave, she smiled down to Suzanne. "Oh no, I know him quite well."

The more Suzanne thought about the woman, the angrier she became. "He told the woman his name was Allen," she whispered to herself. "At least that's not a total lie - Frank Allen Olliver. He appears to care for Rebecca, but now this foolishness. I just can't understand my brother."

13

Splendor of New Orleans

You turned my wailing into dancing; you removed my sackcloth and clothed me with joy, that my heart may sing to you and not be silent. O Lord my God, I will give you thanks forever.
—Psalm 30: 11-12

Wrapped in a couple of blankets, John curled up under his covers, trying to stay warm. He awoke to the sound of a brisk winter's wind blowing outside and the shivering cold of a room with no fire in the stove. Hank had left John's cell door unlocked and had secured the jail by fastening a padlock to the outer door leading to the street. John wrapped himself in one of his blankets and, in his sock feet, tipped over to the stove to see if any ashes remained to rekindle the fire. As he poked the ashes, he found a few red embers and knew he was in luck. In a matter of minutes, a flame was dancing through the split oak wood, and a roaring fire warmed the jail. John returned to his bunk and, with a satisfied sigh, snuggled under his covers. A little past nine o'clock, Hank unlocked the door and rambled inside. Hank was met with warmth and knew John had rebuilt the fire sometime earlier that morning.

"Time to get up, boy. Today's church day," sung Hank.

John slowly pulled himself up and wrapped himself snuggly in a blanket and headed to the window to look down the street. Moments passed without him issuing a word. Hank wondered at his pensive mood, so unusual for John this time of morning.

Hank made a fresh pot of coffee, poured himself a cup and sat down in his padded desk chair. "What's on your mind, John?"

"A lot of things," replied John.

"Like what?"

"I made it pretty good locked up in here as long as I could get outside and work, but with winter, this cell is getting mighty small."

Hank sat silently, sipping on his coffee and sensed there was more to this story. "Boy, you want to talk to me. You got more on your mind than that."

John turned, walked over and pulled a chair near the stove. With tears forming in his eyes, he muttered, "Hank, I just want to go home. I wish that my memory had never returned if it meant burdening me with this feeling. I need to go home."

Hank poured John a cup of coffee and uncovered a basket of ham biscuits and handed one to him. "You might want to write them. I know at first I didn't allow it, but I think you need to write your folks."

John took a bite of biscuit and washed it down with a sip of coffee. "I can't do that, Hank. If I told them I was in jail for taking part in a horse stealing, it would break their hearts. No sir, I can't send that in a letter, and I would have to explain why I can't come home."

"John, I've changed my mind about you taking part in that stealing," Hank said, trying to make John feel better.

"Maybe so, but the judge hasn't changed his. I'm still locked up in here, ain't I?"

Once again, John grew silent and stared into flames that flickered through the open panels of the cast iron stove door. The fading figure of a woman appeared in the flames and vanished. John knew he had to get home, or this woman would fade from his life. Closing his eyes, he strained to get a glimpse of her, but no name, no face appeared.

Hank reached over and shook John. "You alright, boy?"

John straightened up, blinked his eyes and nodded. "I'll be fine. I guess I'd better get cleaned up for church."

Hank headed outside and returned with a bundle for John.

John unwrapped the bundle and found a heavy, red and black plaid woolen coat. "This is really something, Hank. In this kind of weather, it'll come in handy."

John had left his pensive mood behind with the thoughts of church ahead. John knew that the cold weather had kept the congregation from coming because of the small number of horses, buggies and wagons in front. They were met by smiles and handshakes, and John felt that even in the cold of winter, the Spirit was moving.

Angie's eyes brightened upon seeing John, and she rushed to greet him with a light hug. "I bet you thought I'd forgotten about you since I haven't been to visit this past week."

John smiled at her. "It has been a long week. Even Wally hasn't been around lately. He's up with his mother in Paducah."

Leading him down the aisle to their normal seat, she said, "Papa's been sick with the croup all week, and I've been his personal nurse. That's why I didn't come, but I'll be there next week, if you don't mind."

John patted her hand. "Don't mind? I need all the company I can get. You will certainly be welcomed." John noticed how truly beautiful Angie was with her dark brown hair tipping her shoulders, dark brown eyes and her cute slightly turned-up nose. Her quick smile would brighten any man's heart, but as attractive as she was, something kept tugging at John's heart, separating him from a relationship with Angie. Even when he once kissed her, he felt his heart belonged to another. John felt a sense of guilt knowing that Angie was beginning to care for him.

After several congregational hymns were sung, Pastor Wilcox rose to present the Word. This morning his sermon was on the sins of the heart, and he quoted from the book of Proverbs 33:7, "Whatsoever a man thinketh in his heart so is he." As the sermon progressed, Angie noticed that John's mind was preoccupied. He usually sat on the edge of the pew, listening to every word spoken, and would nod his agreement and voice an occasional amen, but not today.

When the sermon ended, John looked throughout the congregation, and suddenly, a wide smile crossed his lips. Nudging Angie, he said, "You see who's back there?"

Angie looked. "I see a lot of people. Who in particular am I suppose to see?"

John pointed to the back of the church. "Doc Jackson did show up. He said he would."

Doc, acknowledging John, smiled and pointed to the cross and nodded his head in approval.

"That's the first time he has ever darkened the doors of our church," whispered Angie.

"May be, but I don't think it will be the last," John said, leaving Angie to welcome his new friend in Christ.

Like a normal Sunday, John ate with Angie and her father and spent a comfortable afternoon talking with them. He enjoyed listening to Angie as she practiced the piano, knowing that she would one day play for the church service.

Waiting for Hank, the two sat in the parlor at the front of the house where they could watch him arrive.

Angie looked into John's eyes and questioned, "What was going on in that mind of yours during church? You weren't yourself."

John dropped his head then turned to look at her. "Was it that obvious?"

"I know you pretty well, John Wilson. It was that obvious."

"Well, I've got a lot of uncertainties, and I can't seem to sort them out. It is a blessing that my memory is almost back, but I have some unanswered questions, and I don't think I can sort them out unless I go home. But that won't happen any time soon."

Angie snuggled closer to John. "You've made a good impression on everyone in our community. You seem like one of us now. Maybe you belong here, John. Maybe the Lord wants you to stay. I know I do. I guess you just have to keep listening to the voice of God leading you to the right path."

"I'm trying, Angie," answered John.

They both sat in silence a moment as they thought of John's future. Angie interrupted the silence and said, "Do you know who dropped by to see me yesterday?"

"No. Who?" John said, smiling.

"Amos Henderson!" she exclaimed. "And you know he seemed a lot different from the way he used to be. Actually, he was very polite. I don't know what has come over him."

"Angie, you are a very attractive young woman. I think he really cares for you."

"John Wilson, today I've only got one man in my life, and it's not my father or Amos."

As John left with Hank, he was deep in thought about his relationship with Angie.

He was well aware of the change in Amos and only hoped it was permanent. When John thought of Angie, a warm feeling stirred inside of him. *If this mystery woman is just a figment of my imagination, I'd be a fool not to pursue Angie. She does seem to care for me, and I enjoy the time I spend with her. Maybe she is another reason the Lord has brought me here*, he reflected.

***

Suzanne was awakened from her deep sleep by a repetitive light tap on the door. Rousing up, she muttered, "Yes."

"It's your mother. You girls need to get up and get dressed for breakfast, because I know you'll want to be on deck when we approach the city."

Suzanne and Rebecca quickly dressed, packed their belongings and hurried down to Judith. As usual, Frankie was nowhere to be seen. After a light breakfast of freshly baked cinnamon rolls, delightful fruit and coffee, the women ventured to the top deck and walked to the bow to get the best view of the river. As they approached New Orleans, there were a multitude of boats. Some were coming toward them while others were headed down stream. Still, their steam ship towered over the others and gave Rebecca a sense of security.

"Won't be long now, girls!" Judith exclaimed, pointing down the river. "Get ready, Rebecca."

Rebecca stood on her tiptoes and stretched as far as she could. Then off to her right, above the tree line, the point of a steeple came into view. "What's that?" exclaimed Rebecca.

Suzanne said, "That's the steeple of the St. Louis Cathedral."

Rebecca gasped. "I've heard of it. I can't wait to see it."

In a matter of moments, the city of New Orleans bathed by a brilliant, morning sunlight lay before them as if welcoming them with open arms. Rebecca was speechless. She thought Natchez was an industrious and glamorous city, but compared to New Orleans, it was nothing. Never had she seen so many boats and ships, and there was a constant hum of chatter as hoards of men worked hastily loading and unloading cargo. Focusing her attention on the city, she saw people, wagons and buggies moving up and down the streets like ants scurrying when their mound has been disturbed. Then all of a sudden, she saw the beautiful structure standing above all buildings.

Judith said, "Isn't it something?"

"I hope I can go inside. Do you think that is possible?" asked Rebecca.

Judith placed her arm around Rebecca and smiled. "Oh yes, child, you will certainly do just that. Could you imagine being married there?"

"No ma'am, I can't."

"Well, I was."

"Are you serious, Mrs. Olliver? You were married in that beautiful church?"

"I was and if any of my children want to be married there, they can be," Judith said, looking directly at Rebecca.

Rebecca blushed, realizing her intent.

Judith looked about. "Wonder where Suzanne went?"

Suzanne hurried down the walkway to meet Frankie as he left his room.

"I've come looking for you. You slept in this morning," she said as he grabbed his light luggage.

"You knew where I was," he grunted as he began to walk away from her.

"Hold up, I think we need to talk," stammered Suzanne.

With a frown on his face, Frankie stopped, turned and dropped his bag. "What is it now, Suzanne? What did I do?" he asked.

Suzanne took him by the arm and led him to a vacant hallway where they could talk in private. Looking him in the eye, she asked, "Who is Angel?"

A little surprised, Frankie squinted his eyes in thought. "Angel, I don't think that rings a bell with me."

"Angel from Natchez. Would you like to connect those two?"

A smile began to form on his face. "I do remember an Angel up there. She was some fine woman. In fact, she looked a lot like you, Sister."

Angered at the comparison, Suzanne, without thinking, slapped Frankie with all her might.

Shocked, he staggered backwards and caught Suzanne's hand before she could strike him again. "What'd you do that for, woman? Have you lost your mind?"

Struggling to free herself, she gasped, "Here, you have Rebecca with you, and you want the company of that woman of the night?"

"Woman of the night. Is that what you think Angel is? Did you think I had some kind of immoral relationship with her?" Frankie said, getting up into her face. "How did you meet her? No, that's not important. Let me tell you about this so-called woman of the night. In those gambling houses in Natchez, they employ women, usually beautiful women to circulate around the tables and talk with their clients as they gamble. These women cater to the gamblers and encourage them to purchase drinks from the bar. As men drink, they become foolish and with their foolishness, they loose fortunes. The gaming establishment wins, and the poor gambler goes home broke. That's how the business works."

"But," interrupted Suzanne.

"Let me finish please. The other night, when I escorted those men, I warned them ahead of time what to expect, and I watched out for them. As the night wore on, I became restless just sitting watching. That's when Angel came over to me, and we struck up a conversation. In between her visits with the patrons, we whiled the night away. I never as much as touched the woman. I guess for that I deserved a slap on the face, didn't I, Suzanne?"

Suzanne looked carefully at Frank, "Well, I'm guess I'm sorry, but you better be telling the truth. This so-called lady of the night implied there was much more between the two of you."

Frankie calmly replied, "I know you love me and care about what I do, but you need to let me take care of my life. Now, let's go claim our luggage and enjoy the city."

As they walked to the lower deck, they saw that Judith and Rebecca had already left the boat and were watching for them from the pier. Suzanne waved to get their attention as Frankie rubbed his face and walked toward their luggage. He motioned to a colored man down the way that they needed assistance. The man loaded their bags on a cart then stepped to the front to take hold of the two poles attached to the body.

Rebecca smiled. "This is like a horse drawn wagon except it is smaller and is pulled by a man. What a clever way to carry luggage."

"Mais, where put dis, syuh," the man asked.

"What did he say?" whispered Rebecca.

"It's Cajun, a mix of French and, I think, Creole," answered Suzanne. "You'll hear a lot of that down here."

"Take them to the Hotel Royal at the end of Bourbon Street. When you get there, tell them the Ollivers have arrived. They'll direct you to our suites. We plan to take our time and do some sight-seeing. Understand?"

"Yais syuh, Hotel Royal and you is the Ollivers," answered the man as he took a strong grip on his cart and pulled it away.

"Hold up! Your compensation." shouted Frankie as he looked for a carriage.

"Since the hotel is only eight blocks up, and it's such a pleasant day, let's just walk and let Rebecca experience the uniqueness of the city," Judith told her son.

"That would be wonderful, Mrs. Olliver," Rebecca said, already mesmerized. The streets of New Orleans were paved with cobbled stones aged by time, and on each side of the street rose two and three story brick dwellings containing upper porches with gracefully crafted wrought iron hand railings. People were buying and selling on the lower level, and in the upper level windows, bedrooms were illuminated. People sat out on the balconies, eating breakfast and often calling to passer-bys below. Rebecca could not always understand what was being spoken, which was Louisiana Creole, a combination of English, French, some Spanish.

Frankie directed Rebecca to the sidewalk where a large, worn set of wooden doors stood. "What do you think is behind these old, weathered doors?"

Rebecca shook her head. "I don't know. Maybe a place for horses and carriages?"

Frankie lifted the latch and eased the doors open.

Rebecca stared in amazement at the stone-floored patio bordered in verdant potted plants. In the center of the garden was a bubbling water fountain encircled with flowers. Near the back she saw a black wrought iron table with four matching chairs. Doors to the bricked wall led to darken apartments.

"I have never seen such beauty inside a house." She gasped.

Frankie smiled as he closed the door and took her hand.

As they weaved their way through the masses, the snappy twang of a banjo caught her attention. Taking Frankie by the hand, she led him to the music; and as they pushed through, Rebecca saw an old Negro sitting on top of a cracker barrel plucking away while a young boy about ten danced to the beat. Her eyes lit up as she listened to the old man play, and the boy, seeing Rebecca's admiration, danced harder. Rebecca applauded them, looked back to Frankie and said, "Could you teach me that step?"

Frankie playfully wrapped his arms around her and laughed, "There's no teaching those steps. They are definitely original."

Back on the street, she exclaimed, "It seems we are surrounded by melodies!"

Frankie laughed again. "You'll hear it twenty-four hours a day."

The group, weary from the excitement, stopped for a cold glass of lemonade and began watching the people. Every race, age and size rushed past, and all were in a hurry to unknown destinations. Some were well dressed and others were barefooted and in rags. Rebecca noticed that even though some of the colored were shabbily dressed, others dressed fashionably.

Nudging Suzanne, Rebecca whispered, "Some of the Negroes are really well dressed. It's not that way back home."

"The wars over, and slavery has ended. There's a new life for the Negroes who are willing to take the challenge, but most seem afraid of the change," explained Frankie.

Rebecca stood outside of Hotel Royal and stared at the four-story building and two large glassed, French doors that led from the street to the lobby. As they entered, she noticed that the floors were white marble and the walls were tan colored stone. Beautiful oil paintings added to the decor while rounded columns supported the lower level of the hotel. French doors reached from the floor to the ceiling and brought fresh air and light into the lobby. Floral printed curtains bordered the openings and outside storm windows of cypress provided strength against expected storms. The lobby had a stoned fountain with cascades of water flowing from upper crevices. Padded chairs and low marbled tables surrounded the fountain.

A well-dressed man behind the marble desk at the back left what he was doing and hurried to meet them. Bowing, he spoke with a French accent. "Welcome Mrs. Olliver, Miss Suzanne, Mr. Olliver. We've been expecting you." Then his eyes turned to Rebecca, and he gently took her hand and touched it with his lips. As he looked over to Frankie, he raised his eyebrows and said, "Is this your Cher Amis? If so, you have done well, Mr. Olliver."

Both Rebecca and Frankie blushed.

"No, she's a friend of ours, Mr. Mercier. This is Rebecca Walker," explained Judith.

"Oh, please accept my apologies, but my heart tells me it may soon be so." Mr.

Mercier smiled pleasantly. "Mrs. Olliver, your suites are ready, and if we can be of any assistance, please let us know."

"Children, we each have a suite to ourselves, and I think you'll find them most comfortable. Rebecca, you will have your own bedroom, bath and living area. Let's freshen up, rest a spell and then have lunch and do some shopping."

Rebecca was speechless when she saw the elegance of her room. "I can't believe we're staying in such a beautiful place. Who owns the Hotel Royal?"

A smile formed on Suzanne's face. "Papére Bourdeau owns it. He built it so he and his guests will have a place to stay. This floor is reserved only for our family."

After Suzanne left, Rebecca walked to the massive bed with posts that almost reached the ceiling, pushed the thin mosquito nets aside, and slid up on the cushioned mattress covered with a purple silk spread. She was startled to see a painting on the ceiling of a large waterfall that gently flowed through a dense evergreen forest. The large living area was arranged with a couch, two chairs and table on a circular woven rug and graced by twin French doors leading to the balcony. Next, she inspected the bathroom and found a beautifully designed sink, toilet, and massive porcelain tub all with running water. The floor was completely covered with pink ceramic tiles that blended with the light purple plastered walls. Rebecca went back to the bed and snuggled a pillow under her neck as she whispered to herself, "What an amazing room. I will keep all of these images in my head forever." Shutting her eyes, she lay in awe of the display of wealth and extravagance. As she began to feel her body relaxing, her thoughts turned to God, and she spoke, "Lord, I don't understand the road I'm traveling. It's like I was Esther in the Bible, and I have been taken from my home to the wealth of Babylon. Lord, I feel like I've been caught up in the tumult of a tempest and am being whirled around and around so that I don't know where I'm headed. All that I've seen is so beautiful but yet so confusing. Lord, I am fragile. Keep me in the palm of your hand and guide my heart to you. Amen."

The peace after prayer and the cool autumn breeze fluffing the nets calmed Rebecca's spirit, and soon, she drifted off to sleep.

Rebecca roused several hours later to the sound of tapping on her door.

"Ready to have some more fun?" came the voice of Suzanne. "It's a little past lunch time."

Rebecca slid off the bed and ran to the bathroom to freshen up. She looked quickly in the mirror and pushed her unruly locks in place, straightened her skirt and said, "I'll be right there. Give me a minute."

After a quick lunch in the hotel restaurant, the girls eagerly contemplated the coming shopping trip. Judith announced that she was treating both girls to several outfits. They took their time as they brushed from one store to another not finding the exact outfits desired. Finally, at the far end of Canal Street, they discovered a newly established women's clothing store named, A Touch of Paris. For the next two hours, Suzanne and

Rebecca tried on one dress after another. They both settled on three dresses each woven from a high quality, imported lightweight cotton.

The women gathered their bundles, thanked the clerks for their patience and left the store. As they headed toward the door, Rebecca noticed two men with ruddy complexions and long braided, black hair, who resembled the native Choctaw of Mississippi. She turned to the gentleman who had been assisting them and asked, "Excuse me, sir, who are those men out front?"

"I don't know them, madam," he answered.

"No, I don't think you understand. What race of people are they?"

"Oh, I see. They're Choctaw. There's quite a few of them here."

"I knew it," exclaimed Rebecca. "I just knew it. How'd they get to New Orleans?"

"From what I've been told, when the war started, they formed a company of Choctaws over in Mississippi and sent them here for training. Well, in the very first battle when the smoke had cleared, the Choctaw had cleared out as well. Folks say they took to the swamps and decided that their war was over, and now that the war has really ended, they're emerging from hiding."

Rebecca thanked the gentleman, and then as she left, spoke a few words of welcome to the Choctaw in their native tongue. The Indians, in return, smiled and, in their native language, thanked her for talking with them.

Judith hurried the girls down the street and said, "That was fun, and I think you made some good choices that you can wear tonight."

"What happens tonight, Mrs. Olliver?" Rebecca asked.

"Tonight, my dear girls, is dinner at the Hotel Royal that boasts of the finest chefs in the city. Then we'll take a stroll down Bourbon Street for a little music unique to New Orleans."

After arriving at the hotel, the women found Frankie discussing politics with a group of men in the lobby. Frankie rose and walked over to meet them.

"Here, let me help you. Looks like you bought the city. I'm sure glad I didn't have to go."

At dinner that night, heads turned at the beauty of Suzanne and Rebecca. Not only did the girls look magnificent, Frankie managed to capture the women's attention with his height of six feet, slender body, broad shoulders and his air of self-confidence. Frankie escorted Rebecca and Suzanne to the table and then returned for his mother, and taking her arm, softly remarked, "You know, you're the most beautiful woman here tonight."

"You're being too kind to your mother," she smiled, relishing the attention given by her son.

Judith's long, slightly streaked hair was pulled back and pinned behind her ears and flowed below her shoulders. From the glances of admiration, it was easy to see that the years had been good to her.

After choosing the Italian seasoned pork roast complimented with cinnamon, sugared baked sweet potatoes, lightly stewed apples and freshly baked rolls, they talked about the day's adventure while enjoying a chilled glass of imported wine.

After dinner, they gathered their light wraps and wandered out onto Bourbon Street. A breeze brushed in from the gulf and brought warmth to the evening, and in the distance, the sound of a trumpet and trombone blared away with a swinging melody announcing the French Quarters of New Orleans.

As night slipped into the city, people lazily meandered through the streets talking and laughing to the beat of the music. Numerous bands echoed their sounds into the night, and the melodies blended into a cacophony of excited twists until no one melody was heard.

Frankie, hoping for a table in one of the clubs, checked each as they approached only to find most already packed with no standing room. When the crowd thinned, a sweet, slow sound of a trumpet led them to a club called the Sleepy Lagoon. Frankie was disappointed that they could not find a table and asked the man at the door, "Anyway I can get a table?"

The man was rough looking, stood over six feet tall and showed muscular strength. He looked down at Frankie, and with no emotion said, "You're kinda late, boy."

Frankie reached inside his coat pocket, pulled a bill from his money pouch, folded it neatly and placed it in the man's hand.

The man looked down at it, stuck it in his shirt pocket and asked, "How many you got?"

Frankie turned, pointed to the group behind him and said, "There are four of us."

The man walked inside and, in a few minutes, returned. "Give me fifteen minutes, and your table will be ready."

Suzanne and Rebecca were surprised that Frankie had been able to get them seated, and he just winked at his mother pleased that he had learned the lesson from his father that Olliver money can buy just about anything.

The room was small with brick walls and floor but had a high ceiling. Tables and chairs were arranged about the floor, and in the back was a long wooden bar where waiters were frantically taking orders and delivering drinks. Up front the band members were all colored with one playing a piano while others played the trumpet, trombone, string bass, clarinet and drums.

Judith raised her voice over the noise and told Rebecca, "They have some excellent drinks here that are non-alcoholic. You could try coffee, tea, lemonade or an excellent fruit drink that I'd recommend. Each ordered, but Rebecca decided to settle with coffee. When Rebecca was brought her cup of coffee, she was surprised that it was only half full. Blowing across the cup to cool it, she took a sip.

Rebecca struggled with the bitter taste and whispered, "What is this drink? It's the strongest coffee I've ever tasted."

Judith, Suzanne, and Frankie couldn't help but laugh as they explained.

"We should have warned you about New Orleans coffee. Most put half a cup of cream in it. That's why it was only half full," Judith explained.

Rebecca added cream and found it quite good.

As they listened to the rhythm and flow of the music coming from the hearts and souls of the musicians, the hours quickly slipped away. To Rebecca's amazement, the band played everything by ear and even seemed to make up parts, but the blend was melodious. A little past midnight Judith leaned over and said, "Children, we've got a long day tomorrow. We best call it a night."

Rebecca asked as they entered the hotel, "How long do the bands play?"

"All night, dear. This is the magic of New Orleans."

Suzanne and Judith decided to go to the diner for one quick cup of coffee, and Rebecca decided to retire to her room for some much needed rest. Frankie saw Rebecca to her room. Taking her key, he slipped it into the lock and eased the door open. Handing the key back to her, their eyes met and a warm feeling surged through Frankie.

Rebecca softly reached up and smoothed his hair back and said, "I want to thank you and your family for this trip. It's one treasure I will remember all of my life. The beauty that I've seen and the kindness that you have shown will always be held in my heart."

Frankie reached out, gently caressed Rebecca's cheek and gave her a soft kiss on her waiting lips. Rebecca looked up into Frankie's eyes, and he leaned closer and with more intensity kissed Rebecca as Rebecca responded to his touch and to his desire. When the kiss ended, Rebecca told Frankie goodnight and quickly turned to enter her room.

"Rebecca," Frankie gently called her back. "I hope you didn't mind."

"No, Frankie. I didn't mind at all. Thank you again for a perfect night."

***

Angie pushed the curtains back to watch John and Hank ride away. John usually would wave to her, but he didn't today. Angie was worried and decided to talk to her father. Perhaps, he would know what was troubling John. Angie hurried to her father's study because she knew that Sunday evenings were devoted to his reflection on the morning sermon and his prayers for the Lord to reveal the next one. She also knew that his time in prayer and study usually ended with a deep nap, so she softened her step and eased his door open. It squeaked as she peeked inside.

"Humph," her father muttered as his eyes shot open.

"Sorry, Father, didn't mean to wake you. I can come back later."

"That's alright. I need to wake up anyway. Come on in, darling," he said, rubbing his eyes.

Angie settled in a chair across from her father. She silently waited with bowed head, contemplating what to say.

Her father reached over and gently lifted her chin until their eyes met.

"What is it, darling?"

Tears formed in her eyes as she looked at him. "Do you think I'm pretty?" Angie asked.

"The Bible says that man looketh at the outside, but God looketh at the heart."

"No, Father. Really, am I pretty?"

"In another verse, it says that life is like a flower that grows, blooms, wilts and is no more." Smiling, he reached over and ran his hand down her face and blotted away her tears.

A smile crossed Angie's face, and she laughed as she said "Okay, Father, so much for the sermon. Now tell me about the bloom."

Her father took her hands and looked at her face until he held her eyes with his own. "You look just like your mother, and she was the most beautiful woman I ever saw. She was always my special bloom," he said, choking back his tears.

"Oh Father, do you really mean that?" she cried, leaning into his open arms.

"With every ounce of my body, you are that and more."

"Then why doesn't he love me?"

"You mean John?"

"Yes, Father, I really think I'm in love with him, and I know he seems to enjoy my company, but -."

"But he hasn't expressed his love for you. Is that right, darling?"

Angie nodded her head.

"Then maybe you need to ask him how he feels."

Angie quickly raised her head and said, "I can't do that! What would he think of me?"

"I guess that's not the best idea, but honesty is. When there is love between a young man and woman, it's got to be both ways. Angie, all I can tell you is that John is a fine young Christian man, and I can see why you are attracted to him, but beyond that smile of his, there is a very troubled boy. The horror of battle plus the hardships he experienced at Camp Douglas and even here in Wycliffe have certainly weighed him down. Since his memory is returning, he longs to connect with his family, and there are issues he still must resolve. He's just not ready for a commitment and may not be for a long time. My advise to you is be patient with him, pray the Lord's will be done and trust that God will bring what is best for both of you."

Angie leaned over, kissed her father on the cheek and said, "Father, I really hope the Lord intends for John to be more than a friend, but if not, I do plan to be a good friend to him."

***

"John, it's gonna be a cold one tonight," Hank said, pointing to the stack of split oak wood piled in the rear of the jail. "You should be fine."

John nodded. "Hank, tell me this? When you lock me up like you do, what am I suppose to do if this place catches on fire? I couldn't get out. I'd get burnt to a frazzle."

Hank ran his fingers through his scraggly graying beard. "Well son, that ain't no problem. You'd just go over to my desk, open the top right drawer, take out that set of keys, unlock the rear door and then you could go outside and start throwing water on the place. I'd say you'd be just fine."

John exclaimed, "You mean I haven't been secured all this time you have been letting me have freedom to roam inside the jail! What about that hasp and lock on the outside door?"

Hank puckered his lips and smiled. "That there lock is for them pesky citizens nosing around here telling me how easy I am on you. It's for them."

"What if I decide to cut and run?" joked John.

"My hounds would catch you 'fore you got good out of sight," he laughed. "See you in the morning."

Now alone, John restoked the fire, brewed a fresh pot of coffee and settled himself in a chair next to the front window. Kicking his feet up on the wide window seal, he sipped his coffee and looked out at the town. Not a soul could be seen, and a thick stillness encircled him. John felt a cold draft seeping from the bottom of the front door and reached up to feel one of the glass windowpanes nearby. It was icy cold, and the sky had turned a solid gray with tiny flakes fluttering through the air.

Oh no, thought John, *if it snows, I'll have to stay in until the weather clears before I can help repair that barn roof. Lord, forbid it.* As dusk settled in, the snow continued to fall and it had now crusted over the streets and sidewalks.

John pulled a chair next to the stove and unwrapped the partial loaf of bread and sliced pork roast that Angie had prepared for him earlier, and giving thanks, began enjoying his meal. With nothing to do, John became restless and decided to sleep. He kicked off his shoes, fluffed his pillow and folding his arms behind his neck, turned over toward the front window to watch the snow falling. His mind traveled from his playful childhood days, through the anxieties of his youth and then to the painful experiences of war. *What a fool I was to join the army just to take care of a friend who never showed up,* he thought to himself. *What if all the fathers had paid someone to take their sons' place in battle? It looks like Olliver money can buy anything. He bought his son's life away from the firing line and put mine in his place."*

John turned his Bible once again to Exodus to the story of Joseph. He wondered why he always headed to Joseph, but he knew. It was the story of a boy unjustly jailed for over two years, freed by the hands of God and rose to be second in power unto Pharaoh, the king of Egypt. This story gave him hope, and hope was all he had.

John closed the Bible, placed it on his small table, blew out the flame of the lantern and settled in his bunk. The fire in the stove sent flickering rays of light dancing on the ceiling as John slept soundly.

Later that night, John was awakened by the rushing sound of winds, and he quickly got up and walked to the front window. To his amazement, there was no snow on the ground, and the gray clouds had been swept away, replaced by high, puffy white ones that raced across the heavens. As he watched, the clouds began to spin and bob as if dancing a waltz. Around and around, they whirled in musical motion. Then the image of the bottom skirt of a woman's long evening gown formed. In seconds, soft rounded shoulders appeared. With the brush of another cloud, lovely, curly auburn hair was spiraling about the dancing woman. John thought he recognized the woman and grasped at the clouds. As hard as he could, he could not stretch far enough to clasp her skirt and pull her to him. Then as if by fate, the clouds were blown closer to him, and he was able to seize the tail of the skirt and, gripping as hard as he could, John began pulling the woman to him. With all his strength, he held her to him tightly, placed his arms around her waist and strained to look into her face. As they whirled about, the woman's floating hair covered her face so that John could not see her, but he held her with one arm and took the other hand to push the veil of hair away. Two sparkling emerald green eyes stared at him, and as he blinked his eyes, he felt the touch of her warm lips upon his. As he held her closely, she spoke without ever moving her lips. In a whisper like a soft breeze, she said, "Why didn't you come home? I waited for you a long time. It's time for you to come home, John." The clouds began to brush away and with it, the woman in John's arms. In a matter of seconds, he was once again, alone.

Waking, he screamed, "I know you! I know who you are! Don't leave me, Rebecca! Don't you ever leave me!"

Shaking and sweating profusely, John sat up in bed and looked around the room. "Where am I?" he asked himself. "Where is Rebecca?"

John rushed to the window, rubbed his eyes and gazed outside. The snow had ceased falling, and the sky had cleared, revealing a heaven of twinkling stars as the reality of Rebecca returned. Angered at first but now in peace, he looked up to the heavens, and knowing his God was in control, John thanked Him for bringing back Rebecca. Then shutting his eyes, he said, "Lord, You still do answer prayers. Your grace is incomprehensible and sufficient."

14

Beauty and the Ballroom

Do not be anxious about anything, but in everything by prayer and petition with thanksgiving present your requests to God. And the peace of God which transcends all understanding will guard your hearts and minds in Christ Jesus.
—Philippians 4:6-7

Suzanne and Rebecca rose early to bathe and perfect their hair and clothes. They found a carriage outside waiting for them. Frankie stepped down from the carriage to assist the girls.

Mrs. Olliver soon joined them and said, "Rebecca, this is Robert. He drives for the family. He's been with us a long time."

The old colored man, dressed in a well-tailored black suit and top hat to match, turned and smiled at her. "Morning, Miss Rebecca. Welcome to dah 'pire."

After he had turned and whipped the horses into motion, Rebecca whispered to Suzanne, "What is the 'pire?"

Frankie laughed and answered, "The 'pire is what the colored folks who work for Papére call the Bourdeau Empire."

It took them over an hour to get through the busy New Orleans streets, but once out of the city, travel became much easier. Unlike the red clay of Newton County, these roads were sandy and rather smooth. As they traveled southwest, farms sprinkled the countryside, and the farther they traveled, swamps with dark green water appeared. Large cypress and live oak trees draped with long strands of Spanish moss bordered the road. The ride down the shadowed lane seemed to be engulfed by an endless levy of water on each side.

"How far is it to the plantation?" questioned Rebecca.

"Tell her, Robert," voiced Frankie jokingly.

"Fuh shore, deres about twenty more miles, Miss Rebecca. Won't be long," he said, pushing the horses forward. "Git 'on up dere, you devils. Times a-wasting."

Rebecca marveled at the scenery, and after noticing a small railroad track that followed close to the road, Rebecca asked, "What kind of tracks are those?"

Mrs. Olliver answered with a smile. "That's Papa's tracks. At one time, he grew cane and processed his own sugar for shipping but found it more profitable to cut and ship the sugarcane to New Orleans by rail, so he built the tracks. In fact, we should pass his train headed for the city soon."

Noting a commotion ahead, Robert pulled the carriage to a stop and stood up. He covered his eyes to shade them from the morning sun in order to get a better look, and with a frustration, he spoke to Mrs. Olliver. "We's gonna be a bit late, Mrs. Olliver."

"Why's that?"

"There's a run going on up the way," he muttered.

"What's a run?" asked Rebecca, stretching up to see it.

"Dat's crawfish, ma'am. Every once in a while, dey decides to move from one bayou slew to another. Only problem for dem is, the road gets in the way," explained Robert.

"Why are we worried about a few crawfish?" inquired Rebecca.

They all broke out in laughter.

"Robert, you best pull on up there and let Rebecca see these few crawfish," directed Mrs. Olliver.

As the carriage neared the crossing, Rebecca's eyes widen. It looked like a huge mass of dark crawling lava flowing over the road, and scores of people, black and white, with bags and baskets were scooping crawfish up as fast as possible.

Confused, Rebecca asked, "What are they going to do with those?"

Robert shook his head and laughed. "Mais, deys some shore enough good eating. You folks up in Miss'sip don't eat 'em?"

Rebecca made a face and shook her head.

They all laughed again, and in about an hour, the run was made, people collected their meals and the journey continued.

After about a half an hour, Robert slowed the horses and stopped. A broad waterway lay before them with a long wooden bridge stretching to the far bank. It seemed connected to a small island of swaying sugarcane. The sound of a whistle and puffs of smoke curling above the sugarcane announced the train's arrival. Slowly, it approached the bridge with car after car stacked with cane. When the final car cleared the bridge, Rebecca said, "I counted seventy-eight." Then she exclaimed, "How long is this bridge?"

Frankie pointed. "The bridge is about four hundred feet long, and in a way, it saved Papére from Yankee destruction during the war."

"How did it do that?" questioned Rebecca.

When Papére got wind the Yankees were going to make a raid on his place and seize his sugar and burn him out, he had the bridge burnt down instead. Since there wasn't any way a Union gunboat could get up here and with an abundance of gators in the water, I think the Yanks just didn't think it was worth it.

"You mean alligators?" exclaimed Rebecca.

"Yep, that put the scare on 'em. Left all that sugar to the old man."

Rebecca reached over and clasped his hand and asked, "How much sugar did he have?"

Mrs. Olliver laughed. "Thousands and thousands of dollars worth were sitting up there for the taking. Papa kept growing, processing and storing sugar all through the war years, and when the South laid down their arms, Papa was one of the richest men in the South. Even now, I'm not sure he knows exactly how much he's worth."

After they crossed the bridge, the land rose gently; and for the first time, Rebecca began to see fields that had been stripped of its cane, and off in the distance, workers were cutting and stacking it up on wagons to be transported to the rail. Live oak trees clustered the roadway, and the land continued to make a slight rise. Up ahead, white tweaked through the tops of the massive oaks.

Frankie covered Rebecca's eyes and said, "How about a surprise, Miss Walker?"

In a matter of minutes, Frankie removed his hand and, pointing, exclaimed, "Welcome to the Oaks, Rebecca."

Rebecca's eyes widened. "Gracious, it's as large as our capital building in Jackson. It is beautiful and such a bright white."

"It is that, Rebecca. The walls are constructed of solid brick, perhaps a foot thick, and to lighten the place up, Papa decided to stucco the outer face and paint it all white."

Several maids scurried to meet the carriage, and a young colored man came running from the barn.

"Morning, Mrs. Olliver," greeted an elderly woman, standing erect and neatly dressed in a black cotton dress and white blouse. "We's been looking for you all. Master Bourdeau is out riding and will be back soon. We's got the rooms ready for you."

"Thank you, Miss Lucy," Mrs. Olliver said, stepping down from the carriage.

Robert cleared his throat and looked toward the young man approaching. "Timmy, you get dere b'longings and get dem on into dat house. You understand?"

"Yes sir, boss, I knows where deys go."

Frankie exited the carriage and walked around to assist the women.

Mrs. Olliver noticed the wonder in Rebecca's eyes and said to Frankie, "While our luggage is being brought up, why don't you take Rebecca on a tour of the house."

The Oaks was three stories high with steps leading up to a columned entrance, plus a basement that housed the carriages and servant quarters. Each floor opened to a wrap around balcony. As Rebecca entered, she found herself in the receiving room floored with a gray tile with ceilings at least sixteen feet high. The plaster walls were off-white, and in the adjoining rooms, the tile gave way to exported Philippine mahogany. Beautiful oil paintings graced the walls, and every window was bordered with curtains of blending pastel shades, and outside shudders were placed over the windows for impending storms. Frankie showed Rebecca the parlor, library, office, Papére's bedroom, and several other rooms used for entertaining guests. He then escorted her up marbled steps to the second floor which held eight bedrooms. Each bedroom contained two large glassed, double French doors that led to the outside balcony. He pointed to a cord hanging from the ceiling next to each bed and explained that with one pull, a servant could be summoned.

"Well, that kind of pampering would be nice, but I can't imagine needing that much help. Thanks for the tour, Frankie." Rebecca smiled.

"Oh no, the best is yet to come," Frankie spoke softly as he took her hand and led her to another set of stairs.

At the top, there were heavy oak doors. Frankie pushed them open to reveal an enormous ballroom with polished oak floors smooth enough to glide across in stocking feet. The walls were lined with glassed French doors identical to the ones below, and when opened, allowed the evening breeze to flow throughout the ballroom. Even more impressive, was a large glassed cupola overhead that revealed the wonders of heaven.

"Well, do you think you might try your waltz on these floors?" he asked, leading Rebecca onto the floor and taking her hand as if for a dance.

"I hope so," Rebecca replied spellbound.

"Good, because if I know my Papére, he has a ball planned for you, Miss Rebecca Walker. But let me take you outside to the walkway.

The sun now was setting, and Frankie pushed open one of the doors to lead Rebecca outside. On the balcony, Rebecca could see the tops of massive oak trees and felt as if she were standing atop of a mountain. At her right, she could see all the way to the long bridge they had crossed earlier and the fields were laid out perfectly. Some that had been cut lay bare while other fields of cane were tossed by the evening breeze. Down to her left next to a stream were rows upon rows of small dwellings.

It looks like a small village over there. Workers, I presume," Rebecca said, pointing toward them. "And what are those white objects beyond the town?"

"Rebecca, those houses are called quarters, and they are homes for our workers. Overall, there are about two hundred Negroes living down there. That counts for men, women and children, and those so-called white objects are tents. They house our temporary workers who are brought in from the city for harvesting."

"I'm a little confused, Frankie. That's a lot of workers. Why so many?"

"Papére has a little over two thousand acres in sugarcane, and since cane is a late maturing crop and a freeze will damage it, when it's ready you have to harvest it fast. That, my dear, takes a lot of harvesters. Now, I want you to walk with me all the way around the walkway," Frankie said, taking her hand.

The two strolled around the balcony and returned to the awaiting door. Frankie said, "Now, what did you see?"

Rebecca was clueless. "I have no idea what you mean."

Frankie stretched his hand out and slowly moved it from left to right. "From up here where we're standing, you can see every inch of Papére plantation. At a glance, he can know exactly what is transpiring at any time. It's hard to believe, isn't it?"

"I bet your grandmother loved this place," Rebecca said.

Frankie nodded. "To her, this was a kingdom. Papére was the king, and she was the queen. He took care of the fields, and she managed the house and their social affairs."

"What was she like?"

"In ways, they were so different. He is French, and she was a beautiful Louisiana woman. He was all business, and she was the most energetic and happiest person I've ever known. Together, they built this kingdom."

"I bet he misses her."

"Every day of his life," Frankie said, noticing dust rising down the road.

As dusk settled in, Frankie and Rebecca noticed a tall thin man bringing his horse to stop. As he dismounted, he handed the reins to a colored man who had rushed out to meet him and turning, he headed up the steps leading to the house.

Frankie leaned over the rail and called down, "You always in this kind of hurry, old man?"

The gentleman stopped, looked up to the voice, squinted his eyes and called back, "At least I ain't a little peeshwank wet behind the ears. Who you got with you?"

"We'll see you downstairs. I've got someone I want you to meet."

Rebecca and Frankie hurried and found his grandfather on the porch beating the dust off his pants with his hat. He smiled to Frankie and then to Rebecca. "Sorry for the dust," he said, extending his hand to Frankie. Turning his attention to Rebecca, he studied her for a moment, then said, "Young lady, you have grown into a beautiful woman. The last time I saw you was when I was up dere about eight years ago. Your father is Thomas Walker, isn't he?"

"Yes sir, he is," Rebecca replied, gazing at the elderly gentleman. With his thick, course white hair, piercing blue eyes and pointed nose, he reminded her of someone, but she couldn't place just who.

Seeing her gazing intently at him, he smiled. "Who do you think I resemble, darling?"

"How did you know I was thinking that?" Rebecca frowned.

"It happens all the time. You'd be surprised at the people who come up to me and ask me if I am Andrew Jackson's son. Can you believe that, Andy Jackson's son?"

Rebecca nodded her head and smiled. "That's exactly who you resemble."

Judith came to greet her father, and hugging him, said, "Suzanne is already in the dining room, and as soon as you get freshened up, dinner will be served.

"Won't take me long. I haven't eaten since breakfast, and I'm starved," exclaimed Mr. Bourdeau. Then turning his attention back to Rebecca, he added, "Frankie, you should have brought this young woman down here long before now. I'm certainly looking forward to getting to know you. We'll do our best to entertain you, won't we, grandson?"

"I'm certain about that," Frankie replied, extending his arm to Rebecca to direct her to the dining room.

Following a southern meal of fried chicken, rice and gravy, sliced and fried sweet potatoes, green beans, and followed with slices of hot apple pie, the party sat around the table for an evening of conversation.

As a servant brought out freshly brewed coffee and began turning the cups over and filling them, Mr. Bourdeau looked toward his daughter. "How long are y'all going to be able to stay?"

"Oh, a week, maybe ten days," she nodded, reaching over and placing her hand on her father's. We want Rebecca to experience your harvest ball."

"I tell you what. It's already near the last of November, you might as well stay for Christmas," joked Mr. Bourdeau, taking a swallow of coffee.

The next few days, Judith, Suzanne and Rebecca rested from their tiring trip and enjoyed the comfort of the Oaks. After another outstanding dinner, Mr. Bourdeau caught Rebecca's eyes and said, "You haven't seen the place yet, have you? I mean the farm."

"Not yet." She smiled. "I think we're all rested up. I would love to see it."

"Do you ride?" Mr. Bourdeau asked.

"Yes sir, I ride," Rebecca answered.

"You will certainly do just fine, young lady." He chuckled. "The mornings are cool. It'll be great for riding. How about you, Suzanne? I know your mother doesn't care for the saddle. You'll certainly ride with us, won't you, granddaughter?"

Suzanne shook her head no. "Too early for me, Papére."

"What about you, grandson?"

Frankie rubbed his nose and frowned. "I was planning to ride the train in with the sugarcane tomorrow, spend the night in New Orleans and ride it back the next day. Colt is coming out with a new center fire pistol that shoots shells like the Spencer rifle, and I thought I'd pick you and me up a couple of 'em, but I can change my plans."

Mr. Bourdeau thought for a moment. "I've read about them. Tell you what, you go get us a set of those pistols, and I will personally escort Rebecca in the morning, that is if she doesn't mind spending a little time with an senile ole Andy Jackson."

Rebecca smiled into the eyes of the old gent and said, "You've got yourself a date, Mr. Jackson. What time should I be ready?"

Suzanne gave Rebecca a set of riding clothes and a pair of boots. Because Rebecca was too excited to sleep, she tipped up to the ballroom, trying not to wake anyone, and pushed the heavy doors open. She found the room illuminated by a half moon resting over the treetops. The floor sparkled like glass. As she opened the outer French doors, she was greeted by a cool autumn breeze, and Rebecca felt the peace of heaven. "Are you up here, John," she whispered to herself. "If you are, you know I miss you, and I'll always love you."

Rebecca found herself once again thinking of Esther as she looked out on the beautiful evening. She could imagine Esther gazing down on the splendor of the hanging gardens of Babylon. Then Rebecca's thoughts turned to Frankie. As she contemplated marriage to Frankie, Rebecca knew she would trade all the wealth in the world to see the one who had already brought immense joy to her life and now heartache.

***

Rebecca and Mr. Bourdeau enjoyed an early breakfast and walked leisurely to the stables. They found two horses saddled, bridled and ready for the morning.

With a kick in the flank, the horses bolted forward and cantered down the path leading to the quarters. Down below bordering a winding creek was a long row of cabins. Each cabin had two rooms, a small covered porch on the front and back and a chimney for heating and cooking. Behind each cabin, lay a plot for a summer vegetable garden. Most impressive was the neatness of each house and yard.

"There sure are a lot of homes here, and they're all nicely kept," Rebecca replied.

"Over a hundred and I expect for them to take care of each one."

"I hope you don't mind me asking, but isn't this still like slavery?"

Mr. Bourdeau pulled the brim of his wide-rimmed straw hat down as the sunrays crossed his face. "Rebecca, that's a good question. When the war ended, I called all my slaves together and told them they were free to go. Almost all of them looked at me and said, 'Where will we go?' Most were born here and didn't want to leave dere home, so I told them if they wanted to stay, that they would have dere lodging, and I would pay dem a salary."

"How many of them left?"

"Seven left and within two months, four returned."

"What about schooling? Do you intend to educate them?" questioned Rebecca.

Mr. Bourdeau shook his head. "Oh no, how would that help dem in the cane fields. Now, how about us heading for the fields?"

Rebecca looked back once more and thought how unfair life was for them working from daylight to dark with no hope of anything better. *Lord, you brought the children of Israel out of bondage and made them a nation. I hope you give the Negro the same mercy.*

After touring the fields, Mr. Bourdeau took Rebecca to see his cattle and horses. Finally nearing the house, they dismounted and reined in their horses at a small stream to water. They sat on a moss-covered area under the shade of a small live oak to rest.

"Well, what do you think of the place?" Mr. Bourdeau asked.

Rebecca smiled. "It's the most beautiful place I've ever seen."

Mr. Bourdeau removed his hat and ran his fingers through his thick gray hair. "One day, this place will be Frankie's," he said.

"How about Suzanne?"

"Darling, I have two more cotton plantations south of Baton Rouge for her and her fellow and enough cash assets for generations to come. I started off as a boy working on the docks in New Orleans, and my papa also left me a piece of land. I have been truly blessed."

As they headed toward the stream, Mr. Bourdeau said, "Rebecca, I've enjoyed getting to know you these past few days, and to be honest with you, I hope you will become a part of our family. I think you are the woman who will shape Frankie into the man I believe he can be. I know he has feelings for you."

Rebecca shyly smiled and pondered his words.

Little snow remained on the ground after two days, except in the shaded areas. To John's delight, Hank reported that barn work awaited him, and John dressed warmly because he knew he would be in the crisp open air. At the site, John was introduced to a local farmer, George Andrews, a widower in poor health, and Hank turned John over to George. They walked to the barn, and they worked together, replacing missing and torn shingles. The job was finished by noon, so they headed to the kitchen for some hot beef stew, cornbread and coffee. As they ate, George mentioned that he needed help with some firewood. John was happy to help and soon had the firewood split and stacked.

John was sad when Hank pulled up, because his day outdoors was such a relief to confinement in the jail. John and George walked out to meet Hank.

"Well, George, how'd he do?"

George answered, "Mighty fine worker. I'd hire him anytime. By the way, how much do I owe you?"

"Today's a gift. You have just received your first Christmas present."

George shook his head. "Thank you, Hank. I thank both of you."

After John climbed onto the wagon, he looked back and said, "There'll be just one cost to you."

"And what is that?' answered George, obviously confused.

"How 'bout us seeing you at church Sunday? You can give the good Lord some thanks."

"I'll do just that, young man."

Hank looked at John after they were down the road and remarked, "If'n you had your way, you'd save every soul in this county, wouldn't you?"

"The Bible tells us that all believers should be missionaries. Every believer should spread the word. That means you too, Hank."

That night, John watched a half moon rise over the roofs across the street, and he was filled with loneliness. Somewhere, someplace, he wondered if Rebecca was looking at the same beautiful sky. Bowing his head he prayed, "Lord, I praise your holy name, and I thank you for your mercy. Lord, your beggar is begging again, and I know all things are possible through you, but if it's Your will, and I know it's going to take a miracle, but I ask you to send me home for Christmas. Amen."

John lay on his bunk, viewing a biology book Doc had dropped off the previous day. Hank rambled in about mid-morning and was not talkative, but he settled in his seat and began rustling through some papers. As the door squeaked open, he looked up to see an elderly, stately man with short, cropped white hair and in his hand was a walking cane.

"Good gracious, General, I thought you'd be home a long time before now. How in the world are you doing? Here take a seat."

The general carefully lowered himself in the seat, using his cane for balance, and said, "It takes a long time to get from Virginia to here, and I took my time. I had some old friends in eastern Kentucky I wanted to visit, and there was no need to hurry. How's my place doing?"

"It's all fine. I kept an eye on it while you were away. Needs just a little cleaning up. I can send John over to help with it."

The general smiled. "That would be thoughtful. Who is John?"

Hank pointed to the cell.

"I'm surprised you have a prisoner. There's usually not much crime around here. What's he in for?"

Hank thought for a second, then answered, "How 'bout meeting the boy and letting him tell you his story. John, come over here. I want you to meet someone."

John laid the book down and walked over to meet the general. He extended his hand and said, "Sir, I'm John Wilson."

"John, this here is General Charles A. Wickliffe. He's one of our locals, and before the war, he served as our county attorney," stated Hank. "In fact, the town is named after him."

John's eyes widened, and he took the general's hand. "Sir, it is indeed a pleasure to meet you. I presume you were with the Confederacy?"

Releasing his hand and pointing to a chair, he motioned for John to have a seat, then replied, "What other is there?"

"John fought for the Confederacy too. Tell 'em your story, son."

John took his time as he told about the engagements he had fought, his wound, how he had been left on the field by the Southern army, and the difficulties he faced at Camp Douglas. He then told how he and his friend had entered Wickliffe looking for work and finally the event that placed him in jail.

When he had finished, the general sat thinking for a moment. "You said you spent two years at Camp Douglas. I don't see how you survived that ordeal. Those Yankees killed a lot of our boys up there by shear meanness. You did say your friend and you were starving when you got here?"

"Yes sir, we were."

"Let me ask you this. Why didn't you boys take the train when the Yankees offered it to you?"

John shook his head. "I guess we were stubborn fools. They told us that if we would sign an amnesty paper and pledge our support to the Union, then they'd give us that ride home. We told them they could keep their papers for the outhouse."

The general smiled. "Good for you, boy, I did the same." He then looked at Hank. "Did the owner get his horse back?"

"Yes sir, he did."

"And the boy who took the horse was killed?"

Hank dropped his head and muttered, "I told him to stop, but you know I can't shoot no pistol worth a flip. I didn't intend to kill the man."

"Let me understand this. The horse was returned, the man who took it was killed, and this here boy is in jail for a year. How about explaining this kind of justice?"

Hank squirmed in his seat. "The boy also stole a ham and some bread."

"Some ham and bread. Did the owners get that back also?" the general questioned.

Hank glanced out to the street and muttered, "Not exactly, I kinda confiscated it, and we used it here in the jail."

"Ham sandwiches, huh. That makes you a thief too."

"Yes sir, I guess you could say that."

"Who was the judge that heard the case?" asked the general.

"Judge Henry."

The general shook his head. "Judge Henry, I figured as well. I would have thought that senile ole rascal might have given up the bench by now. If I know his sentences, I'd say you probably have made a lot of money working this boy."

Hank knew that nothing had been fair about John's sentence.

"Where is the ole cuss now? I'm gonna go pay him a visit," stated the general.

"I'll do some checking and get right back to you," asserted Hank.

"Don't procrastinate, Hank. You're known to do that sometimes. This is important. And do send John over to my place in the morning. By the way, I'll pay the boy, and I want it to stay in his pocket. You understand?"

"Yes sir."

Shaking John's hand, he said, "I noticed you've got a slight limp."

"Yes sir, I took a minie' ball. Luckily, I didn't loose my leg."

The general smiled and pointed to his cane. "Same here. You'll be hearing from me about this matter, Mr. Wilson. See you tomorrow."

***

In the days that followed, Rebecca saw an obvious change in Frankie. Each morning, they mounted their horses and toured the countryside, even crossing the long bridge and venturing miles into the lower bayou. With the rides came picnic lunches spread along meandering streams thick with oaks draped in Spanish moss. On one occasion, Frankie taught Rebecca how to handle and shoot his new forty-five colt revolver.

With luck, the fall frost didn't arrive, and with extra labor, the fields were cleared, and the last of the cane was loaded and ready to be sent to New Orleans. To celebrate his crop safely harvested, Mr. Bourdeau surprised his workers with a pork barbecue in honor of them and all of their hard work. To celebrate Rebecca's visit, Mr. Bourdeau planned a low country boil and a ballroom dance.

"What's a low country boil?" asked Rebecca.

Frankie laughed and placed his arm around Rebecca's shoulders. "That is a surprise you will have to see to believe," he said, giving her a quick kiss on the cheek.

Excitement filled the air as they all feverishly made plans. The house servants dusted and cleaned every inch of the Oaks while other servants raked the yards, weeded the gardens, trimmed the hedges and built a massive platform to be covered with a canvas canopy. Large cast iron kettles were brought onto the grounds and placed on strong iron supports. Oak, split for burning, was stacked near the kettles. As the sun was setting on Friday evening, Mr. Bourdeau called the family together in the parlor. Smiling, he said, "Folks, I think we're ready for the whirlwind that will sweep in here come tomorrow afternoon. My suggestion is that you all sleep as late as you can tomorrow morning because when this ball begins to roll, it'll roll all night long."

"All night?" Rebecca exclaimed.

"That's exactly right, all night long. It'll last until the last person has left."

Saturday dawned bright and sunny with a cool breeze flowing in from the north. Mr. Bourdeau walked out on the front steps and took a deep breath and slowly exhaled the words, "Thank you, Lord. It's a perfect day."

Rebecca and Suzanne were up by eleven and, after a light breakfast, went upstairs to dress for the afternoon. At three o'clock, a continuous caravan of carriages, buggies and lone horsemen began to arrive. Some were Mr. Bourdeau's neighbors, but most were from New Orleans, and a few came from as far as Baton Rouge. Servants worked as quickly as they could while Mr. Bourdeau and Judith welcomed the guests.

Rebecca in an ivory dress was radiant. Suzanne's soft purple dress, dark complexion and shining long black hair, turned many a young man's head as well as some of the older gents. Frankie dressed more casual in light gray pants tucked neatly into a pair of highly polished knee high riding boots. Looking much like his Creole ancestry, the women found him irresistible.

As afternoon wore on, fires were started under the kettles, and the low country boil began. Frankie took Rebecca by the hand and led her to the kettles. Tables were placed near the kettles and each table held different items. One contained a mountain of potatoes that were being sliced into bits. Another held ears of shucked corn while another was covered with diced onions. In several large barrels, Rebecca caught the scent of seafood and walked over to find them filled with shrimp.

"Now how do they put this all together?"

"It's really easy. Since each of the tabled items cook at different rates, you fill the kettles about half full of water, then you first add the potatoes and maybe onions to each of the pots. Later, you add the corn and last the shrimp with a spicy seasoning and you have a low country boil. What do you think about that?"

"I am not sure yet, but will let you know soon." Rebecca laughed.

Rebecca observed servants placing long tables on the floor of the covered platform, then covering them with oil tablecloths. Other servants were in the process of bringing out stacks of plates and napkins. "What about knives and forks?" she questioned.

"You'll see. Show just a little bit of patience," Frankie teased.

The sound of an accordion and violin broke loose from the stage area, and instantly, a guitar and drums followed. Rebecca shook her head and smiled up at Frankie and said, "You don't need to tell me this is the low country of Louisiana. I know the sound."

At six o'clock, Mr. Bourdeau stepped on the large platform to welcome his guest, and then gave thanks and invited them to commence eating. The servants in charge of the boil, quickly strained out the contents from the water with large skimmers and carried them to the tables. They carefully poured the contents on the middle of the oilcloths and spread it out equally. Guests quickly walked to the table, took a plate and napkin, and with their hands, collected their meal.

"You eat with your hands?" she exclaimed. "I've never heard of such."

Frankie laughed and said, "Darling, like you just said. This is the low country and this is a low country boil. Let's go dig in. I hope your hands are clean and everyone else's for that matter," he teased.

Around seven-thirty, the women retired to the rooms to rest and change into more formal clothing while the men stayed downstairs, enjoying their smokes and fellowshipping with one another.

Frankie told Rebecca that he would come for her at nine and for her not to be nervous. Suzanne, having already attended a ball many times, was at ease but excited over the attention she had received from the young men.

Beautifully dressed in her light-tan evening gown with a white blouse that buttoned up to her neck, Rebecca sat impatiently waiting for the knock. Glancing into the mirror across the way, she re-pinned her curly auburn hair behind her ears and straightened her blouse. The knock finally came, and she took a deep breath and went to the door.

"Gracious," he said. "You are beautiful. I feel most honored to be with you tonight."

Rebecca blushed and replied, "Thank you, and I'm looking forward to a night of dancing with you."

As they made their way to the ballroom, they could hear soft sounds of violins, cellos, harp, and a string bass playing a European classic. Rebecca and Frankie were presented as they entered, and Frankie took Rebecca's arm and escorted her to the center of the floor. The crowd applauded then faced the entryway to welcome the next guest. When Suzanne entered, escorted by her grandfather, a roar of approval erupted. After escorting Suzanne, Mr. Bourdeau returned to escort his daughter to the ballroom. Then Mr. Bourdeau gave another welcome and nodded to the band. The first selection was a waltz, and Frankie took Rebecca's hand and led her to the center of the floor as the dance began.

The French doors were opened, allowing the cool December breeze to flow across the floor. Through the glassed cupola, Rebecca saw a star-filled sky and felt like she was gliding across the heavens.

Rebecca noticed the young men surrounding Suzanne and remarked to Frankie, "I don't think your sister is having any problem getting the young men's attention. They seem to be fighting to capture her affection."

After hours of dancing, Frankie asked Rebecca if she would go outside with him. Rebecca was relieved and wanted some fresh air and quietness. A full moon hovered overhead illuminating the night, and all seemed peaceful. The cool northern breeze bathed their faces, and Frankie placed his arm around Rebecca's waist and pulled her close to him. "Isn't it all so beautiful?" he whispered, looking out across the countryside. "It's like heaven on earth."

The music played softly from inside as Rebecca reached up and ran her hand tenderly across his face.

Drawn to her, Frankie leaned down and kissed her, and she placed her arms around him and returned the kiss. There was no blush this time as Rebecca held him, and without speaking, the two walked to a bench located near the path and sat in silence, gazing at the moon and a lone cloud.

Frankie broke the quiet moment with these words, "Rebecca, I know how you loved John, and as his friend, I loved him too. Without a doubt, he would have given his life for me, if needed."

Rebecca gazed into his eyes as he spoke.

"Lord knows, I have my faults, but I do care for you. I've always cared for you."

Rebecca's breath shortened, and her heart beat rapidly as she listened to him.

"What I'm saying is that I would like for you to marry me. I want you to be my wife - that is, if you can love me. I know it may not be the kind of love you had for John, but we could have our own special kind of love."

Rebecca took a deep breath, and with tears forming, reached over and pulled Frankie to her. "I don't know what to say," she whispered, laboring over her words. "I do care for you, but are you sure it's me you want?"

Frankie leaned down and kissed her again. "You're more than I deserve and more than I ever thought would be possible for me."

Silence prevailed as they held each other and sensing an uncertainty, Frankie looked down into her eyes and said, "Marriage is a lifetime commitment, so if you need some time to think about it, take the time you need. I plan to wait for you as long as it takes."

***

The night after the ball and a night's stay at the Hotel Royal in New Orleans, the party boarded the boat for Vicksburg to return home. Rebecca wandered up to the top deck to enjoy the river and sort out her thoughts. She noticed Mrs. Olliver standing nearby.

"Please forgive me for intruding. I love to stand up here and look out as the river rushes by," she said, placing her arm around Rebecca's waist.

Rebecca placed her hand on Mrs. Olliver's hand and said, "Thank you for introducing me to another world, another lifestyle, another culture."

"It was our pleasure. You are a wonderful, sweet, intelligent young woman."

The women stood a moment in silence as the water of the mighty Mississippi rushed, splashed and gurgled its way to the gulf.

Mrs. Olliver then squeezed Rebecca's hand. "Darling, I would love to have you in our family, to be my daughter-in-law. The world you have entered is not a fantasy. It's reality. Your every dream will be at your fingertips. I do want you to give it thought. This empire you have seen can be yours as well as the heart of my son."

Mrs. Olliver left Rebecca to think. Standing alone, the cold wind sweeping off the waters seemed so invigorating. Looking up she prayed, "Lord, clear my eyes, direct my steps and help me to make the right decision. Lord, I can never forget the love I feel for John, but if I need to let go and allow Frankie to fill this place in my heart, please let me know."

15

The Train Home

Ask and it will be given to you; seek and you will find; knock and the door
will be opened to you. For everyone who asks receives; he who seeks finds;
and to him who knocks, the door will be opened.
—Luke 11:9-10

The train gave a loud whistle, and bellows of smoke boiled from the smokestack, as it slowly crept into Newton Station. The Walkers eagerly waited for the train's arrival.

Rebecca wiped away the condensation on her window formed from the bitter cold. She waved continuously at her parents huddled on the walkway of the station.

As soon as the train safely stopped and the conductor placed the steps, Rebecca bounded down to greet her parents with hugs and kisses. The Ollivers collected their baggage and headed toward Rebecca and her parents. After greeting and thanking the Ollivers, Thomas took Rebecca's luggage, placed it in his buggy and assisted the women into their seats. As they pulled from the station, Frankie called out to Rebecca, "Don't forget."

Rebecca nodded her head and waved back to him.

"What was that about?" asked her mother.

"We'll talk later." Rebecca sighed. "It'll be so good to get home."

Rebecca used the eighteen miles from Newton Station to Little Rock to describe in detail the unbelievable events she had experience. Later that evening Rebecca, dressed for bed, threw a shawl around her shoulders and ventured to her parent's bedroom to enjoy the warmth of their fire. Rebecca related again all she had experienced, then grew noticeably quiet as she contemplated telling her parents about Frankie.

"What has got you thinking so hard, darling?"

Rebecca hesitated. "I am not sure how to tell you."

"What do you need to tell us, dear?" her mother questioned.

"Frankie asked me to marry him," she whispered.

"Rebecca!" exclaimed her mother.

"Frankie Olliver asked you to marry him?" echoed her father. "What did you say?"

Rebecca shook her head. "I told him I had to think about it."

"Think about it! Are you out of your mind, daughter! You should have said yes," her father said, reaching over to give her a hug. "You need to let him know your answer is yes as soon as possible."

"Now Thomas, we need to talk soundly about this," Mrs. Walker said, refusing to celebrate yet. "Rebecca, you know the kind of life that Frankie can give you. And because of the war, there is no one left here in Little Rock that could take care of you like Frankie can. But you also have to think about how Frankie feels about you and how you feel about him."

Rebecca listened to her mother's words and reflected, "Mother, I know Frankie has wealth. I've seen how much he will inherit. I know it can be important, but most important is if Frankie loves me and I love him. We both care about each other, and I think it may be enough, but I want to be sure."

Thomas looked into his daughter's eyes and spoke his mind clearly. "Darling, I agree with your mother. There are not many desirable men left around here. Now take Frankie, he's a handsome young man, smart and could offer you things most women only dream about. You marry him, and you'd be the richest woman in Mississippi, maybe in the whole South. You've admitted you care about each other, so put that together and your decision ought to be easy."

"It does seem to make sense, doesn't it? I'm sure Frankie will be by to see me soon."

December 10, 1865

A steady cold rain had fallen for the past three days keeping the people in Wickliffe confined to the comfort of their homes. John stood at the jail window deep in thought, staring at the muddied, vacant street. A week had passed since Mr. Wickliffe talked to him, and he was disappointed he had not heard a word. John glanced at himself in the mirror behind Hank's desk and walked closer. Turning his head from one side to the other, he stated to the image in the mirror, "What's happened to your youth?" He ran his hand across his temple, exposing white hair. "White hair too. When you left home, you weighed one hundred and eighty pounds. Now you probably weigh two hundred. Guess you're going to be as big as your father."

John thought about home and General Wickliffe and continued to talk to his image, "I guess it was all idle talk. Well, at least it gave me some hope."

Hank knocked the mud off his boots at the door, then angrily slung his oilcloth on a peg behind his desk. "I'm tired of rain and cold weather and gummy mud," he complained, moving to the woodstove.

"Say you're tired." John laughed.

"Yep, but I ain't too tired for a game of checkies."

"Checkies, you don't really want to play me. It ain't no fun any more."

"Ain't no fun! What do you mean, boy? You and I has had many a good time playing."

John pulled up a chair facing Hank and explained, "Look at it this way. We play

200

one or two games. I always win, then you get mad and throw the checkie board and checkies all over the place. That ain't exactly what I call fun."

"Heck! That's what I like about it," laughed Hank. "It's getting mad and seeing them checkies fly that makes this game for me. Let's play. Who knows, this might be the day I win one, and then you can throw the checkies."

"Well, I guess I'm still the prisoner. Get the board, and let's go at it," agreed John.

"You know, I'm going to miss you when yore time's up. You sure turned out the work these past months."

Hank laid the checkerboard out and started placing the checkers on their squares.

"Hank, you get any word from the general?"

"Naw, not a word. That ain't unusual. He's a peculiar man."

"I thought sure he would come for me to help him with his place."

"He'll getcha when he wants you. You ready?"

"Hank, do you think he was serious about helping me?"

Hank twisted his neck and looked at John. "He may be a peculiar ole cuss, but he'll shore enough do what he says. Now, let's play. I'm gonna move first."

Hank jumped a few of John's checkers, and, when it looked like he was going to make a run, John slowly made his moves toward cleaning the board. Hank's face turned red with apprehension. With only two of his checkers left on the board, Hank could already sense the outcome. Just as he was about to admit defeat, the door opened.

"Well, what do we have here? You tell him yet," stated Reverend Wilcox with a wide smile.

"Shhh!" whispered Hank. "I ain't beat yet. I still got two left."

Instantly, John made his move and snapped up Hank's last two checkers. "That does it. The board is clean. Games over. You can throw the board now - that is, if'n you want to show the preacher how your temper can get the best of you." John chuckled.

"And Preacher, what was he suppose to tell me?"

"Hank, you haven't given this boy the note from the general?"

Hank dropped his head. "I was about to give it to him. I only got it yesterday," replied Hank, reaching into his coat pocket.

Hank handed John a note, and turned to stare out the window at the rain pounding the boardwalk.

John read the note and quietly folded and placed it in his pocket. Then to the top of his voice, he shouted, "Thank you, Lord! Thank you! I'm finally going home."

Mr. Wickliffe had talked extensively with Judge Henry, and after much chastising, the judge had agreed to drop all charges. John would be released as soon as the paperwork was complete. The judge would then notify John, and he would be free to go.

John embraced the preacher and walked to Hank who stood gazing outside.

"Hank, why didn't you tell me yesterday?"

"When I first met you, I didn't care much for you, but with time, you kind of grew on me. Truth is you've made my life interesting and brought pleasure to this job. I used to hang around this old jail, walk the streets, take a few drunks home to their wives and go work my farm. It was the same day after day. Then, you come along and turned my job upside down. We've got to visit almost all the citizens, and I've always had a friend right here by me day in and day out."

Hank pulled John into his arms, hugged him and, fighting back the tears, muttered, "I'm gonna miss you, and I love you, boy."

"You may be an ornery ole cuss sometimes, but I love you too, Hank."

Pastor Wilcox spoke as he was leaving. "John, my prayers have been with you, and the good Lord has granted my plea. At least, we'll have one more Sunday service together."

John asked Hank after the pastor left, "You think you can spare me some stationary?"

"I think I can handle that for you, boy."

"How about a stamp?"

"You pushing me, but maybe, just maybe you've earned one stamp and the ink. I guess the pen will also be free."

John laughed. "I'm going to write me a letter to one Miss Rebecca Walker at Little Rock, Mississippi, and I'm going tell her that I'm on my way home, and she'd better have those arms open for me. I'm going to tell her that I ain't ever going to leave her for the rest of my life. And I want her to tell Mama and Papa, I'm coming home. How long do you think it will take to get there?"

Hank scratched his head. "It's a long way, boy. It's gonna take a while, I'd say."

***

Frankie rode to the Walker's house after Thomas had closed the store and asked for Rebecca. Mrs. Walker directed him to the parlor, and he anxiously waited. In a few moments, Rebecca entered and sat next to him on the couch.

"I hope you've had a good rest," Frankie said, smiling at her.

"I do feel rested, and the trip to the low country still seems like a fairy tale. It was perfect."

"It was, wasn't it?" Frankie added. "It doesn't have to be a fairy tale, you know. It can become a part of your life."

"I know," she said, looking into his eyes.

"I hope you've considered my offer of marriage."

Rebecca's life was always the same - she got up, dressed, worked at her father's store and came home. Rebecca knew that this could be her only chance to change that. Frankie is a good man, and I really care for him, she thought.

"Frankie, I've decided to marry you," Rebecca whispered.

Frankie took her in his arms, kissed her and whispered, "You've made the right choice. You won't be sorry." Reaching into his pocket, he retrieved a piece of red velvet cloth and opened it revealing a beautiful gold ring with a cluster of sparkling diamonds, mounted high above the band. He gently slipped it onto Rebecca's finger.

"I think I need to speak with your father to ask for his permission," Frankie stated.

Rebecca studied the ring. "It's simply magnificent. It must have cost a fortune."

"I wanted you to have it," Frankie answered, looking at her. "You're so special to me."

Hand in hand, they walked to Rebecca's parent's room, and Frankie asked for Rebecca's hand in marriage.

The Walkers were more than pleased with the proposal and graciously granted their permission. Mrs. Walker suggested a spring wedding, but neither Frankie nor Rebecca wanted to wait that long. They decided to speak with the Ollivers, get their thoughts together and form more definite plans.

***

As the pastor was leaving, he met Doc who held a newspaper over his head and hurried inside out of the rain. Once inside, he stuck out his hand to congratulate John, "News travels fast. I'm proud for you, John."

"You can thank the general for that. It wouldn't have happened without his support," stated John.

"Not so, my boy. Your ole buddy Hank, sent a letter along with Wickliffe's to the judge."

Hank dropped his head, smiled and muttered, "It weren't much."

John turned to him with a sly smile and said, "Didn't know it was in you. I do thank you."

"I'll tell you, John. I'm going to miss you. You're the only one around this place that can give me some mental stimulation," joked Doc.

"Well, I guess you need to go on back to yore practice then. You may have a dab of book sense, but you're a little short on the common," added Hank, wanting the last word.

They all laughed at each other, and Doc grabbed his newspaper and headed back out into the downpour.

Hank rubbed his nose in thought and motioned for John to take a seat. "John, I don't rightly know what to do with you. Basically, you're a free man. I guess until the papers come, you best stay with me."

John shook his head. "This place is like home to me. I'll just stay here."

"Okay, if that's what you want, but I'm not locking up, and you're free to go anywhere you like. Your meals will be with me."

"Hank, you know I can't stand sitting around here with nothing to do. Isn't there something I can help you with while I wait?"

Hank nodded. "Since you've been here, you have shore took my time, and I'm behind with my farm work. I've got plows needing sharpening, harness work, leaking roof on my barn and falling fences."

John turned over his hands palms up. "They're hard as old leather and calloused. I don't mind hard work."

Hank smiled and placed his arm around John's shoulder. "Let's go home and get busy."

"How much you gonna pay me?" teased John.

"Pay you! The food ought to be worth something." He laughed.

Sunday, Hank and John pulled up to the church grounds. People had heard John's news and congregated around his wagon. Congratulations, handshakes and pats on the back made John feel even more assured that his ordeal had ended. Angie watched John entered the church. To her surprise, John walked down the aisle and sat beside her.

She smiled and whispered, "I wasn't sure you would sit with me now you're free."

"Where else would I sit?"

Because John had shared his love of Genesis, Pastor Wilcox opened his Bible and said, "Today, we're going to study the life and trials of Joseph."

John nudged Angie, smiled at the preacher and whispered, "He knows me well."

As he closed his sermon, he looked proudly at John and spoke, "Brothers, Sisters, this sermon today parallels the life of one of our members. John, I want you to come up here with me, if you will."

John slowly rose from his pew, looked around the congregation and walked to the podium.

Placing an arm around John's shoulder, Pastor Wilcox continued, "When John was arrested and his friend killed, we all thought he was a real scoundrel and didn't want anything to do with him, but we were wrong. With his quiet, pleasant disposition and the way he labored tirelessly for us, we began to see the true John Wilson."

"Amen! Amen!" sounded the congregation.

"As you all know, the charges against him have been dropped, and he will soon be on his way home. He's got one problem though."

John frowned with uncertainty.

"The boy has several hundred miles to cover and no money."

John was a little embarrassed for everyone to think about his lack of money.

"Well, John, the Lord works in strange and wonderful ways, and we, as a congregation, would like His ways to start with us, so we took up a collection to help you get home. Who knows, you might even make it by Christmas," he concluded, handing John an envelope.

John smiled with gratitude. He knew times were hard, and he was thankful for their generosity. Holding back tears, he regained his composure and said, "I can't believe all that has happened in my life especially in these past few days. The Lord has covered me with his mercy, and I want to thank this kind and caring congregation for your love and support, and in time, I pray I have the opportunity to help some other soul in need. I'm going to miss you, I'll pray for you, and I love you from depths of my heart."

Tears began streaming down Angie's cheeks as she looked up at the man she had grown to respect and love. He had been her rainbow, her knight in shining armor, and she realized through him, her life had been blessed.

***

After Sister cleared the breakfast table, cleaned and put away the dishes, she untied her apron, hung it on the peg by the stove and looked at the mirror above the washbasin. She brushed off a smudge on her cheek and walked to her parents' bedroom to talk to her mother who was sitting next to the fire darning a pair of socks.

"Can I help you?" Sister asked, pulling a chair close to her mother.

"No, just room for one set of hands here."

"Mama, you remember me asking Papa about celebrating Christmas?"

"I remember."

"It's ten days 'til Christmas and nothing's happened. You think he's changed his mind?"

Sarah laid her work down and answered, "I don't think so. He may be waiting on you. Why don't you go ask him? He's down behind the barn, splitting kindling for the stove."

"I'm afraid to ask him. He might say no," Sister replied quietly.

Sarah smiled at Sister and said, "He's your father, and he loves you more than you know. Now, get yourself wrapped up and go on down and ask him."

Sister grabbed her coat and ran to the back of the barn. She found her father busy splitting wood and placing it in a wheelbarrow to be taken to the house. Lott looked at Sister, smiled and dropped his ax to take a needed rest. He settled on a stump of wood nearby.

"Come to help?" he joked.

Sister shook her head and smiled. "I came to talk to you."

Lott pointed to another stump nearby and, with a twinkle in his eyes, teased, "I bet I know what this is all about. You want me to grant my permission for you to marry that young man you've been courting."

Sister tightened her lips and fussed, "Papa, don't be silly. I'm not ready to leave you or Mama. It's something more important than that."

Lott held his arms upward, lifted his face and said, "Thank you, Lord. I get to keep my precious daughter just a little longer. Now, what is more important than that, dear?"

"Papa, I want us to have Christmas this year," she softly stated. "I want you to let me do some decorating like we used to."

Lott's eyes watered as he looked at his daughter. *What a wonderful child God has blessed me with*, he thought. *How can I be so blind to her needs and her happiness? How can I be such an old fool?*

Lott placed his arms around his daughter and said, "I've been waiting for you to get started. I wondered why you hadn't."

With a big smile, Sister hugged her father, then jumped up and whirled around shouting, "Thank you, Papa, thank you and an early Merry Christmas."

"But remember, no bushes in the house. Too many bugs."

"I know, Papa, but how about a few small cedar branches for the mantle?"

"Long as I don't see no bugs," he muttered, picking up his ax to continue work. "And by the way, I'm going down to Walker's store later today, and I'll pick us up some of those candles like we used to place on the mantle."

Later that afternoon, Lott returned from the store with a paper bag he placed on the bed. Sister had arranged some cedar branches on the mantle above the fireplace. Sister and Sarah joined Lott in front of the mantle, and Lott reached in the paper bag and brought out several large candles. Some were red, and some white. Lott took the old candleholders, and one by one, he lit each candle, dripped a few drops of wax into the base of the holder and pushed each new candle firmly into the holder, then placed them on the mantle. When he finished and the two red and two white candles were burning brightly, he asked, "What do you think?"

Sarah questioned, "We've always used red ones in the past. Were they short on red candles?"

"I don't understand, Papa," added Sister, frowning.

Lott shook his head. "Well, this is the way I see it. Those four red candles in the past represented the lives of our four children - Thomas, James Earl, John and you - and since two of 'em have passed on, I thought I'd represent them in white. Ingenuous, ain't it?"

Sarah rolled her eyes, shook her head and said, "Dear, you amaze me sometimes, but I truly suspect a flaw in your intellect on occasions such as this."

Sister didn't want the moment to be spoiled and spoke up, "I think it's a pretty good idea, Papa. It's nice to have different colors, but let's put the white ones in the middle."

Lott placed his hands on his hips and laughed. "I see you both think my idea is a little strange and that red is the only color Christmas candles should be, but this year, you will have to just put up with me."

***

Meanwhile, at Walker's store, Thomas was busily placing his bills in their designated slots in the cashbox when he heard horses in the distance and a bell ringing. He pushed the drawer closed and hurried to the front of his store. "Stage is early today," he mumbled to himself. "Rebecca usually handles this for me."

He walked outside to meet the stage and took several packages coming in from Meridian and was handed the mailbag. Mr. Walker placed the packages behind the counter to be identified later and emptied the mail on top of the counter. He quickly sorted out the letters to be boxed. All of a sudden, his eyes caught one addressed to Miss Rebecca Walker. Picking it up, he examined it closer. Part of the left corner containing the return address was torn revealing only the city's name, barely legible, Wickliffe, Kentucky. "Wickliffe, Kentucky?" he frowned. "She don't know nobody up that ways," he mumbled. Noticing that the letter was only partially sealed, he figured that a slip of his knife blade would easily open the cover, and with a little glue, it could be resealed. Unable to control his curiosity, he slipped the blade inside the cover. Unfolding the letter, he read the note. His hands began to tremble, his breath shortened and perspiration ran down his face. "Bet!" he called. "You better come in here right now!"

His wife was sorting stock in the back room and called, "Is it really that urgent?"

"Come here!" he shouted. "We've got a problem! A big one!"

Mrs. Walker stopped what she was doing and fussed to herself about the interruption. Thomas waved a letter in his hand. "You've got to read this. This could change all our dreams," he fumed.

Mrs. Walker calmly read the letter and contemplated its meaning. "Well, this is going to be important to Rebecca. She will have another decision to make."

"What are you talking about, woman! This is our decision, and we need to make it right now."

"I don't understand what you mean. How is this our decision?"

"We need to protect Rebecca's future. The way I see it, we need to decide if we are going to let Rebecca read this or not."

"It's hers, she should read it."

They sat silently for a while, then Thomas stated, "I think it's best Rebecca not see this letter. We will carry out the wedding as planned, and her future will be secure."

Betty slowly nodded her head in agreement but still not convinced this was best.

"I think we need to see the Ollivers and talk with Frank Sr. and Judith. Rebecca and Frankie have been wanting to move the wedding date up, and I think that is a must. You know, what could be more appropriate than a Christmas wedding? We could have it here in Little Rock and not in the St. Louis Cathedral. Get your wrap."

Betty took her husband by the hand. "Thomas, what if Rebecca had met the stage like she usually does? What do you think she would have wanted to do?"

"Let's just not think about it." Walking faster, Mr. Walker said, "I'm just glad it was me who saw the letter first."

The Walkers met with the Ollivers. Both couples were upset about the news and agreed that it was best that Rebecca and Frankie never know of the letter. They began making plans for a Christmas wedding using the Little Rock Church. With only ten days left, plans would need to be finalized quickly.

Frank Sr. secretly employed men to watch the Newton Station and placed men on all roads leading into Little Rock. Every traveling person would be scanned and any suspicious person was to be seized and taken to Meridian until further notice. Frank Sr. knew how to get what he wanted and had no doubt this wedding would take place.

As Thomas was dressing for bed, the letter slipped from his pocket. He hurriedly picked it up and placed it in the family Bible. Tomorrow, he and Bet would talk to Rebecca about the Christmas wedding, and he would make sure she never saw the letter.

***

The fire turned to embers, and the glow of the candles flickered light to the ceiling. Sarah and Lott had retired to bed for the night and were in each other's arms, sharing their deep thoughts, a regular ritual. Sarah whispered, "Thank you for what you did today. You made our daughter very happy. I guess that's why I love you like I do."

"You know, I've been an old fool too long. I think the Lord has finally softened my heart. I hope He'll forgive me."

"Have you asked him to?"

"I have."

"Then you don't need to worry. It's getting late. You might want to blow out the candles," Sarah said, giving her husband a kiss.

When Lott came in from work the next day for lunch, he sat down, eased his cold feet up near the fire and relaxed. As he looked at the mantle for any hatched-out bugs, he noticed something unusual. The candles on the mantle were changing colors. One of the white ones had red wax running down the side.

When Sarah came into the room, Lott pointed to the pinkish candle and said, "Did you do something to that candle?"

"Dear, what are you talking about? All I've done since I got up was bake and clean in the kitchen, getting the meals for the day complete."

"What about Sister?"

"She left right after breakfast to spend the day with her friend, Susan."

Lott figured it must be a flaw in the candle, and taking down the pink one, he replaced it with a new white one.

***

Anxiously, John grabbed his coat and waited for Hank to pick him up for work. His disappointment grew because the official document releasing him had not come. Sometimes, it seemed his dream of a Christmas homecoming was just that - a dream. He watched as strong northern winds whipped through the streets carrying leaves and scraps of paper with it. The old folks at church were saying that this was the worst early winter they had known. Hearing the rattling of a wagon, John walked out to meet Hank. After a hot breakfast, they ventured to the shed to repair harnesses and sharpen plowshares. Right before midday, they heard someone calling from around the house.

Hank called out, "Down here, Buddy."

Buddy McMichael was the owner of a dry goods store in town and served as the local postmaster. He waved a letter in his hand and called, "Morning, Hank and John, I think this might be what you been looking for."

John's heart beat rapidly as he watched Hank take the letter and open it. In a moment, he nodded his head, smiled and handed the letter to John.

John read it carefully, closed his eyes in prayer and whispered, "Thank you, Lord. The road home is finally open."

Thanking Buddy, John turned to Hank, extended his hand and said, "Well, this is it old friend. If you'll take me back to the jail, I'll collect my belongings and be headed south.

Hank replied, "Slow down, John. Let's make sure you're ready first."

After lunch, in the warmth of Hank's kitchen, they talked of plans.

"Now, John. How much money did the congregation give you?"

"About sixty dollars."

"Well, it's December twentieth. That gives you five days. The train might be yore answer, but that ain't enough money, so I'm givin' you a little present early – an extra twenty dollars."

"You don't need to do that, Hank."

"Well, it's not really me; it's some of the money you worked for. I'd give you more, but the school took the rest."

People began to flock to Hank's house to wish John well. Doc spent the whole afternoon at Hanks, and to John's surprise, Wally strolled in about mid-afternoon. Dressed in his normal baggy pants, uncombed hair and heavy woolen coat, he entered and saluted. "Reporting for duty, General."

John said in reply, "At ease, Private."

Wally dropped his hand and relaxed. "Wally's going with ya, General. Them Yanks may still be after ya. I'll be yore bodyguard."

John placed his arm around Wally. "No, Private, you best stay here and guard Mr. Hank."

Hank rolled his eyes and shook his head, no.

Wally cast his eyes on Hank, saluted and stated, "Wally's gonna take good care of you, Hank. I might even make you a major."

"You got two more orders, Private Wally," John stated. "First, you need to take care of your mother, and then I want you in church every Sunday."

Wally smiled. "That ain't gonna be hard, General. I been think'n about doing some preaching."

At that, the men began to chuckle.

Wally frowned. "What y'all laughing about? You think there ain't no sinners around here."

John stated, "You're right about that, Wally. We're all sinners turned to saints in the Lord each day."

By dusk, John had returned to the jail to pack his few belongings, when he heard a wagon approach and saw Angie and her father. After the pastor helped his daughter from the wagon, they came in to say goodbye. Angie's father left the jail and walked down the street so Angie would have a moment alone with John. Angie took John's hand

and quietly spoke, "I'm going to miss you, and I want to thank you for your friendship."

"Angie, the pleasure was mine. I could not have made it without you, your father and the church. You know you're special to me, but I guess I gave my heart away a long time ago. You'll find that special man one day."

"John, do you think you could write me when you get home, just as a special friend? Just to let me know how you're doing? Who knows, I might even have some news one day to share with you about finding that special man."

"Angie, I'd really like that. Maybe one day, you will get to meet Rebecca. You both are a lot alike, and I know you'd like her."

John reached over, wiped away her tears and, pulling her close to him, held her in his arms and whispered, "You'll always be my special friend; one who saw me through some difficult times. And I'll always be grateful."

As night approached, John found sleeping difficult, and at first dawn, he was up and waiting to say goodbye to Hank.

The glow of light through the window let Hank know that John was ready. Hank opened the door to find John dressed and next to the woodstove. He held a small bundle tied with a string.

"I see you're ready," Hank said, placing his hands over the stove to warm them.

"I am definitely ready."

"Let's go over what we talked about last night. You take my horse and ride south to Columbus. It's only twenty miles. When you get there, where are you gonna take it?"

"Pope's Stables, south end of town, not far from the station," John replied.

"That's right, Pope's Stables and you ask for Jack. Tell 'em who you are and that I'll be picking my horse up later. You got all that?"

"Yes sir, and I'm grateful to you."

"Now John, you should have enough money to get home, but be careful. In these hard times, there folk's out there that'll take you." Hank pointed to an oilcloth and hat hanging on a peg on the wall. "It's nasty out there, so take that oilcloth and that broad-brimmed hat. That brim will keep the rain from running down your neck. Now you need to get out of here if you have plans to get home by Christmas."

John picked up his bundle, walked over and wrapped his arms around Hank. "Thank you for everything, ole friend."

"Humph," grunted Hank. "I'm gonna miss you, boy."

Releasing him, John smiled. "Well, you're gonna have Wally to keep you company, and you two ought to have some close checkie games."

"I don't know why you put him off on me. You know he gets on my nerves, and for the checkies, I throwed 'em in the stove yesterday," Hank explained with a smirk turning into a smile.

The two embraced once more, and John walked out, mounted Hank's horse and, kicking him in the flanks, headed for home.

Hank took out his handkerchief, blew his nose and thought, *If I had been blessed with a son, I'd want him to be just like that boy.*

John turned the horse back for a moment and waved to Hank and then pushed the horse into a full gallop. As John rode away, he could hear Hank call, "Boy, you've been through some hard times, but remember, beyond the storm, there's often a rainbow."

A light mist fell, but by mid-morning, John had covered the twenty miles, and Columbus came into view. It was a rail town and much larger than Wickliffe. John could see the station and tracks at the far end of town. Buildings lined both sides of the muddied street, and down to his left he saw a sign posted above the entrance of a large barn identifying it as Pope's Stables. Pulling his horse to a stop, he dismounted, secured the reins and walked into the barn. Jack was throwing hay to stalled horses, and John introduced himself and relayed the message from Hank. He then walked the boarded sidewalk to the station. As he passed a clothing store displaying beautiful women's dresses in the window and Simpson's Jewelry Store next door, John's thoughts turned to Rebecca. All of a sudden, he realized there was one thing he needed to purchase before he reached home. He reached in his pocket, took out his money and counted it. He tucked the coins into his pocket and knew it would be tight.

When John reached the station, he found the ticket office and went to the window.

"Sir," John said, getting the clerk's attention.

An elderly man, dressed in a neat dark-blue suit, completely bald and with a long white mustache, adjusted his glasses. "Yes sir. How can I help you?"

"You familiar with the Mississippi lines?"

"I've been here for quite a spell, son," he smiled, readjusting his glasses.

"You ever hear of Newton Station?"

"Yep, where the Yanks came on their raid through Mississippi."

"Can you get me there?" asked John. "By Christmas?"

"It'll cost you."

"How much?"

The old man took his pen and figured for a minute. "Fifty dollars."

"Fifty dollars! That's a lot," exclaimed John.

"Yep, that'll do it, but to get from here to Newton Station by Christmas is going to be pretty near impossible. Maybe if the weather and the state of the tracks are good. The Yankees tore up some of the tracks during the war."

John walked from the window solemnly and settled in a chair nearby. *I have enough money for the ticket, but don't have enough for what I need to buy*, he reasoned. For several moments, he sat silently in thought, then with a smile, went back to the clerk's window.

"Excuse me, sir. Would you mind telling me the route it would take to reach Newton Station?"

"That's not a problem. From here, you would travel southeast to Jackson,

Tennessee. Now, Jackson is a pretty large town, and there the tracks split, and you'd take the train to Corinth, Mississippi. At Corinth, you'd travel south to Meridian and head west twenty miles to Newton Station. Why'd you want to know?"

"Just wondered. How much would a ticket to Corinth be?" John asked hopefully.

"Well, let me see. That would be about thirty-five dollars."

"Thank you, sir, I'll be right back to buy a ticket. I've got to run an errand first.

John knew the train would be soon approaching, so he hurried back down the street.

John quickly found the store and looked at the display in encased glass. He leaned down and studied each one.

"May I help you?" said a gentleman.

John pointed to the display. "I'm interested in purchasing a ring. That's a pretty one with the small diamond," he said. "How much is it?"

The clerk opened the back of the casing, brought out the ring and handed it to John. "You do have good taste. It's one hundred twenty dollars," he stated.

John knew that the others would be out of his price range, but he continued to look and found a pretty opal ring. He carefully held it to the light and thought about how it would look on Rebecca's finger and how surprised she would be. He asked again for a price. "Well, that one is fifty-five dollars, sir."

John handed the ring back to the clerk. "I'm sorry, I don't have that kind of money. Could you show me some others?"

One by one, the clerk brought rings for John to see but like the first ones, they were beyond his means. Finally, John said, "How about just a gold band?"

The clerk asked, "Please forgive me but how much do you have to spend?"

John thought for a moment, then answered, "Sir, I have about forty dollars."

Looking directly at John, he said, "I noticed you had a slight limp when you walked in. I don't suppose it's related to the war, is it?

John glanced down at his leg. "Yankee mini ball," he answered.

A grim look formed on the clerk's face and his said softly, "I lost my son at Shiloh. He was my only son."

"I'm sorry to hear that, sir." Knowing it was futile to waste the man's time, John extended his hand to the clerk and said, "I'm a little short, but I guess I better get the band."

As John stood waiting, the clerk asked, "Is this for someone special?"

"The sweetest and prettiest girl in Mississippi," answered John with a wide smile.

"I think we can work something out here for you," said the clerk.

"It'll be forty dollars, sir," the clerk said, and he chose the very ring that John had looked at so carefully.

John's eyes widened. "Sir, you must be confused. That's the opal, not the gold band."

A smile crossed the clerk's face, and his eyes watered. "I'm not confused. You place it on that young woman's finger, and I pray you have the best Christmas ever."

John thanked the gentleman and murmured to himself, "Thank you, Lord, for granting my desire."

John headed quickly to the train depot, purchased his ticket and was soon headed to Corinth. Now he must think of a way to get to the Newton Station from Corinth.

As John approached Jackson, Tennessee, he remembered to board the Corinth train. John knew the ride to Corinth would be long on his emigrant-priced ticket, but he couldn't complain because he had Rebecca's ring in his pocket. His seating was near the cattle car and somewhat colder than on the previous train. John could tell the weather was turning for the worst.

As daylight slowly broke on Christmas Eve, John, with hunger gnawing in his stomach, stood under a gray overcast sky on the walkway outside the train depot in Corinth, Mississippi. What little money the congregation of Wickliffe had given him was gone. He knew he would have to quickly find someone heading south and catch a ride. He would definitely not make it for Christmas Eve but was determined to get home even if he had to walk every step of the way.

A commotion down the tracks caught John's attention. A train was waiting on the tracks with steam puffing from its smokestack, and the conductors were frowning toward the engine, wondering about the delay. As John approached, he saw a man being lowered to the ground from near the engineer's compartment.

"Just my luck. This train's ready to pull out, and I got a drunk fireman. How can the railroad expect me to stay on schedule with a no-good drunk firing my engine?" complained the engineer.

John immediately pushed through the crowd. "Where's this train headed?" he questioned, stepping up to the man.

"Goin'! We ain't going nowhere till I get somebody sober to fire my boiler."

"Where you goin' then?" pressed John. "You headed south?"

"Yep, we're headed south to Meridian and then west to Jackson. That is, if I get this crate moving."

John shoved his hand toward the engineer. "How about takin' me on? I can fire it. I'm John Wilson, and I need a ride as far as Newton, Miss'sippi. You let me do the firin', and I won't charge you a thing."

The gentleman studied the young man for a few seconds and then extended his hand. "You fought for the Confed'racy, didn't ya?"

"Yes sir. Miss'sippi infantry, and I'm trying to get home," replied John, excitedly.

"Well, Mr. Wilson, you have just been employed. I'm Fred McCleary. Let's see you get up there and fire that thing, and by the way, I rode with Gen'ral Forrest. You heard about him, ain't you?"

"Yes sir."

John knew home was only hours away. By mid-morning, after a two-hour delay, the train was steaming south toward Meridian.

***

The candles had not been lit the previous night, so Sister took a small burning branch from the fire, reached up and lit the candles. Satisfied, she sat and watched the tiny flames dance about the room. Her thoughts traveled to the real reason for Christmas, and she looked at her parents both relaxed and said, "You know, if it hadn't been for Christ, we'd have no hope at all. We would live our life here on earth, die and exist no more. In fact, in a matter of years, no one would even know we ever existed except maybe for our name on a gravestone. But with our faith in Him, we have peace on earth and hope for eternal life with Him. Isn't that wonderful?"

Proud of their daughter's spiritual revelation, Lott and Sarah stopped their reading to respond.

"Sister, what wonderful thoughts. I'm so glad you're thinking about what the Lord really means to us," commented Sarah.

Lott smiled with pride at his daughter's words and pondered the truth she had shared. *Lord*, he prayed, *open my eyes, and help me build my faith in you and be thankful for the hope we have in your Son.*

The next day, Lott checked the cows and carried a load of corn to the mill to be ground. Finally, he headed to his bedroom to relax and get warm. Checking the time on the clock centered on the mantel and admiring the decorations, his heart stopped. Rubbing his eyes, he looked once again.

"Sarah! Sister! I want you in here now!"

Girded with aprons, they hurried in from the kitchen. "What is it, dear?" exclaimed Sarah.

Pointing to the mantle, he muttered, "This has gone far enough. You two are trying to tease me, and it's not funny. I know you wanted red candles, but don't keep changing the colors on these. I've only got one white candle left."

"Papa, are you alright?" Sister asked.

"Look up there," he said, pointing to the mantel.

There it was, two red candles, one white, and one that was slowly changing from white to pink and now even a little red.

"I don't like this," he muttered. "You shouldn't trick me this way."

"Darling, we have done nothing. Perhaps it's a flaw in the candles."

Lott thought for a moment, then went to the mantle, took the flawed one down and moved his last white candle in its place. "That should do it," he said, throwing the pinkish candle into the fire.

***

Frank briefly met with his foreman, Junior Barrett, to discuss his plans.

"Junior," Frank queried, "you got the roads covered?"

Junior, weighing more than two hundred pounds and seldom showing emotion, shook his head. "I got it covered twenty-four hours a day. I got men placed at Newton Station and others on the roads coming in from Union, Decatur, Beulah Church Road, Meridian and two of the less used roads from the north. We got 'em all covered. The way I figure it, is he's coming by rail. If so, we'll get him."

Mr. Olliver smiled, nodded his head and slipping a bundle of money into Barrett's hand, said, "Just be sure you get him, and keep this quiet. Understand?"

What if it takes force?" Junior asked.

"Do whatever it takes."

"What if we have to kill him, Mr. Olliver?"

"Junior, did you not hear what I said? Do whatever it takes," Mr. Olliver said, calmly looking at his foreman.

"I understand. We'll take care of him."

***

On Christmas eve, Sister lighted the candles. "Papa, I hope you don't mind."

Lott shook his head. "You go ahead, dear."

He realized he had been silly about the flawed candle. *Now all will be fine*, he thought. *We can celebrate our two children who live, but we can also celebrate the lives of our other two children who are in heaven with the Lord. That will make Christmas perfect.*

***

John sat on a stack of wood behind the boiler, enjoying the north Mississippi countryside when McCleary turned and shouted, "John, it's gotten mighty cold the past hour. Don't look good."

John shook his head in agreement. "I know it must be might near freezing, and the looks of them low gray clouds means snow," observed John. "It don't usually snow here in December."

"We can't ever predict what the Good Lord's going to send us, but we'll get you to Newton before seven tonight, regardless of the weather," McCleary answered.

John smiled at McCleary, thankful he would be home, but disappointed that he would not be home in time to fulfill his Christmas Eve dream. Even if the train reached Newton by seven, John still faced an eighteen-mile walk.

***

Rebecca, standing on a stool, dressed in her beautiful, white silken wedding dress, tried not to move as her mother tediously made some minor alterations. Tired from standing, Rebecca twisted and gazed out the open window of the parlor. Tiny snowflakes flittered, and she frowned in disbelief and then exclaimed, "Mother, you won't believe this."

"Be still, darling, I might stick myself," her mother answered, tugging her back into position.

"No, Mother, it's snowing outside!"

"You're teasing. It doesn't snow here very often, and when it does, not this early in the winter."

"Well, you better look outside."

Mrs. Walker laid her needle down, and the two went to the window, pulled the curtain aside and looked out.

"Gracious dear, it is snowing," murmured Mrs. Walker.

As if the heavens had opened their gates, large flakes were now drifting and swirling to the ground.

"Isn't it beautiful," Rebecca said. The two silently watched the wonderland in progress.

Then Rebecca asked, "What about my wedding? Will this alter our plans?"

Mrs. Walker shook her head and smiled, "Not at all, dear. It'll be over by morning, and there won't be any problem getting to church."

***

A tall man in a long coat with the collar turned up in the back and a wide brimmed hat with woolen scarf stood under the porch of Newton Station, shivering in the cold. Hands wrapped under his armpits, he stomped around trying to keep his feet from freezing. Lifting the front cover of his coat, he looked at the pistol holstered inside. He moved up and down the platform, observing anyone who approached. With the snow now covering the walkway, he did not look forward to the night.

16

Dreams in the Snow

*He gives strength to the weary and increases the power of the weak. Even youths grow
tired and weary, and young men stumble and fall; but those who hope in
the Lord will renew their strength. They will soar on wings like eagles; they
will run and not grow weary, they will walk and not be faint.*
—Isaiah 40:29-31

The train soon pulled out of the depot and headed west. The sleet that had fallen
for the past hour was now turning to snow. John kept throwing logs into the boiler and
praying they would reach Newton without a problem.

At ten minutes after seven, McCleary pulled the whistle cord that sent a shrill blast
echoing through the darkness.

"John, we're pulling into Newton Station. You think you going to recognize the
place?"

"Sure will, Mr. McCleary. Been down here many a time with my Papa. Seems like
yesterday."

"Well, it's changed some since you last seen it. The Yankees burnt the station and
some of the buildings with it. They had to rebuild the station. A Yank named Grierson
made a raid through here. John, look at the big flakes coming down. I tell ya one thing,
I ain't ever seen snow falling like this in Miss'sippi, not in December. I hope you ain't
planning to go it on foot tonight. You might just freeze out there."

The train came to a slow, screeching stop, and John carefully eased down on a
stool. "Mr. McCleary, it's been might near three years since I seen my folks, and I ain't
going to let snow stop me when I'm as close as I am now."

Most passengers had left the train and hurried to gather their baggage and head to
the warmth of the station. In a matter of minutes, the walkway was cleared, and only the
sluggish chug of the steam engine broke the silence of the evening. Soon, people would
gather to board the train for its next destination.

McCleary looked down the walkway below and saw a man approaching.

Teeth chattering from the cold, he muttered, "You think this is all that's getting
off?"

McCleary looked down the walkway once more and nodded. "I think that's gonna
be it, sir. Can I help you?"

The man glared up at him. "I guess that man up there with you fires yore boiler?"

"Yes, he does," answered McCleary.

The stranger studied the two for a minute then asked, "When's the next train scheduled to arrive?"

McCleary thought for a moment. "In this kind of weather, you can't tell, but probably ten in the morning."

"Humph," grunted the man, walking away. "Ten in the morning. I ain't gonna stay out here all night and freeze. I'm going home."

McCleary followed John to the ground, almost slipping on one of the steps.

"Hold up, John!" he insisted. "I want to thank you for the job you done for me. It sure helped us keep this ole crate moving. I just hope the man I picked up in Meridian can fill your shoes. But I'm more concerned about you being out in this weather. You best stay here in town till morning."

"Can't do that, Mr. McCleary. I've got to get on home. Ain't nothin' gonna stop me now."

"Well, I guess I'd do the same, but if you start getting cold and sleepy, you stop at somebody's house and get out of the cold. Now remember, don't go sleeping out in the cold. You'll freeze. You hear me?"

John shook McCleary's hand. "I hear you. Don't go sleeping out in the cold," repeated John. "And thank you for taking me on with you."

McCleary quickly crawled back up to his compartment and threw a blanket down.

"That old coat and oilcloth might not be enough. This here might help some. You take care now, and a Merry Christmas to you."

"Merry Christmas to you, Mr. McCleary," replied John as the train moved out.

The streets were completely deserted with only a few dim lights from several store windows silhouetting the walkways. The townspeople had already retired to the warmth of their homes.

John suddenly felt a surge of loneliness. With no one in sight and a deep snow covering the ground, John thought, *I've got eighteen miles to go. We marched a lot further than that in the army. All I have to do is just take one step at a time.*

Home for John meant walking nine miles north to the village of Decatur and then another nine miles northeast to Little Rock. This time of the year, roads would be almost impassable by wagon, and several streams would have to be forded. Travel on foot, especially at night, was dangerous.

The snow was now falling heavier than ever and visibility was difficult. Deep ruts in the road helped him find his way through the darkness, and to his surprise, the bridges outside of Newton were still intact. After more than three hours, John reached the outskirts of Decatur. Facing a stream south of the village with no bridge, he had to take off his shoes and wade across. As he reached the opposite bank, he recognized a large bent oak tree up ahead and knew he was only a short distance from the town.

Through the falling snow, a dim light appeared. *Probably Taylor's Tavern*, John thought. The stage stop should be located on the edge of town. The light and the thought of getting out of the cold spurred him on. With hands almost frozen, he pushed the door open and stumbled in. Toward the back of the tavern was a low fire burning in a large fireplace. John's sudden entry startled two elderly men sitting next to the fire, quietly enjoying an evening smoke.

"Boy, where'd you come from?" questioned one as he pushed his chair back so the stranger could get to the fire.

John stood, shivering as steam rolled from his wet clothing. He tried to speak, but was shaking so hard the men could not understand a word he said.

"Jacob, this here boy is 'bout frozen. Here lad, take off that wet blanket, and let me get you sumpthin' dry. You must be some kind of fool to be out on a night like this. I'm Jimmy Taylor. I own this place, and that there is my cousin, Jacob."

After more than an hour, John began to come around. "Want to thank you for the dry blanket, and I ain't a fool. I'm from Little Rock, and I'm on my way home tonight. Been gone for most near three years. I'm John Wilson, son of Lott Wilson."

The old men shook their heads. "We know of Lott Wilson, and I had more than a few run-ins with that Uncle Jake of yours. That is, 'fore he got himself killed," commented Taylor. "You sure don't need to go to Little Rock tonight. You need to stay here. I ain't never seen it like this before. They'll find you frozen dead out there."

John reached for the blanket he had spread out to dry next to the fire. "I'll make it. I've come too far to stop this close to home, but I do thank you for letting me share your fire."

One of the men pointed to a pot hanging near the hearth. "'Fore you leave, there's a little stew left in the pot. You best get a bite to eat, and I still say you're a fool to get out there in that cold. I guess you get some of that foolishness from your uncle. He used to do some outlandish things 'round here."

John carefully wrapped his blanket around his shoulders and again thanked the men for their hospitality. The severe cold and the perils that lay ahead caused him to hesitate momentarily before stepping into the night. When he reached the edge of town, John found the fork in the road that led to Little Rock. Only eight and a half miles more, a short walk from here to his house, and then he would be home.

For the first hour, John had no trouble finding his way, but the freezing temperature soon began to take its toll. He would fall in the ruts, and with each fall, it became harder to regain his balance. Dizzy and confused, he thought, "*I'm spending more time on the ground than I am walking. I've got to stop and rest a while. I've got to find shelter.*"

Up ahead, he saw a tree that had foliage on the low branches. He crawled up the bank and slid under its cover. From the scent, he realized he had found protection under a cedar tree. He curled up drowsily and pulled the blanket over his head. For the first time since leaving the tavern, he began to feel a sense of warmth.

"*I'm just going to take a short nap and rest a spell, then I'm going to get on home,*" thought John. Before losing consciousness, John remembered what McCleary had told him, "Don't go to sleep out there in that snow. You'll freeze."

"*I'll only rest a few minutes,*" John thought.

Later that night, a light wind shook the branches causing snow to come crumpling to the ground. The sound of the wind and the shock of the fallen snow awakened John, and he crept from underneath the branches. He found, to his surprise, that the storm had passed. A clear sky and a full moon reflecting on the snow made the night as light as early dawn.

Suddenly, he heard a horse approaching in the distance, and as the rider drew near, he recognized the markings.

"It was definitely his brother's horse, Lightning. Only one horse in the county looked like that stallion. But what in the world was it doing out in the night, and who was the rider?"

"Hey, hold up there!" commanded John, stepping in front of the rapidly moving stead.

The rider jerked the horse to an abrupt stop, straightened himself in the saddle and stared down at John.

"'Bout time you got home. We all been waiting for ya," replied the rider, removing his hat and dusting the snow from its brim.

"James Earl, what you doing out here?" exclaimed John, rushing to the horse's side. "Am I glad to see you!"

Startled by John's quick movement, the horse bolted forward.

"Woah, Lightning! Woah!" shouted James Earl. "You sure know how to spook a horse, don't ya? What am I doing out here, little brother? It's Christmas Eve, and I'm out serenading that's what I'm doing."

John extended his hand, but his brother seemed more interested in calming his mount.

"James Earl, give me a hand, and help me up. We'll be home in no time. Help me up. I'm 'most froze."

He smiled down at John. "I got places to go 'fore I go home, and Little Rock is right over that rise. You get on home. Mama's been waiting for ya a long time. Every morning and afternoon she rocks on that porch and waits. So don't you go back to sleep. You get on home."

With that, James Earl slapped the side of his mount, and away he galloped.

"James Earl, you got to take me home!" screamed John, running after his brother. "Serenading ain't as important as yore own flesh and blood! We ain't seen each other in years! You're acting crazy!"

The rapidly disappearing rider shouted over his shoulder, "The folks need you. Get on home, John! I love ya, brother."

John couldn't believe that a brother that he hadn't seen in ages wouldn't even help him get home. That just didn't make sense.

"Just wait till I tell Papa 'bout how he left me out here. He's going to be in some kind of trouble," mumbled John angrily, stomping up the hill.

John noticed a figure under a small pine tree up ahead, so he stopped and looked closer. It did indeed look like a man. "Hey!" John called out. "You up there!" Nothing moved. Uneasy, John drew closer and saw a man sitting under the tree. His head was drooped, his hands were in his pockets, and a rifle rested across his lap. His eyes were wide open, and he was glazed over with a sheet of ice and snow. Touching him, John shuddered realizing the man had frozen to death. John wondered why the man had been sitting out there in the cold when he could have easily gone into the village and found refuge. John closed his eyes and prayed, *Lord, I hope his soul is with you and his family is comforted.* Leaving, he looked back once more and said to himself, "I'll send someone up here for you tomorrow."

At the crest, John paused and stared down at the scene. In the valley below, he could make out the winding stream that bordered the western edge of the village, and beyond, he could see stores and homes with swirls of smoke curling upward from the chimneys.

John started running and screaming to the top of his lungs. In a matter of minutes, he had covered the quarter of mile, splashed through the shallow creek, and stood in the center of town. Before him was Walker's store, and up the street, he could see Rebecca's house. She was only a few hundred feet from him.

"*Do I rush over and surprise her, or do I go on home to my folks?*" thought John. Without answering himself, he headed for the Walkers. But as he drew closer to the Walker's fenced yard, he suddenly remembered what James Earl had said, "You get on home. The folks are waiting for you."

John stopped and looked down at himself. He saw that he was filthy from firing the train engine. "Can't see her like this. Got to clean up first. I'll see her first thing in the morning after I've rested and am at my best," reasoned John.

John turned and headed north. The countryside was beautiful in its thick covering of snow and its quietness. It was comforting to know the village was still standing. John had heard that the Yankees had come through Little Rock on the way to make a raid on Meridian, and he was afraid Sherman might have burned the town.

"*Only a half mile to go,*" he thought.

Once more, the cold tore through his body, and the dizziness returned. Pushing on, he realized his feet and hands were completely numb.

"Got to get home. Too close now," John mumbled.

A large stand of timber bordering an open field came into view. He was on Wilson property.

"What happened to the rail fences that used to hold in the stock?" muttered John.

"It won't be long now 'fore I'll spot that big ole log home of ours," thought John. *"Hope it'll still be standing. Maybe the Yankees burnt it. Wonder if Thomas made it back like James Earl."*

Only a few more steps and he would know. He could feel fear building in his stomach, but in the bright night, his home stood like a fortress.

"And look at the barn, it's there too. Thank you, Lord."

As he neared the house, one of the hounds caught the familiar scent and came tearing from underneath the house, barking with every breath. Bolting through the snow, Spot leaped up and knocked John to the ground. Lying there on his back, with the hound licking his face and beating his tail vigorously in the snow, John remembered how he had raised this dog, along with its brother, Joe, from pups and had spent many a night following the dogs as they chased coons through the hills and hollows in the woods nearby.

John brushed himself off and trudged across the front yard and up the front steps. Spot could not leave him alone. He whimpered and brushed against John, making the icy steps treacherous.

As John reached the porch, he knew only the open hall and a thick wooden door separated him from his family. Frozen and numb, he could barely limp down the hall. He tried to lift the door latch, but it was bolted from the inside.

***

Lott heard Spot barking and thought someone must be approaching. But when the barking stopped, Lott just figured some critter had excited the hound.

"That dog ain't never barked like that before," mumbled Lott. "Sounded like he was barking at somebody."

"Barking at somebody?" asked Sarah who had been awakened by her husband's voice. "Lott, hand me the lantern," demanded Sarah. "Got to light it, quick. He's home!"

"Ain't nobody out there, woman. You're dreaming again. If you want to check on that hound, do it yourself. I ain't getting up."

She worked frantically to light the lantern.

"Sarah, you be careful opening that door," warned Lott. "And don't go wandering in that cold."

Finally, the lantern was brought to life, and Sarah hurried to the door and lifted the latch. Cautiously opening the door, she looked into the darkness and was excited to see the figure of a man leaning against the doorway with a snow-covered blanket wrapped around his shoulders. Snow and ice was crusted in his hair and beard, and his face was blistered. Sarah slowly lifted the lantern and detected a familiar twinkle in the man's deep blue eyes.

"'Bout time you got home, son. You running a might late, ain't ya," Sarah said quietly as she placed the lantern on the floor and held her arms open to her son. "I knew you was coming."

John stumbled into his mother's arms as Lott came to the bedroom door.

"What's going on Sarah? Who is this man?" exclaimed Lott, rushing to the intruder and grabbing him by the arm.

Sarah pushed Lott away. "He's home, Dear Lord All Mighty! John's home," cried Sarah with both arms wrapped around her son.

Lott lifted the lantern and studied the man's face carefully.

John shook his head and smiled at his father. "It's me, Papa. I'm home."

"Sister, get out here! Yore brother's home! He did come home!" shouted Lott as he wrapped his arms around his son.

John held his hand out to his astonished sister. "Don't you know me?" he said.

"Mama! Papa! It's John! He's home!" exclaimed Sister, grabbing her brother around the waist.

Suddenly, feeling weak and faint, John sank to his knees.

"Lott, feel of this boy!" Sarah said. "He's might near froze. Go start the fire, and build a big one. His face is like ice. Sister, get some of James Earl's long underwear and thick socks," she instructed. "And make up some hot tea, and bring it to the fireside."

"Yes ma'am. I'm going," replied Sister, so excited she ran out to the front porch.

"Toby!" she screamed. "John's come home! He's here in the house."

Lott soon had a fire going and had helped John into dry clothing. Sarah and Sister placed a thick pallet of quilts in front of the fireplace and wrapped several blankets over him. John was soon able to get the hot tea down and began regaining his strength. Even though he was covered with thick quilts, his whole body continued to shake.

Sarah motioned to Lott. "We best get him to bed. It'll be a lot warmer than this here floor."

John shook his head. "Don't move me, Mama. I dreamt of sleeping in front of this fire for a long time. Just let me be," whispered John as he closed his eyes.

A light tapping was heard at the door.

"Come on in, Toby. We got one big Christmas present here with us," Lott said as Toby shook the snow off his shoes and placed his hat under his arm.

"What ya got there, Mist' Lott?" questioned Toby.

Toby stooped down to see the man at the fire. "Good Lawd, it sho' be Mist' John. Where'd that boy come from, Mist' Lott?" marveled Toby. "He sho' don't look like a boy no more. That boy done gone and made a man. Just wait till I tell Sadie 'bout this. She won't believe it."

Toby soon returned to his wife's bed. Thanks to Lott, she had finally been freed and was now with her husband on the Wilson farm.

Up on the mantle, the clock struck five times.

Light filtered through the windows as dawn approached. Sister, wrapped in a thick quilt, had curled up on the floor next to her brother and was still asleep. Lott sat next to the fireplace watching the fire pop and crackle as he enjoyed an early morning smoke.

"Lott, the boy's done grown a beard," whispered Sarah. "And look at that touch of grey hair, just like yores," she continued as she pushed his hair back. "Lott, come look at this," insisted Sarah, motioning to her husband. "This boy has got a bad scar on the side of his head."

Lott squatted down and gently examined his son. "Sarah, somethin' sure hit this boy. No telling what John's been through nor where he's been."

"Don't care where. Just glad he's come home," whispered Sarah.

Several hours later, John turned over on his side. "Mama, why didn't James Earl bring me on home last night? Just wait till I rest up. We gonna straighten that matter out," grumbled John. "He just left me out in that snow and rode off."

"What do you mean by that, John?" questioned his mother.

"He was out there serenading last night and rode up on me where I'd been asleep. We talked a spell, and then he just rode off into the night on Lightning and left me standing there."

Sarah and Lott were shaken by John's words.

"John, you were just dreaming. It's hard to tell you this, but James Earl died over two years ago. He got real sick up in Virginia. It was right after that big battle in Pennsylvania. He's been gone over two years," explained Sarah. "That cold weather will do things to your mind."

John shook his head. "Ain't no dream, Mama. I seen him clearer than light. He told me to get on home, and that you had been waiting for me a long time. He said you've been rocking on the porch and waiting for me to come home. It weren't no dream," whispered John as he slowly turned toward the fire.

Sarah and Lott sat quietly pondering John's words.

"Sarah, I can understand a man out in the cold seeing things that ain't there, but how'd he know you been rocking on the porch and waiting for him. It's hard not to believe that somethin' happened out there in that snow tonight."

"Lott, like I told you. All those hours talking to the Lord on the porch, I knew the Lord was sending our son back to us, and I can't wonder how he done it. I just know that our boy is lying here, alive and home."

***

Mrs. Walker eased the door open and quietly tipped into Rebecca's room, holding a tray. "Time to get up, Sweetie. It's your wedding day," she said, setting the breakfast tray down on the table near her daughter's bed.

The covers rustled, and a sleepy Rebecca slid the covers back over her head. "I'm so tired. Just let me sleep a little longer."

Pulling the covers down, Mrs. Walker smiled at her daughter who was squinting up at her. "Wedding day, dear. This is the best day of your life," she said.

Rebecca got out of bed, went to the window and looked at the beautiful winter wonderland. Over seven inches of snow blanketed the ground, and the branches of the evergreen trees in the front yard sagged with snow and ice. She walked back to her bed and eased back under the covers. "Mother, I'm so exhausted. I had the most tiring dream last night."

Her mother poured her a cup of coffee and asked, "You want to share it?"

"I dreamed I was up in the sky looking down, and there below me was a man struggling through the snow. Slipping, sliding and falling, the man would get up and fight his way forward as if spirit driven. He never would give up. Disturbed, I would wake myself up knowing it was a dream, clear my thoughts and go back to sleep. But to my anguish, the dream would continue. Over and over, the struggle continued as if it would never end."

Mrs. Walker handed Rebecca the cup of coffee. "Rebecca, you were excited about the snow last evening and your wedding today. I'm sure you're just a little anxious."

Rebecca took a sip and continued, "Mama, at one point it was so real, I got up and looked outside and that man was standing out there beyond our fence. He just stood and looked toward me, then walked away. You know, I really don't know if I was still dreaming or if there really was a man out there."

Mrs. Walker leaned to kiss her daughter on the forehead. "Put this all behind you, darling, because in a few hours, you will be Mrs. Rebecca Ann Olliver."

***

Right at sunup, Toby came running to the house calling for Lot. Lott walked onto the porch. "What's all the shouting about? You're gonna wake the boy."

Out of breath, Toby leaned down with his hands on his knees and gasped for air. "Mist Lott, somebody has up and been riding Lighting. When I went down to the stables, I found the gate open and tracks leading from the stables and ones coming back in."

Lott asked, "Is he in the stable now?"

"Yes suh, he is. Has y'all been up and riding?" questioned Toby, regaining his breath.

A solemn look formed on Lott's face. "You best get on out of this cold. We ain't been out riding."

"But, Mist Lott, who -"

"Go on home, Toby. It's okay," interrupted Lot, and a warm feeling crept into Lott's heart.

With the sun sending rays of light shimmering on the soft snow, Lott looked up above and shutting his eyes prayed, "Lord, I can't understand what's going on here. My dear wife told me that John would be coming home, but I doubted. But Lord, he's in there right now, and I'm out here in one kind of spiritual mess. Lord, I can't understand why you've been so patient with me, the sinner that I am."

As a gentle wind pushed some snow from a limb nearby sending it cascading to the ground, he knew the answer. It was God's grace and love that made his sins forgivable. It was God's grace and love that had brought his son home. With a warm feeling and renewed faith, he walked back to the house smiling.

17

Wedding Day

*Where can I go from your Spirit? Where can I flee from your presence? If I go up to the
heavens, you are there; if I make my bed in the depths, you are there. If I rise
on the wings of the dawn, if I settle on the far side of the sea, even
there your hand will guide me, your right hand will hold me fast.*
—Psalm 139:7-10

At mid-morning the heat of a roaring fire roused John. Throwing off some cover, he turned on his back. Disoriented, he mumbled, "Where am I?"

Lott, who had been watching over him while Sarah and Sister prepared dinner, leaned down and placed his hand on John's shoulder. "You're home, John."

John's drowsy eyes looked around momentarily and resting on his father, he smiled and settled back down into a peaceful sleep. A little before midday, John awoke again and took a moment to study the face of each family member. Then he stirred and pulled his blanket around his shoulders. Feeling no need to speak or ask questions, they sat and breathed in his presence, waiting expectantly for his words. Finally, John took a deep breath, and exhaling, said, "It sure is good to be home with family." Then he asked, "What day is this?"

Unable to restrain herself any longer, Sister blurted out, "It's Christmas Day."

"No, that's not what I mean. What day is this?"

Sarah knelt down next to her son and, running her hand over his blistered face, said, "It's Sunday. It's the Lord's day."

John ran his fingers through his hair and beard and said, "I got to get myself cleaned up. I bet I look a mess, don't I?"

Sister snickered and pinched her nose closed. "You need a bath too."

John smiled and nodded back to her. "That I do. By the way, are they having church today?"

"Why'd you ask that?" Lott asked. "You ain't in no condition to be up and out."

"You're wrong, Papa. If it's the Lord's Day, that's exactly where I need to be. You just don't realize what I've been through. It was by the grace of God that I'm here."

"Tell us about it, son. Tell us all about it," Lott said anxiously, looking at the miracle below.

"I can't right now. I really feel a need to go to church. Will there be a church service today?"

"John, this past week has been the worst weather we've ever seen. We've barely been out of the house," Sarah said, smiling up to him. "A rider did come by here late yesterday and, in his haste to get home, said he heard there would be some kind of service today. He said it would start about mid-afternoon."

"Probably because of the snow," Lott added.

John began looking for his clothes, and seeing them piled up in the corner, he headed that way. Sharp pains in his legs told him the long walk the previous night and the severe cold had taken its toll. He massaged the stiffened muscles and then tried to stretch them out.

"John, you can't wear those things," Sarah said. "They need a good washing. By the way, is your leg hurt?"

Reaching into his coat pocket, John said, "I'm glad you didn't wash them yet, and for my leg, it's just a little stiff." Then retrieving a small item, he clinched it in his fist and walked to the chair next to his father.

Sarah, Lott and Sister were filled with happiness at just the sight of John talking, walking and alive. Sarah's face glowed knowing her prayers had been answered and she had been right about God telling her John was safe and would be home.

"I need a bath, and I've got to do something with my hair and beard. I'm going to need some help," John stated, looking at his family.

Sarah looked at Lott. "Husband, you and Sister go to the kitchen and fill all the boilers you can on the stove. He's gonna need a lot of hot water. I'll drag the washtub in from the back porch and place it in the room next to the kitchen. Dinner is already made, so I'll get that in place. Sister, you're pretty good with the scissors, so cut his hair and crop his beard a little."

"Mama, I don't know about scissors in my sister's hands. That could be dangerous," John teased.

Sister reached over and jerked the blanket from John's shoulders, exposing his baggy long underwear and laughed, "I'll give you your blanket back if you'll apologize."

John lifted his head arrogantly and continued to walk. "You can keep it. It might just be a nice covering for that smart face of yours." He laughed.

Sarah shook her head as she checked the chicken and dumplings in the oven. *It's just like old times with the children teasing each other. I wouldn't want it any other way,* she thought.

Lott checked the fire then glanced at the mantle. There stood four candles based with evergreen branches, two red, one white and one that had turned into a light reddish color. Taking a long breath, he stood for a moment in awe, then murmured, "Lord, you kept sending me messages, but I was just too blind to see. I do thank you, Lord."

Sarah decided that they could eat while the water on the stove was coming to a boil. Bringing out a large pot of chicken and dumplings, she returned to the oven and took out several sweet potatoes and wrapped them in a cloth then placed them in a platter on the table. She returned for the skillet of brown crusted cornbread. Sister poured the hot spiced tea into cups, and the family bowed their heads, held hands, and Lott graced the table. Talking and laughing, they enjoyed the meal and, when Lott, Sarah and Sister had finished, John was still asking for more.

"How long has it been since you've eaten?" Lott asked.

With his mouth full, John motioned, he needed a minute to answer, then swallowing, said, "Don't rightly know. Last night is just a blur to me. Seems like I had something, but I just don't remember."

The water was already boiling, so John decided to bathe first and later let Sister do what she could with his hair and beard. Settling beneath the warm water, John relaxed and thought about Rebecca. For a long while, he just leaned back and soaked, then knowing he needed to hurry, he soaped up well and washed his hair. He got out, dried off and went to the stack of clean clothes his mother had laid out for him to wear. He quickly found that these would not work.

"Mama, I've got a problem," he called out.

"What do you need?" she asked.

"These clothes are too small. I can't button my pants. What am I going to do?"

Sarah looked to Sister. "Whose clothes did you get?"

Sister thought for a second and answered, "Didn't you tell me to get some of James Earl's clothes?"

"Oh no, dear, if I said that, I'm sorry. Go get some of Thomas's things."

Now dressed in larger clothes, John felt better. The pants at the waist were a little large, but a tightening of the belt would solve that problem, and finally settling on a pair of his father's shoes, he felt he was presentable.

"John, why do you want to get out in this snowy mess to go to church?" Sister said, holding up a strand of hair to be clipped. "You're most worn out."

"I've already told you why."

"Is there another reason?" Sister probed.

"You haven't changed a bit, have you? Well, you probably know me too well anyway."

Hair began to fall to the towel below. "You want to see Rebecca, don't you? I wondered when you were going to get around to asking about her?"

John turned, caught Sister's hand and asked, "How is she? She is alright, isn't she?"

Sister pushed his hand away to cut again. "She's fine," Sister said quietly. How could she tell her brother about Rebecca. Even though she didn't know the specifics of the wedding, she knew that Rebecca was engaged to Frankie, and like her parents had agreed, this was not the time to tell John.

When she had finished clipping his hair and beard, John stood up and looked into the mirror. He nodded his approval and thanked his sister. Rubbing his injured leg, he limped into his parent's bedroom and came to attention. "Well, do I pass your inspection?" he asked.

With a wide grin, Lott smiled and thought if the years were rolled back, John would be the spitting image of himself. "You'll do just fine, John," Lott proudly said.

Sarah gave him a hug and whispered, "I will say you've changed a lot, but you're still the most handsome man in this county, Mr. John Wilson." Glancing back to her husband, Sarah added, "Except, maybe for that ole codger sitting over there."

They all laughed at Sarah's humor, and since it was almost three o'clock, they knew they should hurry so as not to be late for the service, so they quickly collected their wraps. Outside, they found that Toby had harnessed the horse to the wagon, and they cautiously made their way down the icy steps. As John was about to climb into the wagon, he suddenly remembered something.

"Hold up for just a second." John said as he turned and walked back inside the house. He headed to the mantle in his parent's bedroom, took the small wrapped package and opened it to see the special opal ring. John smiled as he saw it sparkle, and quickly rewrapping it, he snugly tucked it into his pants pockets and hurried back to the wagon.

The countryside was decorated with a bright cover of white snow, and the church was only a short distance ahead. The sun was now tipping in the west. As he had always remembered, there would be a young woman, standing on the top step waiting for him. Just the thought made his heart leap with joy. He could see those bright green eyes as they looked into his with the special love they shared. He laid his hand against his upper pants leg, and feeling the bundle tucked deep in his pocket, he relaxed and smiled at his sister.

Sister sensed his feelings and hoped that Rebecca would not be at church today.

***

Rebecca had decided to only invite close family members and friends. With the weather as it was and Christmas day an important holiday, most locals were not even aware of the wedding. Rebecca was now dressed and standing by the window. The dream was so vivid. The man seemed real as he stood there. She knew she must refocus on her wedding and forget this dream. Only in the Bible did dreams mean anything.

Mrs. Walker noticed her daughter's pensive mood and was concerned. She placed her hand on Rebecca's shoulder. "Are you alright, darling?"

Rebecca took a deep breath and answered, "I really don't know, Mother. This is not how I thought I would feel."

Pulling her close, her mother softly said, "I know it's a big step, but I felt the same way when I married your father. It's natural."

"Did you love him?"

"Certainly, I loved him! What a silly question. Now, it's about two-thirty, and the carriage is out back waiting for us."

Rebecca kissed her mother on the cheek and solemnly whispered, "Well, I guess it's about time I become Mrs. Rebecca Ann Olliver, isn't it?"

Rebecca, dressed in her wedding dress, looked out the Sunday school classroom window. *What more could I ask for than a wedding on Christmas Day decorated with white puffy snow,* she thought. But her childhood dreams awoke within her, and she thought about the spring wedding with flowers tempting to bloom and the dogwood in full blossom. She saw her childhood love now as a mature man and embracing her in matrimony. A flash of anger entered and she mumbled, "I hate that war. I hate what it did to our country, and I hate what it took from me."

"What'd you say, dear?" questioned her father who was leaning against the wall, smoking his pipe.

"Nothing, Papa." Then smelling the smoke she said, "Papa, do you have to smoke in here? I don't want to be wed smelling like tobacco."

Apologizing, Thomas pushed up the window, knocked the ashes out to the ground below and pushed the window back down.

Frank was standing out front welcoming people as they entered when he saw a horseman gallop up and secure his mount at the fence that bordered the churchyard. Frank, recognizing Junior, his foreman, raised his eyebrows.

"What do you want, Junior? This is my son's wedding day," Frank said harshly.

With a worried look, he said, "Boss, I think we need to talk in private."

"Is it that important?"

"Yes sir, it is."

Directing Junior around to the side of the church, they looked to see if anyone was nearby. Then Frank said, "What's so important?"

Junior looked down and, shuffling his feet in the snow, said, "With the weather like it was last night, most of my men went home about midnight. Well, that is all but one. When I went to check up on George, my man who was watching the road coming in from Decatur, I found him, but he was frozen dead. I went back and got my wagon to get him, and when I placed him in the bed of the wagon, I just threw a blanket over him and took him home."

"You say the man was frozen?" questioned Frank.

"Yes sir, he was."

A hint of a smile crossed Frank's face. "That's good. If it got that cold out there, I don't think we need to worry about that problem any longer, and while you're here, you might as well stay for the wedding."

Since John had been described by Frank as a no-good scoundrel, Junior had advised his men, if at all possible, to shoot to kill. Walking away, Junior shook his head and thought, *The man Olliver fears probably ain't anywhere about, and it cost us a good man's life.*

With the sound of music flowing from the pump organ and the murmuring subsiding inside the sanctuary, Rebecca knew it was almost time. Taking a deep breath, she looked toward her father and said, "Are you ready?"

Clasping their family Bible securely in his hand, he smiled nervously and nodded his head.

***

As the wagon pulled away from the Wilsons, Sister reached up and touched her mother's shoulder. "Isn't it wonderful to have a church service on our Lord's birthday," she said.

Sarah reached back and placed her hand on Sister's. "It can't get any better than this, darling."

To Lott's anguish, the roads were in terrible condition, making travel hazardous. When approaching a gully, he carefully tried to coax his horse at such angles as to not overturn the wagon or get stuck in the thick red clay. Earlier that day, with the roads frozen, it would have been much easier to travel, but with the sun breaking through the clouds, the snow and ice had begun to melt quickly. Pulling out his pocket watch, he glanced down and said, "Looks like we're gonna be a little late. I didn't anticipate the condition of the road."

"Don't worry. We'll only miss some of the early singing. It'll be fine," Sarah assured him.

***

Suzanne had begun singing, accompanied by the organ, so Rebecca knew that as soon as the song was finished, she and her Father would make their entrance. The song seemed to continue forever as she stood waiting. Finally, all was quiet, and then Rebecca heard the wedding song. She took a deep breath, reached for her father's arm and, opening the door, stepped into the sanctuary entrance. Everyone stood and watched as she proceeded down the aisle following two of Suzanne's little cousins who served as flower girls. Since it was winter and no local flowers were available, Mrs. Olliver had ordered artificial ones purchased in New Orleans and imported from France that looked exactly like living ones. Frankie, dressed in a black tuxedo, white ruffled shirt and black bow tie, beamed at the sight of the beautiful girl walking down the aisle toward him. As a boy growing up in the community, he never dreamed that someday, Rebecca Walker would be his wife.

When Rebecca reached the platform, her father assisted her up the steps, and then when the pastor asked who gives this woman in Holy matrimony, Thomas stated, "Her mother and I." Taking her hand, he then reached over and extended it to Frankie who thanked him and then smiled down at Rebecca. With Suzanne serving as maid of honor and a young man from New Orleans who had always been a long time friend of Frankie's as best man, they turned and faced the preacher.

The pastor cleared his throat, and looking out at the congregation, stated, "In Genesis, second chapter, twenty-fourth verse, it says, For this reason a man shall leave his father and his mother, and be joined to his wife; and they shall become one flesh. So in following the Word, we are here today to join this woman, Rebecca Ann Walker, to this man, Frank Allen Olliver Jr, in holy matrimony.

Seeing the two together, Judith placed her hand on Franks. All of her dreams and planning had now actually become a reality. Now her son would have the woman of his dreams.

As they reached the church, Lott looked at his watch again. "Three fifteen," he muttered. "We best hurry."

Sarah noticed that there were not as many wagons or buggies as usual but dismissed it knowing the weather had kept a lot of the members at home.

"Papa," John said. "You get the women in, and I'll secure the wagon. I'll be only a step behind you."

Walking up the steps, no singing was heard, and Sarah wondered why the change of service.

Easing the door open so as not to disturb the service in case someone was praying, the Wilsons edged in. To their dismay, the door hinge squeaked and a gush of cold air flushed through the entrance.

Hearing the squeaking sound and feeling a cold draft, Rebecca turned to see what had caused it. A smile formed on her face as she recognized the Wilsons. She wasn't sure if they had been invited, but she was glad they were here in her support.

Lott, Sarah and Sister lowered their heads, trying to avoid eye contact, and quickly took a seat on a pew in the rear of the church. Most of those present only glanced back, and seeing that it was just a late arrival, turned and once again focused on the couple up front.

John, knocking the snow and mud from his shoes, pushed the door open and entered. As the preacher was about to continue, the door squeaked again as John, embarrassed for his interruption, walked in. As John stood in the aisle, he looked for his parents.

Almost automatically, everyone looked to the back again.

Rebecca gazed quickly at the man standing in the rear of the church. Frustrated, Frankie shook his head and thought, *Why can't people just be on time?*

Before turning back to the preacher, Rebecca took one more look at the man in the rear of the church and shuddered as she realized that he looked much like the one in her dream the previous night.

Realizing that a wedding was in progress, Sarah looked at Lott and mouthed, "What should we do?"

"What can we do?" murmured Lott, looking down at Sister who was obviously upset.

With his wounded leg cramping up again and seeing his parents, John limped down the aisle to where they were sitting. John was embarrassed to look up, but as he started to take a seat, his eyes wandered to the front of the church. To his astonishment, he saw that it was not a regular service taking place. Like someone had taken his breath away, he immediately recognized the bride.

To everyone's surprise, Rebecca turned again and gazed at the man who was still standing in the aisle. A murmur filled the church as the people looked first at Rebecca and then to the stranger.

"What's going on Frank?" Judith said, turning and looking back.

"With a worried look, Frank answered, "I don't have the vaguest idea."

In her mind, Rebecca envisioned a young man, tall with broad shoulders, unruly curly black hair with deep blue eyes that twinkled when he laughed. The man back there was tall, heavyset, bearded and had unruly black hair. Then she began to blend the two into one. "It can't be," she murmured. "It just can't be."

Seeing her distressed, Frankie reached to take her hand. "What in the world is wrong with you? Are you alright?" Then looking back to the stranger, he said, "He's just a stranger, Rebecca. Probably just coming in to see what's going on or just getting of the cold."

It was as if no one in the church existed except for the woman standing before John. Drawn to her, John reached from one pew end to the next to steady himself and slowly edged down the aisle toward Rebecca. With a ray of sun streaming in from a picture window across the way, its light crossed John's face revealing his deep-blue eyes.

Rebecca began to tremble as she realized who the stranger was. Reaching over, she grasped for Suzanne to steady herself. Frankie stood, not knowing exactly what he should do.

Rebecca lifted the front of her dress as not to stumble and carefully tipped down the steps without taking her eyes off the man. Reaching him, they gazed into each other's eyes for a moment, and Rebecca reached up to touch John's face. Then she gazed at the graying hair that streaked from his temples. Dropping her hand, she then looked to each feature of his face, studying each carefully. Reaching down for his hand, she whispered, "Where have you been?"

Tears formed in John's eyes and trickled down his cheek as he replied, "I have so much to explain to you."

"Why didn't you write me?"

"I did write you. I wrote you ten days ago."

Feeling that the man there with Rebecca was none other than John Wilson, Frank turned around to his foreman who was sitting behind him. "Junior, you best get that man out of here," he ordered. "How'd you miss him?"

Junior looked at the stranger and then to Lott who was getting up and walking toward them and said, "Boss, this ain't none of my business. You gonna have to take care of this one yourself."

John took Rebecca's other hand and looking directly into her eyes, asked, "Am I too late?"

Rebecca turned and looked at Frankie. Natchez, New Orleans, and the Oaks came to mind.

Turning back to John, she asked, "Are you?"

Never taking his eyes off her, he answered, "I loved you as a child. I love you more than a man should love a woman, and no matter what happens today, I'll love you as long as I live."

Taking John's hands, Rebecca turned them up and looked at his palms. They were rough, cut and calloused. They were a working man's hands, and the dream of him lying there face down bleeding returned to her.

Holding her hand, John gazed at the beautiful diamond ring on her finger. Seeing the tears on Rebecca's cheek, he took out his handkerchief, wiped them away and said, "I don't own a thing. I don't even own the clothes I'm wearing, but what I can give you is my whole heart."

Rebecca looked back to Frankie who was impatiently waiting and suddenly realized that during the whole time she had been with Frankie, he had never once told her that he loved her nor had she told him.

Rebecca held out her arms to John and pulled him to her. Crying, she said, "Your heart will be just fine. Just don't ever leave me again. You can never imagine how much I have missed you and how I still do love you."

John placed his hands softly to her cheeks, lifted her head, kissed her on each cheek and then felt the tender touch of her lips. That moment for John and Rebecca was an eternity.

The women in the church began to whisper to each other while the men sat in awe. Never had they seen such an unusual series of events as the ones playing out in front of them. Everything had happened so fast, no one knew how to react. Judith's father, Joseph Bourdeau, and her relatives from Louisiana were all whispering, trying to discover the identity of the man and his relationship to Rebecca. Suzanne, completely astounded, had eased down and sat on the top step of the platform, gazing at the spectacle taking place in front of her.

Frankie was motioning to his father and asked, "What should I do?"

Furious, Frank looked up to Frankie and firmly stated, "That's your woman back there, isn't it? I think you should put an end to this nonsense—hat is, if you're man enough. I know I certainly haven't seen any evidence of that in the past."

Judith, angry, reached over and placed her hand firmly on her husband's leg and said, "That statement was wrong and unnecessary. You criticized our son in front of all of our relatives and friends."

Frank pushed her hand away and mumbled, "Then, I'll put an end to it."

Reaching inside his coat, he felt the handle of his double barrel derringer, a New Orlean's gift from Frankie, and as he pulled it from his coat, a large rough hand twisted the pistol away.

Looking down at Frank, Lott muttered, "If you cause any trouble, I'm gonna have to hurt you, and I really don't want to do that, this being the Lord's house." Then looking to Judith, he added, "I'm sorry for what's happened. We had nothing to do with this. I think we should let our children settle the problem for themselves."

Lott then opened the chamber, took out the two shells and placed them into his pants pockets. He handed the derringer to Junior and said, "Put it away. You can give it back to Frank tomorrow. I don't expect any trouble from you. Do you understand me?"

Noting the fury in Lott's face, Junior took the pistol and answered, "I understand, Mr. Wilson. There won't be no trouble from me."

Shamed by his father's words, Frankie turned and said, "You're wrong about me, Father. I am man enough, just not the kind of man you are, and I hope I never will be."

Frankie looked at his father once more and then walked from the platform and up the aisle to John and Rebecca. He placed his hand firmly on John's shoulder. It was not until this moment that John realized that Frankie was the man who had been standing beside Rebecca. At first, John and Frankie just looked each other in the eyes. Then Frankie extended his hand to John. "I'm glad you're alive and home," Frankie said. "I might have married Rebecca today, but I know in my heart that it would be you, dead or alive, that she would always love."

Then looking to Rebecca, he smiled. "You've got a good man here, far better than me. Take care of him."

As Frankie began to walk away, John was saddened by images of their youth - fishing, hunting, and camping. There was a time they had been inseparable, and it was for Frankie that he had joined the army. John whispered, "I'm sorry, Frankie."

Rebecca slipped the ring from her finger and unclasped the necklace and placed them in Frankie's hand. She reached out to Frankie and hugged him. Holding him tight, she whispered, "Thank you for understanding. You will always be a special friend. You are a lot stronger man than your father will ever be, and don't you forget that."

Smiling, Frankie patted John on the back and, facing the guest, said, "Ladies, gentlemen, I think by now you know there ain't gonna be any wedding today. I do thank you for coming." Then Frankie walked down the aisle past his parents and headed out the rear door.

Worried about Frankie and his reaction to losing Rebecca, Judith followed her son, "Where are you going, son?"

"I'm going to Louisiana, Mother."

By the way, Father, I won't be seeing you any time soon. I guess I'm gonna work on becoming a man, and to do that, I need a good man to teach me, and that certainly won't be you."

Next Frankie looked at his grandfather and said, "Papére, I'd like to come live with you so you can teach me to be the man I need to become."

Frankie reached back to hug his mother. "I love you, Mother, and don't worry about me. I think everyone wanted me to marry Rebecca more than I did. She is beautiful, but I've always known her heart belonged to another, and I want someone to love me that way someday."

People slowly got up, whispered and glanced at John and Rebecca as they edged in the aisle to exit the church. When passing, some would speak to John and Rebecca, a few smiled while others completely ignored them. Mrs. Olliver, her father and kin beckoned to Suzanne and quietly left the church by the way of the rear entrance. Not used to being humiliated, Frank walked up to the couple and brashly said, "You could have had it all, girl, but you just tossed it away."

Rebecca, taking no offense, replied, "Mr. Olliver, I wasn't the right girl for Frankie. I'm sorry."

Frank just muttered as he stormed away.

Sarah and Sister had already joined Rebecca and John, and now Lott embraced Rebecca and said, "You've had some kind of a day, Rebecca. I'm sorry."

Rebecca looked up at him and then at John and with tears rolling down her cheeks she said, "It's been the best day of my life."

Thomas and Betty waited until the guests had left and walked over to Rebecca. As they neared, Thomas tripped and dropped his Bible. Hitting the floor, the cover flipped back and an envelope slipped across the floor next to John. John picked up the letter and was in the process of handing it back to Mr. Walker when he recognized his handwriting. Frowning, he looked closer to be sure. Thomas, realizing that he had forgotten to burn the letter, became pale.

John dropped his head and, saying nothing, handed the letter to Rebecca. Opening, she began to read, and when she finished, she looked at her father and asked, "How could you do this to me?"

Rebecca's mother grabbed Thomas by the arm and whispered, "Rebecca, we're so sorry. We just wanted you to have all the things that Frankie could give you, but we know now that's not what is important. We hope you will forgive us."

Deeply hurt, Rebecca began to cry, and trying to get the barely audible words from her lips, she said, "I just don't understand how you could not tell me, Mother."

Betty embraced her daughter and whispered, "I'm so sorry. I love you, daughter."

Then the Walkers quietly left the Wilson family alone in the church.

Lott wiped the perspiration from his brow, pulled out his pocket watch and noting the time, exclaimed, "It's about twenty-five 'til four. A lot has happened in just a little bit of time."

Seeing the comical expression on his face, everyone laughed, which eased the tension.

Feeling both light-headed and with a tightening in his chest, Lott asked to be excused and walked out of the church to the grounds below. Steadying himself by placing his hand on the top railing of the church fence, he raised his head upward, shut his eyes and began taking deep breaths. The cold wind brushing against his face and rushing down into his lungs proved invigorating. In a few moments, his head cleared and he felt much better.

"You praying, old man?" came a deep raspy voice.

Lott's eyes shot open, and with the sun shining directly into his face, he couldn't make out who had spoken to him. Bringing his hand up to shade the glare, he vaguely made out the image of a rider.

"I ain't that old, and if I was praying, which I wasn't, it ain't none of your business," he whipped back."

The rider sat, studying the old man and then countered, "You look mighty old to me, and you seem to be one mean ole cuss."

Angered, Lott walked over to get out of the sun's glare and then took a close look at the man who appeared to be making fun of him. On one of the tallest horses he had ever seen was a large bearded man with long straight brown hair flowing down his shoulders, some kind of furry ankle-length coat, wide-brimmed hat and some of the strangest boots he had ever seen. The toes were pointed, the heels were at least two inches, and massive spurs were extended backwards. A pistol was protruding from a holster on his belt, and a large hunting knife was tucked in a scabbard on the opposite side. Lott remarked, "I may be an ole cuss, but you look like some kind of show clown."

"You getting mighty mouthy, ain't you?" the man smiled.

"Mouthy you say. I may be old, but I ain't too old to tangle with the likes of you."

At that, the stranger began to laugh and taking his hat off, said, "Papa, don't you know your own son?" With the screeching of leather, he dismounted and walked toward Lott.

"What ya doing at church, Papa," he asked, grabbing him around the waist and picking him up, then he set him back down.

"Thomas, I can't believe it. Where'd you come from?"

"I come from the Arizona Territory, and I figured it was time for me to get on home."

"For good," gasped Lott.

"For good, Papa." He smiled. "You don't know how long I've wanted to be in this very spot looking out at you. Where's the rest of the family? In church?"

Lott, barely able to speak, answered, "You best go on in the church. The families all there. I'll be in shortly."

Closing his eyes, Lott couldn't believe the miracles of this Christmas Day. "Lord," he prayed, "I can't understand why you have graced me so. You've showered me with blessings I certainly don't deserve. How can you favor such a sinner as I?" Sensing another presence, Lott opened his eyes, and standing in front of him was the same young man who had mysteriously stopped by and visited him that rainy afternoon. The man he had tried to erase from his memory, but to his surprise, he felt no fear.

"What are you doing here?" Lott asked the man.

"Lott, is that all you have to say?'

"You've caused me a lot of torment."

The man smiled at Lott and shook his head. "I don't think torment is the correct term, and the reason I am here is to say good-bye to you," he explained.

Lott thought for a moment. "Are you a ghost or some kind of spirit?"

"Ghost!" the man laughed. "Is there any mention of ghosts in the Bible?"

Lott rubbed his nose in wonder. "Then tell me this. A man came by here a while back and told me he had been up there in that hospital in Virginia with my son, James Earl, when he passed, and he said there was another soldier in there by the name of Gabe Jacobs, and by his description it was the perfect image of you. He told me that this Gabe passed on right after my son, James. The way I got it figured is that Gabe was you and that makes you nothing but a ghost."

The man laughed at the thought. "I've never been in any army, but I was there."

'"Then what were you doing there?"

"I was just doing my job. I was ministering to your son in time of need," explained the man.

"Then you're some kind of angel, ain't you?" stated Lott, becoming more bold.

"Lott, what is my first name?"

"Gabe."

"That's right, but that's just part of my first name, now think more carefully."

His hand resting on the fence railing began to tremble, and in a whisper he answered, "Gabriel?"

The man shook his head and smiled. "You're doing better."

"Why me? Why show your mercy to me and to my family?"

"You can thank your wife, Sarah. She is a God-fearing woman, and her faith surpasses what most humans display. Her constant prayers were heard."

"What about John? He's part of those prayers. What about him?"

"You ask a lot of questions. Why don't you just enjoy the blessing you've received?"

"Well, it's partly your fault for revealing yourself. You know I'm an inquisitive old cuss."

The man laughed again. "You are at that. I visited with your son one night when he was in jail and tried to encourage him and earlier when he had been thrown into the pit. I told him that he would be home for Christmas. Now, Mr. Wilson, I've got to be going."

A serious expression formed on Lott's face. "Can I ask you one more question?"

At peace, Lott smiled out to Gabe. "Will I ever see you again?"

Turning and walking away, Gabe said, "Oh yes, you'll see me one day. Keep the faith to the end."

"I want to thank you," Lott called out to him.

The man waved and replied, "Don't thank me. I was just following the Master. In fact, you can just call me the Lord's messenger."

The man waved and as he approached the woods, began to fade away. Even his footsteps pressed into the snow began to disappear, and soon, there was no one. All was perfectly quiet, and Lott was alone.

"Pa, you gonna stay out there all day?" questioned Thomas from the church door. "Papa, you need to come in out of the cold."

"I hear you," Lott called out, moving toward his family.

Placing his arm around his father as the two walked up the steps, Thomas said, "Who were you talking to down there? Were you praying?"

Lott cleared his throat. "Yes, I guess you could say I was talking to the Lord, or at least, his messenger."

Satisfied, Thomas excitedly exclaimed, "Why didn't you tell me John was alive? When we was in the army, I told you I'd look out for him. Well, when he come up missing after that battle, I felt responsible, and that's why I quit the army and took to the run. I felt like I failed you."

Lott smiled and gave Thomas a hug and answered, "You didn't fail me. There was no way you could be sure that John was safe in a war. There's only one who can do that. I know you did the best you could. No, son, you have not failed me."

Lott found the family all sitting together, talking. "Where've you been Lott?" questioned Sarah, motioning him to a space beside her.

"Needed some fresh air. This day has been too much for an old man."

The rear door opened, and the preacher came in from outside. Having been compensated by the Ollivers, he had returned to collect his Bible.

Sarah smiled at the thought and called out to him, "You came here for a wedding, didn't you?"

The preacher adjusted his glasses and focused on the Wilsons and Rebecca. "Yes ma'am, I certainly did at that," he answered.

Sarah looked at John with a glimmer in her eyes. "Well, how about it, son?"

Knowing what she was suggesting, John's face glowed, and he smiled over to Rebecca. "Rebecca?"

"Yes, John."

John kneeled beside Rebecca, and pulling out the ring in his pocket, he unwrapped it and said, "Rebecca, I know that this has been a most unusual day, but I know that God has made this day happen in His timing. I have loved you for as long as I can remember. I want to know if you will become Mrs. John Wilson."

"John, I never thought I would get this chance. There have been so many times that I was afraid to hope you would return. The answer is yes. Mrs. John Wilson is who I have always been in my heart, and now I would like to have that title for keeps."

John slipped the ring on Rebecca's finger, a little embarrassed after seeing the ring Frankie had given her. "It's not much, but it holds my whole heart, my whole life."

"It is beautiful and special. I will always cherish it and you."

"Preacher," Lott called out. "Weren't you paid to conduct a wedding?"

In the process of leaving, he turned and answered. "Yes sir, I was."

"Well, it looks like we have one you can conduct."

"Who do you suggest I marry, sir?"

Lott pointed over to Rebecca and John.

"This day has certainly been confusing. Now are you sure, Miss, we have it right this time?"

Rebecca laughed and said, "Yes, preacher. John is definitely the husband I've been waiting for."

"Well, I'm Pastor Phillips from Decatur," he replied as he shook John's hand.

As all gathered in the aisle below the pulpit, the preacher asked, "I guess you haven't filled out the legal papers?"

"No sir, not yet," John said, looking to his father for advice.

"Then I don't know if it would be legal," the preacher explained.

"Preacher, you did say you were ordained, and if that being so, then in the eyes of God, these two young souls would be united in holy matrimony. Ain't that right?" Sarah explained confidently.

The preacher, chuckled and said, "Ma'am, you do have a point."

Turning to John, he spoke, "John, would you promise me you'll go down to the court house first thing in the morning and take care of the paper work? I'll write an official report as the official minister for you to take with you."

"Yes sir, I certainly will," John assured him.

"Then I suggest we proceed with the wedding."

The family gathered below the preacher. Sister and Sarah stood to the left of Rebecca as her bridesmaid, and Lott and Thomas were to John's right. Holding hands, John and Rebecca looked up as the preacher began.

"Dearly beloved, we come together to join this woman, Rebecca Ann Walker, to this man, John Lewis Wilson, in Holy matrimony."

Having finished the vows, the preacher said, "I now pronounce you man and wife. You may kiss the bride."

With a serious expression on his face, Thomas said, "He's already done that, preacher. They were back there kissing a while ago."

"Thomas!" exclaimed his mother.

"Sorry, Mama, I have missed getting to tease my brother and just couldn't hold it back."

As John tenderly kissed Mrs. Rebecca Wilson, the family looked over to Thomas and laughed knowing that the Wilson clan would definitely experience some major changes in the days to come. Smiling, Sarah couldn't wait to enjoy the future with her family. Her eyes met Lott's, and they knew God had been gracious and had intervened in their lives to restore their family.

18

Home

For this reason I kneel before the Father, from whom his whole family in heaven and on earth derives its name. I pray that out of his glorious riches he may strengthen you with power through his Spirit in your inner being, so that Christ may dwell in your hearts through faith. And I pray that you, being rooted and established in love, may have power, together with all the saints, to grasp how wide and long and high and deep is the love of Christ, and to know this love that surpasses knowledge—that you may be filled to the measure of all the fullness of God.
—Ephesians 3:14-19

The family headed to the wagon, and Lott, to give room for Rebecca, rode double with Thomas. John asked Thomas, "When you left here, where have you been?"

"Well, after deserting and coming home, I figured the regulators would be after me, so with some of my other buddies, we headed west. We tried to get as far away as possible, so we rode through Louisiana and Texas and decided it best to head further to the Arizona Territory where folks didn't ask questions. Well, after meeting up with a territory marshal and having no money, we signed up like rangers to help protect the folks out there from the Indians. Funny thing, we went from fighting one kind of war to another, and I'll tell you this, them Yankees couldn't even begin to be the fighters them Apache were. But, you know, after a while, I began to see it a little different. Us white folks, went in there, stole their land, placed them on reservations with no means of support, put 'em under our laws, and killed 'em if they stepped out of line. John, one day when I came in from the field after an ambushing, I'd had enough. I told the marshal, I'd killed my last Apache and was going home."

When Thomas had finished, no one asked any questions, remembering the way the Choctaw had been mistreated here in Mississippi.

As they neared the house, the hounds and protectors of the premises ripped out from underneath the porch, barking as they ran and, recognizing the family, began whimpering and wagging their tales. Rebecca was dressed in her beautiful wedding dress and in a wagon instead of a carriage and was pulling up to a Mississippi log cabin instead of a Louisiana mansion. In all of her dreams, she never knew the feeling of such joy. This was home.

Sister got Rebecca some of her clothes, and after changing, Sister and Rebecca joined Sarah in the kitchen to prepare supper. On such a cold evening, they decided to have scrambled eggs, fried ham, grits, biscuits and the choice of coffee or spiced tea. After enjoying a joyous meal together, they all retired to Lott and Sarah's bedroom to relax and enjoy each other's company. John reluctantly agreed to share his story, and as he spoke, sometimes they would all laugh, and at other times, they sat silently and cried.

"One thing I thought was unusual," John related, "is one night when I was sleeping, I was awaken by a man's voice calling out to me. It was the clearest, purist voice I've ever heard. I don't know whether I was dreaming or not, but he told me he had come in out of the rain to rest a spell, and we began to talk for a while. Then after I had told him all that had happened to me, he told me not to worry that I'd be home for Christmas."

"Well, I guess that dream came true," Sister added.

"The funny thing was when Hank, the town marshal, came in the next day, the door had been locked the whole time. But it really seemed real, not like a dream."

Lott smiled and thought, Looks like we all have had messengers from God. Lott, looking at his family with Thomas sitting to his left, John and Rebecca huddled together on a bench nearby and Sarah and Sister settled to John's right, he thought, the family is complete with the exception of James Earl. He marveled at the day's happiness and knew it was a blessing from the Lord. Lott got up and walked to the lamp table near his bed to pick up his Bible. Handing the Bible to Sarah, he said, "I think it's time for our Christmas story, don't you?"

Sister's eyes brightened as she smiled at her father.

Sarah took the Bible and opened it to the second chapter of Luke and the first verse and read, "Now in those days there went out a decree from Caesar Augustus that all should be taxed . . ." When she had finished the story, she closed the Bible and began to look from one family member to another, then said, "We have a lot to be thankful for. The Lord has truly blessed us this day. A son thought to be dead is here with us. Another who we thought would not be able to return is with us, and the Lord has brought Rebecca and John together, binding their hearts in love. And for you, Sister, you have been our joy and strength when we felt all was lost. With blessings such as we have seen, we must go to the Lord in thanksgiving."

Pulling their chairs into a circle, the family joined hands and each, in sentence prayer, praised the Lord for his mercy, asked for forgiveness of their sins and pledged their lives to building the kingdom of God here on earth.

In preparation for bedtime, Sarah walked across the hall and began straightening James Earl's and Thomas's room, changed the sheets and fluffed up the feather bed to make it as comfortable and presentable as possible for John and Rebecca's wedding night. Since it was the only other room in the house with a fireplace, Lott brought in wood from the porch and started a fire.

Thomas saw his old sword leaning on the wall just beyond the fireplace and asked as he took it in his hands, "What's this old thing still doing here?"

"It's yours. I thought I'd leave it there until you came home. It was my memory of you," explained Lott.

"This thing is an instrument of death. I'm going to put it away because as long as I live, I will never take another man's life."

After putting the sword away, Thomas, exhausted from the long ride, rearranged the pallet of quilts that John had used the night before and, pushing it over next to the wall, took off his boots, pulled a couple of blankets over his body and snuggled down on his pillow. Lott reached over and took Thomas's buffalo coat and draped it over him to protect him from the cold drafts of air that came through the cracks around the windows.

"Sorry, folks; this ole boy is spent. This has been one glorious day. Mama, Papa, Sister, John and especially you Rebecca, I love you all." In a few minutes, his breathing slowed, and he began to snore.

The family quietly continued their conversation. Later, Lott got out of his chair, went to the mantle and took down the white candle that was burning. He blew it out and carried it over to his dresser. Reaching into the top drawer, he laid the white candle down and retrieved a red one. Walking back to the mantle, he picked up the candleholder, placed the red one on its base and lit the new one. Stepping back, he placed his hands on his hips, nodded his head in approval and said, "That should do it."

Sarah sat, wondering why Lott was changing the candles again, and finally asked, "What are you doing now, Lott? These candles have really troubled you."

"Not troubled, my dear, just ignorance on my part," Lott explained. "These candles represent the lives of our four children."

"But Papa, you said the red ones represent life and the white was for the one who had passed," Sister remarked, confused.

Still focusing on the mantle and the four red candles flickering as they slowly burned, Lott spoke these words, "Daughter, as your dear mother has always said, the Lord works in strange and wondrous ways, blessed be the name of the Lord. Earlier tonight when there were three red candles representing you, John, and Thomas and one white candle for James Earl, I realized that James Earl is alive and with his heavenly Father where he rightly should be. So you see, you, John, Thomas, and James Earl are home. Praise be to the Lord, all of my children are home."

Later that night, Lott walked out to the porch and looked across his farm. Feeing the tender touch of God's mercy, he realized that God had been there with them through every trial. He now knew that beyond each storm there is always hope and healing.

Readers Guide

Chapter 1

1. Reread the description about the prison. How would you find hope and encourage others to have hope in a place like this?
2. Camp Andersonville in Georgia was considered a horror, but Camp Douglas in Illinois was found to be even more inhumane. Should prisoners of war be treated with respect, tolerance, strictness, cruelty? Why?
3. Sam tells John, "I think the Lord done turned his back on us. If He loved us, wouldn't things be different?" How do you answer this question for someone who is in a difficult situation and does not feel God close?

Chapter 2

1. Sarah tells Rebecca that angels have been talking to her. How would you react if a close relative or friend made that statement to you? Would you feel hope like Rebecca or worry like Lott?
2. Rebecca says she knows a child should not be held responsible for a parent's actions. What in this chapter makes you thing Frankie's father has had a negative impact on him?
3. John's anger over the murder of the Confederate black man almost cost him his life. When is it important to stand up against injustice? To keep quiet?

Chapter 3

1. After the death of his sons, Lott feels like God has deserted him. Was this true? Why did he feel this way? Give several explanations.
2. Colonel Sweet wanted to invent a situation to make himself look important at the detriment of the prisoners. History shows he never received recognition, and if the South had won, he would probably have been executed because of the atrocities he committed. Pride often makes us lose sight of what is truly important? Instead of praise and recognition, what should people truly seek?

Chapter 4

1. Lott had a belt on a nail in the kitchen. How do you feel about this type of discipline?
2. Sarah tells Lott that he is the spiritual leader of their family. Do you think the husband should be the spiritual leader of a family?
3. The preacher's sermon was about ministering angels. Reread the verse at the beginning of this chapter. Do you believe angels still minister today? Have you ever felt an angel was ministering to you or your family?

Chapter 5

1. John and Sam decided against becoming Union Calvary soldiers to escape life in prison. They remained loyal to the Confederacy and refused a free train ticket home? Do you think they made wise decisions in each circumstance? Why?

2. Were you surprised by the lack of hospitality in Wickliffe, Kentucky? Would you have hired someone who looked ragged and had been a prisoner of war? Why do you think this community had this reaction?

3. John finds himself in prison again and is wrongly accused of thievery. He admits to stealing a cracker which is minor. When is stealing justified?

4. How would you explain Gabe Jacobs? Do you think he was a ministering angel? How did he minister to Lott?

Chapter 6

1. What qualities is John displaying as he accepts punishment for a crime he did not commit and instead works diligently for the town? Would you have been like John or would you have done just enough to get by?

2. Mr. Walker begins pushing Rebecca toward a relationship with Frankie. Do you think he is concerned about her future or is he influenced by the Olliver's wealth?

3. Why do you think Frank, Sr. and Frankie have such a poor relationship? Is Frankie justified in the way he talks to his father?

Chapter 7

1. How do you explain John's visitor in the jail? A dream, a ministering angel, or a man off the street? If this were your child, how would you explain the visitor to him?

2. Fathers are often over-protective of their daughters. How did Sarah get Lott to allow Sister to go to the party? Do you think sixteen is a good age to begin dating? How should parents prepare their children for dating?

3. The people of Wycliffe are at first frightened of John because he was a Confederate soldier and prisoner. What qualities did John exhibit that changed the citizens' opinions?

4. Frankie has many battles going on inside his head. What is his fear about Rebecca? About his friends who became soldiers? About becoming a man like his father?

Chapter 8

1. Lott was sad when he realized his daughter would soon be grown and independent. What are some of the events in your children's lives that make you realize your child does not really belong to you? Why is it important to spend less time working and worrying and more time with your children? Give several reasons.

2. Thomas Walker begins to regret his involvement in Frank's business and knows the love of money was his motivation. Is Mr. Walker, a church goer continuing in wrong, more guilty than Frank, a non-church attender in the wrong?

Chapter 9

1. Do you believe in ghosts? Does the Bible support the belief in ghosts? Toby tells Lott that he figures "haints" are satan's angels. Do you agree with that conclusion?
2. Hank and Angie fervently pray for John who has a severe injury from the fight. How can prayer help both the injured (or sick) and those praying? Do you believe God still heals miraculously in today's world?
3. Mr. Henderson wants revenge on John for his son's broken jaw. This decision is based on pride and not truth. How does pride affect many decisions that lead to our judgment of others?

Chapter 10

1. Thomas Walker probably thought no one would ever find out about his unethical business dealings, but both Rebecca and Lott discovered his wrongful actions. The Bible teaches the truth sets you free. Does repentance come easier after your wrongs have been exposed and confronted? Do you think Mr. Walker will repent?
2. Many times people who are different, especially the mentally challenged, are ridiculed and shunned. When our nation states "All men are created equal" what does this really mean and how does it apply to those outside of what is considered normal?

Chapter 11

1. Hank realized that God does take care of His children when they pray. Does this always seem true? We do not see life from God's perspective and wisdom. If we realize this, can we agree with Hank? Why?
2. Angie desires that John be free to love her, but realizes a solution to her worry about John. What did she conclude and will this help us when we are anxious?
3. How did Frank earn his wealth after the war? Do you think this is smart business or unethical? Why?
4. Mr. Walker's opinion of John is that he is a step away from the poorhouse. Is this the same concern for daughters today? How can parents re-prioritize the requirements they set for the ones their children will marry?

Chapter 12

1. Frankie was tempted to return to Lower Nachez. What steps could he (and you) take to avoid and conquer temptation?
2. If Frankie truly loves Rebecca, would he even consider spending the night with another woman? What could possibly be motivating his fondness for Rebecca?
3. Doc felt his sin was too great for God to forgive. How does a person get rid of immense guilt over a past sin?

Chapter 13

1. New Orleans was an important seaport and had lots of wealth. Rebecca is mesmerized by all she sees. Do you think this will influence her feelings for Frankie? Does wealth and influential people affect your decisions? Why?
2. Rebecca recognizes the opulence of all she has seen and says a prayer in her New Orleans room. Reread that prayer. Why do you think her prayer will keep her grounded?
3. Frankie was glad he had learned the lesson that Olliver money could buy just about anything. What else has Franke learned from his father? We often say, "Like father, like son." Why is it difficult for a son to choose different behaviors than his father?
4. Compare and contrast Angie's relationship to her father and Frankie's relationship to his. What are the qualities of a parent-child relationship that make it a good one?

Chapter 14

1. The Ollivers have brought Rebecca to their plantation to show her the advantages of a life of wealth. When Rebecca contemplates marriage to Frankie, what does she realize about the wealth she has seen?
2. How do you know that Mr. Bordeau was good to his slaves? What is an error in his thinking when it comes to those working in his fields?
3. Reread the prayer that Rebecca prays at the end of this chapter. When and how can the first sentence of the prayer be used in your life?

Chapter 15

1. Rebecca decides to marry Frankie. Do you think love can grow when two people care for each other or should love be a beginning foundation?
2. We know that although God doesn't cause the bad in our life, it sometimes seems He allows it in order to refine us and draw us closer to Him. How have John's tribulations refined him?
3. The Walkers and Ollivers decide to keep John's letter from Rebecca and Frankie. Do parents have the right to hide knowledge that will affect their children's future? Why is honesty the best policy?
4. John tells Wally, "You're right about that, Wally. We are all sinners turned to saints in the Lord each day." Explain what he means by "each day." Do you believe you are a sinner, a saint, neither or both? Why?
5. The jewelry store owner paid it forward. Has there been a time in your life when you helped someone in need and expected nothing in return? Why did you help? Have you been the one who was helped? What was your response?
6. Mr. Olliver tells Junior to do whatever it takes. What does this reveal about his character? Do you think he had Lott's brother killed in order to gain the Choctaw land mentioned earlier?

Chapter 16

1. John continues to head home even when he knows being in the cold and snow will be dangerous. Has there been a time in your life when something was so important to you, you refused to think about safety? When should you put safety first?
2. When John sees James Earl on the horse, is he daydreaming, hallucinating, or is he a ministering angel making sure John does not remain in the snow where he might perish? Why do you think this? Do you think angels minister to us through dreams?
3. John decided to clean up before seeing Rebecca? Was this wise? What would you have done?
4 Sarah was not surprised when John came home. She expected that God would deliver what he promised her. When you pray, do you wait expectantly for the answer? Why is waiting expectantly important? What happens in our lives when we don't expectantly look for God each day?

Chapter 17

1. Lott finally realized that the candle turning red was a message from God. The message meant John was alive, but what was the real message of the red candle?
2. Rebecca stated, "Only in the Bible do dreams mean anything." Do you think God still speaks to His children by dreams? Why or Why not?
3. How did the way Frankie handled John's return affect your opinion of Frankie and the man he would become?
4. What reason did Gabe give to Lott about why angles had been ministering to Lott's family. Do you think that is why so many people do not recognize ministering angels today?

Chapter 18

1. How would John's return to Wycliffe and marriage to Angie have made a good ending?
2. Thomas states that he went from fighting one kind of war to another. Thomas talks about how the Indians were being slaughtered. Do you think that that the Indians have been discriminated against worse than any other group of people in our country?
3. Rebecca was pulling up to a Mississippi log cabin instead of a Louisiana mansion, but yet felt amazing joy? Was there a time in your life when you felt amazing joy regardless of the lack of comfort or wealth?
4 Sarah begins talking about all the blessings they have received amidst their trials. Why is it important to be thankful for blessings?
5. Lott replaces the red candle with a white one and states, "All my children are home." Why should this bring us comfort in times of loss?
6. How did this story affect your belief in ministering angels and your belief in the care of God for His children during suffering and adversity?

www.ingramcontent.com/pod-product-compliance
Lightning Source LLC
Chambersburg PA
CBHW031944010726
47493CB00007B/2064